紅樓夢

A DREAM OF RED MANSIONS

An Abridged Version

Written by Tsao Hsueh-chin and Kao Ngo
Translated by Yang Hsien-yi and Gladys Yang

The Commercial Press

紅樓夢

A DREAM OF RED MANSIONS

An Abridged Version

Written by Tsao Hsueh-chin and Kao Ngo

Translated by Yang Hsien-yi and Gladys Yang

Published by

THE COMMERCIAL PRESS (HONG KONG) LTD.
Kiu Ying Bldg., 2D Finnie St., Quarry Bay, Hong Kong.
and
FOREIGN LANGUAGES PRESS
24 Baiwan Zhuang, Beijing.

Printed by

C & C OFFSET PRINTING CO., LTD.
1/F-9/F., C & C Bldg., 36 Ting Lai Rd., Tai Po, N.T., Hong Kong.

1st Edition 1986
4th Impression 1996
ISBN 962 07 1068 1
Printed in Hong Kong

Translators' Preface to the Abridged Version

Hong Lou Meng or *A Dream of Red Mansions* is generally considered as the greatest Chinese novel ever written. However, because of its size and scope and host of characters, 975 in all, it presents certain difficulties to foreign readers. Towards the end of the 19th century a British consul in China, Bancroft Joly, embarked on a translation; but his two-volume *Dream of the Red Chamber*, published in Hong Kong in 1892-93, comprises less than half of the original. A later English translation by Florence and Isabel McHugh, based on the German version by Franz Kuhn, was published by Routledge and Kegan Paul in 1958. Kuhn's translation of 50 chapters presents about half of the original but carries the story to its end. During the last decade, two new English translations of the novel have appeared. Our version was published by the Foreign Languages Press, Beijing; the other version, *The Story of the Stone*, translated by Professor David Hawkes of Oxford University and Dr. John Minford, is appearing in five volumes in the Penguin Classics series.

For the reader who finds the whole novel daunting, an abridged version should be welcome; so the Foreign Languages Press has arranged with the Commercial Press in Hong Kong to produce this edition. Already in the early thirties one such shortened version translated as *Dream of the Red Chamber* and adapted by Chi-chen Wang appeared with a preface by Arthur Waley; and a second version of Wang's was published in 1959 with a preface by Mark Van Doren. Wang's first version consists of 39 short chapters, his second of 60 short chapters. However, both are more in the nature of an abstract than a translation, while this present version is a faithful abridgement of our complete translation. Those who want to enjoy some of the most moving passages in the original should find

this version reliable ·and satisfactory. The work of abridgement has been ably done, and the credit for this should go to
the editor of the Commercial Press, while for any faults in the
translation we still assume responsibility.

YANG XIANYI and *GLADYS YANG*

1985

Preface

A Dream of Red Mansions (Hong Lou Meng, sometimes translated as The Dream of the Red Chamber), the great classical Chinese novel written by Tsao Hsueh-chin in the mid-eighteenth century during the reign of Emperor Chien-lung of the Ching Dynasty, has been widely popular throughout the last two hundred years and more.

Tsao Hsueh-chin's family were Hans, but they had later become Manchu bannermen. One of his ancestors came south of the Great Wall with the Ching rulers. Subsequently his great-grandfather, grandfather, father and uncle all held one of the posts administering the affairs of the imperial household — Textile Commissioner of Chiangning Prefecture (present-day Nanking and six contiguous counties including Liuho, Kaochun, Chiangpu and others); and his great-grandmother nursed Emperor Kang-hsi. Later, her son, Hsueh-chin's grandfather, accompanied the emperor in his studies. This shows the Tsao family's relationship with the Ching imperial house in general, and with Emperor Kang-hsi in particular.

Towards the end of the reign of Kang-hsi and the beginning of that of Yung-cheng, however, a fierce struggle for the claim to the throne led to a conflict among members of the imperial house. In the fifth year of Yung-cheng (1727) the Tsao family, so favoured by the previous emperor, were charged with the crime of embezzling public funds, their estates were confiscated and they fell into disgrace. After this they moved from the south to Peking; later Tsao Hsueh-chin lived in the western suburb of the city. He was then so poor that his family sometimes had nothing more substantial to eat than porridge. It was in these poverty-stricken circumstances that he started writing his novel. Then the death of his beloved son overwhelmed him with sorrow and he fell ill. Unable to afford good medical treatment, he died in the twenty-eighth year of Chien-lung (1763) without having finished his novel.

Only eighty chapters written by him are extant in manuscript form with comments by Chih-yen Chai. He wrote more than this but unfortunately the manuscripts of the later chapters were lost. The last forty chapters in the present novel were the work of Kao Ngo, who lived after Tsao Hsueh-chin and carried out his plan of making the love story between Pao-yu and Tai-yu end in tragedy; and in this respect his forty chapters have great artistic impact. After Kao Ngo's completion of the novel, this book originally known as *The Tale of the Stone* in eighty manuscript chapters was printed in movable type in 1791 as a complete novel in 120 chapters and renamed *A Dream of Red Mansions*. The printing of this edition increased the circulation of the book and helped to preserve the original eighty-chapter version.

CONTENTS

The Main Characters and Their Relationships

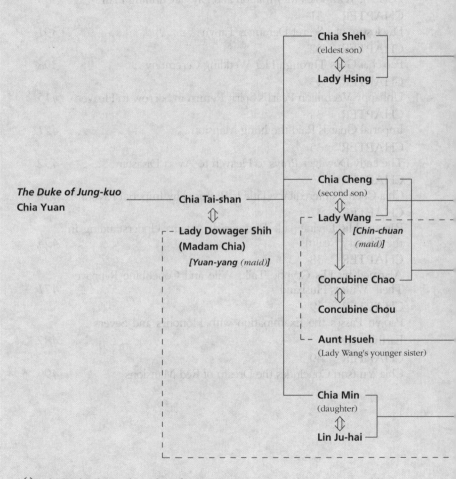

The Duke of Ning-kuo
Chia Yen ——————— Chia Tai-hua ——————— Chia Ching

Chia Sheh
(eldest son)
⇕
Lady Hsing

The Duke of Jung-kuo
Chia Yuan ——————— Chia Tai-shan
⇕
Lady Dowager Shih
(Madam Chia)
[Yuan-yang (maid)]

Chia Cheng
(second son)
⇕
Lady Wang
[Chin-chuan (maid)]
⇕
Concubine Chao
⇕
Concubine Chou

Aunt Hsueh
(Lady Wang's younger sister)

Chia Min
(daughter)
⇕
Lin Ju-hai

⇕   husband–wife/concubine relationship

·········   brothers/sisters of the same father but of different mothers

– – –   other close relatives

Chia Chen (son)
⇕
Madam Yu
   Second Sister Yu (Madam Yu's younger sister,
                Chia Lien's concubine)
   Third Sister Yu (Madam Yu's younger sister)
Chia Hsi-chun (daughter)

Chia Jung (son)
⇕
Chin Ko-ching
Chin Chung
  (Chin Ko-ching's
   younger brother)

Chia Lien (son)
⇕
Wang Hsi-feng (Lady Wang's niece)
  [Ping-erh (maid)]

Chia Ying-chun (daughter)

Sister Chiao
(daughter)

Chia Chu (eldest son)
⇕
Li Wan

Chia Yuan-chun (eldest daughter, titled Worthy and Virtuous Consort)

Chia Pao-yu (second son)
  [Hsi-jen (maid)] [Ching-wen (maid)]

Chia Tan-chun (second daughter)
  [Tai-shu (maid)]

Chia Huan (youngest son)

Hsueh Pao-chai (daughter)
  [Ying-erh (maid)]

Hsueh Pan (son)
⇕
Shia Chin-kui

Lin Tai-yu (daughter)
  [Tzu-chuan (maid)] [Hsueh-yen (maid)]

Shih Hsiang-yun (Lady Dowager Shih's grandniece)

Miao-yu (a nun living in the Grand View Garden)
Chia Yu-tsun (a kinsman of the Chias and a Prefect)
Granny Liu (a distant relative of Lady Wang's maiden family)

Chapter 1
Leng Tzu-hsing Describes the Jung Mansion

Long ago the earth dipped downwards in the southeast, and in that southeast part was a city named Kusu,[1] and the quarter around Chang-men Gate of Kusu was one of the most fashionable centres of wealth and nobility in the world of men. Outside this Chang-men Gate was a certain Ten-*li* Street, off which ran the Lane of Humanity and Purity; and in this lane stood an old temple, which being built in such a narrow space was known from its shape as Gourd Temple. Beside this temple lived a gentleman named Chen Shih-yin. Although neither very rich nor noble, his family was highly regarded in that locality.

Now Chen was in good terms with a poor scholar Chia Yu-tsun, who was a native of Huchow and the last of a line of scholars and officials. His parents had exhausted the family property and died leaving him alone in the world. Since nothing was to be gained by staying at home, he had set out for the capital in the hope of securing a position and restoring the family fortunes. But by the time he had reached here a couple of years ago his money had run out and he had gone to live in the temple where he made a precarious living by working as a scrivener. For this reason Shih-yin saw a good deal of him.

In time the Mid-Autumn Festival came round. After the family meal, Shih-yin had another table laid in his study and strolled over in the moonlight to the temple to invite Yu-tsun over.

When he entered the temple, he overheard Yu-tsun chant the

---

[1]Present-day Soochow.

couplet:

> "The jade in the box hopes to fetch a good price,
> The pin in the casket longs to soar on high."

"I see you have high ambitions, Brother Yu-tsun!" he joked.

"Not in the least," replied Yu-tsun, somewhat embarrassed. "I was merely reciting some lines by a former poet. I don't aspire so high. To what do I owe the pleasure of this visit?"

"Tonight is mid-autumn, commonly known as the Festival of Reunion. It occurred to me that you might be feeling lonely in this temple, brother. I've prepared a little wine in my humble place and wonder if you'd condescend to share it?"

Yu-tsun needed no urging.

"You lavish too much kindness on me, sir," he said. "Nothing would please me better."

They went to the court in front of Shih-yin's study. Soon they had finished their tea and sat down to a collation of choice wine and delicacies. At first they sipped slowly, but their spirits rose as they talked and they began to drink more recklessly. The sound of flutes and strings could be heard from all the houses in the neighbourhood; everywhere was singing; and overhead the bright moon shone in full splendour. The two men became very merry and drained cup after cup.

Yu-tsun, eight-tenths drunk, could not suppress his elation. He improvised a quatrain to the moon and declaimed it:

> "On the fifteenth the moon is full,
> Bathing jade balustrades with her pure light;
> As her bright orb sails up the sky
> All men on earth gaze upwards at the sight."

"Excellent!" cried Shih-yin. "I've always maintained that you were cut out for great things. These lines foretell rapid advancement. Very soon you will be treading upon the clouds. Let me congratulate you."

He filled another large cup. Yu-tsun tossed it off and then sighed.

"Don't think this is just drunken talk," he said. "I'm sure I could acquit myself quite creditably in the examinations; but

I have no money in my wallet for travelling expenses and the capital is far away. I can't raise enough as a scrivener. . . ."

"Why didn't you say so before?" interposed Shih-yin. "I've often wondered about this, but since you never mentioned it I didn't like to broach the subject. If that's how things are, dull as I am at least I know what's due to a friend. Luckily the Metropolitan Examinations are coming up next year. You must go as fast as you can to the capital and prove your learning in the Spring Test. I shall count it a privilege to take care of the travelling expenses and other business for you."

He sent his boy in to fetch fifty taels of silver and two suits of winter clothes.

"The nineteenth is a good day for travelling," he continued. "You can hire a boat then and start your journey westward. How good it will be to meet again next winter after you have soared up to dizzy heights."

Yu-tsun accepted the silver and clothes with no more than perfunctory thanks, then said no more of the matter but went on feasting and talking. They did not part until the third watch, when Shih-yin saw his friend off and returned to his room to sleep until the sun was high in the sky. Then, remembering the previous night's business, he decided to write Yu-tsun two letters of introduction to certain officials in the capital who might put him up.

But the servant sent to ask his friend over brought back word, "The monk says that Mr. Chia left for the capital at the fifth watch this morning. He asked the monk to tell you that scholars are not superstitious about lucky or unlucky days but like to act according to reason; so he had no time to say goodbye in person."

This Shih-yin had to accept.

Yu-tsun, after receiving Shih-yin's gift of silver, had left on the sixteenth for the capital. He did so well in the examinations that he became a Palace Graduate and was given a provincial appointment. He had now been promoted to this prefectship.

But although a capable administrator Yu-tsun was grasping and ruthless, while his arrogance and insolence to his superiors made them view him with disfavour. In less than two years they found a chance to impeach him. He was accused of "ingrained duplicity, tampering with the rites and, under a show of probity, conspiring with his ferocious underlings to foment trouble in his district and make life intolerable for the local people."

The Emperor, much incensed, sanctioned his dismissal. The arrival of this edict rejoiced the hearts of all officials in the Prefecture. But Yu-tsun, although mortified and enraged, betrayed no indignation and went about looking as cheerful as before. After handing over his affairs he gathered together the capital accumulated during his years in office and moved his household back to his native place. Having settled them there he set off, "the wind on his back, moonlight in his sleeves," to see the famous sights of the empire.

One day his travels again took him to Yangchow, where he learned that the Salt Commissioner that year was Lin Hai — his courtesy name was Lin Ju-hai — who had come third in a previous Imperial examination and recently been promoted to the Censorate. A native of Kusu, he had now been selected by the Emperor as a Commissioner of the Salt Inspectorate. He had been little more than a month in this present post.

One of Lin Ju-hai's ancestors five generations earlier had been ennobled as a marquis. The rank had been conferred for three generations; then, as the benevolence of the present gracious Emperor far exceeded that of his noble predecessors, he had as a special favour extended it for one more generation, so that Lin Ju-hai's father had inherited the title as well. He himself, however, had made his career through the examinations, for his family was cultured as well as noble. Unfortunately it was not prolific, although several branches existed, and Lin Ju-hai had cousins but no brothers or sisters. Now he was in his forties and his only son had died at the age of three the previous year. He had several concubines but fate had not granted him another son, and he could not remedy this. By his wife, née Chia, he had a daughter Tai-yu just five years old. Both parents loved her dearly. And because she was as intelligent as she was pretty, they decided to give her a good education to make up for their lack of a son and help them forget their loss.

It so happened that Yu-tsun had caught a chill which laid him up in his inn for a month and more. Exhausted by his illness, and short of funds, he was searching for somewhere to recuperate. Fortunately he had two old friends here who knew that the Salt Commissioner was looking for a tutor. Upon their recommendation Yu-tsun was given the post, which provided the security he needed. He was lucky, too, to have as pupil only one small girl accompanied by two maids. Since the child was so delicate, her lessons were irregular and this meant that his duties were light.

In a twinkling another year went by and then his pupil's mother unexpectedly fell ill and died. The little girl attended her during her illness and then went into strict mourning. Yu-tsun considered resigning, but Lin Ju-hai kept him on so as not to interrupt his daughter's education during the period of mourning. Recently, grief had brought about a relapse in the delicate child's health, and for days at a time she had to abandon her studies. Then Yu-tsun, finding time hang heavy on his hands, used to take a walk after his meals when the weather was fine.

One day he strolled to the outskirts of the city to enjoy the countryside. He came to luxuriant woods and bamboo groves set among hills and interlaced by streams, with a temple half hidden among the foliage. The entrance was in ruins, the walls were crumbling. A placard above the gate bore the inscription: Temple of Perspicacity. And flanking the gate were two mouldering boards with the couplet:

> Though plenty was left after death, he forgot
> to hold his hand back;
> Only at the end of the road does one think of
> turning on to the right track.

"Trite as the language is, this couplet has deep significance," thought Yu-tsun. "I've never come across anything like it in all the famous temples I've visited. There may be a story behind it of someone who has tasted the bitterness of life, some repentant sinner. I'll go in and ask."

But inside he found only a doddering old monk cooking gruel. Not very impressed, Yu-tsun casually asked him a few questions. The man proved to be deaf as well as dim-witted, for his mumbled answers were quite irrelevant.

Yu-tsun went out again in disgust and decided to improve the occasion by drinking a few cups in a village tavern. He had scarcely set foot inside the door when one of the men who was drinking there rose to his feet and accosted him with a laugh.

"Fancy meeting you here!"

It was Leng Tzu-hsing, a curio-dealer whom he had met in the capital. As Yu-tsun admired his enterprise and ability while Tzu-hsing was eager to cultivate one of the literati, they had hit it off well together and become good friends.

"When did you arrive, brother?" asked Yu-tsun cheerfully. "I'd no idea you were in these parts. What a coincidence, meeting you here."

"I went home at the end of last year and stopped here on my way back to the capital to look up an old friend. He was good enough to ask me to stay, and since I've no urgent business I'm breaking my journey for a couple of days. I shall go on about the middle of the month. My friend's busy today, so I came out for a stroll and stopped here to rest. I'd no idea I'd run into you like this."

He made Yu-tsun sit down at his table and ordered more food and wine. Drinking slowly, they spoke of all they had done since parting.

"Is there any news from the capital?" asked Yu-tsun.

"Nothing much," replied Tzu-hsing. "But something rather curious has happened in the house of one of your noble kinsmen."

"I've no kinsmen in the capital. Who do you mean?"

"You have the same surname even if you don't belong to

the same clan."

Yu-tsun asked to whom he alluded.

"The Chia family of the Jung Mansion. You needn't be ashamed of the connection."

"Oh, that family." Yu-tsun laughed. "To tell the truth, our clan is a very large one. Since the time of Chia Fu of the Eastern Han Dynasty its branches have multiplied until now you find Chias in every province. Impossible to keep track of them all. The Jung branch and mine are, however, on the same clan register, but they're so grand that we've never claimed relationship and are gradually drifting further and further apart."

"Don't talk like that, friend. Both the Ning and Jung branches have declined." Tzu-hsing sighed. "They're not what they used to be."

"How is that possible? They used to be enormous households."

"I know. It's a long story."

"Last year when I was in Chinling,"[1] said Yu-tsun, "on my way to visit the Six Dynasty ruins I went to the Stone City[2] and passed the gates of their old mansions. Practically the whole north side of the street is taken up by their houses, the Ning Mansion on the east and the Jung Mansion adjoining it on the west. True, there wasn't much coming and going outside their gates, but over the wall I caught glimpses of most imposing halls and pavilions, while the trees and rockeries of the gardens behind had a flourishing, opulent look. There was nothing to suggest a house in decline."

"For a Palace Graduate you're not very smart." Tzu-hsing chuckled. "A centipede dies but never falls down, as the old saying goes. Although they're not as prosperous as before, they're still a cut above ordinary official families. Their households are increasing and their commitments are growing all the time, while masters and servants alike are so used to lord-

---

[1] Present-day Nanking.
[2] The northwestern section of Nanking.

ing it in luxury that not one of them thinks ahead. They squander money every day and are quite incapable of economizing. Outwardly they may look as grand as ever, but their purses are nearly empty. That's not their worst trouble, though. Who would've thought that each new generation of this noble and scholarly clan is inferior to the last."

"Surely," countered Yu-tsun in surprise, "a family so cultured and versed in etiquette knows the importance of a good upbringing? I can't vouch for our other branches, but I've always heard that these two houses take great pains over the education of their sons."

"It's these two houses I'm talking about," rejoined Tzu-hsing regretfully. "Just hear me out. The Duke of Ningkuo and the Duke of Jungkuo were brothers by the same mother. The Duke of Ningkuo, the elder, had four sons and after his death the oldest of these, Chia Tai-hua, succeeded to the title. The elder of his two sons, Chia Fu, died at the age of eight or nine, leaving the younger, Chia Ching, to inherit the title. But he's so wrapped up in Taoism that he takes no interest in anything but distilling elixirs. Luckily when he was younger he had a son Chia Chen, to whom he's relinquished the title so that he can give all his mind to becoming an immortal; and instead of going back to his native place he's hobnobbing with Taoist priests outside the city. Chia Chen has a son called Jung just turned sixteen. Chia Ching washes his hands of all mundane matters, and Chia Chen has never studied but lives for pleasure. He's turning the Ning Mansion upside down, yet no one dares to restrain him.

"Now for the Jung Mansion, where that curious business I just mentioned took place. After the death of the Duke of Jungkuo, his elder son Chia Tai-shan succeeded to the title and married a daughter of Marquis Shih of Chinling, by whom he had two sons, Chia Sheh and Chia Cheng. Chia Tai-shan has been dead for many years but his wife, Lady Dowager Shih, is still alive. Their elder son Chia Sheh inherited the title. The younger, Chia Cheng, was so fond of studying as a child that he was his grandfather's favourite and he hoped to make a career for himself through the examinations. When Chia Tai-shan died, however, he left a valedictory memorial, and the Emperor out of regard for his former minister not only conferred the title on his elder son but asked what other sons there were, granted Chia Cheng an audience, and as an additional favour gave him the rank of Assistant Secretary with instructions to familiarize himself with affairs in one of the ministries. He has now risen to the rank of Under-Secretary.

"Chia Cheng's wife, Lady Wang, bore him a son called Chia Chu who passed the district examination at fourteen, married before he was twenty and had a son, but then fell ill and died. His second child was a daughter, born strangely enough on the first day of the year. But stranger still was the birth later of a son who came into the world with a piece of clear, brilliantly coloured jade in his mouth. There are even inscriptions on the jade. Isn't that extraordinary?"

"It certainly is. The boy should have a remarkable future."

"That's what everyone says." Tzu-hsing smiled cynically. "And for that reason his grandmother dotes on him. On his first birthday Chia Cheng tested his disposition by setting all sorts of different objects before him to see which he would select. Believe it or not, ignoring everything else he reached out for the rouge, powder-boxes, hair ornaments and bangles! His father was furious and swore he'd grow up to be a dissolute rake. Because of this he's not too fond of the boy, but the child's still his grandmother's darling. He's seven or eight now and remarkably mischievous, yet so clever you won't find his equal in a hundred. And he says the strangest things for a child. 'Girls are made of water, men of mud,' he declares. 'I feel clean and refreshed when I'm with girls but find men dirty and stinking.' Isn't that absurd? He's bound later on to run after women like the very devil."

"That doesn't follow," put in Yu-tsun, grown suddenly grave. "You don't know how he's come into the world. I suspect his father is making a mistake as well if he thinks the boy depraved. To understand him you'd need to be widely read and experienced, able to recognize the nature of things, grasp the Way and comprehend the Mystery."

He spoke so seriously that Tzu-hsing asked him to expand on this.

"All men, apart from the very good and the very bad, are much alike," said Yu-tsun. "The very good are born at a propitious time when the world is well governed, the very bad in times of calamity when danger threatens. Examples of the first are Yao, Shun, Yu and Tang, King Wen and King Wu, Duke Chou and Duke Shao, Confucius and Mencius, Tung Chung-shu, Han Yu, Chou Tun-yi, the Cheng brothers, Chang Chai and Chu Hsi.[1] Examples of the second are Kung Kung, Chieh, Chou, Chin Shih Huang, Wang Mang, Tsao Tsao, Huan Wen, An Lu-shan and Chin Kuai.[2]

"The good bring order to the world, the bad plunge it into confusion. The good embody pure intelligence, the true essence of heaven and ·earth; the bad, cruelty and perversity, the evil essence.

"This is a prosperous, long-enduring reign when the world is at peace and there are many people in the court and in the countryside who are endowed with the good essences. The over-abundance of this good essence, having nowhere to go,

---

[1] Yao and Shun were legendary sage kings of ancient China; Yu, founder of the Hsia Dynasty (21st-16th century B.C.), was the legendary pacifier of flood; Tang founded the Shang Dynasty (16th-11th century B.C.); King Wen and King Wu founded the Western Chou Dynasty (11th century-771 B.C.); Duke Chou and Duke Shao were early Chou statesmen; Tung Chung-shu (179-104 B.C.) was a Confucian philosopher of the Han Dynasty; Han Yu (768-824) a Confucian writer of the Tang Dynasty; Chou Tun-yi, Cheng Hao, Cheng Yi and Chu Hsi were neo-Confucianists of the Northern Sung Dynasty (960-1127); and Chang Chai (1020-77) was a Northern Sung philosopher with some materialist ideas.

[2] Kung Kung, a legendary figure, was considered a rebel by China's feudal rulers; Chieh and Chou were the last rulers of the Hsia and Shang dynasties; Chin Shih Huang (259-210 B.C.) was the founder and First Emperor of the Chin Dynasty; Wang Mang usurped power towards the end of the Western Han Dynasty; Tsao Tsao (155-220) was a poet, statesman and military strategist of the Three Kingdoms Period; Huan Wen (312-373) was an eastern Tsin general; An Lu-shan was a rebel general in the Tang Dynasty, and Chin Kuai was a corrupt prime minister in the Southern Sung Dynasty (1127-1279).

is transformed into sweet dew and gentle breezes and scattered throughout the Four Seas.

"But because there is no place under the clear sky and bright sun for the essence of cruelty and perversity, it congeals in deep caverns and in the bowels of the earth. If wafted by winds or pressed upon by clouds, it is thrown into agitation and traces of it may escape. And should these meet the pure essence, good refuses to yield to evil while evil envies good — neither can prevail over the other. This is like wind, rain, lightning and thunder which cannot vanish into thin air or give way but must battle until they are spent. So in order to find some outlet these essences permeate human beings, who come into the world embodying both. Such people fall short of sages or perfect men, but neither are they out-and-out villains.

"The pure intelligence with which they are endowed sets them above their myriad fellow creatures, but their perversity and unnatural behaviour sink them lower than other men too. Born into rich and noble families, such people will become romantic eccentrics; born into poor but cultured families, they will become high-minded scholars or recluses. Even if born into luckless and humble homes, they will never grow up into yamen runners or servants at the beck and call of the vulgar — they'll turn out celebrated actors or courtesans. People of this type in the past were Hsu Yu, Tao Chien, Yuan Chi, Chi Kang and Liu Ling, the two families of Wang and Hsieh, Ku Kai-chih, Chen Shu-pao, the Tang emperor Ming-huang, the Sung emperor Hui-tsung, Wen Ting-yun, Mi Fei, Shih Yen-nien, Liu Yung and Chin Kuan.[1] More recent examples are Ni Tsan,

---

[1] Hsu Yu, an ancient legendary hermit; Tao Chien (365-427), an Eastern Tsin poet who gave up an official career to live in retirement; Yuan Chi, Chi Kang and Liu Ling, third century poets and eccentrics; the Wang and Hsieh families, nobles of the Eastern Tsin Dynasty (317-420); Ku Kai-chih, a famous Eastern Tsin painter; Chen Shu-pao, last ruler of the Chen Dynasty (557-589); Ming-huang (685-762); Hui-tsung (1082-1135), a Northern Sung emperor, painter and calligrapher; Wen Ting-yun, a romantic poet of the late Tang Dynasty; Mi Fei (1051-1107), a Sung Dynasty painter; Shih Yen-nien, a Sung Dynasty poet; Liu Yung, a Sung poet; Chin Kuan, a Sung poet, author of many love poems.

Tang Yin and Chu Yun-ming.[1] Then there are others like Li Kuei-nien, Huang Fan-cho, Ching Hsin-mo, Cho Wen-chun, Hung-fo, Hsueh Tao, Tsui Ying-ying and Chao-yun.[2] All of these, in their different fields, were essentially the same."

"You're saying that such people may become princes or thieves, depending on whether they're successful or not."

"Exactly. You don't know yet that since my dismissal I've spent two years travelling through different provinces and come across one or two remarkable children. Hence my guess that this Pao-yu you mentioned belongs to the same category. Let me give you an example no further away than Chinling. You know Mr. Chen, who was principal of the Chinling Provincial College?"

"Who doesn't know him? The Chen and Chia families are interrelated and on a very friendly footing. I've done business with the Chens a number of times."

"Last year when I was in Chinling," said Yu-tsun, "someone recommended me to the Chens as a resident tutor. I was surprised to find their household so grand, yet it combined wealth with propriety. Posts like that are not easy to come by. But although my pupil was a beginner, he was harder to teach than a candidate for the Provincial Examination. Here's an example of the absurd things he'd say: 'I must have two girls as company while I study, or I can't learn characters — my brain gets muddled.' He told his pages, 'The word "girl" is so honourable and pure, not even the supreme Buddhist and Taoist titles can compare with it. You with your filthy mouths and stinking tongues must never violate it. Before you utter this word, mind you rinse your mouths with clear water or

---

[1] Ni Tsan, a Yuan scholar and painter; Tang Yin, a Ming painter and poet, celebrated especially for his paintings of beautiful women; Chu Yun-ming, a Ming scholar and calligrapher.

[2] Li Kuei-nien, a Tang musician; Huang Fan-cho, a Tang actor; Ching Hsin-mo, a tenth-century actor; Hung-fo, the beautiful servant girl who married Li Ching, a duke in the early Tang Dynasty; Hsueh Tao, a Tang poetess; Tsui Ying-ying, heroine of *The Western Chamber*; Chao-yun, concubine of the Sung poet Su Tung-po.

fragrant tea. If you don't, your teeth will grow crooked and rip through your cheeks.'

"He had a fearful temper and could be incredibly stubborn and obstreperous; but as soon as classes were over and he joined the girls he became a different person — amiable, sensible and gentle. More than once, because of this, his father thrashed him within an inch of his life, but still that didn't change him. When the pain became too much for him, he would start yelling, 'Sister! Little Sister!' Once the girls in the inner chambers teased him saying, 'Why do you call us when you're being beaten? Do you want us to beg you off? For shame!' You should have heard his answer. He said, 'The first time I called I didn't know it would ease the pain. But then I discovered that it worked like magic. So when the pain's worst, I keep on calling "Sister".' Have you ever heard anything so ludicrous?

"His grandmother indulged him so unwisely that she was often rude to his tutor or blamed her son. That's why I resigned from that post. A boy like that is bound to lose the property he inherits and won't benefit by the advice of teachers and friends. The pity is, all the girls in his family are admirable."

"The three girls in the Chia family aren't bad either," rejoined Tzu-hsing. "Chia Cheng's elder daughter Yuan-chun was chosen to be a Lady-Clerk in the palace of the heir apparent because of her goodness, filial piety and talents. The second, Ying-chun, is Chia Sheh's daughter by a concubine. The third, Tan-chun, is Chia Cheng's daughter by a concubine. The fourth, Hsi-chun, is the younger sister of Chia Chen of the Ning Mansion. The Lady Dowager is so attached to these grand-daughters that she makes them study in the Jung Mansion near her, and I hear good reports of them all."

"I prefer the Chen family's way of giving their daughters the same sort of names as boys instead of choosing flowery names meaning Spring, Red, Fragrant, or Jade," remarked Yu-tsun. "How could the Chia family sink to such vulgarity?"

14

"You don't understand," said Tzu-hsing. "They named the eldest girl Yuan-chun[1] because she was born on New Year's Day, and so the others have *chun* in their names too. But all the girls of the last generation had names like those of boys. For proof, look at the wife of your respected employer Mr. Lin, the sister of Chia Sheh and Chia Cheng in the Jung Mansion. Her name, before she married, was Chia Min.[2] If you don't believe me, check up when you go back."

Yu-tsun pounded the table with a laugh. "No wonder my pupil always pronounces *min* as *mi* and writes it with one or two strokes missing.[3] That puzzled me, but now you've explained the reason. And no wonder she talks and behaves so differently from the general run of young ladies nowadays. I suspected she must have had an unusual mother. If she's a grand-daughter of the Jung family that explains it. What a pity that her mother died last month."

"She was the youngest of four sisters, but now she's gone too." Tzu-hsing sighed. "Not one of those sisters is left. It will be interesting to see what husbands they find for the younger generation."

"Yes. Just now you spoke of Chia Cheng's son born with jade in his mouth, and mentioned a young grandson left by his elder son. What about the venerable Chia Sheh? Has he no sons?"

"After the birth of this son with the jade Chia Cheng had another by his concubine, but I know nothing about him. So he has two sons and a grandson. However, there's no saying how they'll turn out. Chia Sheh has two sons as well. Chia Lien, the elder, is over twenty now. Two years ago he married a relative, the niece of Chia Cheng's wife Lady Wang. This Chia Lien, who has bought the rank of a sub-prefect, takes no interest in books but is a smooth man of the world; so he lives with his uncle Chia Cheng and helps him to manage his

---

[1] Cardinal Spring.

[2] *Min* has the same radical as *Sheh* and *Cheng*.

[3] A parent's name was taboo and had to be used in an altered form.

domestic affairs. Since his marriage he's been thrown into the shade by his wife, who is praised by everybody high and low. I hear she's extremely good-looking and a clever talker, so resourceful and astute that not a man in ten thousand is a match for her."

"That bears out what I was saying. These people we've been discussing are probably all pervaded by mixed essences of both good and evil. They are people of similar ways."

"Never mind about good and evil," protested Tzu-hsing. "We've been doing nothing but reckoning accounts for others. You must drink another cup."

"I've been talking so hard, I'm already slightly tipsy."

"Gossip goes well with wine. Why not drink some more?"

Yu-tsun looked out of the window. "It's growing late. They'll soon be closing the city gates. Let's stroll back and continue our conversation in town."

With that they paid the bill.

Chapter 2
The Lady Dowager Sends for Her Motherless Grand-Daughter

Now there was word from the capital that a request for the reinstatement of former officials had been sanctioned. Yu-tsun was naturally overjoyed.

Leng Tzu-hsing, who had heard the good news, at once proposed asking Lin Ju-hai to enlist the support of Chia Cheng in the capital. Accepting his advice, Yu-tsun went back alone to verify the report from the *Court Gazette*.

The next day he laid his case before Lin Ju-hai.

"What a lucky coincidence!" exclaimed Ju-hai. "Since my wife's death my mother-in-law in the capital has been worried because my daughter has no one to bring her up. She has sent two boats with male and female attendants to fetch the child, but I delayed her departure while she was unwell. I was wondering how to repay you for your goodness in teaching her: now this gives me a chance to show my appreciation. Set your mind at rest. I foresaw this possibility and have written a letter to my brother-in-law urging him to do all he can for you as a small return for what I owe you. You mustn't worry either about any expenses that may be incurred — I've made that point clear to my brother-in-law.

"I've chosen the second day of next month for my daughter's departure for the capital," continued Ju-hai. "It would suit both parties, surely, if you were to travel together?"

Yu-tsun promptly agreed with the greatest satisfaction, and took the gifts and travelling expenses which Ju-hai had prepared.

His pupil Tai-yu, who had just got over her illness, could hardly bear to leave her father, but she had to comply with the wishes of her grandmother.

"I am nearly fifty and don't intend to marry again," Ju-hai told her. "You're young and delicate, with no mother to take care of you, no sisters or brothers to look after you. If you go to stay with your grandmother and uncles' girls, that will take a great load off my mind. How can you refuse?"

So parting from him in a flood of tears, she embarked with her nurse and some elderly maid-servants from the Jung Mansion, followed by Yu-tsun and two pages in another junk.

In due course they reached the capital and entered the city. Yu-tsun spruced himself up and went with his pages to the gate of the Jung Mansion, where he handed in his visiting-card on which he had styled himself Chia Cheng's "nephew".

Chia Cheng, who had received his brother-in-law's letter, lost no time in asking him in. Yu-tsun cut an impressive figure and was by no means vulgar in his conversation. Since Chia Cheng was well-disposed to scholars and, like his grand-father before him, delighted in honouring worthy men of letters and helping those in distress, and since moreover his brother-in-law had recommended Yu-tsun, he treated him uncommonly well and did all in his power to help him. The same day that he presented a petition to the throne Yu-tsun was reha-bilitated and ordered to await an appointment. In less than two months he was sent to Chinling to fill the vacated post of prefect of Yingtien.[1] Taking leave of Chia Cheng he chose a day to proceed to his new post. But no more of this.

To return to Tai-yu. When she disembarked, a sedan-chair from the Jung Mansion and carts for her luggage were waiting in readiness. She had heard a great deal from her mother about the magnificence of her grandmother's home; and during the last few days she had been impressed by the food, costumes and behaviour of the relatively low-ranking attendants escorting her. She must watch her step in her new home, she decided,

---

[1] Another name for Nanking.

18

記內 海薦 西賓 孫貿外情 母惜 孤女

be on guard every moment and weigh every word, so as not to be laughed at for any foolish blunder. As she was carried into the city she peeped out through the gauze window of the chair at the bustle in the streets and the crowds of people, the like of which she had never seen before.

After what seemed a long time they came to a street with two huge stone lions crouching on the north side, flanking a great triple gate with beast-head knockers, in front of which ten or more men in smart livery were sitting. The central gate was shut, but people were passing in and out of the smaller side gates. On a board above the main gate was written in large characters: Ningkuo Mansion Built at Imperial Command.

Tai-yu realized that this must be where the elder branch of her grandmother's family lived.

A little further to the west they came to another imposing triple gate. This was the Jung Mansion. Instead of going through the main gate, they entered by the smaller one on the west. The bearers carried the chair a bow-shot further, then set it down at a turning and withdrew. The maid-servants behind Tai-yu had now alighted and were proceeding on foot. Three or four smartly dressed lads of seventeen or eighteen picked up the chair and, followed by the maids, carried it to a gate decorated with overhanging flowery patterns carved in wood. There the bearers withdrew, the maids raised the curtain of the chair, helped Tai-yu out and supported her through the gate.

Inside, verandahs on both sides led to a three-roomed entrance hall in the middle of which stood a screen of marble in a red sandalwood frame. The hall gave access to the large court of the main building. In front were five rooms with carved beams and painted pillars, and on either side were rooms with covered passageways. Cages of brilliantly coloured parrots, thrushes and other birds hung under the eaves of the verandahs.

Several maids dressed in red and green rose from the terrace and hurried to greet them with smiles.

"The old lady was just talking about you," they cried. "And here you are."

Three or four of them ran to raise the door curtain, and a voice could be heard announcing, "Miss Lin is here."

As Tai-yu entered, a silver-haired old lady supported by two maids advanced to meet her. She knew that this must be her grandmother, but before she could kowtow the old lady threw both arms around her.

"Dear heart! Flesh of my child!" she cried, and burst out sobbing.

All the attendants covered their faces and wept, and Tai-yu herself could not keep back her tears. When at last the others prevailed on her to stop, Tai-yu made her kowtow to her grandmother. This was the Lady Dowager from the Shih family mentioned by Leng Tzu-hsing, the mother of Chia Sheh and Chia Cheng, who now introduced the family one by one.

"This," she said, "is your elder uncle's wife. This is your second uncle's wife. This is the wife of your late Cousin Chu."

Tai-yu greeted each in turn.

"Fetch the girls," her grandmother said. "They can be excused their lessons today in honour of our guest from far away."

Two maids went to carry out her orders. And presently the three young ladies appeared, escorted by three nurses and five or six maids.

The first was somewhat plump and of medium height. Her cheeks were the texture of newly ripened lichees, her nose as sleek as goose fat. Gentle and demure, she looked very approachable.

The second had sloping shoulders and a slender waist. She was tall and slim, with an oval face, well-defined eyebrows and lovely dancing eyes. She seemed elegant and quick-witted with an air of distinction. To look at her was to forget everything vulgar.

The third was not yet fully grown and still had the face of a child.

All three were dressed in similar tunics and skirts with the same bracelets and head ornaments.

Tai-yu hastily rose to greet these cousins, and after the introductions they took seats while the maids served tea. All the talk now was of Tai-yu's mother. How had she fallen ill? What medicine had the doctors prescribed? How had the funeral and mourning ceremonies been conducted? Inevitably, the Lady Dowager was most painfully affected.

"Of all my children I loved your mother best," she told Tai-yu. "Now she has gone before me, and I didn't even have one last glimpse of her face. The sight of you makes me feel my heart will break!" Again she took Tai-yu in her arms and wept. The others were hard put to it to comfort her.

All present had been struck by Tai-yu's good breeding. For in spite of her tender years and evident delicate health, she had an air of natural distinction. Observing how frail she looked, they asked what medicine or treatment she had been having.

"I've always been like this," Tai-yu said with a smile. "I've been taking medicine ever since I was weaned. Many well-known doctors have examined me, but none of their prescriptions was any use. The year I was three, I remember being told, a scabby monk came to our house and wanted to take me away to be a nun. My parents wouldn't hear of it. The monk said, 'If you can't bear to part with her she'll probably never get well. The only other remedy is to keep her from hearing weeping and from seeing any relatives apart from her father and mother. That's her only hope of having a quiet life.' No one paid any attention, of course, to such crazy talk. Now I'm still taking ginseng pills."

"That's good," approved the Lady Dowager. "We're having pills made, and I'll see they make some for you."

Just then they heard peals of laughter from the back courtyard and a voice cried:

"I'm late in greeting our guest from afar!"

Tai-yu thought with surprise, "The people here are so respectful and solemn, they all seem to be holding their breath. Who can this be, so boisterous and pert?"

While she was still wondering, through the back door trooped some matrons and maids surrounding a young woman. Unlike the girls, she was richly dressed and resplendent as a fairy.

Her gold-filigree tiara was set with jewels and pearls. Her hair-clasps, in the form of five phoenixes facing the sun, had pendants of pearls. Her necklet, of red gold, was in the form of a coiled dragon studded with gems. She had double red jade pendants with pea-green tassels attached to her skirt.

Her close-fitting red satin jacket was embroidered with gold butterflies and flowers. Her turquoise cape, lined with white squirrel, was inset with designs in coloured silk. Her skirt of kingfisher-blue crepe was patterned with flowers.

She had the almond-shaped eyes of a phoenix, slanting eyebrows as long and drooping as willow leaves. Her figure was slender and her manner vivacious. The springtime charm of her powdered face gave no hint of her latent formidability. And before her crimson lips parted, her laughter rang out.

Tai-yu rose quickly to greet her.

"You don't know her yet." The Lady Dowager chuckled. "She's the terror of this house. In the south they'd call her Hot Pepper. Just call her Fiery Phoenix."

Tai-yu was at a loss how to address her when her cousins came to her rescue. "This is Cousin Lien's wife," they told her.

Though Tai-yu had never met her, she knew from her mother that Chia Lien, the son of her first uncle Chia Sheh, had married the niece of Lady Wang, her second uncle's wife. She had been educated like a boy and given the school-room name Hsi-feng.[1] Tai-yu lost no time in greeting her with a smile as "cousin".

Hsi-feng took her hand and carefully inspected her from head to foot, then led her back to her seat by the Lady Dowager.

"Well," she cried with a laugh, "this is the first time I've set eyes on such a ravishing beauty. Her whole air is so distinguished! She doesn't take after her father, son-in-law of our Old Ancestress, but looks more like a Chia. No wonder

---

[1] Splendid Phoenix.

our Old Ancestress couldn't put you out of her mind and was for ever talking or thinking about you. But poor ill-fated little cousin, losing your mother so young!" With that she dabbed her eyes with a handkerchief.

"I've only just dried my tears. Do you want to start me off again?" said the old lady playfully. "Your young cousin's had a long journey and she's delicate. We've just got her to stop crying. So don't reopen that subject."

Hsi-feng switched at once from grief to merriment. "Of course," she cried. "I was so carried away by joy and sorrow at sight of my little cousin, I forgot our Old Ancestress. I deserve to be caned." Taking Tai-yu's hand again, she asked, "How old are you, cousin? Have you started your schooling yet? What medicine are you taking? You mustn't be home-sick here. If you fancy anything special to eat or play with, don't hesitate to tell me. If the maids or old nurses aren't good to you, just let me know."

She turned then to the servants. "Have Miss Lin's luggage and things been brought in? How many attendants did she bring? Hurry up and clear out a couple of rooms where they can rest."

Meanwhile refreshments had been served. And as Hsi-feng handed round the tea and sweetmeats, Lady Wang asked whether she had distributed the monthly allowance.

"It's finished," was Hsi-feng's answer. "Just now I took some people to the upstairs storeroom at the back to look for some brocade. But though we searched for a long time we couldn't find any of the sort you described to us yesterday, madam. Could your memory have played you a trick?"

"It doesn't matter if there's none of that sort," said Lady Wang. "Just choose two lengths to make your little cousin some clothes. This evening don't forget to send for them."

"I've already done that," replied Hsi-feng. "Knowing my cousin would be here any day, I got everything ready. The material's waiting in your place for your inspection. If you pass it, madam, it can be sent over."

Lady Wang smiled and nodded her approval.

Now the refreshments were cleared away and the Lady Dowager ordered two nurses to take Tai-yu to see her two uncles.

At once Chia Sheh's wife, Lady Hsing, rose to her feet and suggested, "Won't it be simpler if I take my niece?"

"Very well," agreed the Lady Dowager. "And there's no need for you to come back afterwards."

Lady Hsing assented and then told Tai-yu to take her leave of Lady Wang, after which the rest saw them to the entrance hall. Outside the ornamental gate pages were waiting beside a blue lacquered carriage with kingfisher-blue curtains, into which Lady Hsing and her niece entered. Maids let down the curtains and told the bearers to start. They bore the carriage to an open space and harnessed a docile mule to it. They left by the west side gate, proceeded east past the main entrance of the Jung Mansion, entered a large black-lacquered gate and drew up in front of a ceremonial gate.

When the pages had withdrawn, the curtains were raised, and Lady Hsing led Tai-yu into the courtyard. It seemed to her that these buildings and grounds must be part of the Jung Mansion garden; for when they had passed three ceremonial gates she saw that the halls, side chambers and covered corridors although on a smaller scale were finely constructed. They had not the stately splendour of the other mansion, yet nothing was lacking in the way of trees, plants or artificial rockeries.

As they entered the central hall they were greeted by a crowd of heavily made-up and richly dressed concubines and maids. Lady Hsing invited Tai-yu to be seated while she sent a servant to the library to ask her husband to join them.

After a while the servant came back to report, "The master says he hasn't been feeling too well the last few days, and meeting the young lady would only upset them both. He isn't up to it for the time being. Miss Lin mustn't mope or be homesick here but feel at home with the old lady and her aunts. Her cousins may be silly creatures, but they'll be company for her and help to amuse her. If anyone is unkind to her, she must say so and not treat us as strangers."

Tai-yu had risen to her feet to listen to this message. Shortly after this she rose again to take her leave. Lady Hsing insisted that she stay for the evening meal.

"Thank you very much, aunt, you're too kind," said Tai-yu. "Really I shouldn't decline. But it might look rude if I delayed in calling on my second uncle. Please excuse me and let me stay another time."

"You're quite right," said Lady Hsing. She told a few elderly maids to escort her niece back in the same carriage, whereupon Tai-yu took her leave. Her aunt saw her to the ceremonial gate and after giving the maids some further instructions waited to see them off.

Back in the Jung Mansion, Tai-yu alighted again. The nurses led her eastwards, round a corner, through an entrance hall into a hall facing south, then passed through a ceremonial gate into a large courtyard. The northern building had five large apartments and wings on either side. This was the hub of the whole estate, more imposing by far than the Lady Dowager's quarters.

Tai-yu realized that this was the main inner suite, for a broad raised avenue led straight to its gate. Once inside the hall she looked up and her eye was caught by a great blue tablet with nine gold dragons on it, on which was written in characters large as peck measures:

Hall of Glorious Felicity.

Smaller characters at the end recorded the date on which the Emperor had conferred this tablet upon Chia Yuan, the Duke of Jungkuo, and it bore the Imperial seal.

On the large red sandalwood table carved with dragons an old bronze tripod, green with patina, stood about three feet high. On the wall hung a large scroll-picture of black dragons riding the waves. This was flanked by a bronze wine vessel inlaid with gold and a crystal bowl. By the walls were a row of sixteen cedar-wood armchairs; and above these hung two panels of ebony with the following couplet inset in silver:

Pearls on the dais outshine the sun and moon;
Insignia of honour in the hall blaze like
    iridescent clouds.

Small characters below recorded that this had been written by
the Prince of Tungan, who signed his name Mu Shih and styled
himself a fellow provincial and old family friend.

Since Lady Wang seldom sat in this main hall but used
three rooms on the east side for relaxation, the nurses led
Tai-yu there.

The large *kang* by the window was covered with a scarlet
foreign rug. In the middle were red back-rests and turquoise
bolsters, both with dragon-design medallions, and a long
greenish yellow mattress also with dragon medallions. At each
side stood a low table of foreign lacquer in the shape of plum-
blossom. On the left-hand table were a tripod, spoons, chopsticks and an incense container; on the right one, a slender-
waisted porcelain vase from the Juchow Kiln containing flowers
then in season, as well as tea-bowls and a spittoon. Below
the *kang* facing the west wall were four armchairs, their covers
of bright red dotted with pink flowers, and with four foot-
stools beneath them. On either side were two tables set out
with teacups and vases of flowers. The rest of the room need
not be described in detail.

The nurses urged Tai-yu to sit on the *kang*, on the edge
of which were two brocade cushions. But feeling that this
would be presumptuous, she sat instead on one of the chairs
on the east side. The maids in attendance served tea, and as
she sipped it she studied them, observing that their make-up,
clothes and deportment were quite different from those in other
families. Before she had finished her tea in came a maid
wearing a red silk coat and a blue satin sleeveless jacket with
silk borders. With a smile this girl announced:

"Her Ladyship asks Miss Lin to go in and take a seat over
there."

At once the nurses conducted Tai-yu along the eastern corridor to a small three-roomed suite facing south. On the *kang*

under the window was a low table laden with books and a tea-service. Against the east wall were a none too new blue satin back-rest and a bolster.

Lady Wang was sitting in the lower place by the west wall on a none too new blue satin cover with a back-rest and a bolster. She invited her niece to take the seat on the east. But guessing that this was Chia Cheng's place, Tai-yu chose one of the three chairs next to the *kang*, which had black-dotted antimacassars, looking none too new. Not until she had been pressed several times did she take a seat by her aunt.

"Your uncle's observing a fast today," said Lady Wang. "You'll see him some other time. But there's one thing I want to tell you. Your three cousins are excellent girls, and I'm sure you'll find them easy to get on with during lessons, or when you're learning embroidery or playing together. Just one thing worries me: that's my dreadful son, the bane of my life, who torments us all in this house like a real devil. He's gone to a temple today in fulfilment of a vow, but you'll see what he's like when he comes back this evening. Just pay no attention to him. None of your cousins dare to provoke him."

Tai-yu's mother had often spoken of this nephew born with a piece of jade in his mouth, his wild ways, aversion to study and delight in playing about in the women's apartments. Apparently he was so spoiled by his grandmother that no one could control him. She knew Lady Wang must be referring to him.

"Does aunt mean my elder cousin with the jade in his mouth?" she asked with a smile. "Mother often spoke of him. I know he's a year older than me, his name is Pao-yu, and for all his pranks he's very good to his girl cousins. But how can I provoke him? I'll be spending all my time with the other girls in a different part of the house while our boy cousins are in the outer courtyards."

"You don't understand," replied Lady Wang with a laugh. "He's not like other boys. Because the old lady's always doted on him, he's used to being spoilt with the girls. If they ignore him he keeps fairly quiet though he feels bored. He can always work off his temper by scolding some of his pages. But if the girls give him the least encouragement, he's so elated he gets up to all kinds of mischief. That's why you mustn't pay any attention to him. One moment he's all honey-sweet; the next, he's rude and recalcitrant; and in another minute he's raving like a lunatic. You can't take him seriously."

As Tai-yu promised to remember this, a maid announced that dinner was to be served in the Lady Dowager's apartments. Lady Wang at once led her niece out of the back door, going west along a corridor and through a side gate to a broad road running from north to south. On the south side was a dainty three-roomed annex facing north; on the north a big screen wall painted white, behind which was a small door leading to an apartment.

"That's where your cousin Hsi-feng lives." Lady Wang pointed out the place. "So next time you know where to find her. If you want anything just let her know."

By the gate several young pages, their hair in tufts, stood at attention. Lady Wang led Tai-yu through an entrance hall running from east to west into the Lady Dowager's back courtyard. Stepping through the back door, they found quite a crowd assembled who, as soon as they saw Lady Wang, set tables and chairs ready. Chia Chu's widow, Li Wan, served the rice while Hsi-feng put out the chopsticks and Lady Wang served the soup.

The Lady Dowager was seated alone on a couch at the head of the table with two empty chairs on each side. Hsi-feng took Tai-yu by the hand to make her sit in the first place on the left, but she persistently declined the honour.

"Your aunt and sisters-in-law don't dine here," said her grandmother with a smile. "Besides, you're a guest today. So do take that seat."

With a murmured apology, Tai-yu obeyed. The Lady Dowager told Lady Wang to sit down; then Ying-chun and the two other girls asked leave to be seated, Ying-chun first on the right, Tan-chun second on the left, and Hsi-chun second on the right. Maids held ready dusters, bowls for rinsing the mouth and napkins, while Li Wan and Hsi-feng standing behind the diners plied them with food.

Although the outer room swarmed with nurses and maids, not so much as a cough was heard. The meal was eaten in silence. And immediately after, tea was brought in on small trays. Now Lin Ju-hai had taught his daughter the virtue of moderation and the harm caused to the digestive system by drinking tea directly after a meal. But many customs here were different from those in her home. She would have to adapt herself to these new ways. As she took the tea, however, the rinse-bowls were proffered again, and seeing the others rinse their mouths she followed suit. After they had washed their hands tea was served once more, this time for drinking.

"You others may go," said the Lady Dowager now. "I want to have a chat with my grand-daughter."

Lady Wang promptly rose and after a few remarks led the way out, followed by Li Wan and Hsi-feng. Then her grandmother asked Tai-yu what books she had studied.

"I've just finished the *Four Books*,"[1] said Tai-yu. "But I'm very ignorant." Then she inquired what the other girls were reading.

"They only know a very few characters, not enough to read any books."

The words were hardly out of her mouth when they heard footsteps in the courtyard and a maid came in to announce, "Pao-yu is here."

Tai-yu was wondering what sort of graceless scamp or little dunce Pao-yu was and feeling reluctant to meet such a stupid creature when, even as the maid announced him, in he walked.

He had on a golden coronet studded with jewels and a golden chaplet in the form of two dragons fighting for a pearl. His red archer's jacket, embroidered with golden butterflies and flowers, was tied with a coloured tasselled palace sash.

---

[1] Confucian classics.

Over this he wore a turquoise fringed coat of Japanese satin with a raised pattern of flowers in eight bunches. His court boots were of black satin with white soles.

His face was as radiant as the mid-autumn moon, his complexion fresh as spring flowers at dawn. The hair above his temples was as sharply outlined as if cut with a knife. His eyebrows were as black as if painted with ink, his cheeks as red as peach-blossom, his eyes bright as autumn ripples. Even when angry he seemed to smile, and there was warmth in his glance even when he frowned.

Round his neck he had a golden torque in the likeness of a dragon, and a silk cord of five colours, on which hung a beautiful piece of jade.

His appearance took Tai-yu by surprise. "How very strange!" she thought. "It's as if I'd seen him somewhere before. He looks so familiar."

Pao-yu paid his respects to the Lady Dowager and upon her instructions went to see his mother.

He returned before long, having changed his clothes. His short hair in small plaits tied with red silk was drawn up on the crown of his head and braided into one thick queue as black and glossy as lacquer, sporting four large pearls attached to golden pendants in the form of the eight precious things. His coat of a flower pattern on a bright red ground was not new, and he still wore the torque, the precious jade, a lock-shaped amulet containing his Buddhistic name, and a lucky charm. Below could be glimpsed light green flowered satin trousers, black-dotted stockings with brocade borders, and thick-soled scarlet shoes.

His face looked as fair as if powdered, his lips red as rouge. His glance was full of affection, his speech interspersed with smiles. But his natural charm appeared most in his brows, for his eyes sparkled with a world of feeling. However, winning as his appearance was, it was difficult to tell what lay beneath.

Someone subsequently gave an admirable picture of Pao-yu

in these two verses written to the melody of *The Moon over
the West River*:

> Absurdly he courts care and melancholy
> And raves like any madman in his folly;
> For though endowed with handsome looks is he,
> His heart is lawless and refractory.
>
> Too dense by far to understand his duty,
> Too stubborn to apply himself to study,
> Foolhardy in his eccentricity,
> He's deaf to all reproach and obloquy.
>
> Left cold by riches and nobility,
> Unfit to bear the stings of poverty,
> He wastes his time and his ability,
> Failing his country and his family.
>
> First in this world for uselessness is he,
> Second to none in his deficiency.
> Young fops and lordlings all, be warned by me:
> Don't imitate this youth's perversity!

With a smile at Pao-yu, the Lady Dowager scolded, "Fancy
changing your clothes before greeting our visitor. Hurry up
now and pay your respects to your cousin."

Of course, Pao-yu had seen this new cousin earlier on and
guessed that she was the daughter of his Aunt Lin. He made
haste to bow and, having greeted her, took a seat. Looking
at Tai-yu closely, he found her different from other girls.

Her dusky arched eyebrows were knitted and yet not frowning, her speaking eyes held both merriment and sorrow; her
very frailty had charm. Her eyes sparkled with tears, her
breath was soft and faint. In repose she was like a lovely
flower mirrored in the water; in motion, a pliant willow swaying in the wind. She looked more sensitive than Pi Kan,[1]
more delicate than Hsi Shih.[2]

---

[1] A prince noted for his great intelligence at the end of the Shang
Dynasty.

[2] A famous beauty of the ancient Kingdom of Yueh.

"I've met this cousin before," he declared at the end of his scrutiny.

"You're talking nonsense again," said his grandmother, laughing. "How could you possibly have met her?"

"Well, even if I haven't, her face looks familiar. I feel we're old friends meeting again after a long separation."

"So much the better." The Lady Dowager laughed. "That means you're bound to be good friends."

Pao-yu went over to sit beside Tai-yu and once more gazed fixedly at her.

"Have you done much reading, cousin?" he asked.

"No," said Tai-yu. "I've only studied for a couple of years and learned a few characters."

"What's your name?"

She told him.

"And your courtesy name?"

"I have none."

"I'll give you one then," he proposed with a chuckle. "What could be better than Pin-pin?"[1]

"Where's that from?" put in Tan-chun.

"*The Compendium of Men and Objects Old and New* says that in the west is a stone called *tai* which can be used instead of graphite for painting eyebrows. As Cousin Lin's eyebrows look half knit, what could be more apt than these two characters?"

"You're making that up, I'm afraid," teased Tan-chun.

"Most works, apart from the *Four Books*, are made up; am I the only one who makes things up?" he retorted with a grin. Then, to the mystification of them all, he asked Tai-yu if she had any jade.

Imagining that he had his own jade in mind, she answered, "No, I haven't. I suppose it's too rare for everybody to have."

This instantly threw Pao-yu into one of his frenzies. Tearing off the jade he flung it on the ground.

---

[1] Knitted Brows.

"What's rare about it?" he stormed. "It can't even tell good people from bad. What spiritual understanding has it got? I don't want this nuisance either."

In consternation all the maids rushed forward to pick up the jade while the Lady Dowager in desperation took Pao-yu in her arms.

"You wicked monster!" she scolded. "Storm at people if you're in a passion. But why should you throw away that precious thing your life depends on?"

His face stained with tears, Pao-yu sobbed, "None of the girls here has one, only me. What's the fun of that? Even this newly arrived cousin who's lovely as a fairy hasn't got one either. That shows it's no good."

"She did have one once," said the old lady to soothe him. "But when your aunt was dying and was unwilling to leave her, the best she could do was to take the jade with her instead. That was like burying the living with the dead and showed your cousin's filial piety. It meant, too, that now your aunt's spirit can still see your cousin. That's why she said she had none, not wanting to boast about it. How can you compare with her? Now put it carefully on again lest your mother hears about this."

She took the jade from one of the maids and put it on him herself. And Pao-yu, convinced by her tale, let the matter drop.

Just then a nurse came in to ask about Tai-yu's quarters.

"Move Pao-yu into the inner apartment of my suite," said his grandmother. "Miss Lin can stay for the time being in his Green Gauze Lodge. Once spring comes, we'll make different arrangements."

"Dear Ancestress!" coaxed Pao-yu. "Let me stay outside Green Gauze Lodge. I'll do very well on that bed in the outer room. Why should I move over and disturb you?"

After a moment's reflection the Lady Dowager agreed to this. Each would be attended by a nurse and a maid, while other attendants were on night duty outside. Hsi-feng had already sent round a flowered lavender curtain, satin quilts and embroidered mattresses.

Tai-yu had brought with her only Nanny Wang, her old wet-nurse, and ten-year-old Hsueh-yen, who had also attended her since she was a child. Since the Lady Dowager considered Hsueh-yen too young and childish and Nanny Wang too old to be of much service, she gave Tai-yu one of her own personal attendants, a maid of the second grade called Ying-ko. Like Ying-chun and the other young ladies, in addition to her own wet-nurse Tai-yu was given four other nurses as chaperones, two personal maids to attend to her toilet and five or six girls to sweep the rooms and run errands.

Nanny Wang and Ying-ko accompanied Tai-yu now to Green Gauze Lodge, while Pao-yu's wet-nurse, Nanny Li, and his chief maid Hsi-jen made ready the big bed for him in its outer room.

Hsi-jen, whose original name was Chen-chu, had been one of the Lady Dowager's maids. The old lady so doted on her grandson that she wanted to make sure he was well looked after and for this reason she gave him her favourite, Hsi-jen, a good, conscientious girl. Pao-yu knew that her surname was Hua[1] and remembered a line of poetry which ran, "the fragrance of flowers assails men." So he asked his grandmother's permission to change her name to Hsi-jen.[2]

Hsi-jen's strong point was devotion. Looking after the Lady Dowager she thought of no one but the Lady Dowager, and after being assigned to Pao-yu she thought only of Pao-yu. What worried her, though, was that he was too headstrong to listen to her advice.

That night after Pao-yu and Nanny Li were asleep, Hsi-jen noticed that Tai-yu and Ying-ko were still up in the inner room. She tiptoed in there in her night clothes and asked:

"Why aren't you sleeping yet, miss?"

"Please sit down, sister," invited Tai-yu with a smile.

[1] Flower.
[2] Literally "assails men".

Hsi-jen sat on the edge of the bed.

"Miss Lin has been in tears all this time, she's so upset," said Ying-ko. "The very day of her arrival, she says, she's made our young master fly into a tantrum. If he'd smashed his jade she would have felt to blame. I've been trying to comfort her."

"Don't take it to heart," said Hsi-jen. "I'm afraid you'll see him carrying on even more absurdly later. If you let yourself be upset by his behaviour you'll never have a moment's peace. Don't be so sensitive."

"I'll remember what you've said," promised Tai-yu. "But can you tell me where that jade of his came from, and what the inscription on it is?"

Hsi-jen told her, "Not a soul in the whole family knows where it comes from. It was found in his mouth, so we hear, when he was born, with a hole for a cord already made in it. Let me fetch it here to show you."

But Tai-yu would not hear of this as it was now late. "I can look at it tomorrow," she said.

After a little more chat they went to bed.

Chapter 3
The Spiritual Stone Is Too Bemused to Grasp the Fairy's Riddles

Since Tai-yu's coming to the Jung Mansion, the Lady Dowager had been lavishing affection on her, treating her in every respect just like Pao-yu so that Ying-chun, Tan-chun and Hsi-chun, the Chia girls, all had to take a back seat. And Pao-yu and Tai-yu had drawn closer to each other than all the others. By day they strolled or sat together; at night they went to bed in the same apartment. On all matters, indeed, they were in complete accord.

But now Pao-chai, another cousin of Pao-yu, had suddenly appeared on the scene. She had come to visit the Chia family with her mother, Mrs. Hsueh, who was a sister-in-law of Lady Wang. Although only slightly older, she was such a proper young lady and so charming that most people considered Tai-yu inferior to her. In the eyes of the world, of course, everyone has some merits. In the case of Tai-yu and Pao-chai, one was lovely as a flower, the other graceful as a willow, but each charming in her own way, according to her distinctive temperament.

Besides, Pao-chai's generous, tactful and accommodating ways contrasted strongly with Tai-yu's stand-offish reserve and won the hearts of her subordinates, so that nearly all the maids liked to chat with her. Because of this, Tai-yu began to feel some twinges of jealousy. But of this Pao-chai was completely unaware.

Pao-yu was still only a boy and a very absurd and wilful

one at that, who treated his brothers, sisters and cousins alike, making no difference between close and distant kinsmen. Because he and Tai-yu both lived in the Lady Dowager's quarters, he was closer to her than to the other girls, and being closer had grown more intimate; but precisely because of this he sometimes offended her by being too demanding and thoughtless.

Today the two of them had fallen out for some reason and Tai-yu, alone in her room, was again shedding tears. Sorry for his tactlessness, Pao-yu went in to make it up and little by little contrived to comfort her.

As the plum blossom was now in full bloom in the Ning Mansion's garden, Chia Chen's wife Madam Yu invited the Lady Dowager, Lady Hsing, Lady Wang and the others to a party to enjoy the flowers. She brought Chia Jung and his wife with her to deliver the invitations in person, and so the Lady Dowager and the rest went over after breakfast. They strolled round the Garden of Concentrated Fragrance and were served first with tea then wine; but it was simply an informal gathering of the womenfolk of both houses for a family feast, with nothing of special interest to record.

Soon Pao-yu was tired and wanted to have a nap. The Lady Dowager ordered his attendants to take good care of him and bring him back after a rest.

At once Chia Jung's wife Chin Ko-ching said with a smile: "We have a room ready here for Uncle Pao-yu. The Old Ancestress can set her mind at rest and leave him safely to me." She told his nurses and maids to follow her with their young master.

The Lady Dowager had every confidence in this lovely slender young woman who with her gentle, amiable behaviour was her favourite of all the great-grandsons' wives of the Jung and Ning branches. She was therefore sure Pao-yu would be in good hands.

Ko-ching led the party to an inner room, where Pao-yu noticed a fine painting of "The Scholar Working by Torchlight."[1] Without even seeing who the artist was, he took a dislike to the picture. Then he read the couplet flanking it:

> A grasp of mundane affairs is genuine knowledge,
> Understanding of worldly wisdom is true learning.

These two lines disgusted him with the place for all its refinement and luxury, and he begged to go somewhere else.

"If this isn't good enough, where can we take you?" asked his hostess with a laugh. "Well, come along to my room."

Pao-yu nodded and smiled but one of his nurses protested: "It's not proper for an uncle to sleep in his nephew's room."

"Good gracious!" Ko-ching smiled. "I won't mind his being offended if I say he's still a baby. At his age such taboos don't apply. Didn't you see my brother who came last month? He's the same age as Uncle Pao-yu, but if they stood side by side I'm sure he'd be the taller."

"Why haven't I met him?" asked Pao-yu. "Do bring him in and let me have a look at him."

The women burst out laughing. "He's miles away, how can we bring him? You'll meet him some other time."

Now, having reached the young matron's room, they were met at the threshold by a subtle perfume which misted over Pao-yu's eyes and melted his bones.

"How good it smells here!" he cried.

Entering, he saw on the wall a picture by Tang Yin[2] of a lady sleeping under the blossom of a crab-apple tree in spring. On the two scrolls flanking it, Chin Kuan[3] the Sung scholar had written:

> Coolness wraps her dream, for spring is chill;
> A fragrance assails men, the aroma of wine.

---

[1] A Han Dynasty scholar, Liu Hsiang, was said to have been studying late one night when a god came with a torch to teach him the classics.

[2] See Note 1 on p. 12.

[3] See Note 1 on p. 11.

On the dressing-table was a rare mirror from Wu Tse-tien's[1] Hall of Mirrors. In the gold tray by it, on which Chao Fei-yen[2] once danced, was the quince thrown in fun by An Lu-shan[3] at Lady Yang,[4] which had wounded her breast. At one end of the room stood the couch on which Princess Shou-yang[5] had slept in the Hanchang Palace, and over it hung the curtains strung from pearls by Princess Tung-chang.[6]

"It's nice in here," exclaimed Pao-yu repeatedly in his delight.

"This room of mine is probably fit for a god," rejoined Ko-ching with a smile.

With her own hands she spread a gauze coverlet washed by Hsi Shih[7] and arranged the bridal pillow carried by Hung-niang.[8] Then the nurses and attendants made Pao-yu lie down and slipped out leaving only four maids — Hsi-jen, Mei-jen, Ching-wen and Sheh-yueh — to keep him company. Ko-ching told them to wait on the verandah and watch the kittens and puppies playing there.

Pao-yu fell asleep as soon as he closed his eyes and dreamed that Ko-ching was before him. Absent-mindedly he followed her a long way to some crimson balustrades and white marble steps among green trees and clear streams, in a place seldom trodden by the foot of man, unreached by swirling dust.

In his dream he thought happily, "This is a pleasant spot. If only I could spend my whole life here! For that I'd gladly give up my home where my parents and teachers keep caning me every day."

---

[1] A Tang empress.

[2] A Han emperor's favourite, a light dancer, hence her name "Fei-yen", meaning "Flying Swallow".

[3] See Note 2 on p. 10.

[4] The favourite of the Tang emperor Ming-huang.

[5] The beautiful daughter of Emperor Wu of the Sung Kingdom (420-479), the Northern and Southern Dynasties.

[6] A Tang princess.

[7] See Note 2 on p. 31.

[8] The maid and go-between in the Yuan drama *The Western Chamber*; Huo Hsiao-yu, the heroine of a Tang romance.

His fancy was running away with him when he heard someone singing a song on the other side of a hill:

> Gone with the clouds spring's dream,
> Flowers drift away on the stream.
> Young lovers all, be warned by me,
> Cease courting needless misery.

Pao-yu realized that the voice was a girl's and before the
song had ended he saw the singer come round the hill and
approach him. With her graceful gait and air she was truly
no mortal being. Here is as proof her description:

> Leaving the willow bank, she comes just now through the flowers.
> Her approach startles birds in the trees in the court, and soon her
> shadow falls across the verandah. Her fairy sleeves, fluttering, give
> off a heady fragrance of musk and orchid. With each rustle of her
> lotus garments, her jade pendants tinkle.
>
> Her dimpled smile is peach-blossom in spring, her blue-black hair
> a cluster of clouds. Her lips are cherries and sweet the breath from
> her pomegranate teeth.
>
> The curve of her slender waist is snow whirled by the wind.
> Dazzling her pearls and emeralds and gosling-gold the painted design
> on her forehead.
>
> She slips in and out of the flowers, now vexed, now radiant, and
> floats over the lake as if on wings.
>
> Her mothlike eyebrows are knit yet there lurks a smile, and no
> sound issues from her lips parted as if to speak as she glides swiftly
> on lotus feet and, pausing, seems poised for flight.
>
> Her flawless complexion is pure as ice, smooth as jade. Magnificent
> her costume with splendid designs. Sweet her face, compact of fra-
> grance, carved in jade; and she bears herself like a phoenix or dragon
> in flight.
>
> Her whiteness? Spring plum-blossom glimpsed through snow. Her
> purity? Autumn orchids coated with frost. Her tranquillity? A
> pine in a lonely valley. Her beauty? Sunset mirrored in a limpid
> pool. Her grace? A dragon breasting a winding stream. Her spirit?
> Moonlight on a frosty river.
>
> She would put Hsi Shih to shame and make Wang Chiang[1] blush.
> Where was this wonder born, whence does she come?
>
> Verily she has no peer in fairyland, no equal in the purple courts
> of heaven.
>
> Who can she be, this beauty?

Overjoyed by the apparition of this fairy, Pao-yu made haste
to greet her with a bow.

---

[1] A famous beauty in the Han Dynasty.

"Sister Fairy," he begged with a smile, "do tell me where you are from and whither you are going. I have lost my way. May I beg you to be my guide?"

"My home is above the Sphere of Parting Sorrow in the Sea of Brimming Grief," she answered with a smile. "I am the Goddess of Disenchantment from the Grotto of Emanating Fragrance on the Mountain of Expanding Spring in the Illusory Land of Great Void. I preside over romances and unrequited love on earth, the grief of women and the passion of men in the mundane world. The reincarnations of some former lovers have recently gathered here, and so I have come to look for a chance to mete out love and longing. It is no accident that we have met.

"My realm is not far from here. All I can offer you is a cup of fairy tea plucked by my own hands, a pitcher of fine wine of my own brewing, some accomplished singers and dancers, and twelve new fairy songs called 'A Dream of Red Mansions'. But won't you come with me?"

Forgetting Ko-ching in his delight, Pao-yu followed the goddess to a stone archway inscribed: Illusory Land of Great Void. On either pillar was this couplet:

> When false is taken for true, true becomes false;
> If non-being turns into being, being becomes non-being.

Beyond this archway was a palace gateway with the inscription in large characters: Sea of Grief and Heaven of Love. The bold couplet flanking this read:

> Firm as earth and lofty as heaven, passion from
>   time immemorial knows no end;
> Pity silly lads and plaintive maids hard put to
>   it to requite debts of breeze and moonlight.

"Well, well," thought Pao-yu, "I wonder what's meant by 'passion from time immemorial' and 'debts of breeze and moonlight'. From now on I'd like to have a taste of these things."

Little did he know that by thinking in this way he had summoned an evil spirit into his inmost heart.

He followed the goddess through the second gate past two

matching halls on both sides, each with its tablet and couplet. He had no time to read them all but noticed the names: Board of Infatuation, Board of Jealousy, Board of Morning Tears, Board of Night Sighs, Board of Spring Longing and Board of Autumn Sorrows.

"May I trouble you, goddess, to show me over these different boards?" he asked.

"They contain the records of the past and future of girls from all over the world," she told him. "These may not be divulged in advance to you with your human eyes and mortal frame."

But Pao-yu would not take no for an answer and at last she yielded to his importunity.

"Very well then," she conceded. "You may go in here and have a look round."

Pao-yu was overjoyed. He looked up and saw on the tablet the name Board of the Ill-Fated. This was flanked by the couplet:

> They brought on themselves spring grief and
>   autumn anguish;
> Wasted, their beauty fair as flowers and moon.

Grasping the meaning of this and strangely stirred, Pao-yu entered and saw more than ten large cabinets, sealed and labelled with the names of different localities. Having no interest in other provinces, he was eager to find his native place and soon discovered one cabinet labelled *First Register of Twelve Beauties of Chinling*. When he asked what this meant, Disenchantment told him:

"That is a record of the twelve foremost beauties in your honourable province. That's why it's called the First Register."

"I've always heard that Chinling's a very large place," replied Pao-yu. "Why are there only twelve girls? In our family alone just now, if you count the servants, we must have several hundreds."

"True, there are many girls in your honourable province. Only those of the first grade are registered here. The next two cabinets contain records of those in the second and third grade. As for the rest, they are too mediocre for their lives to be worth recording."

Pao-yu looked at the next two cabinets and saw written on them: *Second Register of Twelve Beauties of Chinling* and *Third Register of Twelve Beauties of Chinling*. He opened the door of this last, took out the register and turned to the first page. This was covered by a painting in ink, not of any figures or landscape but of black clouds and heavy mist. Beside this were the lines:

> A clear moon is rarely met with,
> Bright clouds are easily scattered;
> Her heart is loftier than the sky,
> But her person is of low degree.
> Her charm and wit give rise to jealousy,
> Her early death is caused by calumny,
> In vain her loving master's grief must be.

On the next page Pao-yu saw painted a bunch of flowers and a tattered mat, with the legend:

> Nothing avail her gentleness and compliance,
> Osmanthus and orchid with her fragrance vie;
> But this prize is borne off by an actor,
> And luck passes the young master by.

Unable to make anything of this, he put the album down, opened the door of another cabinet and took out the *Second Register*. This opened at a picture of fragrant osmanthus above withered lotus in a dried-up pond. By this was written:

> Sweet is she as the lotus in flower,
> Yet none so sorely oppressed;
> After the growth of a lonely tree in two soils
> Her sweet soul will be dispatched to its final rest.

Still baffled, Pao-yu put this volume aside and took out the *First Register*. The first page had a painting of two withered trees on which hung a jade belt, while at the foot of a snow-drift lay a broken golden hairpin. Four lines of verse read:

> Alas for her wifely virtue,
> Her wit to sing of willow-down, poor maid!

> Buried in snow the broken golden hairpin
> And hanging in the wood the belt of jade.

Pao-yu could make nothing of this either. He knew the goddess would not enlighten him, yet he could not bring himself to put the book down. So he turned to a painting of a bow from which was suspended a citron. This bore the legend:

> For twenty years she arbitrates
> Where pomegranates blaze by palace gates.
> How can the late spring equal the spring's start?
> When Hare and Tiger meet,[1]
> From this Great Dream of life she must depart.

On the next page was a picture of two people flying a kite, while in a large boat out at sea sat a girl, weeping, covering her face with her hands. With this were the lines:

> So talented and high-minded,
> She is born too late for luck to come her way.
> Through tears she watches the stream
> On the Clear and Bright Day;[2]
> A thousand *li* the east wind blows,
> But her home in her dreams is far away.

Next came a painting of drifting clouds and flowing water with the legend:

> Nought avail her rank and riches,
> While yet in swaddling clothes an orphan lone;
> In a flash she mourns the setting sun,
> The river Hsiang runs dry, the clouds over Chu
>   have flown.

Next was depicted a fine piece of jade dropped in the mud, with the verse:

> Chastity is her wish,
> Seclusion her desire;
> Alas, though fine as gold or jade
> She sinks at last in the mire.

-----

[1] "Tiger" and "Hare" are the third and fourth years in the twelve-year cycle.

[2] The festival, usually on the 5th of April, when the Chinese visited their family graves.

There followed a sketch of a savage wolf pursuing a lovely girl to devour her.   The verdict read:

> For husband she will have a mountain wolf,
> His object gained he ruthlessly berates her;
> Fair bloom, sweet willow in a golden bower,
> Too soon a rude awakening awaits her.

Next was depicted a seated girl reading a sutra alone in an old temple.   This had the legend:

> She sees through the transience of spring,
> Dark Buddhist robes replace her garments fine;
> Pity this child of a wealthy noble house
> Who now sleeps alone by the dimly lit old shrine.

Next came a female phoenix perched on an iceberg, with the verdict:

> This bird appears when the world falls on evil times;
> None but admires her talents and her skill;
> First she complies, then commands, then is dismissed,
> Departing in tears to Chinling more wretched still.

After this was a lonely village with a pretty girl spinning in a humble cottage.   The inscription read:

> When fortune frowns, nobility means nothing;
> When a house is ruined, kinsmen turn unkind.
> Because of help given by chance to Granny Liu,
> In time of need she is lucky a friend to find.

After this was painted a pot of orchids in bloom beside a beauty in ceremonial dress.   The legend ran:

> Peach and plum in spring winds finish seeding,
> Who can bloom like the orchid at last?
> Pure as ice and water she arouses envy,
> Vain the groundless taunts that are cast.

Next came a picture of a beautiful woman hanging herself on a tower, with the verdict:

> Love boundless as sea and sky is but illusion;
> When lovers meet, lust must be king.
> Say not all evil comes from the Jung Mansion,
> Truly, disaster originates from the Ning.

Pao-yu would have read on, but the goddess knowing his

high natural endowments and quick intelligence feared the secrets of Heaven might be divulged. She closed the book therefore and said to him with a smile:

"Why not come with me to enjoy the strange sights here instead of puzzling your head over these silly riddles?"

As if in a daze he left the registers and followed her past pearl portières and embroidered curtains, painted pillars and carved beams. Words fail to describe those brilliant vermilion rooms, floors paved with gold, windows bright as snow and palaces of jade, to say nothing of the delectable fairy flowers, rare plants and fragrant herbs.

As Pao-yu was feasting his eyes on these marvellous sights Disenchantment called with a laugh: "Come out quickly and welcome our honoured guest."

At once out came several fairies, lotus sleeves swaying, feathery garments fluttering, lovely as spring blossom, entrancing as the autumn moon. At sight of Pao-yu they reproached the goddess:

"So this is your guest! Why should we hurry out to meet *him*? You told us that today, at this hour, the spirit of Sister Vermilion Pearl would be coming to revisit her old haunts. That's why we've been waiting all this time. Why bring this filthy creature here instead to pollute this domain of immaculate maidens?"

Pao-yu started at that and wished he could slip away, feeling intolerably gross and filthy, but Disenchantment took him by the hand.

"You don't understand," she explained to the fairies. "I did set off to the Jung Mansion today to fetch Vermilion Pearl, but as I was passing the Ning Mansion I met the spirits of the Duke of Ningkuo and the Duke of Jungkuo who told me, 'Since the start of this dynasty, for some generations, our family has enjoyed a fine reputation as well as riches and rank. But after a hundred years our good fortune is at an end, gone beyond recall. Although we have many descendants, the only one fit to continue our work is our great-grandson Pao-yu.

Even though he is headstrong and eccentric, lacking in intelligence, we nonetheless had certain hopes of him. However, our family's luck has run out and there seemed to be no one to show him the right way. How fortunate we are to have met you, goddess. We beg you to warn him of the dangers of lusting after women, so that he may escape from their snares and set his feet on the right path. Then we two brothers will be happy.'

"Sympathizing with their request, I fetched him here. To begin with I made him look at the three registers of the girls in his own household. When he failed to understand, I brought him here to taste the illusion of carnal delight so that later he may perchance awaken to the truth."

With that she led Pao-yu inside. A subtle perfume hung in the air and he could not help asking what incense was being burned.

"You don't have this scent in the dusty world so you wouldn't know it," Disenchantment told him, smiling. "This is made from the essences of the different exotic young plants which grow in all famous mountain resorts. Distilled with the resin of every precious tree, its name is Marrow of Manifold Fragrance."

As Pao-yu marvelled at this they took seats and young maids served tea with such a pure scent, exquisite flavour and refreshing quality that again he asked its name.

"This tea grows in the Grotto of Emanating Fragrance on the Mountain of Expanding Spring," Disenchantment told him. "Infused with the night dew from fairy flowers and spiritual leaves, its name is Thousand Red Flowers in One Cavern."

Nodding in appreciation Pao-yu looked round him. He saw jasper lutes, rare bronze tripods, ancient paintings, new volumes of verse — nothing was lacking. But what delighted him most was the rouge by the window and the spilt powder left from a lady's toilet. On the wall hung this couplet:

> Spiritual, secluded retreat,
> Celestial world of sweet longing.

Lost in admiration of everything about him, he asked the fairies' names. They were introduced by their different appellations as Fairy of Amorous Dreams, Great Mistress of Passion, Golden Maid Bringing Grief, and Saint of Transmitted Sorrow.

Presently little maids brought in tables and chairs and set out wine and refreshments. Verily, glass vessels overflowed with nectar and amber cups brimmed with ambrosia. No need to dwell on the sumptuousness of that feast. He could not resist inquiring, though, what gave the wine its remarkably pure bouquet.

"This wine is made from the stamens of a hundred flowers and the sap of ten thousand trees mixed with the marrow of unicorns and fermented with phoenix milk," the goddess told him. "We call it Ten Thousand Beauties in One Cup."

As Pao-yu sipped it, twelve dancing girls stepped forward to ask what they should perform.

"The twelve new songs called 'A Dream of Red Mansions,'" ordered Disenchantment.

The dancers assented. Lightly striking their sandalwood castanets and softly plucking their silver lyres, they began:

> At the dawn of creation....

But the goddess interrupted them to tell Pao-yu, "This is not like your romantic dramas in the dusty world in which there are always the fixed parts of scholars, girls, warriors, old men and clowns, and the set nine tunes of the south or north. These songs of ours lament one person or event in an impromptu fashion and are easily set to wind or stringed accompaniments. But no outsider can appreciate their subtle qualities, and I doubt whether you will really understand their meaning. Unless you first read the text, they will seem to you as tasteless as chewed wax."

With that she turned and ordered a maid to bring the words of the "Dream of Red Mansions" songs. She handed the manuscript to Pao-yu, who followed the text as he listened.

FIRST SONG:
PROLOGUE TO THE DREAM OF RED MANSIONS

At the dawn of creation
Who sowed the seeds of love?
From the strong passion of breeze and moonlight
    they came.
So in this world of sweet longing
On a day of distress, in an hour of loneliness,
Fain would I impart my senseless grief

By singing this *Dream of Red Mansions*
To mourn the Gold and the Jade.

SECOND SONG:
A LIFE MISSPENT

Well-matched, all say, the gold and the jade;
I alone recall the pledge between plant and stone.
Vainly facing the hermit in sparkling snow-clad hills
I forget not the fairy in lone woods beyond the
    world.
I sigh, learning that no man's happiness is complete:
Even a pair thought well-matched
May find disappointment.

THIRD SONG:
VAIN LONGING

One is an immortal flower of fairyland,
The other fair flawless jade,
And were it not predestined
Why should they meet again in this existence?
Yet, if predestined,
Why does their love come to nothing?
One sighs to no purpose,
The other yearns in vain;
One is the moon reflected in the water,
The other but a flower in the mirror.
How many tears can well from her eyes?
Can they flow on from autumn till winter,
From spring till summer?

Pao-yu could see no merit in these disjointed and cryptic

songs, but the plaintive music intoxicated his senses. So without probing into the meaning or asking where the songs came from, he listened for a while to pass the time. The singers went on:

FOURTH SONG:
THE TRANSIENCE OF LIFE

At the height of honour and splendour
Death comes for her;
Open-eyed, she has to leave everything behind
As her gentle soul passes away.
So far her home beyond the distant mountains
That in a dream she finds and tells her parents:
"Your child has gone now to the Yellow Spring;
You must find a retreat before it is too late."

FIFTH SONG:
SEPARATION FROM DEAR ONES

Three thousand *li* she must sail through wind
   and rain,
Giving up her home and her own flesh and blood;
But afraid to distress their declining years with tears
She tells her parents: "Don't grieve for your child.
From of old good luck and bad have been predestined,
Partings and reunions are decreed by fate;
Although from now on we shall dwell far apart,
Let us still live at peace;
Don't worry over your unworthy daughter."

SIXTH SONG:
SORROW   AMIDST   JOY

She is still in her cradle when her parents die,
Although living in luxury who will dote on her?
Happily she is born too courageous and open-hearted
Ever to take a love affair to heart.
Like bright moon and fresh breeze in a hall of jade
She is matched with a talented and handsome
   husband;
May she live with him for long years
To make up for her wretched childhood!
But over the Kaotang Tower the clouds disperse,
The river Hsiang runs dry.
This is the common fate of mortal men,
Useless it is to repine.

SEVENTH SONG:
SPURNED BY THE WORLD

By nature fair as an orchid,
With talents to match an immortal,
Yet so eccentric that all marvel at her.
To her, rich food stinks,
Silken raiment is vulgar and loathsome;
She knows not that superiority fosters hatred,
For the world despises too much purity.
By the dim light of an old shrine she will fade away,
Her powder and red chamber, her youth and beauty
     wasted,
To end, despite herself, defiled on the dusty road —
Even as flawless white jade dropped in the mud.
In vain young scions of noble houses will sigh for her.

EIGHTH SONG:
UNION OF ENEMIES

A mountain wolf, a savage ruthless beast,
Mindless of past obligations
Gives himself up to pride, luxury and license,
Holding cheap the charms of a noble family's
     daughter,
Trampling on the precious child of a ducal mansion.
Alas, in less than a year her sweet soul fades away.

NINTH SONG:
PERCEPTION OF THE TRANSIENCE OF FLOWERS

She will see through the three Springs[1]
And set no store
By the red of peach-blossom, the green of willows,
Stamping out the fire of youthful splendour
To savour the limpid peace of a clear sky.
Though the peach runs riot against the sky,
Though the clouds teem with apricot blossom,
Who has seen any flower that can win safely
     through autumn?
Even now mourners are lamenting by groves of
     poplars,
Ghosts are wailing below green maples,
And the weeds above their graves stretch to the
     skyline.
Truly, changes in fortune are the cause of men's toil,
Spring blooming and autumn withering the fate of
     flowers.

---

[1] A pun meaning the three months of Spring and the three elder Chia girls. All the Chia girls had the character *chun* or spring in their names.

Who can escape the gate of birth, the fate of death?
Yet in the west, they say, grows the *sal* tree[1]
Which bears the fruit of immortality.

TENTH SONG:
RUINED BY CUNNING

Too much cunning in plotting and scheming
Is the cause of her own undoing;
While yet living her heart is broken
And after death all her subtlety comes to nothing.
A rich house, all its members at peace,
Is ruined at last and scattered;
In vain her anxious thought for half a lifetime,
For like a disturbing dream at dead of night,
Like the thunderous collapse of a great mansion,
Or the flickering of a lamp that gutters out,
Mirth is suddenly changed to sorrow.
Ah, nothing is certain in the world of men.

ELEVENTH SONG:
A LITTLE ACT OF KINDNESS

Thanks to one small act of kindness
She meets by chance a grateful friend;
Fortunate that her mother
Has done some unnoticed good.
Men should rescue the distressed and aid the poor,
Be not like her heartless uncle or treacherous cousin
Who for love of money forget their own flesh and
blood.
Truly, rewards and punishments
Are meted out by Heaven.

TWELFTH SONG:
SPLENDOUR COMES TOO LATE

Love is only a reflection in a mirror,
Worse still, rank and fame are nothing but a dream,
So quickly youth and beauty fade away.
Say no more of embroidered curtains and love-bird
quilts,
Nor can a pearl tiara and phoenix jacket
Stave off for long Death's summons.
Though it is said that old age should be free
from want,
This depends on the unknown merits laid by for
one's children.

---

[1] It was said that Sakyamuni attained Buddhahood in a grove of *sal* trees.

Jubilant in official headdress
And glittering with a gold seal of high office,
A man may be awe-inspiring and exalted,
But the gloomy way to the Yellow Spring is near.
What remains of the generals and statesmen of old?
Nothing but an empty name admired by posterity.

THIRTEENTH SONG:
GOOD THINGS COME TO AN END

Fragrant dust falls from painted beams at the close
    of spring;
By nature passionate and fair as the moon,
The true root is she of the family's destruction.
The decline of the old tradition starts with Ching,
The chief blame for the House's ruin rests with Ning.
All their sins come about through Love.

EPILOGUE:
THE BIRDS SCATTER TO THE WOOD

An official household declines,
Rich nobles' wealth is spent.
She who did good escapes the jaws of death,
The heartless meet with certain retribution.

Those who took a life have paid with their own lives,
The tears one owed have all been requited in kind.
Not light the retribution for sins against others;
All are predestined, partings and reunions.
Seek the cause of untimely death in a past existence,
Lucky she who enjoys rank and riches in old age;
Those who see through the world escape from the
    world,
While foolish lovers forfeit their lives for nothing.
When the food is gone the birds return to the wood;
All that's left is emptiness and a great void.

After this they would have gone on to sing the second
series, but the Goddess of Disenchantment saw that Pao-yu
was utterly bored.

"Silly boy!" she sighed. "You still don't understand."

Pao-yu asked the fairies then not to sing any more, explaining that he was drunk and would like to sleep off the effects
of the wine.

Disenchantment ordered the feast to be cleared away and
escorted him into a scented chamber hung with silk, more

luxuriously furnished than any he had seen in his life. More amazing still, he saw there a girl whose charm reminded him of Pao-chai, her grace of Tai-yu. He was puzzling over this when Disenchantment said:

"In your dusty world, countless green-windowed chambers and embroidered boudoirs of rich and noble families are desecrated by amorous men and loose women. Worse still, all dissolute wretches since ancient times have drawn a distinction between love of beauty and carnal desire, between love and lust, so as to gloss over their immorality. Love of beauty leads to lust, and desire even more so. Thus every sexual transport of cloud and rain is the inevitable climax of love of beauty and desire.

"And what I like about you is that you are the most lustful man ever to have lived in this world since time immemorial."

"You must be mistaken, goddess," protested the frightened Pao-yu. "My parents are always scolding me because I'm too lazy to study. How dare I risk being called 'lustful' as well? Besides, I'm still young and hardly know what that word means."

"Don't worry," said Disenchantment. "In principle all lust is the same, but it has different connotations. For instance, there are profligates in the world who delight only in physical beauty, singing, dancing, endless merriment and constant rain-and-cloud games. They would like to possess all the beauties in the world to gratify their momentary desires. These are coarse creatures steeped in fleshly lust.

"In your case, you were born with a passionate nature which we call 'lust of the mind'. This can be grasped by the mind but not expressed, apprehended intuitively but not described in words. Whereas this makes you a welcome companion to women, in the eyes of the world it is bound to make you appear strange and unnatural, an object of mockery and scorn.

"After meeting your worthy ancestors the Duke of Ningkuo and the Duke of Jungkuo today and hearing their heartfelt request, I could not bear to let you be condemned by the world for the greater glory of women. So I brought you here to entertain you with divine wine and fairy tea, then tried to awaken you with subtle songs. And now I am going to match you with my younger sister Chien-mei,[1] whose childhood name is Ko-ching, and this very night at the auspicious hour you must consummate your union. This is simply to let you know that after you have proved for yourself the illusory nature of pleasures in fairyland you should realize the vanity of love in your dusty world. From this day on you must understand this and mend your ways, giving your minds to the teachings of Confucius and Mencius and devoting yourself to the betterment of society."

With that she initiated him into the secrets of sex. Then, pushing him forward, she closed the door and left.

Pao-yu in a daze did all the goddess had told him. We can draw a veil over his first act of love.

The next day, he and Ko-ching had become so attached and exchanged so many endearments that they could not bear to part. Hand in hand they walked out for a stroll.

Suddenly they found themselves in a thorny thicket infested with wolves and tigers. In front a black torrent barred their way and there was no bridge across. They were in a quandary when Disenchantment overtook them.

"Stop! Stop!" she cried. "Turn back before it's too late."

Standing petrified Pao-yu asked, "What is this place?"

"The Ford of Infatuation," Disenchantment told him. "It's a hundred thousand feet deep and a thousand *li* wide, and there is no boat to ferry you across. Nothing but a wooden raft steered by Master Wood and punted by Acolyte Ashes, who accept no payment in silver or gold but ferry over those who are fated to cross. You strolled here by accident. If you had fallen in, then all my well-meant advice to you would have been wasted."

Even as she spoke there came a crash like thunder from

---

[1] "Combining the best," i.e., the best features of Pao-chai and Tài-yu.

the Ford of Infatuation as hordes of monsters and river devils rushed towards Pao-yu to drag him in. Cold sweat poured off him like rain. And in his terror he shouted:

"Ko-ching! Save me!"

Hsi-jen hurried in with the other maids in dismay to take him in her arms.

"Don't be afraid, Pao-yu," cried the girls. "We're here."

Chin Ko-ching was on the verandah telling the maids to watch the kittens and puppies at their play, when she heard Pao-yu call her childhood name in his dream.

"No one here knows my childhood name," she thought in surprise. "How is it that he called it out in his dream?"

Truly:

> Strange encounters take place in a secret dream,
> For he is the most passionate lover of all time.

Chapter 4
The Precious Jade of Spiritual Understanding and Pao-chai's Gold Locket

One afternoon, remembering that he had not gone in person to ask after Pao-chai's recent indisposition, Pao-yu decided to pay her a visit.

On reaching Pear Fragrance Court, Pao-yu went first to see Aunt Hsueh, whom he found distributing sewing to her maids. He paid his respects to his aunt, who caught him in her arms and hugged him.

"How good of you to come, dear boy, on a cold day like this." She beamed. "But get up here quickly on the warm *kang*." She ordered hot tea to be served.

"Is Cousin Pan at home?" asked Pao-yu.

"Ah, he's like a horse without a halter," she sighed. "He's for ever rushing about outside. Not a day does he spend at home."

"Is Pao-chai better?"

"Yes, thank you. It was thoughtful of you to send over to ask how she was the other day. She's in her room now. Why not go in and see her? It's warmer there. Go and keep her company and I'll join you as soon as I'm through here."

Pao-yu promptly slipped off the *kang* and went to his cousin's door, before which hung a somewhat worn red silk portière. Lifting this he stepped inside.

Pao-chai was sewing on the *kang*. Her glossy black hair was knotted on top of her head. She was wearing a honey-coloured padded jacket, a rose-red sleeveless jacket lined with brown- and snow-weasel fur, and a skirt of leek-yellow silk.

There was nothing ostentatious about her costume, which was none too new. Her lips needed no rouge, her blue-black eyebrows no brush; her face seemed a silver disk, her eyes almonds swimming in water. Some might think her reticence a cloak for stupidity; but circumspect as she was she prided herself on her simplicity.

As Pao-yu observed her he asked, "Are you better now, cousin?"

Pao-chai looked up and rose swiftly to her feet, saying, "Ever so much better, thank you for your kind concern."

She made him sit on the edge of the *kang* and told Ying-erh to pour tea. As she asked after the old lady and her aunts and cousins, she took in Pao-yu's costume.

He was wearing a golden filigree coronet studded with gems, a gold chaplet in the form of two dragons fighting for a pearl, a yellowish green archer's jacket embroidered with serpents and lined with white fox-fur, and a sash embroidered with many-coloured butterflies. From his neck hung a longevity locket, a talisman inscribed with his name, and the precious jade found in his mouth at the time of his birth.

"I've heard so much about that jade of yours but I've never seen it," said Pao-chai edging forward. "Do let me have a good look at it today."

Pao-yu leaned forward too, and taking the stone from his neck laid it in her hand. She held it on her palm. It was the size of a sparrow's egg, iridescent as clouds at sunrise, smooth as junket, and covered with coloured lines.

The obverse side read:

Precious Jade of Spiritual Understanding
Never Lose, Never Forget,
Eternal Life, Lasting Prosperity.

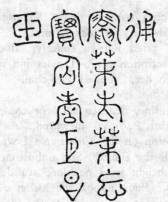

The reverse side:

1. Expels Evil Spirits.
2. Cures Mysterious Diseases.
3. Foretells Happiness and Misfortune.

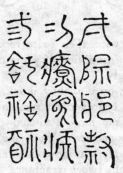

After examining both sides Pao-chai turned the jade over to study the face more closely and read the inscription aloud, not once but twice. Then she turned to ask Ying-erh:

"Why are you standing gaping there instead of getting us tea?"

Ying-erh answered with a giggle, "Those two lines seem to match the words on your locket, miss."

"Why, cousin," cried Pao-yu eagerly, "does that locket of yours have an inscription too? Do let me see it."

"Don't listen to her," replied Pao-chai. "There aren't any characters on it."

"I let you see mine, dear cousin," he countered coaxingly.

Cornered like this, Pao-chai answered, "As it happens, there is a lucky inscription on it. Otherwise I wouldn't wear such a clumsy thing all the time." She unbuttoned her red jacket and drew out a bright gold necklace studded with glittering pearls and jewels. Pao-yu took the locket eagerly and found two inscriptions, one on either side, in the form of eight minute characters.

Never Leave, Never Abandon,   Fresh Youth, Eternally Lasting.

Pao-yu read this twice, then twice repeated his own.

"Why, cousin, this inscription of yours matches mine exactly," he declared laughingly.

"It was given her by a scabby monk," explained Ying-erh. "He said it must be engraved on something made of gold."

Before she could say more Pao-chai called her to task for not bringing them some tea. Then she asked Pao-yu where he had come from. He was now close enough to her to catch whiffs of some cool, sweet fragrance which he could not identify.

"What incense do you use to scent your clothes with?" he asked. "I've never smelt this perfume before."

"I don't like incense perfumes. They just make good clothes

reek of smoke."

"What is that perfume, then?"

Pao-chai thought for a moment. "I know. It must be the pill I took this morning."

"What pills smell so good? Won't you give me one to try?"

"Don't be silly!" She laughed. "You don't take medicine for the fun of it."

Just then a servant outside announced, "Miss Lin is here." And in came Tai-yu.

"Ah!" she exclaimed at sight of Pao-yu. "I've chosen a bad time to come."

Pao-yu rose with a smile to offer her a seat while Pao-chai asked cheerfully, "What do you mean?"

"If I'd known he was here, I wouldn't have come."

"That's more puzzling than ever," said Pao-chai.

"Either everybody comes at once or no one comes," explained Tai-yu mischievously. "If he came one day and I the next, spacing out our visits, you'd have callers every day and would find it neither too lonely nor too distracting. What's so puzzling about that, cousin?"

Pao-yu saw that she was wearing a crimson camlet cloak which buttoned in front. "Is it snowing outside?" he asked.

"It's been hailing for some time," replied the maids.

"Have they brought my cape?"

"Wasn't I right?" cried Tai-yu. "As soon as I come, he must go."

"When did I say a word about going? I just want to be prepared."

"It's snowing and it's getting late now," put in Nanny Li. "Just amuse yourself here with your cousins. Your aunt's prepared refreshments in the other room. I'll send a maid for your cape and tell your pages not to wait."

As Pao-yu agreed to this, his nurse went out and sent the pages away.

Meanwhile Aunt Hsueh had tea and other good things ready for them. When Pao-yu spoke highly of the goose feet and duck tongues served a couple of days before by Madam Yu, she produced some of her own, pickled with distiller's grain, for him to try.

"These taste even better with wine," he hinted, smiling.

His aunt promptly sent for the best wine in the house.

"No wine, please, Madam Hsueh," protested Nanny Li.

"Just one cup, dear nanny," begged Pao-yu.

"No you don't! If the Lady Dowager or Lady Wang were here I wouldn't mind your drinking a whole jarful. But I haven't forgotten the way they scolded me for two days on end just because some irresponsible fool who wanted to get on the right side of you gave you a sip of wine behind my back. You've no idea what a rascal he is, Madam Hsueh. And drinking brings out all the worst in him. On days when the old lady's in a good humour she lets him drink all he wants, but on other days she won't let him touch a drop. And I'm always the one that gets into trouble."

"Don't worry, poor old thing," said Aunt Hsueh, laughing. "Go and have a drink yourself. I'll see that he doesn't drink too much. If the old lady says anything, I'll take the blame." She ordered her maids, "Take the nurses along to drink a few cups now to keep out the cold." So Nanny Li had to join the other servants to enjoy her drink.

As soon as she had gone Pao-yu said, "Don't bother to heat it. I prefer cold wine."

"That won't do," said his aunt. "Cold wine will make your hand shake when you write."

"Brother Pao," put in Pao-chai teasingly, "you've the chance every day to acquire miscellaneous knowledge. How come you don't realize how heating wine is? Drunk hot, its fumes dissipate quickly; drunk cold, it stays in your system and absorbs heat from your vital organs. That's bad for you. So do stop drinking cold wine."

Since this made sense, Pao-yu put down the wine and asked to have it warmed. Tai-yu had been smiling rather cryptically as she cracked melon-seeds. Now her maid Hsueh-yen brought in her little hand-stove.

"Who told you to bring this?" demanded Tai-yu. "Many

thanks. Think I was freezing to death here?"

"Tzu-chuan was afraid you might be cold, miss, so she asked me to bring it over."

Nursing the stove in her arms Tai-yu retorted, "So you do whatever *she* asks, but let whatever *I* say go in one ear and out the other. You jump to obey her instructions faster than if they were an Imperial edict."

Although Pao-yu knew these remarks were aimed at him, his only reply was to chuckle. And Pao-chai, aware that this was Tai-yu's way, paid no attention either. Aunt Hsueh, however, protested:

"You've always been delicate and unable to stand the cold. Why should you be displeased when they're so thoughtful?"

"You don't understand, aunt," replied Tai-yu with a smile. "It doesn't matter here, but people anywhere else might well take offence. Sending a hand-stove over from my quarters as if my hosts didn't possess such a thing! Instead of calling my maids too fussy, people would imagine I always behave in this outrageous fashion."

"You take such things too seriously," said Aunt Hsueh. "Such an idea would never have entered my head."

By now Pao-yu had already drunk three cups, and Nanny Li came in again to remonstrate. But he was enjoying himself so much talking and laughing with his cousins, he refused to stop. "Dear nanny," he coaxed, "just two more cups — that's all."

"You'd better look out," she warned. "Lord Cheng's at home today, and he may want to examine you on your lessons."

With a sinking heart, Pao-yu slowly put his cup down and hung his head.

"Don't be such a spoil-sport," protested Tai-yu. "If uncle sends for you, cousin, we can say Aunt Hsueh is keeping you. This nanny of yours has been drinking and is working off the effects of the wine on us." She nudged Pao-yu to embolden him and whispered, "Never mind the old thing. Why shouldn't we enjoy ourselves?"

"Now, Miss Lin, don't egg him on," cried Nanny Li. "You're

the only one whose advice he might listen to."

"Why should I egg him on?" Tai-yu gave a little snort. "I can't be bothered with offering him advice either. You're too pernickety, nanny. The old lady often gives him wine, so why shouldn't he have a drop more here with his aunt? Are you suggesting that auntie's an outsider and he shouldn't behave like that here?"

Amused yet vexed, Nanny Li expostulated, "Really, every word Miss Lin says cuts sharper than a knife. How can you suggest such a thing?"

Even Pao-chai couldn't suppress a smile. She pinched Tai-yu's cheek and cried, "What a tongue the girl has! One doesn't know whether to be cross or laugh."

"Don't be afraid, my child," said Aunt Hsueh. "I've nothing good to offer you, but I'll feel bad if you get a fright which gives you indigestion. Just drink as much as you want, I'll answer for it. You needn't leave till after supper. And if you do get tipsy you can sleep here." She ordered more wine to be heated, saying, "I'll drink a few cups with you and then we'll have our rice."

Pao-yu's spirits rose again at this.

His nurse told the maids, "Stay here and keep an eye on him. I'm going home to change, then I'll come back." She urged Aunt Hsueh on the sly: "Madam, don't let him have it all his own way or drink too much."

When she had gone the two or three other elderly servants who were left, not being over-conscientious, slipped out to enjoy themselves. There remained only two maids eager to please Pao-yu. But by dint of much coaxing and teasing, Aunt Hsueh kept him from drinking too many cups before the wine was whisked away. Then Pao-yu had two bowls of soup made from pickled bamboo-shoots and duck-skin and half a bowl of green-rice porridge. By this time Pao-chai and Tai-yu had finished too and all of them drank some strong tea, after which Aunt Hsueh felt easier in her mind.

Now Hsueh-yen and three other maids came back from their

own meal to wait on them, and Tai-yu asked Pao-yu:

"Are you ready to go?"

He glanced at her sidewise from under drooping eyelids. "I'll go whenever you do."

Tai-yu promptly rose to her feet. "We've been here nearly all day, it's time we left. They may be wondering where we are."

As they took their leave their wraps were brought, and Pao-yu bent his head for a maid to help him on with his hood. She shook out the crimson hood and started slipping it over his head.

"Stop, stop! Not so roughly, you silly thing," he protested, stopping her. "Have you never seen anyone put on a hood before? Better let me do it myself."

"What a commotion!" Tai-yu stood up on the *kang*. "Come here. Let me see to it."

Pao-yu went up to Tai-yu, who put her hand gently over his coronet and placed the edge of the hood on his chaplet. Then she made the red velvet pompon, the size of a walnut, bob up in front.

"That's better," she said, surveying her handiwork. "Now you can put on your cloak."

As Pao-yu did so his aunt remarked, "None of the nurses who came with you is here. Why not wait a bit?"

"Why should we wait for them?" he asked. "We've the maids to go with us. We shall be all right."

To be on the safe side, however, Aunt Hsueh told two older servants to accompany them. Then Pao-yu and Tai-yu thanked their hostess and made their way to the Lady Dowager's quarters.

The Lady Dowager had not yet dined but was very pleased when she learned where they had been. Observing that Pao-yu had been drinking, she packed him straight off to rest, forbidding him to leave his room again that evening. As she gave orders for him to be well looked after, she wondered who was attending him and asked:

"Where's Nanny Li?"

The maids dared not disclose that she had gone home. "She was here a moment ago," they said. "She must have gone out on some business."

Swaying a little, Pao-yu called over his shoulder, "She has a better time of it than our old lady. Why ask for her? I wish she'd leave me in peace to live a little longer."

While saying this he reached his apartment, where his eye fell on the brush and ink on the desk.

Ching-wen greeted him with a smile, exclaiming, "A fine one you are! You made me grind that ink for you this morning because you were feeling good; but you only wrote three characters, then threw down your brush and marched off. You've kept us waiting for you the whole day. You must set to work quickly now and use up this ink."

Reminded of that morning's happenings, Pao-yu asked, "Where are the three characters I wrote?"

"This fellow's drunk!" Ching-wen laughed. "Just before you went over to the other house you told me to have them pasted above the door, yet now you ask where they are. Not trusting anyone else to do a good job, I got up on a ladder to paste them up myself. My hands are still numb with cold."

"I forgot." Pao-yu grinned. "Let me warm your hands for you." He took Ching-wen's hands in his while they both looked up at the inscription over the lintel.

Just then Tai-yu came in and he asked her, "Tell me honestly, dear cousin, which of these three characters is the best written?"

Tai-yu raised her head and read the inscription: Red Rue Studio.

"They're all good. I didn't know you were such a calligrapher. You must write an inscription for me some time too."

"You're making fun of me again." Pao-yu chuckled. "Where's Hsi-jen?" he asked Ching-wen.

Ching-wen tilted her head towards the *kang* in the inner room, where Pao-yu saw Hsi-jen lying, fully dressed.

"That's good," he said. "But it's rather early to sleep. At breakfast in the other house this morning there was a plate of beancurd dumplings. Knowing you'd like them, I asked Madam

Yu to let me have them for supper, and they were sent over. Did you get them all right?"

"Don't ask!" answered Ching-wen. "I knew at once they were meant for me, but as I'd just finished my breakfast I left them here. Then Nanny Li came and saw them. 'Pao-yu won't be wanting these,' she said. 'I'll take them for my grandson.' She got somebody to send them home for her."

At this point Chien-hsueh brought in tea and Pao-yu said, "Do have some tea, Cousin Lin."

The maids burst out giggling. "She's gone long ago, yet you offer her tea."

After drinking half a cup himself he remembered something else and asked Chien-hsueh, "Why did you bring me *this* tea? This morning we brewed some maple-dew tea, and I told you its flavour doesn't really come out until after three or four steepings."

"I did save that other tea," she replied. "But Nanny Li insisted on trying it and she drank it all."

This was too much for Pao-yu. He dashed the cup to pieces on the floor, spattering the maid's skirt with tea. Then springing to his feet he stormed:

"Is she your grandmother, that all of you treat her so respectfully? Just because she suckled me for a few days when I was small, she carries on as if she were more important than our own ancestors. I don't need a wet-nurse any more, why should I keep an ancestress like this? Send her packing and we'll all have some peace and quiet."

He wanted to go straight to his grandmother to have the old woman dismissed.

Now Hsi-jen had only been shamming sleep, in the hope that Pao-yu would come in to tease her. She hadn't troubled to get up when he asked about the dumplings; but now that he had smashed a cup and flown into a passion she jumped up and came out to smooth things over, just as a maid arrived from his grandmother to ask the reason for the noise.

"I'd just poured out some tea," said Hsi-jen. "I slipped

because of snow on my shoes and the cup was smashed."

Then she turned to calm Pao-yu. "So you've decided to dismiss her. Good. We'd all like to leave. Why not take this chance to get rid of the lot of us? That would suit us, and you'd get better attendants too."

Thus silenced, Pao-yu let them help him to the *kang* and take off his clothes. He was still mumbling to himself but could hardly keep his eyes open, so they put him straight to bed. Hsi-jen took the precious jade off his neck, wrapped it up in her own handkerchief and tucked it under his mattress, so that it should not be cold to the touch when he put it on the next day.

Pao-yu fell asleep as soon as his head touched the pillow. Meantime Nanny Li had come in. Hearing that he was drunk she dared not risk further trouble, and having quietly made sure that he was asleep she left easier in her mind.

Chapter 5
Chia Jui Meets and Lusts After Hsi-feng

Chia Ching's birthday had now arrived. Chia Chen had six large hampers filled with choice delicacies and rare fruit and sent Chia Jung with some servants to deliver them.

"Make sure your grandfather's agreeable before you pay your respects," he cautioned his son. "Tell him that in compliance with his wishes I've not ventured to go, but I am assembling the whole family here to honour him."

After Chia Jung had left the guests began to arrive. First Chia Lien and Chia Chiang. Observing the seating arrangements, they asked what entertainment was to be offered.

"His Lordship originally planned to invite the old master, so he didn't prepare any theatricals," said the servants. "But the day before yesterday, when he heard that the old gentleman wouldn't be coming, he got us to hire some young actors and musicians. They're getting ready now on the stage in the garden."

Next to arrive were Lady Hsing, Lady Wang, Hsi-feng and Pao-yu. They were welcomed in by Chia Chen and Madam Yu, whose mother had already come. After greetings had been exchanged they were urged to be seated. Chia Chen and his wife handed round tea.

"The Lady Dowager is our Old Ancestress," said Chia Chen with a smile. "My father is only her nephew, and we wouldn't have presumed to invite her on his birthday if not for the fact that the weather is refreshingly cool now and all the chrysanthemums in our garden are at their best. We thought it might prove a pleasant distraction for her to watch all her children and grandchildren enjoying themselves. She hasn't favoured us with her presence, however."

"Up to yesterday she meant to come," explained Hsi-feng before Lady Wang could get a word in. "But yesterday evening she saw Pao-yu eating some peaches and she couldn't resist eating nearly a whole peach. She had to get up twice just before dawn, which left her tired out this morning. She asked me to tell you that she couldn't come, but she hopes you'll send her a few delicacies if you have some that are easy to digest."

"That explains it," said Chia Chen. "The old lady is so fond of lively parties, I was sure there must be some reason for her absence."

Lady Wang remarked, "The other day Hsi-feng told me that Jung's wife is indisposed. What's wrong with her?"

"It's a very puzzling illness," replied Madam Yu. "At the Mid-Autumn Festival last month she enjoyed herself half the night with the old lady and you, and came home none the worse. But for a fortnight since the twentieth of last month she's grown weaker and weaker every day and lost all her appetite. And she hasn't had a period for two months."

"Can she be pregnant?" asked Lady Hsing.

Just then the arrival of Chia Sheh, Chia Cheng and the other gentlemen was announced. They were in the reception hall. Chia Chen hurried out.

Madam Yu continued, "Some doctors thought it might mean a happy event. But yesterday she was examined by an excellent physician and according to him it isn't a pregnancy but a serious illness. He made out a prescription, and today after one dose she feels less dizzy but there hasn't been much other improvement."

"If she weren't quite incapable of any exertion, I know she'd have made an effort to be here today," observed Hsi-feng.

"You saw her here on the third," said Madam Yu. "She forced herself to bear up for several hours, because she's so fond of you she couldn't bear to tear herself away."

Hsi-feng's eyes became moist. After a pause she exclaimed,

"Truly, 'Storms gather without warning in nature, and bad luck befalls men overnight.' But life is hardly worth living if such an illness can carry off one so young!"

As she was speaking Chia Jung walked in. Having greeted the visitors he told his mother, "I've just taken the delicacies to my grandfather. I told him my father was waiting on Their Lordships and entertaining the young gentlemen here, and that in compliance with his orders he wouldn't presume to go over. Grandfather was very pleased. He expressed approval and told me to ask you and my father to attend to the elder generation while we entertain the younger. He also wants to have ten thousand copies of his version of *Rewards and Punishments* printed and distributed as quickly as possible. I've already given this message to my father. Now I must hurry and see to the food for all the grand-uncles, uncles and other gentlemen."

"Just a minute, Master Jung," interposed Hsi-feng. "Tell me, how is your wife today?"

"Not well at all." The young man's face clouded. "Do go and see her for yourself, aunt, on your way home." He left without saying any more.

Madam Yu asked Lady Hsing and Lady Wang, "Would you prefer to eat here or in the garden? The actors are preparing out there."

"Why not eat here and then go out?" suggested Lady Wang. "That would be simpler."

Lady Hsing seconded this.

So Madam Yu ordered the meal to be served at once. There was an answering cry in unison outside the door and the maids went to fetch the dishes. Soon the feast was ready. Madam Yu made Lady Hsing, Lady Wang and her mother take the places of honour, while she sat at a side table with Hsi-feng and Pao-yu.

"We came to congratulate the old gentleman on his birthday," remarked Lady Hsing and Lady Wang. "But now it looks, doesn't it, as if we were celebrating our own?"

"The Elder Master is fond of retirement," said Hsi-feng.

"He's lived so long as an ascetic, we can already consider him an immortal. So he'll know by divine intuition what you've just said."

This set the whole company laughing. The ladies, having by now finished their meal, rinsed their mouths and washed their hands. Just as they were ready to go into the garden, Chia Jung turned up to tell his mother:

"All my grand-uncles, uncles and cousins have finished their meal. Lord Sheh has some business at home, and Lord Cheng has also left as he doesn't care for theatricals or anything rowdy. Uncle Lien and Cousin Chiang have taken the others over to watch the performance.

"Cards and gifts have been brought from the four princes of Nanan, Tungping, Hsining and Peiching, from Duke Niu of Chenkuo and five other dukes, as well as from Marquis Shih of Chungching and seven other marquises. I've reported this to my father, had the presents put in the counting-house and the catalogues of gifts placed on file, and my father's 'received with thanks' cards handed to the messengers, who were given the usual tips and a meal before they left.

"Won't you ask the ladies to go and sit in the garden now, mother?"

"We've just finished our meal too," said Madam Yu. "We're coming over."

"I'd like to drop in and see Jung's wife first, madam," said Hsi-feng. "May I join you later?"

"A good idea," approved Lady Wang. "We'd all go if not for fear of disturbing her. Tell her we asked after her."

"My daughter-in-law always does as you ask her, dear sister," said Madam Yu. "I'll feel much easier in my mind if you go and cheer her up. But join us in the garden as soon as you can."

Pao-yu asked permission to go with Hsi-feng.

"Go if you want, but don't be long," said his mother. "Remember she's your nephew's wife."

So Madam Yu took Lady Hsing, Lady Wang and her own

mother to the Garden of Concentrated Fragrance, while Hsi-feng and Pao-yu went with Chia Jung to see Ko-ching.

They entered her room quietly and when she made an effort to rise Hsi-feng protested, "Don't. It would make you dizzy." She hurried forward to clasp Ko-ching's hand, exclaiming, "How thin you've grown, my poor lady, in the few days since last I saw you!"

She sat down on her mattress, while Pao-yu also asked after his niece's health and took a chair opposite.

"Bring in tea at once," called Chia Jung. "My aunt and second uncle had none in the drawing-room."

Holding Hsi-feng's hand, Ko-ching forced a smile.

"Living in a family like this is more than I deserve," she said. "My father-in-law and mother-in-law treat me as their own daughter. And although your nephew's young, we have such a regard for each other that we've never quarrelled. In fact the whole family, old and young, not to mention you, dear aunt — that goes without saying — have been goodness itself to me and shown me nothing but kindness. But now that I've fallen ill all my will power's gone, and I haven't been able to be a good daughter-in-law. I want so much to show how I appreciate your goodness, aunt, but it's no longer in my power now. I doubt if I shall last the year out."

Pao-yu was looking pensively at the picture *Sleeping Under a Crab-Apple Tree in Spring* and Chin Kuan's couplet:

> Coolness wraps her dream, for spring is chill;
> A fragrance assails men, the aroma of wine.

As he raptly recalled his dream here of the Illusory Land of Great Void, Ko-ching's remarks pierced his heart like ten thousand arrows and unknown to himself his tears flowed. Hsi-feng, distressed as she was, did not want to upset the patient even more, knowing it would be better to distract and console her.

"You're a regular old woman, Pao-yu," she scolded. "It's not as bad as your niece would have us believe." She turned to Ko-ching. "How can someone your age give way to such foolish fancies just because of a little illness? Do you want to make yourself worse?"

"She'd be all right if only she'd eat," put in Chia Jung.

"Her Ladyship told you not to be too long," Hsi-feng reminded Pao-yu. "Don't hang about here upsetting Ko-ching and making Her Ladyship worry." She then turned to Chia Jung and said, "Take Uncle Pao to rejoin the others while I stay here a little longer."

So Chia Jung led Pao-yu to the Garden of Concentrated Fragrance while Hsi-feng soothed Ko-ching and whispered some well-meant advice into her ear.

When Madam Yu sent a servant for the third time to fetch her she said to Ko-ching, "Take good care of yourself. I'll come back again to see you. The fact that this good doctor has been recommended to us is a sign that you're going to get better. Don't you worry."

"Even if he were an immortal, he could cure a disease but not avert my fate," retorted Ko-ching with a smile. "I know it's only a matter of time now, auntie."

"How can you get better if you keep thinking like that? You must look on the bright side. In any case, I'm told the doctor said that even if you're not cured there's no danger until the spring. It's only the middle of the ninth month now. You've four or five months yet, quite long enough to recover from any illness. It would be another matter if our family couldn't afford ginseng; but your father and mother-in-law can easily give you two catties of ginseng a day, not to mention two drams. Mind you rest well. I'm off now to the garden."

"I'm sorry I can't go with you, dear aunt," said Ko-ching. "Do come back again when you've time and let's have a few more good talks."

Hsi-feng's eyes smarted again at this. "Of course I'll come whenever I'm free," she promised.

Accompanied by her own maids and some from the Ning Mansion, she took a winding path to the side gate of the garden. There a rare sight met her eyes.

Yellow chrysanthemums carpeted the ground,
Green willows covered the slopes;
Small bridges spanned the brooks
And winding pathways led to quiet retreats.
Clear springs welled from the rocks,
Fragrance was wafted from trellises laden with
    flowers,
While russet tree-tops swayed
In scattered copses lovely as a painting.
The autumn wind was chilly
And the song of golden orioles had ceased,
But crickets were still chirping in the warm sunshine.
At the far southeast end
Cottages nestled among the hills;
On the northwest side
Pavilions brooded over the lake water.
Fluting cast a subtle enchantment over men's senses,
And silk-gowned girls strolling through the woods
Added to the charm of the scene.

Hsi-feng was strolling along enjoying this sight when a man appeared without warning from behind an artificial rockery and accosted her with, "Greetings, sister-in-law!"

She stepped back, startled, and asked, "Is it Master Jui?"

"Who else could it be? Don't tell me you don't know me."

"Of course I do, but you took me by surprise."

"We must have been fated to meet, sister-in-law." He was devouring her with his eyes as he spoke. "I slipped away from the banquet just now for a quiet stroll in this secluded spot. And I meet you here! What is this if not fate?"

Hsi-feng had sense enough to see through him. "No wonder Lien always speaks so highly of you," she rejoined with a smile, feigning pleasure. "From seeing you today and hearing you talk, I can see how clever and understanding you are. I've no time to spare now, I must join Her Ladyship. But perhaps we shall meet again some other day."

"I've often wanted to call and pay my respects. But I thought, being young, you might not welcome me."

"What nonsense." She assumed another smile. "Aren't we of the same family?"

Enraptured by this unexpected good fortune, Chia Jui looked ready to make more indecent advances. But Hsi-feng urged him, "You must hurry back before you're missed, or they'll make you drink forfeits."

Half numbed by this tantalizing remark he walked slowly away, looking back at her over his shoulder. Hsi-feng purposely slowed down until he was out of sight.

"You can know a man's face but not his heart," she reflected. "I'll show the beast! If he tries anything like that with me, I'll sooner or later make him die at my hands, to let him know my ability."

Then, rounding a miniature hill, she met several matrons hurrying breathlessly towards her.

"Our mistress sent us to fetch you, madam," they cried. "She was worried because you didn't come."

"Your mistress is devilish impatient!"

Continuing to saunter along, she asked how many items had been performed. The answer was: Eight or nine. They had now reached the back door of the Pavilion of Heavenly Fragrance, where Pao-yu was amusing himself with some maids.

"No silly tricks now, Cousin Pao-yu," she warned him.

"The ladies are all in the gallery," one of the girls told her. "Just up those stairs, madam."

Hsi-feng gathered up her skirts to mount the stairs and found Madam Yu waiting for her on the landing.

"You and your niece are so thick, I thought you'd never tear yourself away," teased Madam Yu. "You'd better move over tomorrow and stay with her. Sit down now and let me give you a toast."

Hsi-feng asked Lady Hsing and Lady Wang's permission to be seated and exchanged a few polite remarks with Madam Yu's mother, then she sat down beside her hostess to sip wine and watch the performance. Madam Yu sent for the list of their repertoire and asked her to choose a few items.

"How can I presume when Their Ladyships are present?" demurred Hsi-feng.

"Old Mrs. Yu has chosen several already," replied Lady Hsing and Lady Wang. "It's your turn to pick a couple of good ones for us."

Hsi-feng rose to signify obedience. Taking the list she read through it and marked *The Resurrection*[1] and *The Rhapsody*.[2] Handing it back she observed, "When they've finished this *Double Promotion*[3] there'll be just time enough for these two."

"Yes," said Lady Wang. "We must let our hosts have some rest soon. Especially as this is a worrying time for them."

"You come over so seldom," protested Madam Yu, "I do hope you'll stay a bit longer. It's early yet."

Hsi-feng stood up to look below and asked, "Where are the gentlemen?"

"They've gone to drink in the Pavilion of Lingering Dawn," replied one of the matrons. "They took the musicians with them."

"Our presence cramps their style," remarked Hsi-feng. "I wonder what they're up to behind our backs?"

"How can you expect everybody to be as proper as you?" said Madam Yu jokingly.

So they laughed and chatted till the plays came to an end, when the wine was taken away and rice brought in. After the meal they returned to the drawing-room for tea, then ordered their carriages and took their leave of old Mrs. Yu. They were seen to their carriages by Madam Yu, attended by all the concubines and maids, and there they found the young men waiting with Chia Chen. The latter urged Lady Hsing and Lady Wang to come back again the next day, but Lady Wang declined. "We've spent the whole day here and we're tired. We shall have to rest tomorrow."

Chia Jui kept his eyes on Hsi-feng as the visitors got into their carriages and drove off.

Hsi-feng dropped in more often now to see Ko-ching, who seemed slightly better on some days although in general her

---

[1] A scene from *The Peony Pavilion*, by the Ming playwright Tang Hsien-tsu.

[2] A scene from *The Palace of Eternal Youth*, by the Ching playwright Hung Sheng.

[3] A popular opera chosen for its auspicious title.

health did not improve, to the great dismay of her husband and his parents. And Chia Jui, calling several times on Hsi-feng, invariably found she had gone to the Ning Mansion.

The thirtieth day of the eleventh month would be the winter solstice. As it approached, the Lady Dowager, Lady Wang and Hsi-feng sent daily to inquire after Ko-ching and were told each time that she was neither better nor worse.

"It's a hopeful sign," Lady Wang told the Lady Dowager, "if an illness grows no worse at a season like this."

"Yes, of course," replied the old lady. "If anything were to happen to the dear child, I'm sure it would break my heart."

In her distress she sent for Hsi-feng and said, "You and she have always been good friends. Tomorrow's the first of the twelfth month, but the day after that I want you to call on her and see just how she is. If she's any better, come and tell me. That would take a great weight off my mind. And you must have the things she used to like to eat made and sent round."

Hsi-feng promised to do this and after breakfast on the second she went to the Ning Mansion to see Ko-ching. Although the invalid appeared no worse, she had grown very thin and wasted. Hsi-feng sat and chatted with her for some time, assuring her that she had no cause for alarm.

"Whether I'll ever recover or not we'll know when spring comes," said Ko-ching. "Maybe I shall, for the winter solstice has passed and I'm no worse. Please tell the old lady and Lady Wang not to worry. Yesterday I ate two of the yam cakes stuffed with dates that the old lady sent, and I think they did me good."

"We'll send you some more tomorrow," offered Hsi-feng. "Now I must go to see your mother-in-law before hurrying back to tell the old lady how you are."

"Please send my respects to her and Lady Wang."

Promising to do so, Hsi-feng left. She went to sit with Madam Yu who asked, "Tell me frankly, how did you find her?"

Hsi-feng lowered her head for a while. "There seems to be little hope," she said at last. "If I were you I'd make ready the things for the funeral. That may break the bad luck."

"I've had them secretly prepared. But I can't get any good wood for you know what, so I've let that go for the time being."

After drinking some tea and chatting a little longer, Hsi-feng said she must go back to report to the Lady Dowager.

"Don't break it to her yet," said Madam Yu. "We don't want to alarm the old lady."

Hsi-feng agreed to this and took her leave. Home again, she told the Lady Dowager, "Jung's wife sends her respects and kowtows to you. She says she's better and you mustn't worry. When she's a little stronger, she'll come herself to kowtow and pay her respects."

"How did she seem?"

"For the present there's nothing to fear. She's in good spirits."

The Lady Dowager thought this over, then said, "Go and change your clothes now and rest."

Hsi-feng withdrew and reported to Lady Wang before going back to her room. Ping-erh helped her into the informal clothes she had warming by the fire. Then Hsi-feng, taking a seat, asked what had happened during her absence.

"Nothing much." The maid handed her a bowl of tea. "Lai Wang's wife came with the interest on that three hundred taels, which I put away. And Master Jui sent round again to ask if you were in, as he wanted to pay his respects."

"That wretch! He deserves to die." Hsi-feng snorted. "Just see what I do to the beast if he comes!"

"Why does he keep calling?"

Hsi-feng described their meeting and all he had said to her in the Ning Mansion garden during the ninth month.

"A toad hankering for a taste of swan," scoffed Ping-erh. "The beast hasn't a shred of common decency. He deserves a bad end for dreaming of such a thing."

"Let him come," said Hsi-feng. "I know how to deal with

him."

While Hsi-feng was talking to Ping-erh, Chia Jui was announced. She ordered him to be admitted at once.

Overjoyed at being received, he hastened in and greeted her effusively, beaming with smiles. With a show of regard she made him take a seat and offered him tea. The sight of her in informal dress threw him into raptures. Gazing amorously at her he asked:

"Why isn't Second Brother Lien home yet?"

"I wouldn't know," Hsi-feng replied.

"Perhaps he's been caught by someone and can't tear himself away?"

"Perhaps. Men are like that. Bewitched by every pretty face they see."

"Not all of us, sister-in-law. I'm not like that."

"How many are there like you? Not one in ten."

Tweaking his ears and rubbing his cheeks with delight, the young man insinuated, "You must be very bored here day in and day out."

"Yes, indeed. I keep wishing someone would drop in for a chat to cheer me up."

"I have plenty of time. Suppose I were to drop in to amuse you every day?"

"Now you're joking," she replied archly. "You wouldn't want to come and see me."

"I mean every word I say. May a thunderbolt strike me if I don't! I didn't dare come before because I was told you were very strict and took offence at the least little thing. Now I see how charming and how kind you are, you may be sure I'll come, even if it costs me my life."

"You're certainly much more understanding than Chia Jung and his brother. They look so refined one would expect them to be understanding, but they're stupid fools with no insight at all into other people's hearts."

Inflamed by this praise, he edged closer. Staring at the purse hanging from her girdle, he asked if he might look at her rings.

"Take care," she whispered. "What will the maids think?"

He drew back instantly as if obeying an Imperial decree or a mandate from Buddha.

"You had better go now." Hsi-feng smiled.

"Don't be so cruel. Let me stay a little longer."

"This is no place for you during the day with so many people about," she murmured. "Go now but come back again secretly at the first watch. Wait for me in the western entrance hall."

To Chia Jui this was like receiving a pearl of great price. "You're not joking are you?" he demanded. "How can I hide there with people passing back and forth all the time?"

"Don't worry. I'll dismiss all the pages on night duty. Once the gates on both sides are locked, no one can come through."

Hardly able to contain himself for joy, the young man hurried off, convinced he would have his desire and longing for the evening.

That night, sure enough, he groped his way to the Jung Mansion, slipping into the entrance hall just before the gates were bolted. It was pitch dark and not a soul was about. Already the gate to the Lady Dowager's quarters was locked, only the one on the east remaining open.

He waited, listening intently, but no one came. Then with a sudden clatter the east gate was bolted too. Frantic as he was, he dared not make a sound. He crept out to try the gate and found it securely closed. Escape was out of the question, for the walls on either side were too high to climb.

The entrance hall was bare and draughty. As it was the depth of winter the nights were long and an icy north wind chilled him to the bone. He almost froze to death.

At last dawn came and a matron appeared to open the east gate. As she went over to knock on the west gate and was looking the other way, Chia Jui shot out like a streak of smoke, hugging his shoulders. Luckily no one else was up at this early hour. He was able to escape unseen through the postern door.

Chia Jui had been orphaned early and left in the charge of

his grandfather Chia Tai-ju, a strict disciplinarian who allowed him no freedom for fear he drink or gamble outside and neglect his studies. Now that he had stayed out all night his grandfather was furious and suspected him of drinking, gambling or whoring, little guessing the truth of the matter.

In a cold sweat with fright, Chia Jui tried to lie his way out.

"I went to my uncle's house, and because it was late he kept me for the night."

"You have never dared leave home before without permission," thundered his grandfather. "You deserve a beating for sneaking off like that. And a worse one for deceiving me."

He gave Chia Jui thirty or forty strokes with a bamboo, would not let him have any food, and made him kneel in the courtyard to study ten days' lessons. This thrashing on an empty stomach and kneeling in the wind to read essays completed the wretched youth's misery after his freezing night.

But still too blinded by infatuation to realize that Hsi-feng was playing with him, he seized his first chance a couple of days later to call. She reproached him for his breach of faith, earnestly as he protested his innocence; and since he had delivered himself into her hands she could not but devise further means to cure him.

"Tonight you can wait for me in another place — that vacant room off the passage behind this apartment. But mind you don't make any mistake this time."

"Do you really mean it?"

"Of course I do. If you don't believe me, don't come."

"I'll come, I'll come, even if I should die for it."

"Now, you'd better go."

Assuming that this time all would go well, Chia Jui went off.

Having got rid of him, Hsi-feng held a council of war and baited her trap while the young man waited at home impatiently, for to his annoyance one of their relatives called and stayed to supper. By the time he left the lamps were being lit, and Chia Jui had to wait for his grandfather to retire before he could slip over to the Jung Mansion and wait in the place appointed. He paced the room frantic as an ant on a hot griddle, but there was no sight or sound of anyone.

"Is she really coming?" he wondered. "Or shall I be left to freeze for another whole night?"

Just then a dark figure appeared. Sure that it was Hsi-feng, he threw caution to the winds and barely had the figure stepped through the door than he flung himself on it like a ravenous tiger, or a cat pouncing on a mouse.

"Dearest!" he cried. "I nearly died of longing."

He carried her to the *kang*, where he showered kisses on her and fumbled with her clothes, pouring out incoherent endearments. Not a sound came from the figure in his arms.

Chia Jui had just pulled down his pants and prepared to set to work when a sudden flash of light made him look up. There stood Chia Chiang, a taper in his hand.

"What's going on in here?" he demanded.

The figure on the *kang* said with a chuckle, "Uncle Jui was trying to bugger me."

When Chia Jui saw that it was Chia Jung, he wished he could sink through the ground. In utter confusion he turned to run away.

"Oh, no you don't!" Chia Chiang grabbed him. "Aunt Hsi-feng has told Lady Wang that without any reason you tried to make love to her. To escape your attentions she played this trick to trap you. Lady Wang's fainted from shock. I was sent here to catch you. I found you on top of him, you can't deny it. So come along with me to Lady Wang!"

Chia Jui nearly gave up the ghost. "Dear nephew," he pleaded, "do tell her you couldn't find me. I'll pay you well for it tomorrow."

"I might do that. Depends how much you're willing to pay. I can't just take your word for it, I must have it down in writing."

"How can I put a thing like this down in writing?"

"That's no problem. Just write that you borrowed so much silver from the bank to pay a gambling debt."

"All right. But I've no paper or brush."

"That's easy." Chia Chiang disappeared for a moment and promptly returned with writing materials, whereupon the two of them forced Chia Jui to write and sign an I.O.U. for fifty taels which Chia Chiang pocketed. When he urged Chia Jung to leave, however, the latter at first absolutely refused and threatened to lay the matter before the whole clan the next morning. Chia Jui kowtowed to him in desperation. However, with Chia Chiang mediating between them, he was forced to write another I.O.U. for fifty taels of silver.

"I'll get the blame if you're seen leaving," said Chia Chiang. "The Lady Dowager's gate is closed, and the Second Master is in the hall looking over the things which have arrived from Chinling, so you can't get out that way. You'll have to go through the back gate. But if anyone meets you I'll be finished too. Let me see if the coast is clear. You can't hide here, they'll be bringing stuff in presently. I'll find you somewhere to wait."

He blew out the light and dragged Chia Jui out to the foot of some steps in the yard.

"Here's a good place," he whispered. "Squat down there until we come back and don't make a sound."

As the two others left, Chia Jui squatted obediently at the foot of the steps. He was thinking over his predicament when he heard a splash above him and a bucket of slops was emptied over his head. A cry of dismay escaped him. But he clapped one hand over his mouth and made not another sound, though covered with filth from head to foot and shivering with cold. Then Chia Chiang hurried over calling:

"Quick! Run for it!"

At this reprieve, Chia Jui bolted through the back door to his home. By now the third watch had sounded, and he had to knock at the gate. The servant who opened it wanted to know how he came to be in such a state.

"I fell into a cesspool in the dark," lied Chia Jui.

Back in his own room he stripped off his clothes and washed.

王熙鳳毒設
相思局
賈天祥正照
風月鑑

Only then did he realize with rage the trick Hsi-feng had play-ed him, yet the recollection of her charms still made him long to embrace her. There was no sleep for him that night. After-wards, however, although he still longed for Hsi-feng, he steer-ed clear of the Jung Mansion.

Both Chia Jung and Chia Chiang kept dunning him for pay-ment, so that his fear of being found out by his grandfather and the hopeless passion which consumed him were now ag-gravated by the burden of debts, while he had to work hard at his lessons every day. The unmarried twenty-year-old, con-stantly dreaming of Hsi-feng, could not help indulging in "finger-play". All this, combined with the effect of two nights of exposure, soon made him fall ill. Before a year was out he suffered from heartburn, loss of appetite, emissions in his urine and blood in his phlegm; his legs trembled, his eyes smarted; he was feverish at night and exhausted by day. And finally he collapsed in a fit of delirium.

The doctors who were called in dosed him with dozens of catties of cinnamon, aconitum roots, turtle-shell, liriope, poly-gonatum and so forth — but all to no effect. With the coming of spring he took a turn for the worse.

His grandfather rushed to and fro in search of new physi-cians, yet they proved useless. And when pure ginseng was prescribed this was beyond Chia Tai-ju's means: he had to ask for help from the Jung Mansion. Lady Wang told Hsi-feng to weigh out two ounces for him.

"All our recent supply was used the other day in the old lady's medicine," said Hsi-feng. "You told me to keep the remaining whole roots for General Yang's wife, and as it hap-pens I sent them round yesterday."

"If we've none, send to your mother-in-law's for some. Or your Cousin Chen's household may let us have what's needed. If you can save the young man's life, that will be a good deed."

But instead of doing as she was told, Hsi-feng scraped to-gether less than an ounce of inferior scraps which she dispatched with the message that this was all Her Ladyship had. To Lady Wang, however, she reported that she had collected two ounces and sent them over.

Chia Jui was so anxious to recover that there was no medicine he would not try, but all the money spent in this way was wasted.

One day a lame Taoist priest came begging for alms and professed to have specialized in curing diseases due to retribution. Chia Jui heard him from his sick-bed. At once, kowtowing on his pillow, he loudly implored his servants to bring the priest in.

When they complied he seized hold of the Taoist and cried: "Save me, Bodhisattva! Save me!"

"No medicine can cure your illness," rejoined the Taoist gravely. "However, I can give you a precious object which will save your life if you look at it every day."

He took from his wallet a mirror polished on both sides and engraved on its handle with the inscription: Precious Mirror of Love.

"This comes from the Hall of the Illusory Spirit in the Land of Great Void," he told Chia Jui. "It was made by the Goddess of Disenchantment to cure illnesses resulting from lust. Since it has the power to preserve men's lives, I brought it to the world for the use of intelligent, handsome, high-minded young gentlemen. But you must only look into the back of the mirror. On no account look into the front — remember that! I shall come back for it in three days' time, by when you should be cured." He strode off then before anyone could stop him.

"This is a strange business," reflected Chia Jui. "Let me try looking at this Taoist's mirror and see what happens." He picked it up and looked into the back. Horrors! A skeleton was standing there! Hastily covering it, he swore, "Confound that Taoist, giving me such a fright! But let me see what's on the other side."

He turned the mirror over and there inside stood Hsi-feng, beckoning to him. In raptures he was wafted as if by magic into the mirror, where he indulged with his beloved in the sport of cloud and rain, after which she saw him out.

He found himself back in his bed and opened his eyes with

a cry. The mirror had slipped from his hands and the side with the skeleton was exposed again. Although sweating profusely after his wet dream, the young man was not satisfied. He turned the mirror over again, Hsi-feng beckoned to him as before, and in he went.

But after this had happened four times and he was about to leave her for the fourth time, two men came up, fastened iron chains upon him and proceeded to drag him away. He cried out:

"Let me take the mirror with me!"

These were the last words he uttered.

The attendants had simply observed him look into the mirror, let it fall and then open his eyes and pick it up again. This time, however, when the mirror fell he did not stir. They pressed round and saw that he had breathed his last. The sheet under his thighs was cold and wet.

At once they laid him out and made ready the bier, while his grandparents gave way to uncontrollable grief and cursed the Taoist.

"This devilish mirror!" swore Chia Tai-ju. "It must be destroyed before it does any more harm." He ordered it to be thrown into the fire.

A voice from the mirror cried out: "Who told you to look at the front? It's you who've taken false for true. Why should you burn me?"

That same instant in hustled the lame Taoist, shouting, "I can't let you destroy the Precious Mirror of Love!" Rushing forward he snatched it up, then was off like the wind.

Chapter 6
Literary Talent Is Tested by Composing Inscriptions in Grand View Garden

One evening, tired of embroidering, Hsi-feng sat nursing her hand-stove by the lamp and told Ping-erh to warm her embroidered quilt early, after which they both went to bed. Ping-erh fell fast asleep. And Hsi-feng's eyelids were drooping drowsily when to her astonishment in came Ko-ching.

"How you love to sleep, aunt!" cried Ko-ching playfully. "I'm going home today, yet you won't even see me one stage of the way. But we've always been so close, I couldn't go without coming to say goodbye. Besides, there's something I'd like done which it's no use my entrusting to anyone else."

"Just leave it to me," replied Hsi-feng, rather puzzled.

"You're such an exceptional woman, aunt, that even men in official belts and caps are no match for you. Is it possible you don't know the sayings that 'the moon waxes only to wane, water brims only to overflow,' and 'the higher the climb the harder the fall'? Our house has prospered for nearly a hundred years. If one day it happens that at the height of good fortune the 'tree falls and the monkeys scatter' as the old saying has it, then what will become of our cultured old family?"

Quick to comprehend, Hsi-feng was awe-struck. "Your fears are well-founded," she said. "But how can we prevent such a calamity?"

"Now you're being naive, aunt." Ko-ching laughed caustically. "Fortune follows calamity as disgrace follows honour. This has been so from time immemorial. How can men prevent it? The only thing one can do is to make some provision for lean years in times of plenty. All's well at present except for two things. Take care of them and the future will be secure."

Hsi-feng asked what she had in mind.

"Although seasonal sacrifices are offered at the ancestral tombs there's no fixed source of income for this, and although we have a family school there's no definite fund for it. Of course, while we're still prosperous, we don't lack the where-withal for sacrifices, but where's it to come from once we fall on hard times?

"I'd like to suggest that while we're still rich and noble we should invest in some farms and estates near our ancestral tombs to provide for sacrifices. The family school should be moved to the same place.

"Let the whole family, old and young alike, draw up rules whereby each branch of the family will take it in turn to manage the land, income and sacrifices for a year. Taking turns will prevent disputes and malpractices like mortgages or sales.

"Then even if the family property were confiscated because of some crime, the estate for ancestral worship would be exempted and in those hard times the young people could go there to study and farm. They'd have something to fall back on, and there would be no break in the sacrifices.

"It would be very short-sighted not to take thought for the future in the belief that our present good fortune will last for ever. Before long something marvellous is going to happen which will really 'pour oil on the flames and add flowers to brocade.' But it will simply be a flash in the pan, a brief moment of bliss. Whatever happens don't forget the proverb, 'Even the grandest feast must have an end.' Take thought for the future before it is too late."

"What marvellous thing is going to happen?" asked Hsi-feng.

"Heaven's secrets mustn't be divulged. But because of the love between us let me give you some parting advice, and do remember it, aunt!" With that she declaimed:

"After the three months of the spring, all flowers will fade
And each will have to find his own way out."

Before Hsi-feng could ask more she was woken with a start
by four blows on the chime-bar at the second gate. And a servant announced, "Madam Chia Jung of the East Mansion has
passed away."

Hsi-feng broke into a cold sweat. When she had recovered
from her stupefaction, she dressed quickly and hurried over to
Lady Wang.

By that time the whole household was lamenting, distressed
by this shocking news. The old people recalled Ko-ching's filial
behaviour, the young people her affectionate ways and the
children her kindness; while not one of the servants but wept
for grief recollecting her compassion for the poor and humble
and her loving goodness to old and young alike.

Now it was Chia Cheng's birthday and both households had
gathered to congratulate him. At the height of the festivities
the gateman suddenly rushed in to announce:

"His Excellency Hsia, Chief Eunuch of the Six Palaces, has
come with a Decree from the Emperor!"

This startled Chia Sheh, Chia Cheng and the rest, who did
not know what it could mean. They at once called a halt to
the theatricals and had the feast cleared away. A table was
set out with incense. Then, throwing open the central gate they
knelt down to receive the Decree.

Soon Hsia Shou-chung the Chief Eunuch arrived on horseback, followed by a considerable retinue of eunuchs. He was
not carrying an Imperial Edict, however. Having alighted in
front of the main hall, he mounted the steps with a beaming
smile and, facing south, announced:

"By special order of the Emperor, Chia Cheng is to present
himself at once for an audience in the Hall of Respectful
Approach." This said, without even taking a sip of tea, he remounted his horse and rode off.

Chia Sheh and the others could not guess what this portend-
ed. Chia Cheng lost no time in putting on his court robes and

going to the Palace, leaving the whole family in dire suspense. The Lady Dowager sent one mounted messenger after another in search of news; but it was four hours before Lai Ta and a few other stewards came panting through the inner gate, crying:

"Good news! His Lordship asks the old lady to go at once to the Palace with the other ladies to thank His Majesty."

The Lady Dowager had been waiting anxiously in the corridor outside the great hall with Lady Hsing, Lady Wang, Madam Yu, Li Wan, Hsi-feng and the Chia girls, as well as Aunt Hsueh. On hearing this, they called Lai Ta over and demanded more details.

"We had to wait in the outer court," Lai Ta told them. "So we had no idea what was going on inside. But then Chief Eunuch Hsia came out. He congratulated us on the promotion of our eldest young lady. She's to be Chief Secretary of the Phoenix Palace with the title of Worthy and Virtuous Consort. And then His Lordship came out and confirmed this. Now he has gone to the East Palace and he begs Your Ladyship and the other ladies to go at once to offer thanks."

They were all so relieved that their faces shone with delight as each dressed in the ceremonial robes appropriate to her rank. And presently four large sedan-chairs, with the Lady Dowager's at the head, followed by Lady Hsing's, Lady Wang's and Madam Yu's, were making their way to the Palace. They were escorted by Chia Sheh and Chia Chen, also in court robes, as well as Chia Jung and Chia Chiang.

Then high and low alike in both mansions were filled with joy. Their faces radiant with pride, they broke into a tumult of talk and laughter.

But let us return to Chia Lien, who had accompanied Tai-yu to attend her father's funeral, was back home now. After he had greeted the rest of the family he went to his own quarters; and busy as Hsi-feng was, with not a moment to herself, she set everything aside to welcome her husband back from his long journey.

Once they were alone she said jokingly, "Congratulations, Your Excellency, kinsman of the Imperial House! Your Excellency must have had a tiring journey. Your handmaid, hearing yesterday that your exalted carriage would return today, prepared some watery wine by way of welcome. Will the Imperial Kinsman deign to accept it?"

"You honour me too much," Chia Lien replied with a chuckle. "I am quite overwhelmed."

When Ping-erh and the other maids had paid their respects and served tea, Chia Lien asked his wife what had happened during his absence and thanked her for looking after things so well.

At this point a page from the inner gate reported that Chia Cheng was waiting for Chia Lien in the big library. The young man hastily straightened his clothes and went out.

When Chia Lien returned, Hsi-feng called for wine and dishes, and husband and wife took their seats opposite each other.

"What did your uncle want you for just now?" asked Hsi-feng.

"It was about this Imperial visitation."

"Has permission been granted then?" she asked eagerly.

"Not quite, but ten to one it will be."

"What a great act of Imperial kindness!" She beamed. "I never heard of such a thing in any book or opera about the old days."

Chia Lien explained. "Our present Emperor is concerned for all his subjects. No duty is higher than filial piety, and he knows that all, irrespective of rank, have the same family feeling. Though he himself waits day and night upon his Imperial parents, he considers this too little to express all his filial devotion; and he realizes that the secondary consorts and ladies-in-waiting in the Palace who have been away from their parents for many years must naturally be longing to see them again, for it's only right for children to miss their parents. But if the parents at home fall ill or even die of longing for their daughters, this must impair the harmony ordained by Heaven. So he requested Their Most High Majesties to allow the female relatives of the court ladies to visit them in the Palace on the days ending in two and six each month.

"His Majesty's parents were delighted by the Emperor's piety, humanity and manifestion of Heaven's will on earth. In their infinite wisdom the two venerable sages moreover decreed that, since court etiquette might prevent the mothers of the Palace ladies from gratifying all the wishes of their hearts during such visits, they should be granted an even greater favour. Then in a special Edict it was decreed that, apart from the favour of these visits on certain days of the month, all those court ladies with adequate accommodation at home for the reception of an Imperial retinue might ask for a Palace carriage to visit their families. In this way they can show their affection and enjoy a reunion with their dear ones.

"All were so grateful for this Decree, they leapt for joy. The father of the Imperial Lady of Honour Chou has already started building a separate court for her visit home; and Wu Tien-yu, father of the Imperial Concubine Wu, is looking for a site outside the city. Doesn't this show that the thing is practically certain?"

Just then Lady Wang sent to inquire if Hsi-feng had finished her meal, and realizing that she was wanted she hastily ate half a bowl of rice and rinsed her mouth. She was starting out when some pages from the inner gate reported the arrival of Chia Jung and Chia Chiang, whereupon Chia Lien rinsed his mouth and Ping-erh brought him a basin to wash his hands. As soon as the young men came in he asked what they wanted, and Hsi-feng stayed to hear Chia Jung's reply:

"My father sent me to tell you, uncle, that the old gentlemen have settled on a plan. We've measured the distance from the east wall through the garden of the East Mansion to the north, and it comes to three *li* and a half, enough to build a separate court for the visit. Someone has been commissioned to draw a plan which should be ready tomorrow. Since you must be tired after your journey, please don't think of coming over. If you've any proposals, you can make them first thing tomorrow."

"Kindly thank your father for his consideration," replied Chia Lien. "I shall do as he says and not call on him now.

This is the best possible scheme, the easiest and the simplest to carry out. Any other site would entail more work without such good results. Tell him when you get back that I thoroughly approve, and if the old gentlemen have second thoughts I hope he will dissuade them from looking for another site. When I come tomorrow to pay my respects we can talk it over in detail."

The next morning, after calling on Chia Sheh and Chia Cheng, Chia Lien went to the Ning Mansion. With some old stewards, secretaries and friends he inspected the grounds of both mansions, drew plans for the palaces for the Imperial visit and estimated the number of workmen required.

Before long all the craftsmen and workmen were assembled, and endless loads of supplies were brought to the site: gold, silver, copper and tin, as well as earth, timber, bricks and tiles. First they pulled down the walls and pavilions of the Garden of Concentrated Fragrance in the Ning Mansion to connect it with the large eastern court of the Jung Mansion; and all the servants' quarters there were demolished.

Formerly a small alley had separated the two houses, but since this was private property and not a public thoroughfare the grounds of both could now be thrown into one.

As a stream already ran from the northern corner of the Garden of Concentrated Fragrance, there was no need to bring in another. And though there were not enough rocks or trees, the bamboos, trees and rockeries as well as the pavilions and balustrades in the original garden of the Jung Mansion where Chia Sheh lived were brought over. The proximity of the two mansions made amalgamation easy, in addition to saving much labour and expense. On the whole, not too many new features had to be added.

Some time later Chia Chen came to report to Chia Cheng that the work on the new garden had been completed and Chia Sheh had inspected it.

"All is ready for you to look over, sir," he announced. "If there is anything unsuitable, we can have it changed before the inscriptions for different places are chosen."

Chia Cheng reflected for a while, then said, "The inscriptions *do* present a problem. By rights, we should ask the Imperial Consort to do us the honour of composing them, but she can hardly do this without having seen the place. On the other hand, if we leave the chief sights and pavilions without a single name or couplet until her visit, the garden, however lovely with its flowers and willows, rocks and streams, cannot fully reveal its charm."

"You are absolutely right, sir," agreed his cultured companions.

"I have an idea," said one. "The inscriptions for different places can't be dispensed with, but neither can they be fixed in advance. Why not briefly prepare some tentative couplets and names to suit each place? We can have them painted on lanterns in the shape of plaques and scrolls for the time being. Then, when Her Highness favours us with a visit, we can ask her to decide on permanent names. Wouldn't this be a way out of the dilemma?"

"A sound idea," agreed Chia Cheng. "Let us have a look round then today and think up some inscriptions. If suitable, they can be used; if unsuitable, we can ask Chia Yu-tsun over to help."

"Your suggestions are bound to be excellent, sir," they countered. "Why need we call in Yu-tsun?"

"Frankly, I was never a good hand even in my young days at writing verse about nature — flowers, birds and scenery. Now that I'm old and burdened with official duties I've quite lost the light touch required for belles-lettres. Any efforts of mine would undoubtedly be so clumsy and pedantic that they would fail to bring out the garden's beauty — they might even have the opposite effect."

"Have no fears about that," his secretaries assured him. "We can put our wits together. If each of us uses his ingenuity and we then choose the best suggestions, discarding the rest, we should be able to manage."

"Very well. Luckily it's a fine day for a stroll."

Chia Cheng rose to his feet and set off at the head of the party, while Chia Chen went on in advance to let everyone in the garden know they were coming.

It so happened that Pao-yu had just arrived in the garden. Chia Chen, coming upon him, warned him jokingly, "You'd better clear out! Lord Cheng is on his way here."

Pao-yu rushed out like a streak of smoke, with his nurse and pages behind him. But just round the corner he ran into Chia Cheng's party. Since escape was impossible, Pao-yu stepped to one side.

Now Chia Cheng had recently heard Pao-yu's tutor speak highly of his skill in composing couplets, remarking that the boy, though not studious, showed considerable originality. Having happened upon him like this, Chia Cheng ordered his son to accompany them. Pao-yu had to comply, not knowing what his father wanted.

At the entrance to the garden, they found Chia Chen with a group of stewards lined up in wait.

"Close the gate," said Chia Cheng. "Let us see what it looks like from outside before we go in."

Chia Chen had the gate closed and Chia Cheng inspected the gatehouse, a building in five sections with an arched roof of semi-circular tiles. The lintels and lattices, finely carved with ingenious designs, were neither painted nor gilded; the walls were of polished bricks of a uniform colour, and the white marble steps were carved with passion-flowers. The garden's spotless whitewashed wall stretching to left and right had, at its base, a mosaic of striped "tiger-skin" stones. The absence of vulgar ostentation pleased him.

He had the gate opened then and they went in, only to find their view screened by a green hill. At this sight his secretaries cried out in approval.

"If not for this hill," observed Chia Cheng, "one would see the whole garden as soon as one entered, and how tame that would be."

"Exactly," agreed the rest. "Only a bold landscape gardener could have conceived this."

On the miniature mountain they saw rugged white rocks resembling monsters and beasts, some recumbent, some rampant, dappled with moss or hung about with creepers, a narrow zigzag path just discernible between them.

"We'll follow this path," decided Chia Cheng. "Coming back we can find our way out at the other side. That should take us over the whole grounds."

He made Chia Chen lead the way and, leaning on Pao-yu's shoulder, followed him up through the boulders. Suddenly raising his head, he saw a white rock polished as smooth as a mirror, obviously intended for the first inscription.

"See, gentlemen!" he called over his shoulder, smiling. "What would be a suitable name for this spot?"

"Heaped Verdure," said one.

"Embroidery Ridge," said another.

"The Censer."[1]

"A Miniature Chungnan."[2]

Dozens of different suggestions were made, all of them stereotyped clichés; for Chia Cheng's secretaries were well aware that he meant to test his son's ability. Pao-yu understood this too.

Now his father called on him to propose a name.

Pao-yu replied, "I've heard that the ancients said, 'An old quotation beats an original saying; to recut an old text is better than to engrave a new one.' As this is not the main prominence or one of the chief sights, it only needs an inscription because it is the first step leading to the rest. So why not use that line from an old poem:

> A winding path leads to a secluded retreat.

A name like that would be more dignified."

---

[1] The Censer Peak of Mount Lushan in Kiangsi Province.

[2] The scenic Chungnan Mountain in Shensi Province.

"Excellent!" cried the secretaries.

"Our young master is far more brilliant and talented than dull pedants like ourselves."

"You mustn't flatter the boy," protested Chia Cheng with a smile. "He's simply making a ridiculous parade of his very limited knowledge. We can think of a better name later."

They walked on through a tunnel into a ravine green with magnificent trees and ablaze with rare flowers. A clear stream welling up where the trees were thickest wound its way through clefts in the rocks.

Some paces further north, on both sides of a level clearing, rose towering pavilions whose carved rafters and splendid balustrades were half hidden by the trees on the slopes. Looking downwards, they saw a crystal stream cascading as white as snow and stone steps going down through the mist to a pool. This was enclosed by marble balustrades and spanned by a stone bridge ornamented with the heads of beasts with gaping jaws. On the bridge was a little pavilion in which the whole party sat down.

"What would you call this, gentlemen?" asked Chia Cheng.

One volunteered, "Ouyang Hsiu's[1] *Pavilion of the Old Drunkard* has the line, 'A winged pavilion hovers above.' Why not call this Winged Pavilion?"

"A delightful name," rejoined Chia Cheng. "But as this pavilion is built over the pool there should be some allusion to the water. Ouyang Hsiu also speaks of a fountain 'spilling between two peaks.' Could we not use that word 'spilling'?"

"Capital!" cried one gentleman. " 'Spilling Jade' would be an excellent name."

Chia Cheng tugging thoughtfully at his beard turned with a smile to ask Pao-yu for his suggestion.

"I agree with what you just said, sir," replied his son. "But if we go into this a little deeper, although 'spilling' was an apt epithet for Ouyang Hsiu's fountain, which was called the Brewer's Spring, it would be unsuitable here. Then again, as

---

[1] A Sung Dynasty writer.

大觀園試才題對額　榮國府歸省慶元宵

this is designed as a residence for the Imperial Consort we should use more courtly language instead of coarse, inelegant expressions like this. Could you not think of something more subtle?"

"Do you hear that, gentlemen?" Chia Cheng chuckled. "When we suggest something original he is all in favour of an old quotation; but now that we are using an old quotation he finds it too coarse. Well, what do *you* propose?"

"Wouldn't 'Seeping Fragrance' be more original and tasteful than 'Spilling Jade'?"

Chia Cheng stroked his beard again and nodded in silence while the others, eager to please him, hastened to commend Pao-yu's remarkable talent.

"The selection of two words for the tablet is easy," said his father. "Go on and make a seven-character couplet."

Pao-yu rose to his feet and glanced round for inspiration. Then he declaimed:

> "Willows on the dyke lend their verdancy
> to three punts;
> Flowers on the further shore spare a
> breath of fragrance."

His father nodded with a faint smile amid another chorus of approval.

They left the pavilion then, crossed the bridge and strolled on, admiring each rock, each height, each flower and each tree on the way, until they found themselves before the whitewashed enclosing walls of a fine lodge nestling in a dense glade of fresh green bamboos. With cries of admiration they walked in.

From the gate porch a zigzag covered walk with a cobbled path below and parallel to it wound up to a little cottage of three rooms, with the cottage door in the middle one and furniture made to fit the measurements of the rooms. Another small door in the inner room opened on to the back garden with its large pear-tree, broad-leafed plantain and two tiny side courts. Through a foot-wide opening below the back wall flowed a brook which wound past the steps and the lodge to the front court before meandering out through the bamboos.

"This is pleasant. If one could study at this window on a moonlit night one would not have lived in vain," observed Chia Cheng. He glanced at Pao-yu, who hung his head in confusion while the others quickly changed the subject, one of them suggesting:

"We need a four-character inscription here."

"What four characters?" asked Chia Cheng.

"Shades of the River Chi?"[1]

"Too commonplace."

"Traces of the Sui Garden?"[2]

"That is equally hackneyed."

Chia Chen proposed, "Let Cousin Pao make a suggestion."

"Before he makes any suggestion," objected Chia Cheng, "the impudent fellow criticizes other people's."

"But his comments are correct. How can you blame him?"

"Don't pander to him like that." He turned to his son. "We're putting up with your wild talk today, so let's have your criticisms first before we hear your own proposals. Were either of these gentlemen's suggestions appropriate?"

"I didn't think so, sir."

His father smiled sardonically. "Why not?"

"Since this will be the first place where our Imperial visitor stops, we should pay some tribute to Her Highness here. If we want a four-character inscription there are plenty of old ones ready at hand, why need we compose anything new?"

"Aren't 'The River Chi' and 'The Sui Garden' both classical allusions?"

"Yes, but they sound too stiff. I propose 'Where the Phoenix Alights.'"

The rest were loud in their praise and Chia Cheng nodded.

"You young rascal," he said, "with your pitiful smattering of knowledge. All right, now let's hear your couplet."

Pao-yu declaimed:

---

[1] According to the *Book of Songs,* the area around the River Chi, in the northern part of present-day Honan, abounded with bamboo in ancient time.

[2] Garden of Prince Hsiao of Liang in the Han Dynasty.

"Still green the smoke from tea brewed in a
   rare tripod;
Yet cold the fingers from chess played by
   quiet window."

Chia Cheng shook his head. "No better either!"

He was leading the party on when a thought struck him and turning to Chia Chen he said, "All these compounds and lodges are furnished with tables and chairs, but what about curtains, blinds, knick-knacks, curios and so forth? Have appropriate ones for each place been prepared?"

"We have got in a large stock of ornaments which will be properly set out in due course," replied Chia Chen. "As for the curtains and blinds, Cousin Lien told me yesterday that they are not all ready yet. We took exact measurements from the building plans for each place when the work started, and sent out our designs to be made up. By yesterday about half of them were finished."

Since he was clearly ignorant of the details, Chia Cheng sent for Chia Lien and asked him, "What are the different items? How many are ready and how many are not?"

Chia Lien promptly pulled out a list from the leg of one boot. After referring to it he replied, "Of the one hundred and twenty satin curtains embroidered with dragons and brocade hangings large and small with different designs and colours, eighty were ready yesterday and forty are still to come. Two hundred blinds were delivered yesterday. Beside these, there are two hundred portières of crimson felt, two hundred of red lacquered bamboo with gold flecks, two hundred of black lacquered bamboo, and two hundred woven with coloured silks. Half of each kind is ready, the rest will be finished by the end of autumn. Then there are chair-covers, table-drapes, valances and stool-covers — one thousand two hundred of each — which we already have."

As they walked on talking, their eyes fell on some green hills barring their way. Skirting these they caught sight of brown adobe walls with paddy-stalk copings and hundreds of apricot-trees, their blossoms bright as spurting flames or sunlit clouds. Inside this enclosure stood several thatched cottages. Outside grew saplings of mulberry, elm, hibiscus and silkworm-thorn trees, whose branches had been intertwined to form a double green hedge. Beyond this hedge, at the foot of the slope, was a rustic well complete with windlass and well-sweep. Below, neat plots of fine vegetables and rape-flowers stretched as far as eye could see.

"I see the point of this place," declared Chia Cheng. "Although artificially made, the sight of it tempts one to retire to the country. Let us go in and rest a while."

Just as they were on the point of entering the wicker gate they saw a stone by the pathway which was obviously intended for an inscription.

"That's the finishing touch," they cried, chuckling. "A plaque over the gate would have spoilt the rustic flavour, but this stone here adds to the charm. It would take one of Fan Cheng-ta's poems[1] on country life to do justice to this place."

"What shall we call it then, gentlemen?"

"As your worthy son just remarked, 'An old quotation beats an original saying.' The ancients have already supplied the most fitting name — Apricot Village."

Chia Cheng turned with a smile to Chia Chen, saying, "That reminds me. This place is perfect in every other respect, but it still lacks a tavern-sign. You must have one made tomorrow. Nothing too grand. Just a tavern-sign of the sort used in country places. Let it be hung on a bamboo pole from a tree-top."

Chia Chen readily agreed to this, then suggested, "Other birds would be out of place here, but we ought to have some geese, ducks, hens and so on."

When this proposal had met with general approval, Chia Cheng observed, " 'Apricot Village' is first-rate, but since it is the name of a real place we should have to get official permission to use it."

"True," agreed the others. "We shall have to think of some-

---

[1] Fang Cheng-ta, a Sung Dynasty poet, is famous for his poems on country life.

thing else. What shall it be?"

Without giving them time to think or waiting to be asked by his father, Pao-yu blurted out, "An old poem has the line, 'Above flowering apricot hangs a tavern-sign.' Why not call this 'Approach to Apricot Tavern'?"

"'Approach' is superb," they cried. "It suggests the idea of Apricot Village too."

"'Apricot Village' would be too vulgar a name." Pao-yu smiled scornfully. "But an old poet wrote 'A wicker gate by a stream sweet with paddy.' How about 'Paddy-Sweet Cottage'?"

Again the secretaries clapped in approbation but his father sternly silenced him. "Ignorant cub! How many ancient writers have you read and how many old poems have you memorized that you dare show off in front of your elders? I put up with your nonsense just now to test you in fun — don't take it seriously."

With that he led the party into one of the cottages. It was quite free of ostentation, having papered windows and a wooden couch. Secretly pleased, he glanced at his son and asked, "Well, what do you think of *this* place?"

The secretaries nudged the boy to induce him to express approval. But ignoring them he answered, "It can't compare with 'Where the Phoenix Alights'."

"Ignorant dolt!" Chia Cheng sighed. "All you care for are red pavilions and painted beams. With your perverse taste for luxury, how can you appreciate the natural beauty of such a quiet retreat? This comes of neglecting your studies."

"Yes sir," replied Pao-yu promptly. "But the ancients were always using the term 'natural'. I wonder what they really meant by it?"

Afraid his pig-headedness would lead to trouble, the others hastily put in, "You understand everything else so well, why ask about the term 'natural'? It means coming from nature, not due to human effort."

"There you are! A farm here is obviously artificial and out

of place with no villages in the distance, no fields near by, no mountain ranges behind, no source for the stream at hand, above, no pagoda from any half hidden temple, below, no bridge leading to a market. Perched here in isolation, it is nothing like as fine a sight as those other places which were less far-fetched. The bamboos and streams there didn't look so artificial. What the ancients called 'a natural picture' means precisely that when you insist on an unsuitable site and hills where no hills should be, however skilfully you go about it the result is bound to jar. . . ."

"Clear off!" thundered Chia Cheng. "Stop. Come back. Make up another couplet. If it's no good I'll slap your face on both accounts."

Pao-yu had to comply. He declaimed:

> "The green tide fills the creek where clothes
>   are washed;
> Clouds of fragrance surround the girls plucking
>   water-cress."

"Worse and worse," growled Chia Cheng, shaking his head as he led the company out.

The path now curved around a slope, past flowers and willows, rocks and springs, a trellis of yellow roses, an arbour of white ones, a tree-peony pavilion, a white peony plot, a court of rambler roses and a bank of plantains. Suddenly they heard the plash of a spring gushing from a cave overhung by vines, and saw fallen blossoms floating on the water below. As they cried out in delight, Chia Cheng asked them to suggest another inscription.

"What more apt than 'The Spring of Wuling'?" said one.

"Too hackneyed. Besides, it's also the name of a real place," objected Chia Cheng with a smile.

"Then how about 'The Refuge of a Man of Chin'?"[1]

"Even more impossible," cried Pao-yu. "How can we use

---

[1] Both "The Spring of Wuling" and "The Refuge of a Man of Chin" refer to the imaginary land beyond the peach-blossom stream at Wuling described by the Tsin poet Tao Yuan-ming.

something that implies taking refuge in time of trouble? I suggest 'Smartweed Bank and Flowery Harbour'."

"That makes even less sense," scoffed his father. He strolled to the water's edge and asked Chia Chen, "Do you have any boats here?"

"There will be four punts for lotus-gathering and one pleasure boat, but they aren't ready yet."

"What a pity we can't cross."

"We can make a detour by the path over the hills," said Chia Chen, and proceeded to lead the way.

The others followed, clinging to creepers and trees as they clambered up. There were more fallen blossoms now on the stream, which appeared more translucent than ever as it swirled down its circuitous course. It was flanked by weeping willows and peach and apricot trees which screened the sun, and there was not a mote of dust in the air.

Presently, in the shade of the willows, they glimpsed an arched wooden bridge with scarlet railings. Once over this a choice of paths lay before them; but their attention was caught by an airy house of smooth brick with spotless tiles and an ornamental wall on one of the lesser slopes of the main hill.

"That building seems very out of place here," remarked Chia Cheng.

But stepping over the threshold he was confronted by tall weathered rocks of every description which hid the house from sight. In place of trees and flowers there was a profusion of rare creepers, vines and trailers, which festooned the artificial mountains, grew through the rocks, hung from the eaves, twined round the pillars and carpeted the steps. Some seemed like floating green belts or golden bands; others had berries red as cinnabar and flowers like golden osmanthus which gave off a penetrating scent, unlike the scent of ordinary flowers.

"This is charming!" Chia Cheng could not help exclaiming. "But what are all these plants?"

"Climbing fig and wistaria?" someone suggested.

"But they don't have such a strange fragrance, do they?"

"They certainly don't," interposed Pao-yu. "There *are* climbing fig and wistaria here, but the fragrance comes from alpinia and snakeroot. That one over there is iris, I fancy, and here we have dolichos, dwarf-mallow and glyrcyrrhia. That crimson plant is purple rue, of course; the green, angelica. A lot of these rare plants are mentioned in the *Li Sao* and *Wen Hsuan*,[1] plants with names like *huona, chiangtan, tsulun* and *chiangtzu; shihfan, shuisung* and *fuliu; luyi, tanchiao, miwu* and *fenglien*. But after all these centuries scholars can no longer identify these plants, for which new names have been found. . . ."

"Who asked *your* opinion?" roared his father.

Pao-yu stepped back nervously and said no more.

Covered corridors ran along both sides of this court and Chia Cheng led his party down one of these to a cool five-section gallery with roofed verandahs on four sides, green windows and painted walls, more elegant than any they had yet seen.

"One could brew tea here and play the lyre without having to burn rare incense." He sighed appreciatively. "This is certainly unexpected. We need a good inscription, gentlemen, to do it justice."

"What could be apter than 'Wind in the Orchids and Dew on Angelicas'?" one ventured.

"I suppose we have no other choice. Now what about a couplet?"

"I have thought of one," said another. "The rest of you must correct it.

> Fragrance of musk-orchids fills the court at dusk,
> Scent of alpinia floats to the moonlit island."

"Very good," they commented. "Only the reference to

---

[1] *Li Sao*, long narrative poem by the Chu poet Chu Yuan in the fourth century B.C.; *Wen Hsuan*, an anthology of literature compiled by a prince of Liang in the sixth century.

'dusk' seems inappropriate."

He quoted the old poem then with the line, "The alpinia in the court weeps in the dusk."

"Too sad, too sad," they protested.

"Here's one for your consideration," said another.

> "Along three paths white angelica scents the breeze,
> In the court a bright moon shines on golden orchids."

Chia Cheng thoughtfully tugged at his beard and seemed about to propose a couplet himself when, raising his head, he caught sight of Pao-yu, now afraid to open his mouth.

"Well?" he said sternly. "When it's time to speak you say nothing. Are you waiting to be begged for the favour of your instruction?"

"We have no musk, moon or islands here," said Pao-yu. "If you want allusive couplets of that kind, we can easily compose hundreds."

"Who is putting pressure on you to use those words?"

"Well then, I suggest 'Pure Scent of Alpinia and Iris.' And for the couplet:

> Singing on cardamons makes lovely poetry;
> Sleeping beneath roses induces sweet dreams."

Chia Cheng laughed. "You got that from the line 'Write on plantain leaves and green is the writing.' This is mere plagiarism."

"There's nothing wrong with plagiarism provided it's well done," countered the others. "Even Li Po copied from *Yellow Crane Pavilion*[1] when he wrote his *Phoenix Tower*. If you consider this couplet carefully, sir, it is livelier and more poetical than the original. It even looks as if the other line plagiarizes this by our young master."

"Preposterous!" Chia Cheng smiled.

From there they went on some way until ahead of them

---

[1] A poem by Tsui Hao, another Tang poet.

loomed towering pavilions enclosed by magnificent buildings, all of them connected by winding passageways. Green pines brushed the eaves, white balustrades skirted the steps, the animal designs glittered like gold and the dragon-heads blazed with colour.

"This must be the main reception palace," observed Chia Cheng. "Its one fault is that it is too luxurious."

"Unavoidably so," they reasoned. "Although Her Royal Highness prizes frugality, this is no more than is due to her present exalted rank."

They were now at the foot of a marble arch finely carved with rampant dragons and coiling serpents.

"What should be inscribed here?" asked Chia Cheng.

" 'The Fairy Land of Penglai'?"

He shook his head and said nothing.

As for Pao-yu, he felt strangely stirred by this sight, as if he had seen a place of this kind before — though just when he could not remember. Called upon to compose an inscription, he was too preoccupied to think of anything else. The others, not knowing this, imagined that his wits were wandering and he was exhausted after his long ordeal. Fearing that if he were pressed too hard the consequences might be serious, they urged his father to give him a day's grace.

Chia Cheng, aware that his mother might well be anxious, said with an ironic smile, "So sometimes you are at a loss too, you young rascal. Very well, I'll give you until tomorrow. But if no inscription is ready then, so much the worse for you. This is the most important place, so mind you do your best."

They continued with the tour of inspection and had covered little more than half the grounds when a servant reported that someone had arrived with a message from Yu-tsun.

"We can't see the rest of the places," said Chia Cheng. "But by going out the other way we can at least get a general idea, even if we don't see them all."

He led the way to a large bridge above a crystal curtain of cascading water. This was the sluice admitting water from outside. Chia Cheng asked for a name for it.

"Since this is the source of the River of Seeping Fragrance it could be called 'Seeping Fragrance Lock,' " Pao-yu suggested.

"Rubbish," said his father. "We just won't have 'Seeping Fragrance.' "

On they went past quiet lodges and thatched huts, stone walls and pergolas of flowers, a temple secluded in the hills and a convent half hidden among the trees, long covered walks, meandering grottoes, square mansions and round kiosks, none of which they had time to enter. However, it was so long since their last rest that all were footsore and weary by the time they saw another lodge in front, and Chia Cheng said, "Here we must rest a little."

He led the way in past some double-flowering peach in blossom and through a moon-gate made of bamboo over which climbed flowering plants. Whitewashed walls and green willows confronted them then. Along the walls ran covered corridors, and the rockery in the centre of the courtyard was flanked on one side by plantains, on the other by a red multi-petalled crab-apple tree, its branches trained in the shape of an umbrella, with green trailing tendrils and petals red as cinnabar.

"What superb blossoms!" they exclaimed. "We have never seen such a splendid one before."

"This is a foreign variety called 'Maiden Apple',' Chia Cheng told them. "Tradition has it that it comes from the Land of Maidens, and that it blossoms profusely in that country; but that is nothing but an old wives' tale."

"If so, how did the name come to be handed down?" they wondered.

"Quite likely the name 'Maiden' was given by some poet," said Pao-yu, "because this flower is as red as rouged cheeks and as frail as a delicate girl. Then some vulgar character made up that story and ignorant people believed it."

"A most plausible explanation," said the others.

They sat down on some benches in the corridor and Chia

Cheng at once asked for another inscription.

" 'Plantains and Storks'?" one proposed.

"Or 'Towering Splendour and Shimmering Radiance.' "

Chia Cheng and the rest approved, as indeed did Pao-yu, adding, "It's a pity, though. . . ." Asked to explain himself, he said, "Plantain and crab-apple blossom suggest both red and green. It's a pity to refer to one and not the other."

"What do you suggest then?" demanded his father.

"Something like 'Red Fragrance and Green Jade' would bring out the charm of both, I think."

"Too feeble!" Chia Cheng shook his head.

He led the way into the building. It was unusually set out with no clear-cut divisions between the different rooms. There were only partitions formed of shelves for books, bronze tripods, stationery, flower vases and miniature gardens, some round, some square, some shaped like sunflowers, plantain leaves or intersecting arcs. They were beautifully carved with the motifs "clouds and a hundred bats" or the "three companions of winter" — pine, plum and bamboo — as well as landscapes and figures, birds and flowers, scrollwork, imitation curios and symbols of good fortune or long life. All executed by the finest craftsmen, they were brilliantly coloured and inlaid with gold or precious stones. The effect was splendid, the workmanship exquisite. Here a strip of coloured gauze concealed a small window, there a gorgeous curtain hid a door. There were also niches on the walls to fit antiques, lyres, swords, vases or other ornaments, which hung level with the surface of the wall. Their amazement and admiration for the craftsmen's ingenuity knew no bounds.

After passing two partitions Chia Cheng and his party lost their way. To their left they saw a door, to their right a window; but when they went forward their passage was blocked by a bookshelf. Turning back they glimpsed the way through another window; but on reaching the door they suddenly saw a party just like their own confronting them — they were looking at a big mirror. Passing round this they came to more doorways.

"Follow me, sir," urged Chia Chen with a smile. "Let me take you to the back courtyard and show you a short cut."

He conducted them past two gauze screens out into a courtyard filled with rose trellises. Skirting round the fence, Paoyu saw a clear stream in front.

All exclaimed in astonishment, "Where does this water come from?"

Chia Chen pointed to a spot in the distance.

"It flows from that lock we saw through the ravine, then from the northeast valley to the little farm, where some is diverted southwest. Here both streams converge to flow out underneath the wall."

"Miraculous!" they marvelled.

Now another hill barred their way and they no longer had any sense of direction; but Chia Chen laughingly made them follow him, and as soon as they rounded the foot of the hill they found themselves on a smooth highway not far from the main entrance.

"How diverting," they said. "Really most ingenious."

And so they left the garden.

Chapter 7
Yuan-chun Visits Her Parents on the Feast of Lanterns

For Lady Wang and her helpers the days passed in a flurry of preparations until, towards the end of the tenth month, all was ready. The stewards had handed in their accounts; antiques and precious objects had been set out; the pleasure grounds were well-stocked with cranes, peacocks, deer, rabbits, chicken and geese to be reared in appropriate places; Chia Chiang had twenty operas ready; and the little Buddhist and Taoist nuns had memorized various sutras and incantations.

Then Chia Cheng, able at last to breathe more freely, invited the Lady Dowager to make a final inspection of the Garden and see that all was in order with nothing overlooked. This done, he chose an auspicious date and wrote a memorial, and the very same day that it was presented the Son of Heaven acceded to his request. The Imperial Consort Yuan-chun would be permitted to visit her parents for the Feast of Lanterns on the 'fifteenth of the first month the following year. This threw the whole household into such a commotion that, hard at work day and night, they scarcely had time to celebrate the New Year.

In a twinkling the Feast of Lanterns would arrive. On the eighth of the first month eunuchs came from the Palace to inspect the general layout of the Garden and the apartments where the Imperial Consort would change her clothes, sit with her family, receive their homage, feast them and retire to rest. The eunuch in charge of security also posted many younger eunuchs as guards by the screened and curtained entrances to the retiring rooms. Detailed instructions were given to all members of the household as to where they should withdraw, where they should kneel, serve food or make announcements — all the exact etiquette to be observed. Outside, officers from the Board of Works and the Chief of the Metropolitan Police had the streets swept and cleared of loiterers. Chia Sheh superintended the craftsmen making ornamental lanterns and fireworks, and by the fourteenth everything was ready. But no one, high or low, slept a wink that night.

Before dawn the next day all those with official ranks from the Lady Dowager downwards put on full ceremonial dress. Everywhere in the Garden were hangings and screens brilliantly embroidered with dancing dragons and flying phoenixes; gold and silver glittered, pearls and precious stones shimmered; richly blended incense burnt in the bronze tripods, and fresh flowers filled the vases. Not a cough broke the solemn silence.

Chia Sheh and the other men waited outside in the west street entrance, the Lady Dowager and the women outside the main gate, the ends of the street and the alleys leading to it all having been screened off.

They were growing tired of waiting when a eunuch rode up on a big horse. The Lady Dowager welcomed him in and asked for news.

"It will be a long time yet," the eunuch told her. "Her Highness is to dine at one, pray to Buddha in the Palace of the Precious Spirit at half past two, and at five go to feast in the Palace of Great Splendour and look at the display of lanterns before asking leave from the Emperor. She can hardly set out until seven."

This being the case, Hsi-feng suggested that the Lady Dowager and Lady Wang should go inside to rest and come back later.

So the Lady Dowager and others retired, leaving Hsi-feng in charge. She ordered the stewards to conduct the eunuchs to where refreshments were waiting. Then she had loads of candles carried in for all the lanterns.

It was not until the candles had been lit that a clatter of hooves was heard in the street. The next moment up panted ten or more eunuchs, clapping their hands as they ran. At this signal the other eunuchs said, "Her Highness is coming!" They all rushed to their posts.

For a long time they waited in silence, Chia Sheh and the young men of the family by the entrance of the west street, the Lady Dowager and the women in front of the main gate.

Then two eunuchs wearing scarlet uniforms rode slowly up to the entrance of the west street. Dismounting, they led their horses behind the screens, then stood to attention, their faces turned towards the west. After some time another pair appeared, then another, until there were ten pairs lined up and soft music could be heard in the distance.

And now a long procession approached: several pairs of eunuchs carrying dragon banners, others with phoenix fans, pheasant plumes and ceremonial insignia, as well as gold censers burning Imperial incense. Next came a curved-handled yellow umbrella on which were embroidered seven phoenixes, and under this a head-dress, robe, girdle and slippers. After this came attendant eunuchs bearing a rosary, embroidered handkerchiefs, a rinse-bowl, fly-whisks and the like.

Last of all, borne slowly forward by eight eunuchs, came a gold-topped palanquin embroidered with phoenixes.

All present, including the Lady Dowager, hastily fell to their knees by the side of the road. Eunuchs rushed over to help up the old lady as well as Lady Hsing and Lady Wang.

The palanquin was carried through the main gate to the entrance of the courtyard on the east, where a eunuch holding a whisk knelt down and invited the Imperial Consort to dismount and change her clothes. Then the palanquin was borne inside and the eunuchs withdrew, leaving Yuan-chun's ladies-in-waiting to help her alight.

She observed that the courtyard was brightly lit with ornamental lanterns of every kind, all exquisitely made of finest gauze. The highest, a rectangular lantern, bore the inscription: Fraught with Favour, Basking in Kindness.

Yuan-chun entered the robing room and changed, then remounted her palanquin which was carried into the Garden. She found it wreathed with the perfumed smoke of incense, splendid with flowers, brilliant with countless lanterns, melodious with strains of soft music. Words fail to describe that scene of peaceful magnificence and noble refinement.

Now, as she gazed from her palanquin at the dazzling display both within and without the Garden, the Imperial Consort sighed softly:

"This is too extravagant!"

Then a eunuch with a whisk knelt down by the palanquin and invited her to proceed by boat. As she alighted she saw before her a clear waterway winding like a dragon. From the marble balustrades on either bank lanterns of crystal and glass of every description shed a silvery light, clear as snow. The wintry boughs of the willows and apricot trees above them were festooned with artificial flowers and leaves made of rice-paper and silk, and from every tree hung lanterns. Lovely too on the water were the lotus flowers, duckweed and water-fowl made out of shells and feathers. Lanterns high and low seemed trying to outshine each other. It was truly a world of crystal and precious stones! The boats were magnificent too, with lanterns, rare miniature gardens, pearl portières, embroidered curtains, rudders of cassia and oars of aromatic wood, which we need not describe in detail.

By now they had reached a marble landing-stage. The lantern-sign above it bore the words, "Smartweed Bank and Flowery Harbour."

Regarding this name, Reader, and others such as "Where the Phoenix Alights" from the last chapter in which Chia Cheng tested Pao-yu's literary talent, you may wonder to find them actually used as inscriptions. For the Chias, after all, were a scholarly family all of whose friends and protégés were men of parts. Moreover they could easily find well-known writers to compose inscriptions. Why then make shift with phrases tossed off by a boy? Let me explain this to you.

The Imperial Consort, before she entered the Palace, had

been brought up from childhood by the Lady Dowager. And after Pao-yu was born, as Yuan-chun was his elder sister and Pao-yu her younger brother, bearing in mind that their mother had given birth to him late in life, she loved him more than her other brothers and lavished all her care on him. They both stayed with their grandmother and were inseparable. Even before Pao-yu started school, when he was hardly four years old, she taught him to recite several texts and to recognize several thousand characters. She was more like a mother to him than an elder sister. After she entered the Palace she often wrote letters home reminding her parents to educate him well, for unless strictly disciplined he would not amount to much, but if treated too sternly he might also give them cause for anxiety. Her loving concern for him had never ceased.

Chia Cheng, earlier on, had scarcely believed the tutor's report that Pao-yu had a flair for literary composition. As the Garden happened then to be ready for inspection, he had called on his son for inscriptions in order to test him. And although Pao-yu's childish efforts were far from inspired, at least they were passable. The family could easily enough have enlisted the help of famous scholars; but it seemed to them that a special interest attached to names chosen by a member of the house. Besides, when the Imperial Consort learned that these were the work of her beloved younger brother, she would feel that he had not fallen short of her hopes. For these reasons Pao-yu's inscriptions were adopted.

When the Imperial Consort saw this name, she commented with a smile: "Just 'Flowery Harbour' would do. Why 'Smartweed Bank' too?"

As soon as the eunuch in attendance heard this, he hastily disembarked and went ashore to report to Chia Cheng, who immediately had the alteration made.

Meanwhile the boat had reached the further shore and again Yuan-chun mounted her palanquin. Before her now there towered the beautiful hall of an imposing palace. The marble archway in front of it bore the inscription: "Precious Realm for the Immortal." At once she ordered this to be changed to "House of Reunion."

As she entered this temporary palace, she saw torches in the courtyard flaring to the sky, powdered incense strewing the ground, flaming trees, jasper flowers, gilded windows and jade balustrades, to say nothing of screens as fine as the shrimp's antennae, carpets of otter-skin, musk burning in tripods, and fans made from pheasant plumage. Truly this was:

> An abode with golden gates and jade doors fit
>   for immortals,
> Its cassia and orchid chambers a worthy setting
>   for the Imperial Consort.

After glancing around she asked, "Why has this place no name?"

The eunuch attendant fell on his knees. "Because this is the main palace," he replied, "no subject outside the Court dared suggest a name."

The Imperial Consort nodded and said nothing.

Another eunuch, the Master of Ceremonies, knelt and begged her to sit in a chair of state to receive the obeisances of her family. On both sides of the steps music was played as two eunuchs ushered in Chia Sheh and the men of the family to range themselves below the dais; but when a lady-in-waiting relayed the Imperial Consort's command to dispense with this ceremony they withdrew. Then the Lady Dowager of the Jung Mansion and the female relatives were led up the east flight of steps to the dais, but they too were exempted from the ceremony and shown out.

After tea had been served three times, Yuan-chun descended from the throne and the music ceased while she went into a side chamber to change her clothes. Meanwhile a carriage had been prepared to drive her out of the Garden to visit her parents.

First she went to the Lady Dowager's reception room to pay her respects as a grand-daughter of the house; but before she could do so her grandmother and the others knelt to prevent her. The Imperial Consort's eyes were full of tears as her family drew near to greet her. As she clasped the hands of her grandmother and mother, the hearts of all three were too full to speak — they could do nothing but sob. Lady Hsing, Li Wan, Hsi-feng, Yuan-chun's half sister Tan-chun and her cousins Ying-chun and Hsi-chun also stood beside them weeping silently. But at last the Imperial Consort mastered her grief and forced a smile as she tried to comfort them.

"Since you sent me away to that forbidden place, it hasn't been easy getting this chance today to come home and see you all again," she said. "But instead of chatting and laughing, here we are crying! Soon I shall have to leave you, and there is no knowing when I can come back again." At this she broke down afresh.

Lady Hsing and the others did their best to console her and the Lady Dowager asked her to take a seat, after which she exchanged courtesies with each in turn and more tears were shed. Next the stewards and attendants of both mansions paid their respects outside the door, and so did their wives and the maids.

This ceremony at an end, Yuan-chun asked why Aunt Hsueh, Pao-chai and Tai-yu were missing.

Lady Wang explained that they were afraid to presume, not being members of the Chia family and having no official status.

The Imperial Consort asked them to be invited in at once, and they were about to pay homage according to Palace etiquette when she exempted them too and chatted with them.

Next Pao-chin and the other maids whom Yuan-chun had taken with her to the Palace kowtowed to the Lady Dowager, who hastily stopped them and sent them off to have some refreshments in another room. The senior eunuchs and ladies-in-waiting were also entertained by members of the staff of both mansions, leaving only three or four young eunuchs in attendance.

When the ladies of the family had spoken with feeling about their separation and all that had happened since, Chia Cheng from outside the door-curtain asked after the health of his daughter, and she in turn paid her respects.

With tears she told him, "Simple farmers who live on pickles and dress in homespun at least know the joys of family life together. What pleasure can I take in high rank and luxury when we are separated like this?"

With tears too he replied, "Your subject, poor and obscure, little dreamed that our flock of common pigeons and crows would ever be blessed with a phoenix. Thanks to the Imperial favour and the virtue of our ancestors, your Noble Highness embodies the finest essences of nature and the accumulated merit of our forbears — such fortune has attended my wife and myself.

"His Majesty, who manifests the great virtue of all creation, has shown us such extraordinary and hitherto unknown favour that even if we dashed out our brains we could not repay one-thousandth part of our debt of gratitude. All I can do is to exert myself day and night, loyally carry out my official duties, and pray that our sovereign may live ten thousand years as desired by all under heaven.

"Your Noble Highness must not grieve your precious heart in concern for your ageing parents. We beg you to take better care of your own health. Be cautious, circumspect, diligent and respectful. Honour the Emperor and serve him well, so as to prove yourself not ungrateful for His Majesty's bountiful goodness and great kindness."

Then it was Yuan-chun's turn to urge her father to devote himself to affairs of state, look after his health and dismiss all anxiety regarding her.

After this Chia Cheng informed her, "All the inscriptions on the pavilions and lodges in the Garden were composed by Pao-yu. If you find one or two of the buildings not too tame, please condescend to re-name them yourself, that would make us extremely happy."

The news that Pao-yu was already able to compose inscriptions made her exclaim with delight, "So he's making progress!"

When Chia Cheng had withdrawn, the Imperial Consort observed that Pao-chai and Tai-yu stood out from their girl cousins, being truly fairer than flowers or finest jade. Then she inquired why Pao-yu had not come to greet her. The Lady Dowager explained that, unless specially summoned, as a young man without official rank he dared not presume.

At once the Imperial Consort sent for him and a young eunuch ushered him in to pay homage according to Palace etiquette. His sister called him to her and took his hand. Drawing him close to her bosom, she stroked his neck and commented with a smile, "How you have grown!" But even as she spoke her tears fell like rain.

Madam Yu and Hsi-feng stepped forward then to announce, "The banquet is ready. We beg Your Highness to favour us with your presence." Then she rose and told Pao-yu to lead the way.

Accompanied by all the rest she walked into the Garden, where the magnificent sights were lit up by lanterns. Past "Where the Phoenix Alights", "Crimson Fragrance and Green Jade", "Approach to Apricot Tavern" and "Pure Scent of Alpinia and Iris" they strolled, mounting pavilions, crossing streams, climbing miniature hills and enjoying the view from various different points. All the buildings were distinctively furnished, and each corner had such fresh, unusual features that Yuan-chun was lavish with her praise and approval. But she cautioned them:

"You mustn't be so extravagant in future. This is far too much!"

When they reached the main reception palace she desired them to dispense with ceremony and take their seats. It was a sumptuous banquet. The Lady Dowager and the rest sat at tables on either side, while Madam Yu, Li Wan and Hsi-feng passed round dishes and poured the wine. Meanwhile Yuan-chun asked for writing-brush and inkstone and with her own hand wrote names for the spots she liked best. For the main reception palace she wrote the inscription: Recalling Imperial Favour, Mindful of Duty. And the couplet:

Compassion vast as the universe extends to old and young,
Grace unknown before honours every state and land.

The pleasure grounds were named the Grand View Garden.
"Where the Phoenix Alights" was renamed "Bamboo
Lodge," "Crimson Fragrance and Green Jade" was changed
to "Happy Red and Delightful Green" and also called Happy
Red Court. The name "Pure Scent of Alpinia and Iris" was
altered to "Alpinia Park", the "Approach to Apricot Tavern"
became "Hemp-Washing Cottage". The main pavilion became
"Grand View Pavilion", its eastern wing "Variegated Splendour Tower", that on the west "Fragrant Tower". Other
names given were "Smartweed Breeze Cot," "Lotus Fragrance
Anchorage," "Purple Caltrop Isle" and "Watercress Isle."
She composed a dozen or so other inscriptions too such as
"Pear Blossom in Spring Rain", "Plane Trees in Autumn Wind"
and "Artemisia in Evening Snow". The rest of the inscriptions
cannot all be recorded here. The other former inscriptions at
her order remained unaltered.

Then the Imperial Consort wrote this verse:

Enfolding hills and streams laid out with skill —
What labour went to build this pleasure ground!
For these, the finest sights of earth and heaven,
No fitter name than "Grand View" can be found.

With a smile she showed this to the girls and said, "I have
never had a ready wit or any skill in versifying, as all of you
know, but tonight I had to try my hand at a verse in honour
of these pleasure grounds. Some day when I have more time,
I promise to write a *Description of Grand View Garden* and
a panegyric called *The Family Reunion* to commemorate this
occasion."

Yuan-chun had junket, ham and other delicacies presented to
Pao-yu and Chia Lan, who was too young to do more than pay
his respects after his mother and uncles, for which reason he
has not been previously mentioned.

Chia Huan had not yet recovered from an illness contracted
over New Year and was still convalescing in his own apartments; this is why no mention has been made of him either.

All this time Chia Chiang was waiting impatiently down below with his twelve young actresses. But now a eunuch ran down to him, exclaiming, "They have finished their poems. Give me your programme, quick!"

Chia Chiang lost no time in handing him a programme with a brocade cover and a list of the stage names of the twelve players. Presently four pieces were chosen: "The Sumptuous Banquet,"[1] "The Double Seventh Festival,"[2] "Meeting the Immortals"[3] and "The Departure of the Soul."[4]

Chia Chiang put on the first item without delay. All his players sang bewitchingly and danced divinely; thus although this was merely a stage performance they conveyed genuine grief and joy.

Then they left the banqueting hall to visit the places Yuan-chun had not yet seen, among them a Buddhist convent set among hills, where she washed her hands before going in to burn incense and worship Buddha. She chose as inscription for this convent the words, "Ship of Mercy on the Sea of Suffering". And here she gave additional gifts to the Buddhist nuns and Taoist priestesses.

Soon a eunuch knelt to report that the list of gifts was ready for her approval. She read it through, found it satisfactory, and gave orders that the presents should be distributed. This was done by the eunuchs.

The Lady Dowager received two *ju-yi*[5] sceptres, one of gold, the other of jade; a staff made of aloeswood; a chaplet of sandalwood beads; four lengths of Imperial satin with designs signifying wealth, nobility and eternal youth; four lengths of silk with designs signifying good fortune and long life; ten bars of gold with designs signifying "May Your Wishes Come True",

---

[1] From *A Handful of Snow* by the Ming playwright Li Yu.

[2] From *The Palace of Eternal Youth* by the early Ching playwright Hung Sheng.

[3] From *The Dream at Hantan* by the Ming playwright Tang Hsien-tsu.

[4] From *The Peony Pavilion* by Tang Hsien-tsu.

[5] Meaning "as you wish."

and ten silver bars with fish and other designs to symbolize felicity and abundance.

Lady Hsing and Lady Wang received the same gifts with the exception of the sceptres, staff and chaplet.

Chia Ching, Chia Sheh and Chia .Cheng each received two new books of His Majesty's own composition, two cases of rare ink-sticks, four goblets, two of gold and two of silver, and lengths of satin identical with those described above.

Pao-chai, Tai-yu and the other girls each received one new book, a rare mirror and two pairs of gold and silver trinkets of a new design.

Pao-yu received the same.

Chia Lan received one gold and one silver necklet, a pair of gold and a pair of silver medallions.

To Madam Yu, Li Wan and Hsi-feng were given two gold and two silver medallions and four lengths of silk.

In addition, twenty-four lengths of satin and a hundred strings of newly minted cash were allotted to the women-servants and maids in attendance on the Lady Dowager, Lady Wang and the girls.

Chia Chen, Chia Lien, Chia Huan and Chia Jung each received one length of satin and a pair of gold medallions.

A hundred rolls of variegated satin, a thousand taels of gold and silver, with various delicacies and wine from the Palace were given to those in both mansions responsible for the construction and maintenance of the Garden, the furnishing and upkeep of the various houses in the Garden, the theatre management and the preparation of lanterns. Five hundred strings of newly minted cash were also given as largesse to the cooks, actresses and jugglers.

It was nearly three in the morning by the time all had expressed their thanks, and the eunuch in charge announced that it was time to leave. At once Yuan-chun's eyes filled with tears again, but forcing a smile she clasped the hands of her grandmother and mother and could not bring herself to let them go.

"Don't worry about me," she begged them. "Just take good care of yourselves. Thanks to the Emperor's kindness you can now come to the Palace once a month to see me, so we shall have many chances to meet again. There is no need to be upset. If next year by Imperial grace I'm allowed another visit home, you must promise not to be so extravagant."

The Lady Dowager and other women were sobbing too bitterly to make any reply. But although Yuan-chun could hardly bear to leave, she could not disobey the Imperial regulations and had no alternative but to re-enter her palanquin which carried her away. The whole household did their best to console the Lady Dowager and Lady Wang as they helped them out of the Garden.

Chapter 8
A Song Awakens Pao-yu to Esoteric Truths

After spending several days in the Jung Mansion it was time for Hsiang-yun, the Lady Dowager's grandniece, to go home, but the Lady Dowager urged her to wait until after Pao-chai's birthday and the performance of operas. So Hsiang-yun, having to stay on, sent home for two pieces of her embroidery as a birthday-present for her cousin.

The fact was that the Lady Dowager had taken a fancy to Pao-chai since her arrival on account of her steady, amiable behaviour. And as this would be her first birthday in their house, the old lady summoned Hsi-feng and gave her twenty taels of silver from her own coffer for a feast and an opera.

Hsi-feng teased, "When an Old Ancestress wants to celebrate some grandchild's birthday, no matter how grandly, who are we to protest? So there's to be a feast and opera too, is there? Well, if you want it to be lively you'll have to pay for it yourself instead of trying to play host with a mouldy twenty taels. I suppose you expect me to make up the rest? If you really couldn't afford it, all right. But your cases are bursting with gold and silver ingots of every shape and size — the bottoms of the chests are dropping out, they're so full. Yet you're still squeezing *us*. Look, aren't all of us your children? Is Pao-yu the only one who'll carry you as an immortal on his head to Mount Wutai,[1] that you keep everything for him? Even if the rest of us aren't good enough, don't be so hard on us. Is this enough for a feast or theatricals?"

The whole company burst out laughing.

---

[1] Mount Wutai was a holy Buddhist mountain.

"Listen to that tongue of hers!" The old lady chuckled. "I'm not exactly tongue-tied myself but I'm no match for this monkey. Not even your mother-in-law would think of arguing with me, but you give me tit for tat."

"My mother-in-law dotes on Pao-yu just as much as you do," retorted Hsi-feng with a smile. "So I've no one to take my side. Instead, you make me out a termagant."

That set the old lady crowing with laughter and put her in the highest of spirits.

That night, after the family had gathered to pay their evening respects to the Lady Dowager and then gone on to chat, she asked Pao-chai to name her favourite operas and dishes. Knowing the old lady's partiality for lively shows and sweet, pappy food, Pao-chai gave these as her own preferences, adding even more to the Lady Dowager's pleasure.

The first thing next day she had presents of clothing and trinkets sent to the girl. Lady Wang, Hsi-feng, Tai-yu and the others also sent theirs according to the status of each. But these need not be enumerated in detail.

On the twenty-first a small stage was set up in the Lady Dowager's inner courtyard and a new troupe of young actresses had been hired who were able to perform both *Kunchu* and *Yiyang* operas. Tables were laid in the hall for a family feast, to which no outsiders were asked: apart from Aunt Hsueh, Hsiang-yun and Pao-chai, who were guests, all the rest would be members of the family.

Not seeing Tai-yu that morning, Pao-yu went to look for her and found her curled up on her *kang*.

"Come on to breakfast," he said. "The show will soon be starting. Tell me which opera you'd like and I'll ask for it."

Tai-yu smiled disdainfully.

"If that's how you feel, you'd better hire a special company to play my favourite pieces instead of expecting me to cash in on someone else's birthday."

"That's easy, we'll hire a company next time and let the rest of them cash in on us."

He pulled her up and they went off hand in hand.

After breakfast it was time to choose the plays and the Lady Dowager called on Pao-chai to name her choice. The girl declined the honour at first but finally, to the old lady's delight, named a scene from *Pilgrimage to the West*. Next, Hsi-feng was ordered to take her pick. And knowing the old lady's liking for lively plays, especially comedies and burlesques, she pleased her even more by selecting *Liu Erh Pawns His Clothes*.

Tai-yu, told to choose next, deferred to Aunt Hsueh and Lady Wang.

"I planned today as a treat for you girls," said the Lady Dowager. "So make your choice and never mind your aunts. I didn't lay on this show and feast for them. They're lucky to be here at all, able to watch and eat free of charge, but I won't let them choose any items."

All laughed at that, and then Tai-yu suggested one piece. She was followed by Pao-yu, Hsiang-yun, the three Chia girls and Li Wan, and their choices were put on in turn.

When the feast was ready the Lady Dowager told Pao-chai to select another opera, and she asked for *The Drunken Monk*.

"You always choose something rowdy," objected Pao-yu.

"You've been watching operas all these years for nothing if you don't know how good this is," retorted Pao-chai. "Besides being spectacular it has some magnificent lines."

"I never could stand noisy shows," he persisted.

"If you call this noisy that just shows how little you know about opera," she rejoined. "Come over here and let me explain. This opera has most stirring arias sung in the northern mode *Tien Chiang Chun*, which needless to say is an excellent melody; and the verses set to *Chi Sheng Tsao* are quite superb, did you but know it."

Pao-yu edged closer then and begged her to recite them to him.

Pao-chai declaimed:

> "Dried are the hero's tears,

My patron's house left behind;
By grace divine
Tonsured below the Lotus Throne.
Not destined to stay,
I leave the monastery in a flash,
Naked I go without impediment;
My sole wish now
To roam alone in coir cape and bamboo hat,
And in straw sandals with a broken alms bowl
To wander where I will."

Pao-yu pounded his lap to the rhythm of the verse and nodded appreciatively, loud in his praise of these words as well as of her erudition.

"Do be quiet and watch," said Tai-yu. "Before we've seen *The Drunken Monk* you're playing *The General Feigns Madness.*"

This set Hsiang-yun giggling.

They went on watching operas until dusk. By then the Lady Dowager had taken a special fancy to the girl who played the part of the heroines and the one who took the clown's role. She had them brought to her and on closer inspection found them even sweeter. All marvelled when it was disclosed that the heroine was only eleven, the clown only nine. The old lady rewarded them with some extra delicacies and two additional strings of cash.

"When that child's made up she's the living image of someone here," remarked Hsi-feng. "Have none of you noticed?"

Pao-chai knew whom she meant but she just smiled. Pao-yu too had guessed but did not dare to speak out.

Hsiang-yun, however, blurted out, "I know! She looks just like Cousin Tai-yu."

Too late Pao-yu shot her a warning glance, for by now everyone had noticed the resemblance and laughingly declared that it was most striking. Soon afterwards they scattered.

That evening while undressing, Hsiang-yun ordered Tsui-lu to pack her things.

"What's the hurry?" asked the maid. "We can start packing when it's time to leave."

"We're leaving tomorrow morning. Why should we stay here and put up with dirty looks?"

Pao-yu overheard this exchange and hurried in to take Hsiang-yun by the hand.

"Dear cousin, you've got me wrong," he said. "Tai-yu is so terribly sensitive that the others didn't name her for fear of upsetting her. How could she help being annoyed, the way you blurted it out? I looked at you warningly because I didn't want you to hurt her feelings. It's ungrateful as well as unfair of you to be angry with *me*. If it had been anybody else but you, I wouldn't care how many people she offended."

Hsiang-yun waved him crossly away.

"Don't try to get round me with your flattering talk. I'm not in the same class as your Cousin Tai-yu. It's all right for other people to make fun of her, but I'm not even allowed to mention her. She's a grand young lady, I'm a slave — how dare I offend her?"

"I was only thinking of you, yet now you put me in the wrong." Pao-yu was desperate. "If I meant any harm, may I turn into dust this instant and be trampled on by ten thousand feet!"

"Stop talking such nonsense just after the New Year. Or go and rave if you must to those petty-minded creatures who are so quick to take offence, and who know how to manage you. Don't make me spit at you!"

She flounced off to the Lady Dowager's inner room and threw herself down angrily on a couch.

After this snub Pao-yu went to look for Tai-yu, but scarcely had he set foot in her room than she pushed him out and closed the door in his face. Mystified, he called in a subdued voice through the window:

"Dear cousin!"

But Tai-yu simply ignored him.

He hung his head then in dejected silence. Hsi-jen knew it would be useless to reason with him just then. So he was standing there like a fool when Tai-yu opened the door, thinking him gone. When she saw him still standing there, she hadn't the heart to shut him out again. She turned away and curled up on her bed, while he followed her into the room.

"There's always a reason for everything," he said. "If you'd explain, people wouldn't feel so hurt. What's upset you suddenly?"

"A fine question to ask!" Tai-yu gave a short laugh. "*I* don't know. For you I'm a figure of fun, to be compared with an actress in order to raise a laugh."

"But why be angry with *me*? I didn't make the comparison. I didn't laugh."

"I should hope not, indeed! But what you did was even worse than the others laughing and making comparisons."

Pao-yu did not know how to defend himself and was silent.

"I wouldn't have minded so much if you hadn't made eyes at Hsiang-yun," Tai-yu went on. "Just what did you mean by that? That she'd lower and cheapen herself by joking with me? She's the daughter of a noble house, I'm a nobody. If she were to joke with me and I answered back, that would be degrading for her — was that the idea? That was certainly kind on your part. Too bad she didn't appreciate your thoughtfulness, but flared up all the same. Then you tried to excuse yourself at my expense, calling me 'petty-minded and quick to take offence.' You were afraid she might offend me, were you? But what is it to you if I get angry with her? Or if she offends me?"

Pao-yu realized that she had overheard his conversation with Hsiang-yun. He had intervened in an attempt to prevent bad feeling between them but, having failed, was now held to blame by both sides. This reminded him of the passage in *Chuang-tzu*:

> "The ingenious work hard, the wise are full of care; but those without ability have no ambition. They enjoy their food and wander at will like drifting boats freed from their moorings."

And again:

> "Mountain trees are the first to be felled, clear fountains the first to be consumed."

The more he thought the more depressed he grew.

"If I can't even cope now with just these two, what will it be like in future?" he reflected. At this point it seemed quite useless to attempt to justify himself, so he started back to his room.

Tai-yu realized that he must be very dejected by what had occurred to go off so sulkily without a word. But this only made her angrier than ever.

"Go, then!" she cried. "And don't ever come back! Don't speak to me again!"

Pao-yu paid no attention. Returning to his room, he lay down on his bed staring fixedly before him. Although Hsi-jen knew what had happened, she dared not mention it and tried to distract him with some more cheerful subject.

"Today's plays are bound to lead to others," she prophesied. "Miss Pao-chai is sure to give a return party."

"What do I care whether she does or not?" he snapped back, quite unlike his usual self.

"What do you mean?" asked Hsi-jen. "This is the beginning of a new year when all the ladies and girls are enjoying themselves. Why carry on like this?"

"I don't care whether they're enjoying themselves or not."

"If they are so obliging to each other, shouldn't you be obliging too? Wouldn't that be pleasanter for everyone?"

"For everyone? Let *them* oblige each other while 'naked I go without impediment.'"

Tears ran down his cheeks and, seeing them, she said no more.

Pao-yu, pondering the significance of that line, suddenly burst out sobbing. Getting up, he went to his desk, took up a brush and wrote this verse in the style of a Buddhist *gatha*:

> Should you test me and I test you,
> Should heart and mind be tested too,
> Till there remained no more to test,
> That test would be of all the best.
> When nothing can be called a test,
> My feet will find a place to rest.

For fear that others might not grasp the meaning, he then appended a verse after the melody *Chi Sheng Tsao* and read the whole through again. Then he went to bed, feeling less frustrated, and slept.

Now some time after Pao-yu's abrupt departure Tai-yu came, ostensibly to see Hsi-jen, to find out how things were. Told that he was asleep she was turning to leave when Hsi-jen said with a smile:

"Just a minute, miss! He wrote something you might like to look at."

She quietly fetched and handed Tai-yu the verses Pao-yu had just written, and the girl was both touched and amused to see what he had tossed off in a fit of pique.

"It's just a joke, nothing serious," she told Hsi-jen.

She took it back to her own room and showed it to Hsiang-yun. Next day she showed it to Pao-chai as well. Pao-chai read the second verse. It ran:

> If there's no "I," then neither is there "you,"
> If she misunderstands you then why rue?
> Freely I come and freely too I go,
> Giving myself to neither joy nor woe,
> Close kin or distant — it's the same to me.
> What did it serve, my assiduity?
> Today I see its true futility.

Having read this she read the first verse, then laughed.

"So that's the enlightenment he's attained! This is all my fault for reciting that song to him yesterday. There's nothing so apt to lead people astray as these Taoist teachings and Zen paradoxes. If he really starts taking such nonsense seriously and gets it fixed in his head just because of that song I quoted, I'm the first to blame."

She tore up the verses and told her maids to burn them at once.

"You shouldn't have done that," protested Tai-yu with a smile. "I've some questions to ask him. Come with me, both of you. We'll soon cure him of this nonsense."

So the three girls went together to Pao-yu's rooms. Tai-yu

opened the attack by saying:

"Listen, Pao-yu. *Pao* means that which is most precious, and *yu* that which is most solid. But in what way are you precious? In what way are you solid?"

When Pao-yu could not answer, the girls clapped their hands and laughed.

"And this stupid fellow wants to dabble in metaphysics!"

Tai-yu continued, "The last two lines of your verse are all very well —

> When nothing can be called a test
> My feet can find a place to rest.

But it seems to me they still lack a little something. Let me add two more:

> When there's no place for feet to rest,
> That is the purest state and best."

"Yes, that shows *real* understanding," put in Pao-chai. "In the old days when the Sixth Patriarch Hui-neng of the Southern Sect went to Shaochow in search of a teacher, he heard that the Fifth Patriarch Hung-jen was in the monastery on Mount Huangmei, so he took a job as cook there. The Fifth Patriarch, on the look-out for a successor, ordered each of his monks to compose a Buddhist *gatha*. His senior disciple Shen-hsiu recited:

> 'The body is a Bodhi tree,
> The mind a mirror clear;
> Then keep it cleaned and polished —
> Let no dust settle there.'

"Hui-neng heard this as he was hulling rice in the kitchen and commented, 'Very fine, but it needs rounding off.' With that he declaimed:

> 'The Bodhi tree is no tree,
> The mirror no mirror clear;
> Since nothing actually exists,
> Where can any dust appear?'

Then the Fifth Patriarch passed on his robe and alms bowl to him. Your verse amounts to much the same thing. But what about the conundrum you set him just now? He hasn't answered it yet.   How can you leave it at that?"

"Failure to answer promptly means defeat," said Tai-yu.
"And even if he answered it now it would hardly count.   But
you mustn't talk about Zen any more.   You know even less
about it than the two of us yet you dabble in metaphysics."

Pao-yu had in fact fancied that he had already attained
enlightenment, but now that he had been floored by Tai-yu,
and Pao-chai had quoted Buddhist lore that he had never
suspected her of knowing, he thought to himself, "They understand more about these things than I do, yet still they haven't
attained full enlightenment.   Why should I trouble my head
over such matters?" Thereupon he said with a laugh:

"I wasn't dabbling in metaphysics.   I just wrote that for
fun."

So the four of them made it up.

Chapter 9
A Song from "Peony Pavilion"
Distresses a Tender Heart

After Yuan-chun's return to the Palace from her visit to Grand View Garden she gave instructions that Tan-chun should copy out all the poems written that day for her to arrange in order of merit, because she wished them to be inscribed on the tablets in the Garden as a lasting memorial to that splendid occasion.

While she was editing the poems on Grand View Garden, it occurred to her that it would be a pity if her father locked up such charming pleasure grounds after her visit in deference to her, so that nobody could go there. The more so when the girls of the family had a taste for poetizing, and if they were to move there the Garden would make a perfect setting for them while its flowers and willows would not lack admirers. Then she reflected that Pao-yu was unlike other boys, having been brought up among girls, so that if he alone were excluded he would feel left out in the cold, and this might distress the Lady Dowager and Lady Wang. She had better give directions for him to move in there too.

Having reached this decision, she sent the eunuch Hsia Chung to the Jung Mansion with the order: "Pao-chai and the other young ladies are to live in the Garden, which is not to be closed. Pao-yu is to move in as well to continue his studies there."

This edict was received by Chia Cheng and Lady Wang. As soon as the eunuch had left, they reported it to the Lady Dowager and sent servants to clean up the Garden and prepare the buildings, hanging up blinds, portières and bed-curtains.

The others took the news fairly calmly, but Pao-yu was beside himself with joy. He was just discussing it with his grandmother, demanding this, that and the other, when a maid announced that his father wanted him. At this bolt from the blue he turned pale, his spirits quite dashed. He clung like a limpet to the Lady Dowager, too terrified to leave her.

"Go, my treasure," she urged him. "I won't let him be hard on you. Besides, it's because you wrote so well that Her Highness has said you should move into the Garden, and I dare say your father only wants to warn you to behave yourself when you're there. Just say 'Yes' to whatever he tells you and you'll be all right."

She called two old nurses and ordered them to take Pao-yu there and see that he was not frightened.

The nurses complied and Pao-yu left with dragging steps. It so happened that Chia Cheng was discussing some business in his wife's room while her maids Chin-chuan, Tsai-yun, Tsai-hsia, Hsiu-luan and Hsiu-feng were standing outside under the eaves. At sight of Pao-yu they smiled knowingly, and Chin-chuan caught hold of his sleeve.

"I've just put some scented rouge on my lips," she whispered. "Do you want to taste it?"

Tsai-yun pushed her away.

"Don't tease him when he's feeling low," she scolded. "Go in quickly, while the master's in a good mood."

Pao-yu sidled fearfully in. His parents were in the inner room. The concubine Chao raised the portière, and with a bow he entered. His father and mother sat facing each other on the *kang* talking, while on a row of chairs below sat Ying-chun, Tan-chun, Hsi-chun and Chia Huan, all of whom except Ying-chun rose to their feet at his entrance.

Chia Cheng glanced up and saw Pao-yu standing before him. The boy's striking charm and air of distinction contrasted so strongly with Chia Huan's vulgar, common appearance that he was reminded of his dead son Chu. He glanced at Lady

Wang. She had only this one son left and she doted on him. As for him, his beard was already turning grey. Bearing all this in mind, he forgot his usual aversion to Pao-yu. After a pause he said:

"Her Highness has ordered you to study and practise calligraphy with the girls in the Garden, instead of fooling around outside and neglecting your studies. Mind that you apply yourself there to your lessons. If you go on misbehaving, watch out!"

"Yes, sir," agreed Pao-yu hastily.

Then his mother drew him over to sit beside her while Chia Huan and the other two sat down again. Stroking her son's neck fondly Lady Wang asked:

"Have you finished those pills prescribed for you the other day?"

"All but one."

"You must fetch ten more tomorrow. Get Hsi-jen to see that you take one each evening at bedtime."

"Ever since you ordered it, madam, Hsi-jen has been giving me one every evening."

"Who is Hsi-jen?" demanded Chia Cheng.

"One of the maids," his wife told him.

"A maid can be called anything, I suppose. But who thought up such a suggestive name for her?"

To shield Pao-yu from his father's displeasure Lady Wang said, "It was the old lady's idea."

"Such a name would never occur to the old lady. This must have been Pao-yu's doing."

Since there was no hiding the truth Pao-yu rose to confess: "I remembered that line of an old poem:

> When the fragrance of flowers assails men
> we know the day is warm.

As this maid's surname is Hua (Flower), I called her Hsi-jen."[1]

"You must change it when you go back," put in Lady Wang

---

[1] "Assails men."

quickly. Then she turned to her husband. "Don't be angry, sir, over such a little thing."

"It doesn't really matter, there's no need to change it. But this shows that instead of studying properly Pao-yu gives all his time to romantic trash." Then he said sternly to Pao-yu: "What are you standing there for, you unnatural monster?"

"Run along," urged Lady Wang. "The old lady is probably waiting for you for supper."

Pao-yu assented and slowly withdrew. Once outside he grinned and stuck out his tongue at Chin-chuan before hurrying off with the two nurses.

One day, about the middle of the third month, carrying a copy of *The Western Chamber* Pao-yu strolled after breakfast across the bridge above Seeping Fragrance Lock. There he sat down on a rock to read under a blossoming peach-tree. He had just reached the line

Red petals fall in drifts

when a gust of wind blew down such a shower of petals that he and his book were covered with them and the ground near by was carpeted with red. Afraid to trample on the flowers if he shook them off, Pao-yu gathered them into the skirt of his gown and carried them to the water's edge where he shook them into the brook. They floated and circled there for a while, then drifted down the River of Seeping Fragrance.

Going back, he found the ground still strewn with blossoms and was wondering how to dispose of these when a voice behind him asked:

"What are you doing here?"

He turned and saw Tai-yu, a hoe over one shoulder, a gauze bag hanging from the hoe, and a broom in her hand.

"You're just in time to sweep up these petals and throw them into the water," cried Pao-yu. "I've just thrown in a pile."

"Not into the water," objected Tai-yu. "It may be clean here, but once it flows out of these grounds people empty all sorts of dirt and filth into it. The flowers would still be spoiled. I've a grave for flowers in that corner over there. I'm sweeping them up and putting them in this silk bag to bury them there. In time they'll turn back into soil. Wouldn't that be cleaner?"

Pao-yu was delighted by this idea.

"Just let me put this book somewhere and I'll help," he offered.

"What book's that?"

He hastily tucked it out of sight.

"Just the *Doctrine of the Mean* and *The Great Learning*."[1]

"You're trying to fool me again. You'd have done better to show me in the first place."

"I don't mind showing *you*, dear cousin, but you mustn't tell anyone else. It's a real masterpiece. You won't be able to give a thought to eating once you start reading it." He passed her the book.

Tai-yu laid down her gardening tools to read, and the more she read the more enthralled she was. In less time than it takes for a meal she had read all the sixteen scenes. The sheer beauty of the language left a sweet taste in her mouth. After finishing reading she sat there entranced, recalling some of the lines.

"Well, don't you think it's wonderful?" he asked.

She smiled.

"It's certainly fascinating."

"I'm the one 'sick with longing','" he joked. "And yours is the beauty which caused 'cities and kingdoms to fall'."[2]

Tai-yu flushed to the tips of her ears. Knitting her sulky brows, her eyes flashing with anger beneath half-drooping lids, she pointed a finger at Pao-yu in accusal.

"You really are the limit! Bringing such licentious songs in here and, what's more, insulting me with nasty quotations from them." Her eyes brimmed with tears. "I'm going to tell uncle

---

[1] Two of the Confucian *Four Books*.

[2] Lines from *The Western Chamber*.

西廂記
妙詞通戲
語牡丹亭
艷曲警芳
心

and aunt."

She turned to go.

In dismay Pao-yu barred her way.

"Forgive me this once, dear cousin! I shouldn't have said that. But if I meant to insult you, I'll fall into the pond to-morrow and let the scabby-headed tortoise swallow me, so that I change into a big turtle myself. Then when you become a lady of the first rank and go at last to your paradise in the west, I shall bear the stone tablet at your grave on my back for ever."

Tai-yu burst out laughing at this and wiped her eyes.

"You're so easy to scare, yet still you indulge in talking such nonsense," she teased. "Why, you're nothing but 'a flower-less sprout', 'a lead spearhead that looks like silver'."

It was Pao-yu's turn to laugh.

"Now listen to *you*! I'll tell on you too."

"You boast that you can 'memorize a passage with one read-ing'. Why can't I 'learn ten lines at a glance'?"

Laughing he put the book away.

"Never mind that. Let's get on with burying the flowers."

No sooner had they buried the blossom than Hsi-jen appeared.

"So here you are," she said. "I've been looking all over for you. The Elder Master is unwell and all the young ladies have gone to inquire after his health. The old lady wants you to go too. Come back quickly and change."

Then Pao-yu, taking his book, took leave of Tai-yu and went back to his own room with Hsi-jen.

With Pao-yu gone and the other girls all out too, Tai-yu did not know what to do and decided to go back to her own room. As she rounded the corner of Pear Fragrance Court where the twelve actresses were rehearsing, she heard sweet fluting and singing over the wall. Normally the words of operas made little appeal to her, so she did not listen carefully; but now as she proceeded on her way two lines carried to her distinctly:

> What a riot of brilliant purple and tender crimson,
> Among the ruined wells and crumbling walls.

Strangely touched by this, she stopped to listen. The singer went on:

> What an enchanting sight on this fine morning,
> But who is there that takes delight in the spring?

Tai-yu nodded and sighed.

"So there are fine lines in these operas," she thought. "What a pity that people just care for the spectacle without understanding the meaning."

Then, sorry to have missed a stanza through her preoccupation, she listened again and heard:

> For you are as fair as a flower
> And youth is slipping away like flowing water.

Tai-yu's heart missed a beat. And the next line

> Alone you sit in your secluded chamber

affected her so much that she sank down on a rock to ponder the words.

> For you are as fair as a flower
> And youth is slipping away like flowing water.

They reminded her of a line in an old poem:

> Water flows and flowers fall, knowing no pity. . . .

and the lines from another poem:

> Spring departs with the flowing water and
>   fallen blossom,
> Far, far away as heaven from the world of men.

She compared this with the lines she had just read in *The Western Chamber*:

> Flowers fall, the water flows red,
> Grief is infinite. . . .

As she brooded over the meaning of all these verses, her heart ached and tears coursed down her cheeks.

Chapter 10
Tai-yu Weeps over Fallen Blossom by the Tomb of Flowers

Pao-yu felt so lackadaisical that he curled up as if for a nap. Hsi-jen seated herself on the edge of his bed and nudged him.

"You mustn't fall asleep again," she said. "If you're feeling bored, why not go out for a stroll?"

"I would." Pao-yu took her hand. "But I can't bear to leave you."

"Get up, quick!" she answered laughingly, pulling him up.

"But where shall I go? I'm thoroughly fed up."

"You'll feel better once you're out. If you just stay moping here, you'll only get more fed up."

Pao-yu listlessly took her advice and pottered out. After playing for a while with the birds in the gallery, he strolled beside the River of Seeping Fragrance to have a look at the goldfish. As he did so, two fawns came bolting from the hillside opposite, and he was wondering what could have frightened them when he saw Chia Lan give chase, a small bow in his hand. Seeing Pao-yu ahead of him, the boy stopped short.

"So you're at home, uncle," he said cheerfully. "I thought you'd gone out."

"What mischief are you up to now?" asked Pao-yu. "Why shoot at those harmless creatures?"

"I've finished my lessons and I've nothing to do. I thought I'd practise archery."

"I suppose you won't stop," said Pao-yu, "till you've knocked out your teeth."

His feet carried him on then to the gate of a courtyard.

Bamboos dense as phoenix plumage there made a rustling music. And the board above the gate bore the inscription: Bamboo Lodge. Strolling in he found the bamboo portière down. Not a voice could be heard. As he approached the window a subtle fragrance drifted through the green gauze. He pressed his face against the gauze and heard a long faint sigh, followed by the words:

Day after day a drowsy dream of love.[1]

Pao-yu felt his heart strangely stirred. And looking more closely, he could make out Tai-yu, who was stretching herself on her bed.

He laughed.

"Why 'Day after day a drowsy dream of love'?" he called, then raising the portière walked in.

Blushing to think she had given herself away, Tai-yu hid her face with her sleeve and turned towards the wall, pretending to be asleep. As Pao-yu went up to her to turn her over, her nurse and two other old women followed him in.

"Your cousin's asleep, sir. We shall ask you in when she wakes up."

Tai-yu promptly turned over and sat up with a laugh.

"Who's asleep?"

The three old women smiled.

"Our mistake, miss."

They left after calling Tzu-chuan to attend to her young mistress.

"What do you mean by coming in when people are asleep?" Tai-yu challenged Pao-yu with a smile as, sitting on the bed, she smoothed her hair.

The sight of her soft flushed cheeks, and her starry eyes now faintly misted over, enraptured Pao-yu. He sank smiling into a chair.

"What was that you were saying just now?"

---

[1] This line and the two quoted later by Pao-yu come from *The Western Chamber*.

"I didn't say anything."

"Yes, you did. I heard you."

Tzu-chuan appeared at this point.

"Tzu-chuan," said Pao-yu, "pour a cup of that good tea of yours for me, will you?"

"What good tea have we got?" she retorted. "If you want good tea, better wait till Hsi-jen comes."

"Pay no attention to him," said Tai-yu. "First go and get me some water."

Tzu-chuan laughed.

"He's a guest, so of course I must get him tea before I fetch you water."

As she left to do this Pao-yu exclaimed, "Good girl!

> Should I share the bridal curtains with your
>   sweet mistress,
> How could I give you the task of preparing
>   the bed?"

At once Tai-yu's face clouded over.

"What's that you said?" she demanded.

"I didn't say anything, did I?" Pao-yu chuckled.

Tai-yu began to cry.

"So this is your latest diversion," she sobbed. "All the dirty talk you hear outside, you repeat to me; and any disgusting books you read, you quote to make fun of me. A laughing-stock for you gentlemen, that's what I've become!"

Scrambling off the bed she walked away in tears. Pao-yu followed her in alarm.

"Dear cousin, it was very wrong of me, but please don't tell!" he begged. "May it blister my mouth and rot my tongue if I dare say such things again."

Just then Hsi-jen came in.

"Quick," she said. "Come back and change. The master wants you."

This summons fell on his ears like a clap of thunder. Forgetting all else he rushed back to change, and hurried out of the Garden.

Tai-yu too had been worried on Pao-yu's behalf when she heard that he had not come back all day after being sent for by his father. After dinner she learned of his return and decided to find out from him what had happened. As she strolled over she saw Pao-chai going into Happy Red Court before her. But noticing some unusually beautiful water-fowl of various species unknown to her splashing about in the pool by Seeping Fragrance Bridge, she stopped for a while to admire their brilliant colours. By the time she reached Happy Red Court the gate was closed and she was obliged to knock.

It so happened that Ching-wen was in a bad humour, having just quarrelled with Pi-hen, and at Pao-chai's arrival she transferred her anger to the visitor. She was grumbling in the courtyard:

"She keeps coming here and sitting around for no reason, keeping us up till the third watch at night."

Now this fresh knocking on the gate only incensed her further.

"They've all gone to bed," she cried, not troubling to ask who it was. "Come back tomorrow."

Tai-yu knew the maids' ways and the tricks they played on each other. Assuming that the girl in the courtyard had failed to recognize her voice and taken her for another maid, she called out again more loudly.

"It's me. Open the gate!"

Still Ching-wen did not recognize her voice.

"I don't care who you are," she said crossly. "Master Pao's given orders that no one's to be admitted."

Rooted indignantly to the spot and tempted to let fly at her, Tai-yu reflected, "Although my aunt's house is a second home to me, I'm after all an outsider here. With both my parents dead, I've no one to turn to except this family. It would be foolish to start a real rumpus."

As she thought thus, tears ran down her cheeks. She was wondering whether or not to go back when the sound of talk and laughter inside — she distinguished the voices of Pao-yu and Pao-chai — upset her even more. She thought back then to the events of the morning.

"Pao-yu must be angry with me, thinking I told on him," she reflected. "But I never did! You ought to investigate before flying into a temper like this. You can shut me out today, but shall we not see each other still tomorrow?"

The more she thought, the more distressed she felt. Oblivious of the cold dew on the green moss and the chill wind on the path, standing under the blossom by the corner of the wall she gave way to sobs.

As Tai-yu was weeping, the gate creaked open and out came Pao-chai escorted by Pao-yu, Hsi-jen and other maids. Tai-yu was tempted to accost Pao-yu, but not wanting to embarrass him in public she stepped aside until Pao-chai had left and the others had gone in, when she came back and shed more tears before the closed gate. Then she went back in low spirits to her room and prepared listlessly for bed.

Tzu-chuan and Hsueh-yen knew their young mistress' ways. She would often sit moodily frowning or sighing over nothing or, for no apparent reason, would give way to long spells of weeping. At first they had tried to comfort her, imagining that she missed her parents and home or that someone had been unkind; but as time went by and they found this was her habit they paid little further attention. So tonight they withdrew to bed, leaving her to brood by herself.

Tai-yu leaned against her bed-rail, clasping her knees. Her eyes were brimming with tears. There she stayed motionless as a statue, not lying down until after the second watch.

The next day was the twenty-sixth of the fourth month, the Festival of Grain in Ear. It was the time-honoured custom on this day to offer all manner of gifts and a farewell feast to the God of Flowers, for this festival was said to mark the beginning of summer when all the blossom had withered and the God of Flowers had to resign his throne and be seen off. As this custom is most faithfully observed by women, all the inmates of Grand View Garden rose early that day. The girls used flowers and osiers to weave small sedan-chairs and horses, or made pennants and flags of silk and gauze which they tied with gay ribbons to every tree and flower, turning the whole Garden into a blaze of colour. They decked themselves out so prettily, too, as to put the very flowers and birds to shame. But time forbids us to dwell on that splendid scene.

Now Pao-chai, the three Chia girls, Li Wan and Hsi-feng were enjoying themselves in the Garden with Hsi-feng's little daughter as well as Hsiang-ling and the other maids. Only one person was missing, and that was Tai-yu.

"Why isn't Cousin Lin here?" asked Ying-chun. "Surely the lazy creature isn't still sleeping?"

"I'll go and rouse her," volunteered Pao-chai. "The rest of you wait here and I'll soon bring her."

She set off instantly for Bamboo Lodge.

On the way she met the twelve young actresses headed by Wen-kuan, who greeted her and chatted for a while. Then Pao-chai told them how to find the others and, having explained her own errand, followed the winding path towards Tai-yu's quarters. As she approached Bamboo Lodge she saw Pao-yu enter the courtyard. That made her pause and lower her head in thought.

"Pao-yu and Tai-yu grew up under one roof," she reflected. "They're so free and easy together, they don't care how they tease each other or show their feelings. And Tai-yu's rather jealous and petty-minded. If I follow Pao-yu in, he may not like it and she may resent it. I'd better go back."

She went back to rejoin the other girls.

Let us return to Tai-yu, who had risen late after a sleepless night. When she heard that the other girls were farewelling the God of Flowers in the Garden, for fear of being laughed at for laziness she made haste to dress and go out. She was crossing the courtyard when Pao-yu came in.

"Dear cousin, did you tell on me yesterday?" he greeted her laughingly. "You had me worrying the whole night long."

Tai-yu turned away from him to Tzu-chuan.

"When you've tidied the rooms, close the screen windows," she instructed. "As soon as the big swallows come back, you can let down the curtains. Hold them in place by moving the lions against them. And cover the censer once the incense is lit."

As she said this, she walked on.

Pao-yu attributed this cold behaviour to the lines he had quoted at noon the previous day, having no idea of the incident in the evening. He bowed and raised his clasped hands in salute, but Tai-yu simply ignored him, walking straight off to find the other girls.

Pao-yu was puzzled.

"Surely what happened yesterday can't account for this?" he thought. "And I came back too late in the evening to see her again, so how else can I have offended her?"

With these reflections, he trailed after her.

Tai-yu joined Pao-chai and Tan-chun, who were both watching the storks dancing, and the three girls were chatting together when Pao-yu arrived.

"How are you, brother?" asked Tan-chun. "It's three whole days since last I saw you."

"How are you, sister?" he rejoined. "The other day I was asking our elder sister-in-law about you."

"Come over here. I want to talk to you."

The pair of them strolled aside under a pomegranate tree away from the other two.

"Has father sent for you these last few days?" asked Tan-chun.

Pao-yu smiled.

"No, he hasn't."

"Oh, I thought someone told me he sent for you yesterday."

"That someone must have misheard. He didn't."

Tan-chun chuckled.

"These last few months I've saved a dozen strings of cash. I want you to take them. Next time you go out you can buy me some good calligraphy and paintings, or some amusing toys."

"In my strolls through the squares and temple markets inside and outside the city," Pao-yu told her, "I haven't seen anything novel or really well made. Nothing but curios of gold, jade, bronze or porcelain, which would be out of place here. Or things like silk textiles, food and clothing."

"That's not what I mean. No, but things like you bought me last time: little willow baskets, incense-boxes carved out of bamboo roots, and tiny clay stoves. They were so sweet, I just loved them! But then other people fell in love with them too and grabbed them as if they were treasures."

Pao-yu laughed.

"If that's what you want, those things are dirt cheap. Just give five hundred cash to the pages and they'll fetch you two cartloads."

"Those fellows have no taste. Please choose some things which are simple without being vulgar, and genuine instead of artificial. Do get me a whole lot more, and I'll make you another pair of slippers. I'll put even more work into them than last time. How's that?"

"That reminds me." Pao-yu grinned. "I was wearing your slippers one day when I met father. He asked me disapprovingly who'd made them. It wouldn't have done to tell him it was you, sister; so I said they were a present from Aunt Wang on my last birthday. There wasn't much he could say to that, but after an awful silence he commented, 'What a waste of time and energy and good silk.' When I told Hsi-jen she said: 'Never mind that, but the concubine Chao's been complaining bitterly, "Her own younger brother Huan's shoes and socks are in holes yet she doesn't care. Instead she embroiders slippers for Pao-yu." ' "

Tan-chun frowned.

"Did you ever hear such nonsense?" she fumed. "Is it *my* job to make shoes? Doesn't Huan have his fair share of clothes, shoes and socks, not to mention a whole roomful of maids and servants? What has *she* got to complain of? Who's she trying to impress? If I make a pair of slippers in my spare time, I can give them to any brother I choose and no one has any right to interfere. She's crazy, carrying on like that."

Pao-yu nodded and smiled.

"Still, it's natural, you know, for her to see things rather differently."

This only enraged Tan-chun more. She tossed her head.

"Now *you're* talking nonsense too. Of course she sees things differently with that sly, low, dirty mind of hers. Who cares what *she* thinks? I don't owe any duty to anyone except our parents. If my sisters, brothers and cousins are nice to me, I'll be nice to them too, regardless of which is the child of a wife or the child of a concubine. Properly speaking, I shouldn't say such things, but really that woman's the limit!

"Let me tell you another ridiculous thing too. Two days after I gave you that money to buy knick-knacks, she complained to me she was hard up. I paid no attention, of course. But after my maids left the room, she started scolding me for giving my savings to you instead of to Huan. I didn't know whether to laugh or lose my temper. So I left her and went to Her Ladyship."

But now Pao-chai called to them laughingly: "Haven't you talked long enough? It's clear you're brother and sister, the way you leave other people out in the cold to discuss your private affairs. Aren't we allowed to hear a single word?"

They smiled at that and joined her.

Meanwhile Tai-yu had disappeared, and Pao-yu knew she was avoiding him. He decided to wait a couple of days for the storm to blow over before approaching her again. Then, lowering his head, he noticed that the ground was strewn with balsam and pomegranate petals.

"She's too angry even to gather up the blossom," he sighed. "I'll take these over and try to speak to her tomorrow."

At this point Pao-chai urged them to take a stroll.

"I'll join you later," he said.

As soon as the other two had gone, he gathered up the fallen flowers in the skirt of his gown and made his way over a small hill, across a stream and through an orchard towards the mound

154

滴翠亭寶釵戲彩蝶
埋香塚黛玉泣殘紅

where Tai-yu had buried the peach-blossom. Just before rounding the hill by the flowers' grave he caught the sound of sobs on the other side. Someone was lamenting and weeping there in a heart-rending fashion.

"Some maid's been badly treated and come here to cry," he thought. "I wonder which of them it is."

He halted to listen. And this is what he heard:

> As blossoms fade and fly across the sky,
> Who pities the faded red, the scent that has been?
> Softly the gossamer floats over spring pavilions,
> Gently the willow fluff wafts to the embroidered screen.
>
> A girl in her chamber mourns the passing of spring,
> No relief from anxiety her poor heart knows;
> Hoe in hand she steps through her portal,
> Loath to tread on the blossom as she comes and goes.
>
> Willows and elms, fresh and verdant,
> Care not if peach and plum blossom drift away;
> Next year the peach and plum will bloom again,
> But her chamber may stand empty on that day.
>
> By the third month the scented nests are built,
> But the swallows on the beam are heartless all;
> Next year, though once again you may peck the buds,
> From the beam of an empty room your nest will fall.
>
> Each year for three hundred and sixty days
> The cutting wind and biting frost contend.
> How long can beauty flower fresh and fair?
> In a single day wind can whirl it to its end.
>
> Fallen, the brightest blooms are hard to find;
> With aching heart their grave-digger comes now
> Alone, her hoe in hand, her secret tears
> Falling like drops of blood on each bare bough.
>
> Dusk falls and the cuckoo is silent;
> Her hoe brought back, the lodge is locked and still;
> A green lamp lights the wall as sleep enfolds her,
> Cold rain pelts the casement and her quilt is chill.
>
> What causes my two-fold anguish?
> Love for spring and resentment of spring;
>
> For suddenly it comes and suddenly goes,
> Its arrival unheralded, noiseless its departing.
>
> Last night from the courtyard floated a sad song —
> Was it the soul of blossom, the soul of birds?
> Hard to detain, the soul of blossom or birds,
> For blossoms have no assurance, birds no words.

I long to take wing and fly
With the flowers to earth's uttermost bound;
And yet at earth's uttermost bound
Where can a fragrant burial mound be found?

Better shroud the fair petals in silk
With clean earth for their outer attire;
For pure you came and pure shall go,
Not sinking into some foul ditch or mire.

Now you are dead I come to bury you;
None has divined the day when I shall die;
Men laugh at my folly in burying fallen flowers,
But who will bury me when dead I lie?

See, when spring draws to a close and flowers fall,
This is the season when beauty must ebb and fade;
The day that spring takes wing and beauty fades
Who will care for the fallen blossom or dead maid?

Pao-yu, listening, flung himself wretchedly down on the ground, scattering his load of fallen flowers, heart-broken to think that Tai-yu's loveliness and beauty must one day vanish away. And it followed that the same fate awaited Pao-chai, Hsiang-ling, Hsi-jen and all the rest. When at last they were all gone, what would become of him? And if he had no idea where he would be by then, what would become of this place and all the flowers and willows in the Garden and who would take them over? One reflection led to another until, after repeated ruminations, he wished he were some insensible, stupid object, able to escape all earthy entanglements and be free from such wretchedness despite the —

Shadows of blossom all around,
Birdsong on every side.

Tai-yu, giving way to her own grief, heard weeping now on the slope.

"Everyone laughs at me for being foolish. Is there someone else equally foolish?" she asked herself.

Then, looking up, she saw Pao-yu.

"So that's who it is." She snorted. "That heartless, wretched. . . ."

But the moment the words "wretched" escaped her she covered her mouth and moved quickly away with a long sigh.

When Pao-yu recovered sufficiently to look up she had gone, obviously to avoid him. Getting up rather sheepishly, he dusted off his clothes and walked down the hill to make his way back again to Happy Red Court. Catching sight of Tai-yu ahead, he overtook her.

"Do stop!" he begged. "I know you won't look at me, but let me just say *one* word. After that we can part company for good."

Tai-yu glanced round and would have ignored him, but was curious to hear this "*one* word", thinking there must be something in it. She came to a halt.

"Out with it."

Pao-yu smiled.

"Would you listen if I said two words?" he asked.

At once she walked away.

Pao-yu, close behind her, sighed.

"Why are things so different now from in the past?"

Against her will she stopped once more and turned her head.

"What do you mean by 'now' and 'the past'?"

Pao-yu heaved another sigh.

"Wasn't I your playmate when you first came?" he demanded. "Anything that pleased me was yours, cousin, for the asking. If I knew you fancied a favourite dish of mine, I put it away in a clean place till you came. We ate at the same table and slept on the same bed. I took care that the maids did nothing to upset you; for I thought cousins growing up together as such good friends should be kinder to each other than anyone else. I never expected you to grow so proud that now you have no use for me while you're so fond of outsiders like Pao-chai and Hsi-feng. You ignore me or cut me for three or four days at a time. I've no brothers or sisters of my own — only two by a different mother, as well you know. So I'm an only child like you, and I thought that would make for an affinity between us. But apparently it was no use my hoping for that. There's nobody I can tell how unhappy I am." With that, he broke down again.

This appeal and his obvious wretchedness melted her heart. But though shedding tears of sympathy, she kept her head lowered and made no reply.

This encouraged Pao-yu to go on.

"I know my own faults. But however bad I may be, I'd never dare do anything to hurt you. If I do something the least bit wrong, you can tick me off, warn me, scold me or even strike me, and I won't mind. But when you just ignore me and I can't tell why, I'm at my wits' end and don't know what to do. If I die now I can only become a 'ghost hounded to death', and not even the masses of the best bonzes and Taoists will be able to save my soul. I can only be born again if you'll tell me what's wrong."

By now Tai-yu's resentment over the previous evening was completely forgotten.

"Then why did you tell your maids not to open the gate when I called last night?" she asked.

"Whatever do you mean?" he cried in amazement. "If I did such a thing, may I die on the spot."

"Hush! Don't talk about dying so early in the morning. Did you or didn't you? There's no need to swear."

"I honestly knew nothing about your coming. Pao-chai did drop in for a chat, but she didn't stay long."

Tai-yu thought this over.

"Yes," she said more cheerfully, "I suppose your maids felt too lazy to stir and that made them answer rudely."

"That's it, for sure. I shall find out who it was when I get back and give them a good scolding."

"Those maids of yours deserve one, although of course that's not for me to say. It doesn't matter their offending *me*, but think what trouble there'll be if next time they offend your precious Pao-chai!"

She compressed her lips to smile, and Pao-yu did not know whether to grind his teeth or laugh.

Chapter 11
An Absurd, Loving Girl Falls Deeper in Love

When the first of the fifth month arrived, the road before the Jung Mansion was thronged with carriages, sedan-chairs, attendants and horses. As this mass had been paid for by the Imperial Consort and the Lady Dowager was going in person to offer incense, and as moreover it was just before the Double Fifth Festival, all the preparations were on a more lavish scale than usual.

Presently the ladies of the house emerged. The old lady's large sedan-chair had eight bearers; those of Li Wan, Hsi-feng and Aunt Hsueh, four apiece. The carriage shared by Pao-chai and Tai-yu was gay with a green awning, pearl-tassels and designs of the Eight Precious Things; that shared by the three Chia girls had crimson wheels and an ornamented covering.

Behind them followed their maids and some old nurses from the different apartments, as well as some stewards' wives. The whole street was nearly hidden from sight by all their conveyances. Even after the Lady Dowager's sedan-chair had gone a considerable distance, these attendants were still mounting their carriages at the gate. And as Pao-yu rode up on horseback before the Lady Dowager's sedan-chair, spectators lined the street.

As they neared the abbey gate, they heard the peal of bells and the roll of drums. Abbot Chang in his robes of office, holding a tablet, was waiting with his priests by the roadside to welcome them. The Lady Dowager's sedan-chair had just been borne through the gate when, at sight of the clay images

of gods guarding the temple gate, those of two messenger gods
— one with eyes able to see a thousand *li*, the other with ears
able to catch each breath of rumour — together with local
tutelary gods, she ordered her bearers to halt. Chia Chen and
the young men of the family advanced to receive her. And
Hsi-feng, knowing that Yuan-yang and the others were too far
behind to help the old lady alight, got down from her own
chair to do this. As she did so, an acolyte of twelve or
thirteen, holding a case of scissors for cutting the candle-wicks,
came darting out to see the fun and ran full tilt into her. She
boxed his ears so hard that he pitched to the ground.

"Look out where you're going, little bastard!" she swore.

Too frightened to pick up his scissors, the boy scrambled to
his feet to run outdoors. Just then Pao-chai and the other girls
were dismounting from their carriages, escorted by a multitude
of matrons and stewards' wives. At sight of the little fugitive,
the attendants shouted:

"Catch him! Beat him!"

"What's happened?" asked the Lady Dowager.

Chia Chen hurried over to make inquiries, while Hsi-feng
gave the old lady her arm.

"It's an acolyte who trims the wicks," she explained. "He
didn't get out of the way in time and was rushing wildly
about."

"Bring him here. Don't frighten him," the Lady Dowager
ordered. "Children of humble families are well sheltered by
their parents, they have never seen anything so grand before.
It would be too bad to frighten him out of his wits — his father
and mother would never get over it." She told Chia Chen, "Go
and bring him gently here."

Chia Chen had to drag the boy over. His scissors now in one
hand, trembling from head to foot, he fell on his knees. The
old lady made Chia Chen help him up.

"Don't be afraid," she said. "How old are you?"

But he was speechless with fright.

"Poor little thing!" she exclaimed, then turned to Chia Chen.

"Take him away, Chen, and give him some cash to buy sweet-meats. Don't let anyone bully him."

Chia Chen assented and led the boy away, while the Lady Dowager moved on with her train to see the different shrines.

The pages outside had just observed them enter the third gate when out came Chia Chen with the acolyte and ordered them to take him away, give him a few hundred cash and not illtreat him. Several servants promptly came forward and led him off.

Standing on the steps Chia Chen demanded, "Where is the steward?"

All the pages shouted in unison, "Steward!"

At once Lin Chih-hsiao came running over, holding on his cap with one hand.

"Although this is a large place," Chia Chen told him, "there are more people here than we expected. Keep those you need in this courtyard, send those you don't need to the other, and post some boys at the two main gates and side gates ready to carry out orders and run errands. You know, don't you, that all the ladies have come today, so not a single outsider must be allowed in."

"Yes, sir. Right, sir. Very good, sir," agreed Lin Chih-hsiao hastily.

"You may go."

As he was turning back to the hall he found Chang the Taoist standing beside him.

"In view of my special position I ought to attend the ladies inside," the priest observed with a smile. "But it's such a hot day, with so many young ladies here too, that I don't like to presume without your permission. I'd better wait here in case the old lady may want me to show her round."

Chia Chen knew that though this Taoist had been the Duke of Jungkuo's substitute,[1] later he had been made Chief

---

[1] By this superstitious practice rich people used to pay poor families' sons to be priests or monks in their stead in order to ward off evil.

Warder of the Taoist Script, with the title "Saint of the Great Illusion" verbally conferred by the previous Emperor, and now being Keeper of the Taoist Seal and entitled "Man of Final Truth" by the Emperor he was addressed as "Immortal" by nobles and officials alike. It would not do to slight him. Besides, during his frequent visits to the two mansions he had already made the acquaintance of all the ladies there, both young and old.

So Chia Chen responded with a smile, "What sort of talk is this among friends? Stop it at once or I shall pull out your beard. Come along in with me."

Laughing heartily the Taoist followed him in.

Chia Chen found the Lady Dowager and with a bow informed her: "Grandfather Chang has come to pay his respects."

"Bring him here," she rejoined at once.

Chia Chen led in the priest, chortling.

"Buddha of Infinite Longevity!" he exclaimed. "I hope the Old Ancestress has been enjoying good fortune, long life, health and peace, and that all the ladies and young ladies have been happy too. I haven't called on you to pay my respects, but Your Ladyship looks in better health than ever."

"And are you well, Old Immortal?" she responded with a smile.

"Thanks to my share in your good fortune, yes. I keep feeling concerned about your grandson, though. How has he been keeping all this time? Not long ago, on the twenty-sixth of last month, we celebrated the birthday of the Prince who Shades the Sky. As few people would be coming and everything was quite clean, I sent to invite Master Pao to come; but they told me he wasn't at home."

"It's true, he wasn't."

The old lady called for her grandson.

Pao-yu, just back from the privy, hurriedly stepped forward to say, "How do you do, Grandad Chang?"

The priest took him in his arms and asked after his health.

"Yes," he remarked to the Lady Dowager, "he looks as if he's putting on weight now."

"He may look all right but he's really delicate. And his father is ruining his health, the way he keeps the boy poring over his books."

"I've seen some of his calligraphy and poems in different places recently. They're so remarkably good I can't understand why His Lordship should still complain he's idle. I'd say he's doing all right." Then, with a sigh, the old Taoist observed, "To me, with his face and figure, his bearing and way of talking, Master Pao seems the image of the old duke." Tears welled from his eyes as he spoke.

The old lady was painfully affected too.

"You're right," she agreed. "Of all my sons and grandsons, Pao-yu is the only one who takes after his grandfather."

The priest then remarked to Chia Chen, "Of course, sir, your generation were born too late to see the duke. I don't suppose even Lord Sheh and Lord Cheng remember too well what he looked like." He burst out laughing again before turning back to the Lady Dowager. "The other day in a certain family I saw a young lady of fifteen, a pretty girl. It seems to me time to arrange a match for the young master. And that young lady would do, as far as looks, intelligence and family go. But not knowing how Your Ladyship feels, I didn't like to do anything rash. I can go and broach the subject if Your Ladyship gives the word."

"A bonze told us this boy isn't fated to marry too early," she replied. "So we'll wait until he's older to settle things. But by all means keep your eyes open. Riches and rank are immaterial. Only if you find a girl pretty enough, come and let us know. Even if the family's poor it doesn't matter, we can always let them have a few taels of silver. But good looks and a sweet disposition are hard to find."

Thereupon the priest withdrew, while the Lady Dowager and her party went upstairs to sit in the main balcony, Hsi-feng and her companions occupying that to the east. The maids, in the west balcony, took turns waiting on their mistresses.

Presently Chia Chen came to report that lots had been drawn before the shrine for the operas, and the first was to be *The White Serpent*.

"What's the story?" asked the old lady.

"It's about the First Emperor of Han who killed a serpent, then founded the dynasty. The second is *Every Son a High Minister*."[1]

"So that's the second?" The Lady Dowager nodded, smiling. "Well, if this is the wish of the gods, what must be must be. And what's the third?"

"*The Dream of the Southern Tributary State*."[2]

At this she made no comment. Chia Chen withdrew to prepare the written prayers, burn incense and order the actors to start. But no more of this.

Pao-yu, seated next to his grandmother upstairs, told one of the maids to bring him the tray of gifts. Having put on his own jade again he rummaged through his presents, showing them one by one to the old lady. Her eye was struck by a gold unicorn decorated with turquoise enamel, which she picked up.

"I'm sure I've seen something like this on one of the girls," she remarked.

"Cousin Hsiang-yun has one like that, only a little smaller," Pao-chai told her.

"So that's it!" exclaimed the Lady Dowager.

"All this time she's been staying with us, how come I've never noticed it?" asked Pao-yu.

"Cousin Pao-chai's observant," chuckled Tan-chun. "She never forgets anything either."

"She's not so observant about other things," remarked Tai-yu cuttingly. "But she's *most* observant about other people's trinkets."

Pao-chai turned away and pretended not to have heard.

---

[1] A story about Kuo Tzu-yi of the Tang Dynasty.

[2] Based on a Tang story in which a scholar had a dream of great wealth and splendour; then he woke up and found it was just an empty dream.

As soon as Pao-yu knew that Hsiang-yun had a unicorn too, he picked this one up and slipped it into his pocket. Then, afraid people might see through him, he glanced surreptitiously round. The only one paying any attention was Tai-yu, who was nodding at him with a look of speculation in her eyes. Embarrassed by this, he took the unicorn out again and showed it to her.

"This is rather fun," he said with a smile. "I'll keep it for you till we get home, then put it on a cord for you to wear."

Tai-yu tossed her head.

"I don't fancy it."

"If you really don't, in that case I'll keep it for myself." He put it away again.

Before he could say more, Madam Yu and Jung's second wife — Chia Chen's wife and daughter-in-law — arrived to pay their respects.

"You shouldn't have come," protested the old lady. "I'm just out for a little jaunt."

The next second it was announced that messengers had come from General Feng. For as soon as Feng Tzu-ying heard that the Chia family were celebrating a mass in the abbey he had prepared gifts of pigs, sheep, incense, candles and sweetmeats and had them sent along. The moment Hsi-feng knew this she hurried over to the main balcony.

"Aiya!" she exclaimed, clapping her hands. "I wasn't prepared for this. We just looked on this as an outing, but they've sent offerings under the impression that we're making a serious sacrifice of it. It's all our old lady's fault. Now I shall have to prepare some tips."

That same instant up came two stewards' wives from the Feng family. And before they had left more presents arrived from Vice-Minister Chao, to be followed in quick succession by gifts from all their relatives and friends who had heard that the ladies of the Chia family were holding a service in the abbey.

The Lady Dowager began to regret the whole expedition.

"This isn't a regular sacrifice," she said. "We just came out for fun, but we've put them to all this trouble."

So after watching only one performance she went home that same afternoon and refused to go back the next day.

"Why not go the whole hog?" Hsi-feng reasoned. "Since we've already put everybody out, we may as well amuse ourselves again today."

But Pao-yu had been sulking ever since Chang the Taoist broached the subject of his marriage to his grandmother. He was still fulminating against the priest and puzzling other people by muttering: "I never want to set eyes on him again." As for Tai-yu, she had been suffering since her return from a touch of the sun. For these reasons the old lady remained adamant. When Hsi-feng saw that she would not go, she took some others back with her to the abbey.

Pao-yu was so worried on Tai-yu's account that he would not touch his food and kept going over to find out how she was. Tai-yu, for her part, was worried about him.

"Why don't you go and see the shows?" she asked. "Why should you stay at home?"

The Taoist's officiousness still rankled with Pao-yu, and when Tai-yu said this he thought: "I could forgive others for not understanding me, but now even *she* is making fun of me." So his resentment increased a hundredfold. He wouldn't have flared up had it been anyone else, but Tai-yu's behaving this way was a different matter. His face clouded over.

"All right, all right," he said sullenly. "We've known each other all these years in vain."

"I know that too." She laughed sarcastically. "I'm not like those others who own things which make them a good match for you."

He went up to her then and demanded to her face, "Does this mean you really want to invoke Heaven and Earth to destroy me?" Before she could fathom his meaning he went on, "Yesterday I took an oath because of this, and today you provoke me again. If Heaven and Earth destroy me, what good will it do you?"

Tai-yu remembered their previous conversation and realized she had blundered. She was conscience-stricken and frantic.

"If I wish you harm, may Heaven and Earth destroy me too," she sobbed. "Why take on like this? I know. When Chang the Taoist spoke of your marriage yesterday, you were afraid he might prevent the match of your choice. And now you're working your temper off on me."

Now Pao-yu had always been deplorably eccentric. Since childhood, moreover, he had been intimate with Tai-yu, finding her a kindred spirit. Thus now that he knew a little more and had read some improper books, he felt none of the fine girls he had seen in the families of relatives and friends fit to hold a candle to her. He had long since set his heart on having her, but could not admit as much. So whether happy or angry, he used every means to test her secretly.

And Tai-yu, being rather eccentric too, would disguise her feelings to test him in return.

Thus each concealed his or her real sentiments to sound the other out. The proverb says, "When false meets false, the truth will out." So inevitably, in the process, they kept quarrelling over trifles.

So now Pao-yu was reflecting, "I can forgive *others* not understanding me, but *you* ought to know you're the only one I care for. Yet instead of comforting me you only taunt me. It's obviously no use my thinking of you every minute of the day — you've no place for me in your heart." To tell her this, however, was beyond him.

As for Tai-yu, she was reflecting, "I know I've a place in your heart. Naturally you don't take that vicious talk about gold matching jade seriously, but think of me seriously instead. Even if I raise the subject, you should take it perfectly calmly to show that it means nothing to you, that the one you really care for is me. Why get so worked up at the mention of gold and jade? This shows you're thinking about them all the time. You're afraid I suspect this when I mention them, so you put on a show of being worked up — just to fool me."

In fact, to start with their two hearts were one, but each of them was so hyper-sensitive that their longing to be close ended in estrangement.

Now Pao-yu was telling himself, "Nothing else matters to me so long as you're happy. Then I'd gladly die for you this very instant. Whether you know this or not, you can at least feel that in my heart you're close to me and not distant."

Tai-yu meanwhile was thinking, "Just take good care of yourself. When you're happy, I'm happy too. Why should you be upset because of me? You should know that if you're upset, so am I. It means you won't let me be close to you and want me to keep at a distance."

So their mutual concern for each other resulted in their estrangement. But as it is hard to describe all their secret thoughts, we shall have to content ourselves with recording their actions.

Those words "the match of your choice" infuriated Pao-yu. Too choked with rage to speak, he tore the jade from his neck and dashed it to the floor.

"You rubbishy thing!" he cried, gnashing his teeth. "I'll smash you to pieces and have done with it."

The jade was so hard, however, that no damage was done. So he looked around for something with which to smash it.

Tai-yu was already weeping.

"Why destroy that dumb object?" she sobbed. "Better destroy me instead."

Tzu-chuan and Hsueh-yen dashed in to stop this quarrel. Seeing Pao-yu hammering at the jade they tried to snatch it away from him but failed. And since this was more serious than usual they had to send for Hsi-jen, who hurried in and managed to rescue the stone.

Pao-yu smiled bitterly.

"I can smash what's mine, can't I? What business is it of yours?"

Hsi-jen had never before seen him so livid with rage, his whole face contorted.

"Because you have words with your cousin is no reason to smash this up," she said coaxingly, taking his hand. "Suppose you broke it, think how bad she'd feel."

This touched Tai-yu's heart, yet it only made her more wretched to think that Pao-yu had less consideration for her than Hsi-jen. She sobbed even more bitterly, so distraught that she threw up the herbal medicine she had just taken. Tzu-chuan hastily brought her a handkerchief which soon was completely soaked through. Hsueh-yen meanwhile massaged her back.

"No matter how angry you are, miss, do think of your health!" Tzu-chuan urged. "You were feeling a little better after the medicine; it's this tiff with Master Pao that's made you retch. If you fall ill, how upset Master Pao will be."

This touched Pao-yu's heart, yet also struck him as proof that Tai-yu had less consideration for him than Tzu-chuan. But now Tai-yu's cheeks were flushed and swollen. Weeping and choking, her face streaked with tears and sweat, she looked most fearfully frail. The sight filled him with compunction.

"I should never have argued with her and got her into this state," he scolded himself. "I can't even suffer instead of her." He, too, shed tears.

Hsi-jen's heart ached to see how bitterly both of them were weeping. She felt Pao-yu's hands. They were icy cold. She wanted to urge him not to cry, but feared that bottling up his resentment would be bad for him; on the other hand, comforting him might seem like slighting Tai-yu. Thinking that tears might calm them all, she wept in sympathy.

Tzu-chuan, who had cleaned up and was gently fanning Tai-yu, was so affected by the sight of the three of them weeping in silence that she had to put a handkerchief to her own eyes.

So all four of them wept in silence until Hsi-jen, forcing a smile, said to Pao-yu:

"Just because of the tassel on your jade, if not for any other reason, you shouldn't quarrel with Miss Lin."

At this Tai-yu forgot her nausea and rushed over to snatch

the jade, seizing a pair of scissors to cut off the tassel. Hsi-jen and Tzu-chuan intervened too late to save it.

"All my work for nothing," sobbed Tai-yu. "He doesn't care for it. He can get someone else to make him a better one." Hsi-jen hastily took the jade from her.

"Why do that?" she protested. "It's *my* fault. I should have held my tongue."

"Go ahead and cut it up," Pao-yu urged Tai-yu. "I shan't wear it anyway, so it doesn't matter."

During this commotion, some old nurses had bustled off without their knowing to inform the Lady Dowager and Lady Wang. For having heard Tai-yu crying and vomiting and Pao-yu threatening to smash his jade, they did not want to be held responsible should any serious trouble come of it. Their flurried, earnest report so alarmed the old lady and Lady Wang that both came to the Garden to see what dreadful thing had happened. Hsi-jen was frantic and blamed Tzu-chuan for disturbing their mistresses, while Tzu-chuan held Hsi-jen to blame.

When the Lady Dowager and Lady Wang found both the young people quiet and were told there was nothing amiss, they vented their anger on their two chief maids.

"Why don't you look after them properly?" they scolded. "Can't you *do* something when they start quarrelling?"

The two maids had to listen meekly to a long lecture, and peace was only restored when the old lady took Pao-yu away.

The next day, the third of the month, was Hsueh Pan's birthday, and the whole Chia family was invited to a feast and theatricals. Pao-yu had not seen Tai-yu since he offended her and was feeling too remorseful and depressed to enjoy any show. He pleaded illness, therefore, as an excuse not to go.

Tai-yu was not seriously ill, simply suffering from the heat. When she heard of Pao-yu's refusal to go she thought, "He has a weakness for feasts and theatricals. If he's staying away today, it must either be because yesterday's business still rankles or because he knows *I'm* not going. I should never have cut that tassel off his jade. I'm sure he won't wear it again now unless I make him another." So she felt thoroughly conscience-stricken too.

The Lady Dowager had hoped they would stop sulking and make it up while watching operas together. When both refused to go she grew quite frantic.

"What sins have I committed in a past existence to be plagued with two such troublesome children?" she lamented. "Not a day goes by without something to worry about. How true the proverb is that 'Enemies and lovers are destined to meet.' Once I've closed my eyes and breathed my last, they can quarrel and storm as much as they like. What the eye doesn't see the heart doesn't grieve for. But I'm not at my last gasp just yet." With that she wept too.

When word of this reached Pao-yu and Tai-yu, neither of whom had heard that proverb before, they felt as if a great light had dawned on them. With lowered heads they pondered its meaning and could not hold back their tears. True, they were still apart: one weeping to the breeze in Bamboo Lodge, the other sighing to the moon in Happy Red Court. But although apart, at heart they were as one.

Hsi-jen scolded Pao-yu, "It's entirely your fault. You used to blame boys who quarrelled with their sisters, or husbands who disputed with their wives, for being too stupid to understand girls' hearts. Yet now you're being just as bad yourself. The day after tomorrow, the fifth, is the festival. If you two go on looking daggers at each other that will make the old lady even angrier and no one will have any peace. Do get over your temper and apologize! Let bygones be bygones. Wouldn't that be better for both sides?"

Tai-yu for her part was also remorseful after her quarrel with Pao-yu, but could think of no pretext to go and make it up. So she spent all day and night in a state of depression, feeling as if bereft. Tzu-chuan, who guessed how she felt, tried to reason with her.

"The fact is you were too hasty the other day, miss," she

said. "*We* should know Pao-yu if no one else does. After all, it's not the first time there's been a rumpus over that jade."

"So you side with the others and blame me," snapped Tai-yu. "In what way was I hasty?"

"Why did you cut off the tassel for no reason? That put you more in the wrong than Master Pao. I know how devoted he is to you, miss. All this comes of your touchiness and the way you twist his words."

Before Tai-yu could retort they heard someone calling at the outer gate.

"It's Pao-yu's voice." Tzu-chuan smiled. "He must be coming to apologize."

"Don't let him in."

"That wouldn't be right, miss. It's a scorching day. We don't want him to get sunstroke."

She went and opened the gate, ushering Pao-yu in with a smile.

"I thought you'd never cross this threshold of ours again," she remarked. "But here you are."

"You take things far too seriously." He chuckled. "Why shouldn't I come? Even if I were dead, my ghost would haunt you a hundred times a day. Tell me, is my cousin better?"

"In her health, yes. Not in her feelings."

"I know what's the trouble with her."

He went in and found Tai-yu indulging in a fresh fit of weeping on her bed, so much had his arrival touched her.

Walking cheerfully up to her bedside he asked, "Are you feeling a little better?"

When she simply wiped her tears without answering, he sat down on the edge of the bed.

"I know you're not really angry with me," he told her. "But if I stayed away others might think we'd quarrelled again and come to act as peacemakers, as if the two of us were strangers. So beat me or scold me as much as you like but for pity's sake don't ignore me, dear cousin, sweet cousin!"

Tai-yu had in fact determined to ignore him, but this speech proving that she was dearer to him than anyone else, and all the endearments he now poured out, made her break down again.

"You needn't flatter me," she sobbed. "I shall never dare be friends with you again. Behave as if I'd gone."

"Where would you go?" Pao-yu laughed.

"Home."

"I'd go with you."

"What if I should die?"

"I'd become a monk."

"What a thing to say!" She frowned sternly. "Why talk such nonsense? Think of all the sisters and girl cousins you have. Do you have so many lives that you can become a monk every time one of them dies? Wait and see what the others say when I tell them this."

Pao-yu could have kicked himself for this fresh blunder. Flushing red he hung his head without a word, thankful that no one else was in the room. Too angry to speak, she fixed him with furious eyes until his cheeks were burning. Then, clenching her teeth, she stabbed with one finger at his forehead.

"You. . . ."

But this exclamation ended in a sigh as she took out her handkerchief and wiped her tears.

Pao-yu's heart was very full and he was ashamed of speaking so foolishly. When she struck him then sighed and wept without a word, he too was reduced to tears. He started to wipe them with his sleeve, having forgotten to bring a handkerchief, and Tai-yu noticed through her own tears that he was wearing a new lilac blue linen gown. While dabbing at her own eyes she turned and took a silk handkerchief from her pillow, tossed him this in silence and covered her face again.

Pao-yu took the handkerchief and wiped his tears, then stepped forward to clasp her hand.

"You're breaking my heart with your weeping," he declared. "Come, let's go and see the old lady."

"Take your hands off me!" She pulled away. "You're not a child any more, yet you still carry on in this shameless way. Can't you behave yourself?"

She was interrupted by the cry "Thank goodness!"

The two of them started, then turned to see Hsi-feng sweeping gaily in.

"The old lady's fulminating against Heaven and Earth," she informed them. "She insisted I come to see if you'd made it up. I told her, 'No need, they'll be friends again in less than three days.' But she scolded me for being too lazy to stir, so I had to come. Well, what did I say? I can't see what you two have to quarrel about. Friends one day, squabbling the next, you're worse than children. *Now* you're holding hands and crying, but yesterday you were like fighting cocks. Come along with me, quick, to your grandmother to set the old lady's mind at rest."

She caught hold of Tai-yu meaning to lead her away. Tai-yu turned to call her maids but not one was there.

"What do you want *them* for?" asked Hsi-feng. "*I'll* look after you."

With that she pulled her out. And Pao-yu followed them out of the Garden to the Lady Dowager's quarters.

"I said don't worry, they'll make it up themselves," announced Hsi-feng cheerfully. "Our Old Ancestress didn't believe me, and insisted I go along as peacemaker. I found they'd already asked each other's forgiveness, and were clinging together like an eagle sinking its talons into a hawk. They didn't need any help."

This set the whole room laughing. Pao-chai was also there. Tai-yu said nothing but took a seat by the Lady Dowager.

To make conversation Pao-yu told Pao-chai: "I *would* have to be out of sorts on your brother's birthday; that's why I haven't sent any present over or even gone to offer congratulations. If he doesn't know I'm unwell, he may think I couldn't be bothered and be offended. Do explain to him, will you, cousin?"

"You're over-punctilious," said Pao-chai. "We wouldn't dare put you to any trouble even if you wished to go, much less so when you're unwell. As cousins you're always seeing so much of each other, you've no call to behave like strangers."

"So long as you understand and will overlook it." He added, "But why aren't *you* watching the operas, cousin?"

"I feel the heat. After watching two pieces I couldn't stand it any longer. But as the guests hadn't left, I had to pretend to be feeling unwell in order to slip away."

This sounded to Pao-yu like a reflection on him. In his embarrassment he said with a sheepish smile:

"No wonder they compare you to Lady Yang, you're both 'plump and sensitive to the heat.' "[1]

Pao-chai was so enraged by this remark that she could have flown into a temper, but she restrained herself. This quip rankled so much, however, that she reddened and laughed sarcastically.

"If I'm so like Lady Yang," she retorted, "it's too bad I've no brother or cousin able to be another Yang Kuo-chung."[2]

She was interrupted by one of the young maids, Tien-erh, who had mislaid her fan.

"You must have hidden it, miss," she said playfully. "Do let me have it back."

"Behave yourself!" cried Pao-chai sharply, wagging one finger at her. "Have *I* ever played such tricks with you, that you should suspect me? You should ask the other young ladies who are always joking with you."

This rebuff frightened Tien-erh away.

Pao-yu knew he had made another gaffe, in public too. Even more embarrassed than earlier on with Tai-yu, he turned away to talk to the others.

---

[1] Lady Yang, favourite of Emperor Ming-huang of the Tang Dynasty, was supposed to be rather plump.

[2] Lady Yang's cousin who through nepotism became prime minister. Corrupt and lawless, he was put to death by the Imperial Guards during the Tang general An Lu-shan's rebellion.

Tai-yu had been delighted to hear him make fun of Pao-chai. She would, indeed, have joined in if not for Pao-chai's retort regarding the fan. She decided, as it was, to change the subject.

"What were the two operas you saw, cousin?" she asked.

Tai-yu's enjoyment of her discomfiture at Pao-yu's remark had not escaped Pao-chai, who smiled at this question.

"One was that piece," she answered, "in which Li Kuei abuses Sung Chiang and then apologizes."[1]

Pao-yu laughed.

"Why, cousin," he cried, "surely you're sufficiently well versed in ancient and modern literature to know the title of that opera. Why do you have to describe it? It's called *Abject Apologies*."

"*Abject Apologies*, is it?" retorted Pao-chai. "*You* two are the ones well versed in ancient and modern literature, so of course you know all about 'abject apologies' — that's something quite beyond *me*."

As both Pao-yu and Tai-yu were conscience-stricken, they immediately blushed. And Hsi-feng, although she did not understand such allusions, could guess from their expressions what was afoot.

"Who's been eating ginger in such hot weather?" she asked.

The others were mystified.

"No one's been eating ginger."

Hsi-feng put both hands to her cheeks with a show of astonishment.

"In that case, why are some people so red in the face?"

This embarrassed Pao-yu and Tai-yu even more. And when Pao-chai saw Pao-yu so out of countenance, she simply smiled and let the matter drop. So did the others, who had not caught on to this exchange between the four of them.

Presently Pao-chai and Hsi-feng left. Then Tai-yu turned with a smile to Pao-yu.

"Now you've come up against someone with a sharper

---

[1] From the novel *Shui Hu*. Li Kuei was a peasant rebel. Sung Chiang, the leader of the outlaws, was a capitulationist.

tongue than mine. Not everyone's as simple and tongue-tied as *I* am, so easy to tease."

Pao-yu was already put out by Pao-chai's annoyance, and this fresh provocation added to his ill humour. But not wanting to annoy Tai-yu too, he kept his temper and sulkily left the room.

Chapter 12
A Torn Fan Wins a Smile from a Maid

It was now mid-summer. The days were so long that after lunch masters and servants alike were exhausted. His hands behind his back, Pao-yu strolled through the grounds and did not hear a sound. From the Lady Dowager's quarters he wandered west through the passage hall to Hsi-feng's compound; but the gate there was closed and he knew he had better not call as she usually took a nap after lunch in the summer. So he sauntered through a side gate to his mother's apartments, where some maids were dozing with needlework in their hands while Lady Wang slept on a couch in the inner room. Chin-chuan, sitting by her to massage her legs, was nodding drowsily too.

Pao-yu tiptoed up to her and flicked one of her earrings, whereupon she opened her eyes.

"You sleepy-head!" he whispered.

She pouted, smiled and motioned him away, then closed her eyes again; but Pao-yu was reluctant to leave her. He stole a glance at his mother. Her eyes were closed. Then he took a peppermint pastille from his pouch and slipped it between Chin-chuan's lips. She accepted it without opening her eyes. At that Pao-yu pressed closer and took her hand.

"I'll ask your mistress for you tomorrow," he said softly. "Then we can be together."

Chin-chuan made no reply.

"Or rather I'll ask her as soon as she wakes."

The girl opened her eyes then and pushed him away.

"What's the hurry? 'A gold pin may fall into the well, but if it's yours it remains yours.' Can't you understand that proverb? I'll tell you something amusing to do. Go to the small east courtyard and see what your brother Huan and Tsai-yun are up to."

"I don't care what they're up to. It's *you* I'm interested in."

At this point Lady Wang sat up and slapped Chin-chuan's face.

"Shameless slut!" she scolded. "It's low creatures like you who lead the young masters astray."

Pao-yu had vanished like smoke as soon as his mother sat up. Chin-chuan's cheek was tingling but she dared say nothing and the other maids, hearing their mistress's voice, hurried in.

"Yu-chuan!" ordered Lady Wang. "Go and tell your mother to come at once and take your sister away."

At these words Chin-chuan fell on her knees and burst into tears.

"I shan't let it happen again, madam," she cried. "Whip me, scold me or punish me as you please, but for pity's sake don't send me away! I've been with Your Ladyship more than ten years. If you dismiss me now, how can I look anyone in the face again?"

Lady Wang was generally speaking too good-natured and easy-going to beat the maids; but the shameless way in which Chin-chuan had behaved was the one thing she could not abide. That was why, flaring up, she had slapped and cursed her. Although the maid pleaded hard she refused to keep her, and her mother, old Mrs. Pai, had to take her away. So Chin-chuan went home in disgrace.

Now as this was the eve of the Double Fifth Festival, the twelve young actresses had been given a holiday and were amusing themselves in different parts of the Garden. Pao-kuan who played young scholars and Yu-kuan who played young ladies were enjoying themselves in Happy Red Court with Hsi-jen, when it came on to rain. They stopped up the drain to make water collect in the yard and caught some water-fowl —

green-headed ducks, speckled mallards and mandarin ducks. Having tied their wings they let these loose in the yard, after which they bolted the gate.

While they stood on the verandah enjoying the fun, Pao-yu arrived back only to find the gate closed. The girls were laughing too much to hear his knock, so that he shouted and pounded for a long time before they finally heard. And of course they were not expecting him back at this time.

"Who's that at the gate?" asked Hsi-jen. "Who'll go and see?"

"It's I!" cried Pao-yu.

"Sounds like Miss Pao-chai," said Sheh-yueh.

"Nonsense!" exclaimed Ching-wen. "Miss Pao-chai wouldn't come at this hour."

"I'll peep through a crack," offered Hsi-jen, "to see if it's somebody we should let in. If it's not, we'll let whoever it is get a soaking."

She went along the covered corridor to the gate and discovered Pao-yu there, drenched as a drowned cock. Torn between concern and amusement she hastily opened the gate, then doubled up with laughter, clapping her hands.

"How were we to know you were back?" she spluttered. "Where have you been, running about in such a downpour?"

Pao-yu, in a foul temper, had decided to punish whoever opened the gate. Without waiting to see who it was, and assuming that this was one of the younger girls, he kicked Hsi-jen so hard in the side that she let out a cry.

"You low creatures!" he stormed. "I treat you so well that you've lost all sense of respect. Now you dare make fun of me!"

At this point he lowered his head and heard Hsi-jen's cry. He realized then what a blunder he had made.

"Oh, is it you?" He smiled apologetically. "Where did I kick you?"

Hsi-jen had never had so much as a harsh word from Pao-yu. Now that he had lost his temper and kicked her — in public too — she felt overwhelmed with shame, resentment and pain.

But sure that he hadn't done this deliberately, she did her best to control herself.

"It's all right," she answered. "Go in and change your clothes."

Once inside he said contritely, "This is the first time in my life I've lashed out in a temper — and it had to be at *you*."

Still wincing she helped him out of his wet clothes.

"I'm your number one maid," she answered jokingly, "so I should have first share of everything big or small, good or bad. I just hope you won't make a habit of kicking people."

"I didn't mean to do it."

"I'm not saying you did. Usually it's the younger ones who go to the gate. They're all so spoilt that nobody can stand them, and they're not afraid of anyone either. It would have served them right if you'd kicked one of them to frighten them. Today I'm to blame for not letting them open the gate."

By now the rain had stopped. Both Pao-kuan and Yu-kuan had left. What with the pain in her side and her vexation, Hsi-jen ate nothing that evening. And when she undressed to have her bath she was frightened by the bruise, the size of a bowl, below her ribs, but could hardly remark on it. The pain continued after she was in bed and made her groan in her sleep.

Though Pao-yu had not kicked her deliberately, Hsi-jen's obvious discomfort disturbed him. And hearing her cry out during the night he realized how badly he must have hurt her. He slipped out of bed, took the lamp, and went over to have a look. Just as he reached her bedside she coughed, then brought up some phlegm and opened her eyes with a gasp.

"What are you doing?" she asked in surprise when she saw him.

"You were groaning in your sleep. I must have hurt you badly. Let me have a look."

"I feel dizzy and there's a bitter-sweet taste in my throat. Throw the light on the floor, will you?"

Pao-yu did as she asked and saw that she had coughed blood.

"How dreadful!" he exclaimed.

When Hsi-jen saw the blood on the floor her heart failed her, for she had often heard tell: Spitting blood while young means an early death or infirmity for life. So her dreams of future honour and splendour had gone up in smoke! She could not help shedding tears. Pao-yu's heart ached too.

"How are you feeling?" he asked.

She forced a smile.

"All right."

He would have called someone at once to heat Shaohsing wine and fetch pills compounded with goat's blood, but Hsi-jen restrained him.

"If you make such a fuss that people come flocking in, they'll blame me for getting above myself," she explained. "At present not a soul knows, but to noise it abroad would be damaging for us both. Just send a boy tomorrow to ask Doctor Wang for some medicine, and that will set me right. Far better keep the whole business quiet."

Since this made sense Pao-yu had to agree. He fetched tea for Hsi-jen to rinse her mouth and, knowing how worried he was, she lay there quietly letting him wait on her, for otherwise he would have roused the others.

Next day, at the crack of dawn, Pao-yu scrambled into his clothes. Not stopping to wash or comb his hair, he went off to find Wang Chi-jen whom he plied with questions. When the doctor heard what had happened, he assured him it was simply a contusion and prescribed some pills, giving directions as to their use which Pao-yu carried out on his return to the Garden. But no more of this.

This was the day of the Double Fifth Festival. The doors were hung with mugwort and rushes, everyone wore tiger-charms, and Lady Wang gave a family feast at midday to which Aunt Hsueh and her daughter were invited.

Pao-yu noticed that Pao-chai was cold-shouldering him because of what had happened the previous day. His own low spirits were ascribed by his mother to embarrassment over yesterday's episode with Chin-chuan, and therefore she deliberately ignored him. Tai-yu, for her part, assumed that his dejection was the result of having offended Pao-chai, and that displeased her too. As for Hsi-feng, she had heard the evening before from Lady Wang about Pao-yu and Chin-chuan, and in deference to her aunt's displeasure was not her usual cheerful, laughing self, making the atmosphere even more constrained. As Ying-chun and the other Chia girls were affected by the general lack of spirits, the company soon dispersed.

Now Tai-yu naturally preferred solitude to society. She reasoned, "Coming together can only be followed by parting. The more pleasure people find in parties, the more lonely and unhappy they must feel when the parties break up. So better not forgather in the first place. The same is true of flowers: they delight people when in bloom, but it's so heart-rending to see them fade that it would be better if they never blossomed." For this reason she grieved over what others enjoyed.

Pao-yu, on the other hand, wished that parties need never break up, flowers never fade; and although he could neither stop a feast from ending nor flowers from withering, he grieved every time this happened.

So whereas Tai-yu did not care when the feasters parted in low spirits today, Pao-yu went back to his room feeling so gloomy that he did nothing but sigh. When Ching-wen, who was helping him change, dropped his fan and broke it he sighed:

"How stupid you are! What's to become of you when in future you have a home of your own? Surely you can't go on being so careless then."

"How bad-tempered you've grown lately," she retorted with a snigger. "Always throwing your weight about. The other day you even beat Hsi-jen, and now you're picking on me. You can kick or beat us as much as you like, of course, but what's so dreadful about dropping a fan? Plenty of glass vases and agate bowls have been smashed before without your flaring up. It seems pointless to make such a fuss over a fan. If you're fed up with us, you can send us packing and get some better attendants. But why not part company in a peaceful, friendly way?"

"Don't worry," he cried, fairly trembling with rage. "We shall part sooner or later."

Hsi-jen, who had overheard them, now hurried in.

"Why take on again for no reason?" she asked Pao-yu. "Didn't I tell you, the moment my back's turned there's trouble."

"If you're so clever," sneered Ching-wen, "you should have come earlier to prevent this tantrum. You're the one who's looked after him since ancient times — I never did. It's because you're so *good* at it that you got kicked right under your heart yesterday. Heaven knows what punishment is waiting tomorrow for *me*, unfit as I am to wait on him."

Annoyance and mortification tempted Hsi-jen to make a sharp retort. She only controlled herself because Pao-yu was already livid with rage.

"Run along and amuse yourself outside, good sister," she said, pushing Ching-wen away. *"We're* the ones to blame."

This "we," obviously meaning Pao-yu and herself, made Ching-wen even more jealous.

"I don't know what you mean by 'we,' " she cried with a scornful laugh. "Don't make me blush for you. What you're up to on the sly is no secret to me. The fact of the matter is, you've not even earned the grade of a concubine yet, so you're no better than I am. How can you talk of '*we*'?"

Hsi-jen flushed crimson over her indiscretion.

"If the rest of you are so jealous," raged Pao-yu, "I'll raise her status just to spite you."

Hsi-jen caught him by the hand to restrain him.

"Why argue with a silly girl? You're usually broad-minded enough to overlook plenty of worse things than this. What's got into you today?"

"I'm too silly to be up to talking to you," snorted Ching-wen.

"Are you quarrelling with me, miss, or with Master Pao? If I annoy you just tell me, instead of squabbling with him. If

Master Pao annoys you, don't make such a row that everybody hears. I came in to try to smooth things over and save everybody's face, but then you set on *me*. Which of us are you mad at, him or me? What's the idea, lashing out in all directions? Well, I'll say no more. It's up to you now."

With that she walked away.

"There was no need to fly into such a temper," said Pao-yu to Ching-wen. "I know what's on your mind. I'll tell the mistress you've reached the age to be sent home. How about that?"

"Why should I go home?" Tears of distress welled up in Ching-wen's eyes. "How can you trump up an excuse to get rid of me just because you've taken a dislike to me?"

"I've never been through such a scene before. You're obviously set on going. So I'd better ask my mother to send you away."

He was starting out when Hsi-jen barred the way.

"Where are you off to?" she asked.

"To tell my mother."

"What nonsense!" She smiled at him coaxingly. "How can you have the heart to shame her so? Even if she really wanted to leave, you should wait until she's cooled down and then mention it to the mistress casually. If you rush over now as if this were something urgent, Her Ladyship's bound to start imagining things."

"Not her. I'll just tell her that she insists on leaving."

"When did I insist on leaving?" sobbed Ching-wen. "You fly into a rage, then put words into my mouth. All right, go and report it. But I'll dash out my brains sooner than leave this house."

"That's strange!" he fumed. "If you won't go, what's all this fuss about? I can't stand these rows. Far simpler if you left."

He was so set on telling his mother that Hsi-jen saw no way to stop him. She fell on her knees to plead. This was the signal for Pi-hen, Chiu-wen and Sheh-yueh, who had been listening with bated breath outside, to rush in and kneel down beside her.

Pao-yu pulled Hsi-jen to her feet, sank with a sigh on to his bed, and sent the other girls out.

"What am I to *do*?" he demanded. "I've worn my heart out, yet nobody cares."

He wept and Hsi-jen shed tears in sympathy. Ching-wen beside them was trying to speak through her sobs when Tai-yu's arrival made her slip away.

"What's all this crying during the festival?" asked Tai-yu mockingly. "Are you fighting for sticky rice dumplings?"

The two of them laughed.

"Since *you* won't tell me I'll find out from *her*." Tai-yu patted Hsi-jen's shoulder. "What's happened, dear sister-in-law? I suppose you two have been squabbling again. Tell me what's wrong and I'll act as peacemaker."

"You're joking, miss." Hsi-jen pushed her away. "Don't talk such nonsense to us servant-girls."

"You may call yourself a servant-girl, but I regard you as my sister-in-law."

"Why give her another name for people to jeer at?" protested Pao-yu. "There's enough gossip already without *your* joining in."

"You don't know how I feel, miss," said Hsi-jen. "I'll never have any peace until I can die and be done with it!"

"I can't say what *others* would do if you died." Tai-yu smiled. "I'd die first of crying."

"I'd become a monk if you died," Pao-yu declared.

"Do be quiet," cried Hsi-jen. "That's no way to talk."

Tai-yu held out two fingers with a smile.

"That's twice, so far, you've become a monk. I must keep track of how many times you do it."

Pao-yu knew she was referring to their conversation the other day, and with a smile he let the matter drop.

Soon after that Tai-yu left and Pao-yu received an invitation from Hsueh Pan, which he could hardly decline, to a drinking party. He was unable to leave before the end. Dusk had fallen by the time he came back, slightly tipsy, and as he lurched into his courtyard he noticed someone lying on a couch there. Assuming that it was Hsi-jen, he sat down beside her and nudged her.

"Has the pain stopped?" he asked.

The figure on the couch sat up.

"Why are you back to plague me again?" she demanded.

It was not Hsi-jen but Ching-wen. He made her sit beside him.

"You're growing more and more spoilt," he teased. "When you dropped that fan and I just said a couple of words, you launched into such a tirade. I don't mind your scolding *me*, but was it right to drag Hsi-jen into it too when she meant so well?"

"It's so hot, keep your hands to yourself," countered Ching-wen. "What would people think if they saw? I'm not fit to be sitting here with you anyway."

"Then why were you sleeping here?" he asked with a grin. She giggled.

"It was all right before you came, but not now that you're here. Get up and let me have my bath. I'll call Hsi-jen and Sheh-yueh — they've already had theirs."

"After all the wine I've drunk I need a bath too. If you've not had yours, fill the tub and we'll bath together."

Ching-wen waved this proposal aside with a laugh.

"Not I. I wouldn't dare. I remember what happened that time Pi-hen helped you bath. Two or three hours it took and we couldn't go in — heaven knows what you were up to. When you'd finished and we had a look, the floor right up to the legs of the bed was all over water — even the bed mat was sopping. Goodness knows what sort of bath you had! It kept us laughing for days. I haven't the time to mop up after you, and see no need for you to bath with me. Besides, it's so cool now I don't think you ought to have a bath; I'll just get you a basin of water to wash your face and comb your hair. Yuan-yang brought in a lot of fruit not long ago which is being chilled in

188

撕扇子作千金一笑
因麒塵伏白首雙星

that crystal bowl. I'll tell them to bring it for you."

"In that case, you mustn't bath either. Just wash your hands and bring the fruit."

Ching-wen laughed.

"If I'm so careless that I even break fans, how can I fetch fruit? If I broke a plate too, I'd never hear the end of it."

"You can if you want. Such things are meant to be used. You may like one thing, I another. People's tastes differ. For instance, fans are meant for fanning; but if I choose to break one for fun, what's wrong with that? But we shouldn't break things to work off a fit of temper. It's the same with cups or plates which are for serving things in. If you smash them because you like the sound, all right. Just don't work off your temper on them. That's what's called caring for things."

"If that's so, get me a fan to tear up. I love ripping things apart."

With a smile he handed her his own. Sure enough, she ripped it in two, then tore it to pieces.

Pao-yu chuckled.

"Well done! Try and make a bigger noise."

Just then along came Sheh-yueh.

"What a wicked waste!" she cried. "Stop it."

Pao-yu's answer was to snatch her fan from her and give it to Ching-wen, who promptly tore it up and joined in his loud laughter.

"What's the idea?" demanded Sheh-yueh. "Spoiling my fan — is that your idea of fun?"

"Just pick another from the fan case," Pao-yu told her. "What's so wonderful about a fan?"

"You'd better bring the case out here then and let her tear the whole lot up."

"You bring it." Pao-yu chuckled.

"I won't do anything of the sort. She's not broken her wrist, let *her* fetch it."

"I'm tired." Ching-wen lay back laughing. "I'll tear up some more tomorrow."

"You know the ancient saying," put in Pao-yu. " 'A thousand

pieces of gold can hardly purchase a smile.' And what are a few fans worth?"

He called for Hsi-jen, who came out having just changed into clean clothes and got little Chia-hui to clear away the broken fans. Then they sat outside for a while enjoying the cool.

Chapter 13
An Avowal Leaves Pao-yu Bemused

Tai-yu had discovered Hsiang-yun's whereabouts and knew that Pao-yu had hurried back, no doubt to talk about the gold unicorns he found the other day. That set her thinking. In most of the romances Pao-yu had recently acquired, a young scholar and beautiful girl came together and fell in love thanks to lovebirds, phoenixes, jade rings, gold pendants, silk handkerchiefs, embroidered girdles or other baubles of the sort. So Pao-yu's possession of a gold unicorn like Hsiang-yun's might lead to a romance between them. She slipped over to 'see what was happening and judge of their feelings for each other, arriving just as Hsiang-yun was speaking of worldly affairs, and in time to hear Pao-yu answer, "Miss Lin never talks such disgusting nonsense. If she did, I'd have stopped having anything to do with her."

This surprised and delighted Tai-yu but also distressed and grieved her. She was delighted to know she had not misjudged him, for he had now proved just as understanding as she had always thought. Surprised that he had been so indiscreet as to acknowledge his preference for her openly. Distressed because their mutual understanding ought to preclude all talk about gold matching jade, or she instead of Pao-chai should have the gold locket to match his jade amulet. Grieved because her parents had died, and although his preference was so clear there was no one to propose the match for her. Besides, she had recently been suffering from dizzy spells which the doctor had warned might end in consumption, as she was so weak and frail. Dear as she and Pao-yu were to each other, she might not have long to live. And what use was their affinity if she were fated to die? These thoughts sent tears coursing down her cheeks. And therefore instead of entering she turned away, wiping her tears.

Pao-yu hurried out after changing his clothes to see Tai-yu walking slowly ahead, apparently wiping her tears. He overtook her.

"Where are you going, cousin?" he asked with a smile. "What, crying again? Who's offended you this time?"

Tai-yu turned and saw who it was.

"I'm all right." She gave a wan smile. "I wasn't crying."

"Don't fib — your eyes are still wet."

He raised his hand instinctively to wipe away her tears. At once she recoiled a few steps.

"Are you crazy? Can't you keep your hands to yourself?"

"I did it without thinking." Pao-yu laughed. "I was dead to all around me."

"No one will care when *you're* dead, but what about the gold locket and unicorn you'll have to leave behind?"

This remark made Pao-yu frantic.

"How can you talk like that! Are you trying to put me under a curse, or set on annoying me?"

Reminded of what had happened the previous day, Tai-yu regretted her thoughtlessness.

"Don't get so excited," she begged. "Why work yourself up over a slip of the tongue? The veins on your forehead are all swollen with anger, and what a sweat you're in!"

So saying, she too stepped forward without thinking and reached out her hand to wipe his perspiring face. Pao-yu fixed his eyes on her.

After a while he said gently, "You mustn't worry."

Tai-yu gazed at him in silence.

"Worry?" she repeated at last. "I don't understand. What do you mean?"

"Don't you really understand?" He sighed. "Could it be

that since I've known you all my feelings for you have been wrong? If I can't even enter into *your* feelings, then you're quite right to be angry with me all the time."

"I really don't understand what you mean by telling me not to worry."

"Dear cousin, don't tease." Pao-yu nodded and sighed. "If you really don't understand, all my devotion's been wasted and even your feeling for me has been thrown away. You ruin your health by worrying so much. If you'd take things less to heart, your illness wouldn't be getting worse every day."

These words struck Tai-yu like a thunderbolt. As she turned them over in her mind, they seemed closer to her innermost thoughts than if wrung from her own heart. There were a thousand things she longed to say, yet she could not utter a word. She just stared at him in silence. As Pao-yu was in similar case, he too stared at her without a word. So they stood transfixed for some time. Then Tai-yu gave a choking cough and tears rolled down her cheeks. She was turning to go when Pao-yu caught hold of her.

"Dear cousin, wait. Just let me say one word."

She dried her tears with one hand, repulsing him with the other.

"What more is there to say? I understand."

She hurried off without one look behind, while he just stood there like a man in a trance.

Now Pao-yu in his haste had forgotten his fan, and as Hsi-jen ran after him with it she caught sight of Tai-yu face to face with him. As soon as Tai-yu left, the maid walked up to Pao-yu, still standing there as if rooted to the ground.

"You forgot your fan," she said. "Luckily I noticed it. And here it is."

Too bemused still to know who was speaking, he seized her hands.

"Dear cousin, I never ventured before to bare my heart to you," he declared. "Now that I've summoned up courage to speak, I'll die content. I was making myself ill on account of you, but I dared not tell anyone and hid my feelings. I shan't recover till you're better too, I can't forget you even in my dreams."

"Merciful Buddha, save me!" cried Hsi-jen in consternation. Shaking him she asked, "What sort of talk is this? Has some evil spirit taken possession of you? Go quickly!"

When Pao-yu came to himself and saw Hsi-jen there, blushing all over his face he snatched the fan and ran off without a word.

As the maid watched him go it dawned on her that his avowal had been meant for Tai-yu, in which case it must surely lead to trouble and scandal. That would be truly fearful.

Chapter 14
A Worthless Son Receives a Fearful Flogging

Hsi-jen was still lost in thought when Pao-chai appeared.

"Why are you standing here dreaming?" asked Pao-chai. "This sun is scorching."

"Two sparrows were fighting over there," improvised Hsi-jen hastily. "It was so amusing that I stayed to watch."

"Where has Cousin Pao rushed off to all dressed up? I saw him passing and thought of stopping him; but because nowadays he often talks so wildly, I decided not to call out."

"The master sent for him."

"Aiya! On such a sweltering day. What for? Could it be that something's made him angry and he's sent for Cousin Pao to lecture him?"

"It's nothing like that," replied Hsi-jen with a laugh. "I think a guest wants to see him."

"A guest with no sense." Pao-chai appeared amused. "Why gad about in such hot weather instead of staying indoors and keeping cool?"

While she was speaking an old maid-servant came panting up to them.

"Just imagine!" she gasped. "That girl Chin-chuan, for no reason at all, has drowned herself in the well."

Hsi-jen gave a start.

"Which Chin-chuan?"

"How many Chin-chuans are there? The girl who worked for the mistress, of course. The other day, we don't know why, she was dismissed. She wept and sobbed at home but no one took any notice, till they found she'd disappeared. Just now one of the water-carriers was drawing water from that well in the southeast corner when he discovered a corpse. He fetched people to get it out, and it was Chin-chuan. Her family's trying frantically to bring her round, but of course it's too late."

"This is rather odd!" exclaimed Pao-chai.

Hsi-jen nodded and sighed, and the thought of her friendship with Chin-chuan made tears run down her cheeks. She went back to Happy Red Court while Pao-chai hurried off to condole with Lady Wang.

All was strangely quiet in Lady Wang's apartments, where she sat in the inner chamber shedding tears all by herself. Not wanting to mention the maid's suicide, Pao-chai sat by her aunt in silence until asked where she had come from.

"From the Garden," was her reply.

"Did you see your Cousin Pao?"

"Yes, I saw him just now going out in formal clothes, but I don't know where he's gone."

Lady Wang nodded tearfully.

"Did you hear this extraordinary business about Chin-chuan suddenly drowning herself in the well?"

"Why should she do a thing like that for no reason? It's very strange."

"The other day she broke something of mine, and in a fit of anger I struck her and sent her away. I was meaning to punish her for a couple of days and then to have her fetched back. I'd no idea she'd fly into such a passion she'd jump into the well. This is all my fault."

"You feel that way, auntie, because you're so kind-hearted. But I can't believe she drowned herself in a tantrum. She was playing by the well, more likely, and fell in. After being rather confined in your rooms she'd want to play around once she left, stands to reason. How could she work herself into such a passion? If she did, that was very foolish. She doesn't deserve any pity."

Lady Wang nodded.

"But even if you're right," she sighed, "I still feel bad about it."

"Don't take it so much to heart, auntie. If you feel bad about it, just give them a few extra taels of silver for her burial and you'll be doing all a kind mistress could."

"Just now I gave her mother fifty taels. I wanted to give them two sets of your cousins' new clothes to lay her out in as well; but according to Hsi-feng the only ones ready are two new sets for your Cousin Lin's birthday. She's such a sensitive child, so delicate too, that wouldn't she think it unlucky to have the clothes made for her birthday made over to a dead girl? So I've told the tailors to make two new sets as fast as they can. If it had been any other maid, I'd have felt a few taels of silver would be enough; but Chin-chuan was with me for some time and was just like a daughter to me." As she was speaking she could not help shedding more tears.

"There's no need to hurry the tailors," said Pao-chai. "The other day I had two sets made. I can easily fetch them for her. That would save lots of trouble. When she was alive she wore my old clothes and they were a perfect fit."

"But aren't you afraid it may bring bad luck?"

Pao-chai smiled.

"Don't worry, auntie. I'm not superstitious."

She rose to go, and Lady Wang sent two maids along with her.

When Pao-chai returned with the clothes a little later she found Pao-yu sitting in tears beside his mother. Lady Wang had been scolding him, but at Pao-chai's entrance she stopped.

Pao-yu had been cut to the heart by the news that her disgrace had driven Chin-chuan to suicide. He had nothing to say in reply to his mother's scolding, but Pao-chai's arrival gave him a chance to slip out. He wandered aimlessly along, his hands behind his back, hanging his head and sighing, until he found himself by the front hall. He was skirting the door-screen when as ill luck would have it he bumped full tilt into someone who shouted to him to stop.

Pao-yu started and, looking up, saw to his dismay that it was no other than his father. He had to stand aside respectfully, gasping with fright.

"Why are you moping like this?" demanded Chia Cheng. "It took you a long time to come out when Yu-tsun asked for you; and when you did come, you had nothing spirited or cheerful to say but looked quite down in the mouth, the picture of gloom. And now you're sighing again. What have *you* to moan about? Is anything wrong? Why are you carrying on in this way?"

Pao-yu normally had a ready tongue, but now he was so distressed by Chin-chuan's death that he wished he could follow her straight to the other world. He heard not a word his father said but just stood there in a daze. His stupefied silence — so unlike Pao-yu — exasperated Chia Cheng, who had not to begin with been angry. Before he could say more, however, an officer from the household of Prince Chungshun was announced.

Somewhat taken aback Chia Cheng wondered what this meant, for in general they had no dealings with this prince. He ordered the man to be shown in at once and, hurrying to meet him, found that it was the chief steward of the prince's household. He hastily offered him a seat in the reception hall and tea was served.

The chief steward did not beat about the bush.

"Excuse the presumption of this intrusion," he said. "I come at the order of the prince to request a favour. If you, my lord, will grant it, His Highness will remember your kindness and I shall be infinitely indebted to you."

More mystified than ever, Chia Cheng rose to his feet with a smile.

"What instructions have you for me, sir, from the prince?" he asked. "I beg to be enlightened so that I may do my best to carry them out."

The chief steward gave a faint smile.

"There is no need for you, my lord, to do more than say one word," he answered. "There is in our palace an actor by the name of Chi-kuan, who plays female roles. He had never previously given any trouble, but several days ago he disappeared. After searching the city for him without success, we instituted careful inquiries. We are told by eight out of every ten persons questioned that he has recently been on the closest terms with your esteemed son who was born with jade in his mouth. Of course, we could not seize him from your honourable mansion as if it were an ordinary household. So we reported the matter to His Highness, who says he would rather lose a hundred other actors than Chi-kuan, for this clever well-behaved lad is such a favourite with our master's father that he cannot do without him. I beg you, therefore, to ask your noble son to send Chi-kuan back, in compliance with the prince's earnest request and to save me from wearing myself out in a fruitless search."

He concluded this speech with a bow.

Alarmed and scandalized, Chia Cheng summoned Pao-yu, who hurried in without knowing why he was wanted.

"You scoundrel!" thundered his father. "Not content with shirking your studies at home, you commit such wicked crimes outside! Chi-kuan is in the service of Prince Chungshun; how dare a wretch like you lure him away and bring calamity on me?"

Pao-yu on hearing this was consternated.

"I know nothing about it," he cried. "I've never even heard the name Chi-kuan, let alone lured him away."

He burst into tears.

Before Chia Cheng could speak again the chief steward said with a sardonic smile:

"It is useless to keep it a secret, sir. Tell us whether he is hiding here or where else he has gone. A prompt avowal will save us trouble and win you our gratitude."

Still Pao-yu denied any knowledge of the matter.

"You may have been misinformed, I'm afraid," he muttered.

The steward gave a scornful laugh.

"Why deny it when we have proof? What good can it do you to force me to speak out before your noble father? If you never heard of this actor, how is it that you wear his red sash round your waist?"

Pao-yu was thunderstruck and stood aghast. "How did they find out?" he wondered. "If they've even found out such secrets, it's not much use trying to keep the rest from them. Better send him off before he does any more blabbing."

So he said, "If you know so much, sir, how is it you are ignorant of something as important as his purchase of property? I am told that twenty *li* to the east of the city, in a place called Sandalwood Castle, he has bought a house and a few *mu* of land. I should think he might possibly be there."

The chief steward's face brightened.

"He must be there if you say so. I shall go and investigate. If we find him, well and good. If not, we shall come back for further enlightenment."

He took a hasty leave.

Chia Cheng's eyes were nearly bursting from his head with rage. As he followed the chief steward out, he turned to order Pao-yu:

"Stay where you are. I shall deal with you presently."

He escorted the steward all the way to the gate, and was just starting back when he saw Chia Huan racing past with a few pages. In his fury he ordered his own pages to beat them.

The sight of his father paralysed Huan with fright. He pulled up short, hanging his head.

"What are you rushing about for?" demanded Chia Cheng. "Where are all the people supposed to look after you? Have they gone off to amuse themselves while you run wild?"

As he shouted for the servants who accompanied Huan to school, the boy saw a chance to divert his father's anger.

"I wasn't running to begin with," he said. "Not until I passed the well where that maid drowned herself. Her head's swollen up like this, and her body's all bloated from soaking in the water. It was such a horrible sight that I ran away as fast as ever I could."

Chia Cheng was astounded.

"What maid here had any reason to throw herself into a well?" he wondered. "Such a thing has never happened before in this house. Since the time of our ancestors we have always treated our subordinates well. Of late, though, I've neglected household affairs and those in charge must have abused their power, resulting in this calamitous suicide. If word of this gets out, it will disgrace our ancestors' good name."

He called for Chia Lien, Lai Ta and Lai Hsing.

Some pages were going to fetch them when Huan stepped forward and caught hold of his father's gown, then fell on his knees.

"Don't be angry, sir!" he begged. "No one knows about this except those in my lady's apartment. I heard my mother say...."

He stopped and looked around, and Chia Cheng understood. At a glance from him the servants on both sides withdrew.

"My mother told me," Huan went on in a whisper, "that the other day Brother Pao-yu grabbed hold of Chin-chuan in my lady's room and tried to rape her. When she wouldn't let him, he beat her. That's why she drowned herself in a fit of passion."

Before he had finished Chia Cheng was livid with fury.

"Fetch Pao-yu! Quick!" he roared.

He strode to his study fuming, "If anybody tries to stop me *this* time, I'll make over to him my official insignia and property and let him serve Pao-yu! How can I escape blame? I'll shave off these few remaining hairs and retire to a monastery, there to atone for disgracing my ancestors by begetting such a monster."

His secretaries and attendants bit their lips or fingers in dismay and hastily withdrew as they heard him raging at Pao-yu again. Then Chia Cheng, panting hard, his cheeks wet with tears, sat stiffly erect in his chair.

"Bring Pao-yu in!" he bellowed. "Fetch the heavy rod! Tie him up! Close all the doors. Anyone who sends word to the inner apartments will be killed on the spot."

The servants had to obey. Some pages went to fetch Pao-yu.

Pao-yu knew he was in for trouble when ordered by his father to wait, but he had no idea of the tale Huan had since told. He paced helplessly up and down the hall, wishing some-one would carry the news to the inner apartments; but it so happened that nobody was about — even Pei-ming had dis-appeared. As he was looking round anxiously, an old nanny finally appeared. He seized on her as if she were a treasure.

"Go in quick!" he cried. "Tell them the master's going to beat me. Do hurry! This is urgent!"

He was too terrified to speak distinctly and the old woman, being hard of hearing, mistook the word "urgent" for "drowning."

"She chose drowning herself," she told him soothingly. "What does it matter to you?"

Her deafness made Pao-yu frantic.

"Go and get my page to come," he begged.

"It's over now. Over and done with. And the mistress has given them clothes and silver too. Don't fret."

Pao-yu was stamping his foot in desperation when his father's servants arrived and he had perforce to go with them.

Chia Cheng's eyes blazed at the sight of him. He did not even ask his son what he meant by playing about outside and exchanging gifts with actors, or by neglecting his studies at home and attempting to rape his mother's maid.

"Gag him!" he roared. "Beat him to death!"

The attendants dared not disobey. They thrust Pao-yu down on a bench and gave him a dozen strokes with the heavy rod. His father, thinking these strokes too light, kicked aside the man with the rod and snatched it up himself. With clenched teeth he rained down dozens of vicious blows until his secre-taries, foreseeing serious consequences, stepped forward to in-tervene. But Chia Cheng refused to listen.

"Ask *him* if such conduct as his can be pardoned," he cried. "You're the ones who've been spoiling him. When it comes to this do you still intercede for him? Will you still persist when he commits regicide or parricide?"

Realizing from this tirade that their master was quite beside himself with rage, they hurried away, feeling constrained to send word to the inner apartments. Lady Wang dared not tell her mother-in-law at once. Having dressed in haste she ran towards the study, regardless of who was about, while men-servants and secretaries fled out of her way in confusion.

His wife's arrival roused Chia Cheng to still greater fury and he belaboured his son yet more mercilessly. The two servants holding Pao-yu instantly withdrew, but the boy was already incapable of moving. Before his father could beat him any further, Lady Wang seized the rod with both hands.

"This is the end!" roared Chia Cheng. "You're determined to be the death of me today."

"I know Pao-yu deserves a beating," sobbed Lady Wang. "But you mustn't wear yourself out, sir. It's a sweltering day and the old lady isn't well. Killing Pao-yu is a small matter, but should anything happen to the old lady that would be serious."

"Spare me this talk." Chia Cheng gave a scornful laugh. "I've already proved an unfilial son by begetting this degenerate. When I discipline him all of you protect him. I'd better strangle him now to avoid further trouble."

With that he called for a rope. Lady Wang hastily threw her arms around him.

"You're right to chastise your son, sir, but have pity on your wife!" she cried. "I'm getting on for fifty and this wretch is my only son. If you insist on making an example of him, how dare I dissuade you? But if you kill him today, it means you want *me* to die too. If strangle him you must, take this rope and strangle me first, then strangle him. Mother and son, we won't dare hold it against you, and at least I shall have some support in the nether world."

She threw herself down on Pao-yu and gave way to a storm of weeping.

Chia Cheng heaved a long sigh and sat down, his tears falling like rain. Lady Wang, clasping Pao-yu in her arms, saw that his face was white, his breathing weak, and his green linen underclothes were soaked with blood. When she undid them she cried out in distress at the sight of his buttocks and legs beaten black and blue, with every inch bruised or bleeding.

"Ah, my poor child!" she wailed.

As she wept for her "poor child" she remembered her first son and called Chia Chu's name.

"If you were still living," she sobbed, "I shouldn't care if a hundred others died."

Lady Wang's departure had roused the inner apartments, and she had been joined by Li Wan and Hsi-feng as well as Ying-chun and Tan-chun. Chia Chu's name did not affect the others so much, but it reduced his widow to sobs. And the chorus of lamentation made Chia Cheng weep more bitterly himself.

In the middle of this commotion a maid suddenly announced, "The old lady is coming!"

And they heard her quavering voice outside the window, "Kill me first and then kill him. That will be a clean sweep."

Chia Cheng rose in dismay and distress to greet his mother, who entered on a maid's arm, gasping for breath. At once he stepped forward to bow respectfully.

"Why should you vex yourself, mother, and come over on such a hot day? If you have any instructions, just send for your son."

The Lady Dowager halted to catch her breath.

"Were you addressing me?" she demanded sternly. "Yes, I have some instructions. The pity is I've borne no filial son to whom I can speak."

Appalled by this rebuke, Chia Cheng fell on his knees, tears in his eyes.

"If your son disciplines *his* son, it is for the honour of our ancestors," he pleaded. "How can I bear your reproaches?"

The Lady Dowager spat in disgust.

"So you can't bear one word from me, eh? Then how does Pao-yu bear your lethal rod? You talk of disciplining your son for the honour of your ancestors, but how did *your* father discipline you in the past?"

手足耽耽
枕動唇
小不肯種
吾種大承
答撓

Her eyes filled with tears.

"Don't grieve, mother," he begged. "I was wrong to lose my temper. I shall never beat him again."

The old lady snorted.

"You needn't try to work off your rage on me. It's not for me to stop you beating your son. I suppose you're tired of us all, and we'd better leave now to save trouble all round."

She ordered the servants to prepare sedan-chairs and horses, telling them, "Your mistress and Pao-yu are going back to Nanking with me this instant."

The attendants had to make a show of complying with her orders. Then the Lady Dowager turned to her daughter-in-law.

"Don't cry," she urged Lady Wang. "Pao-yu's still a child now and you love him; but when he grows up and becomes a high official he may not have any consideration for his mother either. Better not be too fond of him now if you want to avoid heartache later."

When Chia Cheng heard this he knocked his head on the floor.

"What place is there for me on earth, mother," he wailed, "if you reproach me like this?"

The Lady Dowager smiled sarcastically.

"You're making it clear that there's no place for *me*, and yet *you* start complaining. We are simply going away to save you trouble and leave you free to beat anyone you please."

She ordered attendants to pack up at once and make ready for the journey, while Chia Cheng kowtowed and earnestly begged her forgiveness.

But while storming at her son the old lady was worried about her grandson, and now she hurried over to look at the boy. She was further pained and enraged by the severity of his flogging today. Clasping him to her she wept bitterly. Lady Wang and Hsi-feng were hard put to it to soothe her. Then some of the maids who had assembled there took Pao-yu's arms, meaning to help him out.

"Stupid creatures!" scolded Hsi-feng. "Have you no eyes?

He's in no state to walk. Go and fetch that wicker couch."

They hastily did as they were told. Pao-yu was laid on the couch and carried to the old lady's room accompanied by his grandmother and mother. As the Lady Dowager was still incensed Chia Cheng dared not withdraw but followed them, aware from a glance at Pao-yu that this time he had flogged him too severely. He turned to his wife, who was now lamenting even more bitterly.

"My child, my darling!" she wailed. "Why didn't you die as a baby in Chu's place? Then your father wouldn't be so angry, and all my trouble wouldn't have been in vain. If anything happens to you now I shall be left all alone, with no one to depend on in my old age!"

These lamentations interspersed with reproaches against her "worthless son" dismayed Chia Cheng and made him repent that he had beaten Pao-yu so mercilessly. But when he tried to mollify his mother she rounded on him with tears in her eyes.

"Why don't you leave us? What are you hanging around for? Won't you be satisfied until you've made sure that he dies?"

Then Chia Cheng was forced to withdraw.

Chapter 15
Moved by Affection, Pao-yu Moves His Cousin

By now Aunt Hsueh, Pao-chai, Hsiang-ling, Hsi-jen and Hsiang-yun had gathered there too. Hsi-jen was simmering with indignation which she could not express outright. And since Pao-yu was surrounded by people, some giving him water to drink, some fanning him, there seemed nothing for her to do. She therefore slipped out and went to the inner gate, where she told some pages to go and fetch Pei-ming.

"There was no sign of trouble earlier on. How did this start?" she asked him. "And why didn't you come to report it earlier?"

"It just happened that I wasn't there," explained Pei-ming frantically. "I only heard about it half-way through the beating. At once I asked people how the trouble had started. It was over the business of Chi-kuan and Sister Chin-chuan."

"How did the master come to hear about it?"

"In the case of Chi-kuan, it looks as if Master Hsueh Pan was behind it. Having no other way to vent his jealous spite, he got somebody from outside to come and tell His Lordship — then the fat was in the fire. As for Chin-chuan, it was young Master Huan who blabbed. Or so His Lordship's men told me."

Both stories seemed likely and Hsi-jen was convinced. She went back to find everyone ministering to Pao-yu. When there was no more to be done for him, the Lady Dowager ordered them to carry him carefully back to his own room. All lent a hand to convey him to Happy Red Court, where they laid him on his own bed. And after some further bustle the others gradually dispersed, leaving Hsi-jen able at last to wait on him hand and foot. She sat down by Pao-yu's side and with tears in her eyes asked the reason for this fearful beating.

"Oh, nothing special. What's the use of asking?" Pao-yu sighed. "The lower part of my body hurts terribly. Do see how serious the damage is."

Hsi-jen gently set about removing his underwear, but the least movement made him grit his teeth and groan so much that she stopped. Only after three or four attempts did she succeed in undressing him. Then she clenched her teeth at the sight of his thighs, all black and purple with weals four fingers wide.

"Heavens! How could he be so cruel?" she exclaimed. "But, you know, this would never have happened if you'd paid the least attention to my advice. Well, it's lucky no bones are broken. What if you'd been maimed for life?"

Just then Pao-chai was announced. As there was no time to clothe Pao-yu again, Hsi-jen threw a lined gauze coverlet over him as Pao-chai walked in, a pill in one hand.

"Dissolve this drug in wine this evening and apply it as a salve," she told Hsi-jen. "That will draw the heat and poison from the bruise and help to cure him."

Having handed her the pill, she asked, "Is he any better?"

Pao-yu gratefully assured her that he was and asked her to take a seat. Seeing he was now able to open his eyes and talk, Pao-chai nodded in relief.

"If you'd listened to our advice, this wouldn't have happened," she sighed. "Now you've not only upset the old lady and your mother; when the rest of us see you like this, our hearts ache too...."

She broke off abruptly, regretting her indiscretion, and hung her head with a blush.

She had spoken with such intimate, tender concern, although attempting to hide her deep emotion, and she looked so indescribably charming in her bashful confusion as she hid her blushing face and fingered her sash, that Pao-yu completely forgot his pain in his elation. "I just get given a few strokes," he thought, "and they show such sweet distress and sympathy. How good and kind they are! How admirable! If I were to meet with some accident and die, they'd surely be quite overcome with grief. But it would be worth dying, even with nothing to show for my life, provided I'd won their hearts. Indeed, it would be silly if I wasn't a happy and contented ghost."

His thoughts were interrupted by a question Pao-chai put to Hsi-jen: "What's the reason for this sudden row and beating?"

Hsi-jen passed on what Pei-ming had said, and this was Pao-yu's first inkling of Chia Huan's tale-telling. But when Hsueh Pan's name came up he was afraid Pao-chai would be upset.

"Cousin Hsueh would never do such a thing!" he interposed quickly. "Stop making such wild guesses."

Pao-chai understood why he had silenced Hsi-jen. "How tactful and cautious you are in spite of your pain after such a dreadful beating," she thought. "If you can be so considerate of *our* feelings, why not pay equal attention to important matters outside? For then your father would be pleased, and you wouldn't get into hot water like this. You cut Hsi-jen short for fear of hurting me, but do you suppose I don't know my brother's wild, lawless ways? If such a rumpus was raised that time because of Chin Chung, much worse things are possible now."

After these reflections she turned to Hsi-jen with a smile. "Why pin the blame on this person or that?" she said. "I think the master was angry because Cousin Pao doesn't behave well and keeps bad company. Even if my brother did let fall some careless remark about Cousin Pao, he can't have meant to make trouble. For after all, in the first place, it was the truth; in the second, he's the type who can't be bothered to gossip. You're used to Cousin Pao who's so considerate. You haven't met my brother, who fears neither Heaven nor Earth and blurts out whatever happens to be in his mind."

Pao-yu's interruption when she spoke of Hsueh Pan had made Hsi-jen realize that her tactlessness must have embarrassed Pao-chai, whose last remarks abashed her even more. As for Pao-yu, he could see that while saying what was right and proper Pao-chai was also trying to put him at his ease. He felt even more touched. But before he could speak again she rose to leave.

"I'll come back tomorrow to see how you are," she assured him. "Have a good rest. I've given Hsi-jen something to make you a salve tonight, and that should help."

With that she left, and Hsi-jen escorted her out of the courtyard.

"Thank you, miss, for taking so much trouble," she said. "When Master Pao's better he'll come himself to thank you."

Pao-chai turned and smiled.

"There's nothing to thank *me* for. Just persuade him to rest properly and not let his imagination run away with him. We don't want the old lady and the mistress and everyone disturbed. For if word of it reached the master's ears, even if he did nothing for the time being, there'd be trouble later on."

So saying, she went off. With a warm sense of gratitude to her, Hsi-jen returned to Pao-yu. Finding him in a dreamy, drowsy state, she went to the other room to tidy herself.

Although Pao-yu lay as still as he could, his buttocks were smarting as if scorched by fire, pricked by needles, or cut by knives. The slightest movement wrung a groan from him. Dusk was falling, Hsi-jen had gone, and he dismissed the other maids saying that he would call if he wanted anything.

Dozing off, he dreamed that Chi-kuan had come to tell of his capture by Prince Chungshun's steward; after which Chinchuan appeared, in tears, to explain why she had thrown herself into the well. Half sleeping and half waking, he paid only scant attention. But then he felt himself shaken and caught the faint sound of sobbing. He opened his eyes with a start to see Tai-yu. Suspecting at first that this was another dream, he propped himself up to look at her more closely. Her eyes were swollen, her face was bathed in tears: it was Tai-yu beyond a doubt. He would have gazed at her longer, but the pain in his legs was so unbearable that he fell back with a groan.

"You shouldn't have come," he said. "Though the sun's set, the ground is still hot. Walking here and back may make you unwell again. I'm not in any pain after my beating, just putting on an act to fool them so that word of it will get out to my father. I'm shamming actually. Don't you worry about me."

Tai-yu was not crying aloud. She swallowed her tears in silence till she felt as if she would choke. She had a thousand replies to make to Pao-yu, but not one word could she utter. At long last she sobbed:

"Never do such things again."

"Don't you worry," replied Pao-yu with a long sigh. "Please don't talk this way. I would die happily for people like them, and I'm still alive."

At this point some maids in the courtyard announced Hsi-feng's arrival. Tai-yu at once stood up.

"I'll go out the back way and drop in again later," she said.

Pao-yu caught her hand protesting, "That's a strange thing to do. Why should you be afraid of her?"

Tai-yu stamped one foot in desperation.

"Look at my eyes," she whispered. "She'd make fun of me if she saw."

At once he released her and she slipped past his bed and out through the back court just as Hsi-feng came in from the front.

"Are you better?" she asked Pao-yu. "If you fancy anything to eat, send someone to my place for it."

Aunt Hsueh called next. And then the Lady Dowager sent maids to inquire after the invalid. When it was time to light the lamps, Pao-yu swallowed two mouthfuls of soup and soon dozed off. Then came some of the older maid-servants, the wives of Chou Jui, Wu Lung-teng and Cheng Hao-shih, who were in the habit of calling and had dropped in after hearing of today's trouble. Hsi-jen hurried out to greet them with a smile.

"You're a second too late, aunties," she whispered. "Master Pao has just gone to sleep."

She offered them tea in the outer room and after sitting quietly for a while they left, having asked her to let Pao-yu know that they had called.

As Hsi-jen was coming back from seeing them off, one of Lady Wang's women accosted her with the message that her mistress wanted to see one of Master Pao's maids. Hsi-jen came to a quick decision. Turning softly she told Ching-wen, Sheh-yueh, Tan-yun and Chiu-wen:

"The mistress has sent for one of us. You see to things here. I'll be back presently."

She went with the other woman out of the Garden to Lady Wang's apartments, where she found her fanning herself with a palm-leaf fan on the couch.

"Why didn't you send one of the others?" asked Pao-yu's mother. "Who'll look after him in your absence?"

"Master Pao's sound asleep now, and the other girls know how to look after him," Hsi-jen answered confidently. "Please don't worry, madam. I thought perhaps you had some instructions which one of the others might not understand, and that might hold things up."

"I've no special instructions. I just wanted to know how he is now."

"Miss Pao-chai brought us a salve, and after I applied it he seemed better. At first the pain kept him awake, but now he's sleeping soundly. It shows he's on the mend."

"Did he eat anything?"

"Only two mouthfuls of the soup the old lady sent. He complained he was parched and asked for some sour plum juice. But I thought to myself: Sour things are astringent, and when he was beaten and couldn't cry out some choleric humours must have rushed to his viscera; plum juice might affect them, bringing on a serious illness, and that would never do. Finally I talked him out of it and gave him some candied rose petals instead. He only ate half a bowl, though, then found it cloying and insipid."

"Why didn't you send and let me know before?" cried Lady Wang. "The other day I was sent a couple of bottles of scented flower juice and meant to give them to him, but thought he might waste them. If he finds rose petals cloying, take him these. One tea-spoon in a bowl of water is delicious." She told Tsai-yun, "Fetch those bottles of juice which were brought the other day."

"Two bottles will be plenty," Hsi-jen assured her. "More would be wasted. We can always come and ask for more when it's finished."

Tsai-yun went off on this errand, returning presently with two bottles which she handed to Hsi-jen. They were tiny glass bottles barely three inches high, with silver caps which screwed on, and yellow labels. On one was written "Pure Osmanthus Juice", on the other "Pure Rose Juice".

"What luxury objects!" Hsi-jen laughed. "Such small bottles can't hold much."

"They're for the Imperial use," explained Lady Wang. "Don't you see the yellow label? Mind you keep them carefully for him. Don't waste any of the juice."

Hsi-jen assented and was about to leave when Lady Wang told her to wait.

"There's something else I want to ask you," she said.

Having made sure that no one else was about she continued, "There's talk that the master beat Pao-yu because of some tale Huan told. Did you hear that? If you did, just tell me what it was. I won't make a rumpus about it. No one will know that it was you who told me."

"No, I didn't hear that," replied Hsi-jen. "I heard it was because Master Pao kept an actor from some prince's mansion, and they came to ask His Lordship to send him back."

Lady Wang shook her head.

"That was *one* reason, but there was another too."

"If there's anything else I really don't know it," rejoined Hsi-jen. She added, "May I make so bold, now that I'm here, to suggest something, madam? . . ."

She broke off at this point.

"Go on."

With a sly smile she went on, "I hope Your Ladyship won't think it presumptuous."

"Of course not. What is it?"

"Actually, Master Pao *does* need to be taught a lesson. If His Lordship doesn't discipline him, there's no knowing what may happen in future."

On hearing this, Lady Wang clapped her hands together, exclaiming "Gracious Buddha!" Then although so eager to hear more, she confided, "Dear child, I'm glad you are so understanding — that's exactly how I feel. Of course I know the importance of discipline. I haven't forgotten how strict I was with Master Chu. But there's a reason for my indulgence now. I'm getting on for fifty, and I've only the one son left; besides, he's rather delicate and the old lady dotes on him. If I were too strict so that something happened to him, or if the old lady were upset, the whole household would be turned upside down and that would be even worse. *That's* why he's been spoiled. I'm always scolding him, pleading with him, getting angry with him or crying over him, but after a short improvement back he slips. He'll never mend his ways unless he's made to smart. Yet if he's badly injured, I'll have no one to depend on in the future."

With this she burst into tears. And Hsi-jen, seeing her distress, wept in sympathy.

"He's your son, madam, of course you take this to heart. Even those of us who wait on him would be happy if everyone could keep out of trouble. If things go on like this we'll have no peace either. Not a day goes by but I reason with Master Pao, yet it has no effect. It's not *his* fault if people of that sort make up to him, and he loses patience when we reason with him. Since you've brought this up, madam, I'd like to ask your advice about something that's been worrying me for a long time. I've never raised it before for fear you might misunderstand. In that case, not only would I be wasting my breath but taking an outrageous liberty."

Lady Wang realized there was something behind this.

"Just say what's on your mind, my child," she urged. "I've heard nothing but good of you recently from everyone. I assumed it was just because you looked after Pao-yu well and were pleasant to everybody. Such thoughtfulness in little things is good. That's why I treated you like one of the old nurses. Now I see you have principles too and your views coincide with mine. Just say whatever's on your mind, but don't let it go any further."

"It's nothing else, only that I was hoping Your Ladyship might arrange for Master Pao to move out of the Garden."

Lady Wang was shocked. She caught hold of Hsi-jen's hand.

"Has Pao-yu been up to anything improper?"

"No, no, madam. Don't misunderstand me. Nothing of that sort. But in my humble opinion, now that he and the young ladies are no longer children and, what's more, Miss Lin and Miss Pao aren't members of the family, cousins of different sexes should live apart. When they spend all their time together every day, it's not convenient for them and we can't help worrying. Besides, it doesn't look good to people outside. As the proverb has it: Best be prepared for the worst. A lot of foolishness is quite innocent, but suspicious people always think the worst. Better make sure in advance that there's no trouble.

"*You* know, madam, what Master Pao is like and how he enjoys amusing himself with us girls. If no precautions are taken and he does something the least bit foolish — no matter whether it's true or not — there's bound to be talk. Low-class people *will* gossip. When they're well disposed, they laud you to the skies; when they're not, they talk as if you were worse than a beast. If people speak well of him, that's as it should be. If a single slighting remark is passed, not only shall we deserve a thousand deaths — that's not important — but his reputation will be ruined for life and how will you answer for it to His Lordship? Another proverb says: A gentleman should show providence. Better guard against this now. You're naturally too busy, madam, to think of these things, and they might not occur to us either. But if they do and we fail to mention it, that would be very remiss. Lately this has been preying on my mind day and night, but I couldn't mention it to anyone else. Only my lamp at night knew how I worried!"

Lady Wang felt thunderstruck on hearing this, borne out as it was by the case of Chin-chuan. The more she thought, the more grateful she felt to Hsi-jen.

"What a wise child you are to see so far!" she exclaimed. "Of course I've given some thought to this myself, but lately I've had too much else on my mind. Now you've reminded me. I'm glad you're so concerned for our reputation. I really had no idea what a good girl you are! All right, you may go now. Leave everything to me. But I tell you this: after what you've said today, I mean to entrust Pao-yu to you. You must look after him and keep him safe. That way, you'll be safe-guarding *me* as well, and I shan't forget our obligation to you."

Hsi-jen hastily assented and withdrew. Back in Happy Red Court, she found Pao-yu had just woken up. When she told him about the juice he was delighted. He asked to taste some and pronounced it delicious.

Because Pao-yu had Tai-yu on his mind he was eager to send someone over to her, but for fear of Hsi-jen he had to resort to a trick. He dispatched Hsi-jen to Pao-chai to borrow some books, and as soon as she had left called for Ching-wen.

"Go and see what Miss Lin is doing," he said. "If she asks after me, tell her I'm better."

"I can't just go there without any excuse. Is there no message that you want to send?"

"Not that I can think of."

"Give me something to take then, or ask to borrow something. Otherwise what am I going to say when I see her?"

After a little thought Pao-yu picked up two handkerchiefs and tossed them to her.

"All right, tell her I sent you to give her these."

"This is even odder!" cried Ching-wen. "What would she want two old handkerchiefs for? She'll flare up again and say you're teasing her."

"Don't worry. She'll understand."

So Ching-wen took his gift to Bamboo Lodge, where she found Chun-chien hanging some handkerchiefs to dry on the balustrade.

Chun-chien held up a warning finger.

"She's gone to bed."

Ching-wen slipped into the dark room where the lamps were not yet lit. Tai-yu, lying on the bed, asked who it was.

"It's me, Ching-wen."

"What do you want?"

"Master Pao has sent you some handkerchiefs, miss."

Why should he send me handkerchiefs? Tai-yu wondered.

"Who gave these to him?" she asked. "I suppose they're specially fine ones. Tell him to keep them for someone else, I don't need them for the time being."

"They're not new," replied Ching-wen giggling. "He's often used them."

Tai-yu was even more mystified at this, but some careful thought cleared up the riddle for her.

"Leave them then," she said quickly. "You may go."

So Ching-wen put down the handkerchiefs and left, puzzling her head all the way back over this gift.

Meanwhile Tai-yu, touched by the meaning of this gift, was lost in reverie. Pleased as she was by Pao-yu's insight and sympathy, it was sad to think that all her concern for him might come to nothing. This unexpected present of two used handkerchiefs was rather laughable if it were not for the fact that she understood the thought behind it; yet it was scandalous that he should send and she accept a secret gift. And it made her ashamed of her habit of crying so much. As she mused in this way, her heart was very full, her mind in a turmoil. Having ordered the lamps to be lit, without any thought of the possible consequences she ground some ink on the inkstone, dipped her brush in it and quickly wrote these lines on the handkerchiefs:

> Vain are all these idle tears,
> Tears shed secretly — for whom?
> Your kind gift of a foot of gauze
> Only deepens my gloom.
>
> By stealth I shed pearly tears,
> Idle tears the livelong day;
> Hard to wipe them from sleeve and pillow,
> Then suffer the stains to stay.
>
> No silk thread can string these pearls;
> Dim now the tear-stains of those bygone years;
> A thousand bamboos grow before my window —
> Is each dappled and stained with tears?[1]

She would have written more but her whole body was afire, her face burning. Going to the mirror-stand she removed its silk cover and saw that her flushed cheeks were redder than peach blossom, but failed to realize that this was the first symptom of consumption. She went to bed with the handkerchiefs clasped in her hands and lost herself in dreams.

---

[1] Referring to a kind of bamboo with dark spots. According to a Chinese legend, after King Shun died, his two wives mourned for him and their tears made dark spots on the bamboo.

Chapter 16
Hsi-feng, Taken by Surprise, Gives Way to Jealousy

The Lady Dowager was not really ill but had simply caught a chill that day in the Garden. Knowing that a visit from the doctor and some medicine had set her right, Lady Wang stopped worrying and sent for Hsi-feng whom she told to prepare some things to be taken to Chia Cheng. While they were discussing this, the old lady summoned them and they both hurried over.

"Are you feeling better, madam?" asked Lady Wang.

"Much better," replied the Lady Dowager. "Just now I tried some of that quail soup you sent, and found it tasty. I ate a few mouthfuls of the flesh too, and enjoyed it."

"That was a filial offering from Hsi-feng," said Lady Wang. "It shows a proper respect for her elders and due gratitude for all your kindness to her."

"It's good of her to be so thoughtful." The old lady nodded. "If there's any left not yet cooked, I'd like a few slices fried, because being salty it goes well with porridge. The soup doesn't, although it's good."

Hsi-feng promised to see to this at once and had the order passed on to the kitchen.

Meantime the Lady Dowager told Lady Wang, "I'll tell you why I sent for you. The second of next month is Hsi-feng's birthday. Last year and the year before that I meant to celebrate it, but each time something urgent cropped up and I let matters slide. This year everyone's here and nothing's likely to happen, so let's all have some good fun."

"Just what I was thinking," replied Lady Wang. "If that's what you want, madam, why not settle on it?"

In no time it was the second of the ninth month. All the inmates of the Garden knew that Madam Yu had arranged for a grand party with not only operas but acrobatics and blind story-tellers too, both men and women. They were looking forward to a delightful time.

As this was a special occasion, the Lady Dowager was determined that Hsi-feng should have a whole day of unalloyed pleasure. Feeling unequal to joining the feasters herself, she reclined on a couch in the inner room to watch the opera from there with Aunt Hsueh, from time to time nibbling some of her favourite titbits set out on the teapoy beside her as they chatted. The two tables of food prepared for her she made over to the maids and serving-women who had no share in the feast, with instructions not to stand on ceremony but to sit in the verandah outside and eat and drink as much as they pleased.

Lady Wang and Lady Hsing sat at the high table in the old lady's room, the girls at tables in the outer room.

The Lady Dowager reiterated to Madam Yu, "Hsi-feng must take the seat of honour. And mind you play hostess well for me to show our appreciation of her hard work all the year round."

"I'll do my best, madam," promised Madam Yu. "But she says she's not used to sitting in the seat of honour. She feels out of place there and won't drink anything."

"If *you* can't make her drink," chuckled the old lady, "I'll go out presently and toast her myself."

Hsi-feng hurried in to protest, "Don't believe her, Old Ancestress. I've had quite a few cups already."

The old lady jokingly ordered Madam Yu, "Drag her out, quick, and force her on to her seat, then take it in turns to toast her. If she still refuses to drink, I shall really come out."

Madam Yu gaily carried out these instructions and ordered a mug to be filled.

"From one end of the year to the other you've been dutifully filial to the old lady, Lady Wang and me," she told Hsi-feng. "I've no gift for you today, so I'll offer you a mug of wine with my own hands. Drink up now like a good girl."

"If you really want to show appreciation you must kneel down, then I'll drink," was Hsi-feng's laughing retort.

"Don't be carried away by all the compliments paid you. I can tell you, such good luck is very rare. Who knows if a day like this will ever come again? So make the most of it, and now drink two cups."

Hsi-feng had no choice but to do as she was told. Next, all the girls presented cups and she had to sip from each. Then Lai Ta's mother, seeing the Lady Dowager in such high spirits, decided to join in the fun and led some old serving-women in to toast Hsi-feng, who again could not refuse them. By the time Yuan-yang and the younger maids came to drink her health, she had really had all she could take.

"Good sisters, let me off," she begged. "I'll drink with you some other time."

"So we have no face, is that it?" protested Yuan-yang. "Why, even the mistress condescends to drink with us. You usually show us more consideration, but now in front of all these people you're putting on the airs of a mistress. Well, it's my fault for coming. If you won't drink, we'll leave you." She turned to go.

Hsi-feng hastily stopped her, crying, "All right, good sister, I'll drink."

She picked up the winepot, filled her cup to the brim, and tossed it off. Then Yuan-yang withdrew with a smile.

After seating herself again, Hsi-feng felt the effects of the wine. Her heart was beating so fast that she decided to go home for a rest. As the jugglers had just come in, she asked Madam Yu to see about tipping them while she went and had a wash.

Madam Yu nodded and, since no one else detained her, Hsi-feng left the table and slipped out the back way. Watchful Ping-erh quickly followed her and took her arm. They were just approaching the covered walk when they noticed one of their young maids standing there, but at sight of them she turned and ran. This made Hsi-feng suspicious. She called to her to stop. At first the girl pretended not to hear, but when Ping-erh called to her too she had to come back.

Hsi-feng, more suspicious than ever now, stepped with Ping-erh into the entrance hall and told the maid to join them and close the partitions. Seating herself on the steps leading to the small courtyard, she made the girl kneel down.

"Get two boys from the inner gate to bring ropes and whips," she sharply ordered Ping-erh. "We'll give this impudent little bitch a good flogging."

The girl, frightened out of her wits, burst into tears and knocked her head on the ground as she begged for mercy.

"I'm not a ghost," snapped Hsi-feng. "Why didn't you stand to attention when you saw me? Why run away?"

"I didn't see you, madam," sobbed the maid. "I ran because I remembered there was no one in our apartments."

"If so, why did you come here in the first place? Even if you didn't see me, we called you at the top of our voices a dozen times, but that only made you run the faster. We weren't far off and you're not deaf. How dare you answer back?"

She slapped the girl so hard on the face that she staggered, then gave her another slap on the other side. At once the girl's cheeks began to swell up and turn purple.

"Mind you don't hurt your hand, madam," urged Ping-erh.

"Hit her for me then. Make her say why she ran away. If she won't, tear her lips!"

The maid went on protesting her innocence until Hsi-feng threatened to brand her mouth with a red-hot iron. Then she confessed with tears:

"The master's home. He sent me here to watch out for you and let him know as soon as I saw you coming, madam. He didn't think you would be back so soon."

Hsi-feng guessed that there was more to it than this. "Why

did he ask you to do that?" she demanded. "Why should he be afraid of my return? There must have been a reason. If you tell me straight out, I'll be good to you; but if you won't talk, I'll get a knife this instant and carve you up." She drew a pin from her hair as she spoke and jabbed viciously at the maid's mouth.

Shrinking back in fright the girl sobbed, "I'll tell you, madam. But please don't let the master know that I told."

Ping-erh, trying to pacify Hsi-feng, urged the maid to hurry up.

"The master came home not long ago and had a short nap," she said. "After he woke up he sent someone to see what you were doing, madam. She reported that you'd just started the feast and wouldn't be back for some time. Then the master opened a case and took out two pieces of silver, two hairpins and two bolts of satin. He told me to take them secretly to Pao Erh's wife and ask her to come over. She took the things and came; then the master told me to watch out for you, madam. What happened after that I don't know."

Trembling with rage, Hsi-feng sprang to her feet and hurried towards her compound. Another young maid was stationed at the gate, and at sight of Hsi-feng she ducked back and ran. Hsi-feng called her by name to stop, and this girl had more sense: seeing that there was no escape, she came running out instead.

"I was just coming to report to you, madam," she said with a smile. "But luckily here you are."

"What were you coming to report?"

"Our master's back. . . ." She went on to repeat the story told by the other.

Hsi-feng spat in disgust. "And what have you been doing all this time?" she cried. "You're only trying to clear yourself because I caught you."

She dealt the maid a blow which made her stagger, then tiptoed into the courtyard and up to the window to listen.

She heard the woman inside say laughingly, "If only that

hellish wife of yours would die!"

"What if she did?" replied Chia Lien. "I'd marry another who might be just as bad."

"When she dies, you can promote Ping-erh and make her your wife. She should be easier to handle."

"Nowadays she won't even let me touch Ping-erh," said Chia Lien. "Ping-erh resents it too, but she dares not complain. What a fate, being saddled with a hell-cat like her!"

Hsi-feng was convulsed with fury, convinced by their praise of Ping-erh that the latter must have been complaining about her behind her back too. By now the wine had quite gone to her head and, not stopping to think, she rounded on Ping-erh and slapped her. Next she kicked open the door and burst into the room. Without a word she caught hold of Pao Erh's wife and pummelled her, then posted herself at the door to cut off Chia Lien's retreat.

"Dirty whore!" she cursed. "You steal your mistress' husband and plot to murder your mistress. And Ping-erh, you come here! You whores and bitches have ganged up against me, yet you make such a public show of trying to please me."

With that she struck Ping-erh again. Having no one to whom to complain of this injustice, Ping-erh holding back her tears nearly choked with rage.

"Can't you wallow in the muck by yourselves without dragging me in for no reason at all?" she stormed. She started scratching and slapping Pao Erh's wife too.

Chia Lien, coming home in high spirits after drinking, had allowed himself to be caught off his guard so that when his wife burst in he was quite at a loss. Now that Ping-erh was making a scene too he flew into a drunken passion. When Hsi-feng beat Pao Erh's wife he could only look on furiously and sheepishly, but as soon as Ping-erh joined in he charged forward and kicked her.

"You slut! Who are *you* to raise your hand against her?"

Ping-erh fearing that he would beat her promptly left off, protesting tearfully, "When you talk behind our backs, why drag me in?"

Ping-erh's fear of Chia Lien made Hsi-feng angrier than ever. She rounded on her and struck her again, insisting that she go on beating Pao Erh's wife. In desperation, Ping-erh ran out of the room to find a knife with which to kill herself, but the serving-women and maids outside hastily stopped her and tried to dissuade her.

When Hsi-feng saw Ping-erh bent on suicide, she rammed her head against Chia Lien's chest and screamed, "You've all ganged up to do me in, and when I find out you all try to frighten me. Strangle me and have done with it!"

In a towering rage Chia Lien snatched a sword from the wall.

"She needn't kill herself," he bellowed. "I've had all I can take. I'll kill the lot of you and pay with my life. Make a clean sweep!"

This uproar was at its height when Madam Yu and some others arrived on the scene.

"What does this mean?" they exclaimed. "A moment ago all was well. What's the row about?"

Their presence emboldened Chia Lien, half drunk as he was, to bluster even more wildly and swear to kill Hsi-feng. For her part, at their arrival she had stopped storming and slipped away tearfully to enlist the support of the Lady Dowager.

By this time the opera was over. Hsi-feng ran to the old lady and threw herself into her arms.

"Save me, Old Ancestress! Lien wants to kill me."

The old lady, Lady Hsing and Lady Wang immediately asked what had happened.

"When I went home just now to change," Hsi-feng sobbed, "I heard him talking to someone. Not liking to intrude if he had a guest, I listened outside the window. It was Pao Erh's wife there, and the two of them were plotting to poison me because I'm a shrew and put Ping-erh in my place. Angry as I was, I dared not quarrel with *him*; I just gave Ping-erh a couple of slaps and asked her why she should want to murder me. He flared up then and threatened to kill me."

The Lady Dowager and the others believed her story.

"How monstrous!" exclaimed the old lady. "Bring the wretch here."

That same moment Chia Lien rushed in with his sword, followed by a crowd of people. Counting on the Lady Dowager's usual indulgence and the helplessness of both his mother and aunt, he ranted and raged with a great show of bravado.

Lady Hsing and Lady Wang angrily barred his way. "Have you gone mad, you degenerate?" they scolded. "How dare you behave like this in the old lady's presence?"

He cast them a sidelong glance. "It's the old lady who's spoiled her," he retorted, "So now she even has the nerve to swear at me."

Lady Hsing wrathfully snatched away his sword and ordered him out of the room. But he simply went on blustering and storming.

"I know you have no respect for *us*," snapped the Lady Dowager. "Send someone to fetch his father, and see if he'll go then."

Then Chia Lien slunk off. Too angry to go home, he went to his outside study.

Meanwhile Lady Hsing and Lady Wang had been remonstrating with Hsi-feng.

"Don't take it so seriously," said the old lady, smiling. "He's only a boy and as greedy as a cat. This sort of thing can't be helped. All young men go through such stages. It's my fault for making Hsi-feng drink so much — the wine's turned to vinegar."

At this everybody laughed.

"Don't worry," the old lady told Hsi-feng. "Tomorrow I'll make him come here to apologize to you. Don't go back today to embarrass him. As for that wretch Ping-erh, I thought she was a good girl — how could she turn out so sly?"

"Ping-erh's not to blame," put in Madam Yu soothingly.

"Hsi-feng was just making a whipping-boy of her. Husband and wife couldn't very well fight each other, so both worked off their temper on her. Ping-erh feels most terribly wronged. Don't you go blaming her too, madam!"

"So that's how it is," said the Lady Dowager. "Yes, I never thought the child was one of those vamps. Well then, poor thing, her mistress stormed at her for no reason. Here, Hu-po! Go and tell Ping-erh from me: I know she's been unfairly treated and tomorrow I'll get Hsi-feng to apologize; but she mustn't make a scene today because it's her mistress' birthday."

Long before this Li Wan had led Ping-erh into Grand View Garden, but she was still sobbing too much to speak.

"You're an intelligent girl," reasoned Pao-chai. "You know how well Hsi-feng's always treated you. Today she just happened to have too much to drink and whom could she vent her anger on if not you? People are laughing at her for getting drunk. If you go on taking it so much to heart, it'll look as if all your good qualities are a pretence."

Just then Hu-po arrived with the Lady Dowager's message which vindicated Ping-erh and made her feel rather better. She did not go back, however, to Hsi-feng's apartments.

Ping-erh spent the night with Li Wan and Hsi-feng with the Lady Dowager. Thus Chia Lien, going home that evening, found the place uncannily quiet. But since he could hardly fetch them he had to spend that night alone. The next morning, too late, he regretted the scene he had made. So when Lady Hsing came over early, distressed by his drunken behaviour the previous day, he accompanied her to the old lady's apartments. Going in sheepishly, he fell on his knees before the Lady Dowager.

"Well?" she asked.

With an apologetic smile he said, "Yesterday I drank too much and disturbed you, madam. I've come now to be punished."

She spat in disgust and swore, "You degenerate! After swigging you might at least stretch out on your bed quietly like a corpse instead of beating your wife. Hsi-feng's a regular saucebox and likes to lord it over everyone, but how you frightened the poor thing yesterday! If not for me you might have killed her. What do you intend to do now?"

Chia Lien had to accept this reproach, much as it rankled, and did not venture to vindicate himself.

"Aren't Hsi-feng and Ping-erh both beauties? Aren't they enough for you?" the old lady demanded. "You never stop philandering, dragging every stinking bit of filth to your room. Fancy beating your own wife and concubine for a whore like that! How can the son of a good family behave so disgracefully? If you've any respect for me, get up. I'll forgive you on condition that you apologize to your wife and take her home. That's the way to please me. Otherwise just take yourself off, I won't have you kneeling to me."

During this lecture Chia Lien saw Hsi-feng standing there, not in her usual finery but with her eyes swollen from weeping, her pale face unpainted and unpowdered, looking more pathetic and lovely than ever before. He thought, "I may as well apologize and make it up. That will please the old lady too."

He therefore replied with a smile, "To hear is to obey, madam. But I'm afraid this will only make her more headstrong."

"Nonsense," retorted the Lady Dowager. "She has the strongest sense of what's fitting, I know, and won't burst out like this again. If she offends you in future, of course I'll give you permission to make her submit to your authority."

Chia Lien rose to his feet then and bowed to Hsi-feng.

"It was my fault, madam," he said. "Please forgive me."

At that the whole company laughed.

"Don't make a scene now, Hsi-feng," said the old lady smiling. "If you do, I shall be cross."

Next she sent for Ping-erh and ordered Chia Lien and Hsi-feng to make their peace with *her*. This Chia Lien was very ready to do. He promptly stepped forward and said:

"I'm the one to blame for the unjust way you were treated yesterday, miss, and because of me your mistress wronged you too. So let me apologize for myself as well as for your mistress." With that he bowed again, making the Lady Dowager and Hsi-feng laugh.

Then the old lady told Hsi-feng it was her turn, but already Ping-erh had kowtowed to her mistress.

"I deserve death, madam," she said, "for offending you on your birthday."

Hsi-feng was thoroughly ashamed of having drunk so much the previous day that she had forgotten their long friendship and lost her temper, humiliating Ping-erh quite groundlessly just because of something a third party had said. Seeing the maid kowtow now, she hastily raised her to her feet, shedding tears of contrition and distress.

Ping-erh was weeping too. "In all the years I've served you, madam, you've never laid a finger upon me," she said. "I don't blame you for striking me yesterday. It was all the fault of that bitch. How could you help being angry?"

The Lady Dowager ordered attendants to escort the three of them to their own apartments.

"If anyone raises the subject again," she said, "report it to me at once. And no matter who it is, I'll take my cane and give him a good beating."

The three of them, having kowtowed once more to the old lady, Lady Hsing and Lady Wang, were seen back by some old nurses.

As soon as they were alone Hsi-feng demanded, "Just why am I hellish? A hell-cat? When that bitch cursed me and wished me dead, you joined in. In a thousand and one days I must be good at least one day; yet it seems, after all this time, I'm less to you than a whore. How can I have the face to go on living now?" By now she was weeping again.

"What more do you want?" cried her husband. "Just think a bit who was most to blame yesterday? Yet today it was *I* who knelt down and begged your pardon in front of all those people. You've got quite enough face, so stop nagging now. Do you expect me to kneel to you *again*? It's no good going too far."

This silenced Hsi-feng and she giggled.

"That's better." He grinned. "I honestly don't know how to cope with you."

Just then a serving-woman came in to report that Pao Erh's wife had hanged herself. They were both shocked to hear this. But after her initial fright Hsi-feng put on a bold face.

"If she's dead, she's dead," she retorted. "What's all the fuss about?"

Presently, however, Lin Chih-hsiao's wife came in and whispered to her, "Pao Erh's wife has hanged herself, madam. And her people are threatening to sue you."

"That's fine." Hsi-feng gave a scornful laugh. "I've been waiting for a chance to go to court."

"We've all been trying to talk or frighten them out of it," said Mrs. Lin. "They're willing to drop the matter if you'll give them a few strings of cash."

"I haven't a cent, and I wouldn't give it to them if I had. Let them go ahead and arraign me. Don't try to talk them round or scare them away. Just let them go ahead. But if they lose their case I shall sue them for blackmail."

Mrs. Lin was in a quandary when Chia Lien glanced at her significantly and, catching on, she withdrew to wait outside.

"I'll go and see what can be done," he told Hsi-feng.

"You're not to pay them anything," she warned.

He went to talk the business over with Lin Chih-hsiao, then sent people to negotiate and finally hushed the matter up by paying two hundred taels. To give them no chance to change their minds, however, Chia Lien also sent stewards to ask Wang Tzu-teng for some runners and sergeants to help with the funeral. When the dead woman's family knew this, they dared make no further move but simply had to swallow their resentment.

Chia Lien also told Lin Chih-hsiao to deduct the two hundred taels from their housekeeping funds, under cover of various items in their daily expenditure. In addition he gave Pao Erh some money too, and promised to find him a good wife later on. Pao Erh raised no objection, naturally, having received both money and consideration. He continued in Chia Lien's service as before.

As for Hsi-feng, although inwardly uneasy she pretended outwardly to be unconcerned.

Chapter 17
A Plaintive Poem Is Written One
Windy, Rainy Evening

Tai-yu, who suffered from a bad cough around every spring
and autumn solstice, had overtaxed her strength this year by
going out more than usual, because of the Lady Dowager's
good spirits, and had recently started coughing again worse
than ever. She therefore stayed in her own rooms to rest.
Sometimes she grew bored and wished the girls would drop
in for a chat to while away the time; yet when Pao-chai and
the rest called to see how she was, a short conversation was
enough to exhaust her. Knowing how delicate and hyper-
sensitive she was, they all made allowances for her, overlooking
any lack of hospitality and courtesy.

Today Pao-chai came to visit her and turned the conversation
to her illness.

"Though the doctors who come here aren't bad, their prescriptions don't seem to be doing you much good," said Pao-
chai. "Why don't you ask a real authority to come and examine
you and see if he can't cure you? You can't go on like this,
having trouble every spring and summer. After all, you're not
an old woman or a child."

"It's no use," was Tai-yu's reply. "I have a hunch I shall
never get over this. You know how poorly I am at the best
of times, let alone when I'm ill."

"That's true." Pao-chai nodded. "The ancients said, 'Food
is life,' yet what you normally eat doesn't give you energy or
strength, and that's a bad sign."

"Life and death are determined by fate, rank and riches

decreed by Heaven," quoted Tai-yu with a sigh. "It's beyond the power of man to alter fate. It seems to me my illness is worse this year." This short speech had been punctuated by several bouts of coughing.

"I saw your prescription yesterday," said Pao-chai. "It struck me there was too much ginseng and cinnamon in it. Although they stimulate the vital forces, you shouldn't have anything too hot either. To my mind, the first essential is to calm your liver and improve your digestion. Once the fire in your liver is quelled so that it can't overcome the 'earth' element your digestion will be better and you'll be able to assimilate your food. When you get up each morning, you should take an ounce of the best quality bird's-nest boiled into a gruel with half an ounce of crystal sugar in a silver pot. Taken regularly, this is a better tonic than any medicine."

"How good you always are to others!" Tai-yu exclaimed with a sigh. "I'm so touchy that I used to suspect your motives. I really began to appreciate you that day when you warned me against indiscriminate reading and gave me such good advice. I can see now I'd misjudged you all along. My mother died early and I've no sisters or brothers so, come to think of it, in all my fifteen years no one ever advised me as you did the other day. No wonder Hsiang-yun speaks so highly of you. I used to be sceptical when she sang your praises, but not after my own recent experience. For instance, when you said anything I always answered back, but instead of taking offence you offered me good advice. That showed that I'd been wrong. If I hadn't realized this the other day, I wouldn't be confiding in you now.

"You just said I should eat bird's-nest. Bird's-nest is easy to buy, but my health is so poor that I fall ill every year and while it's nothing serious I've already caused plenty of trouble, what with sending for doctors and preparing medicine with ginseng and cinnamon. If I started demanding bird's-nest now, the old lady, Lady Wang and Hsi-feng wouldn't say anything, but those below would be bound to think me too pernickety.

Look how jealous these people are and how much gossip there is here because the old lady favours Pao-yu and Hsi-feng. In *my* case, they'd resent it even more. After all, I'm not a daughter of the house, I'm here because I've nowhere else to go. They resent me enough as it is. If I should push myself forward, they'd all start cursing me."

"Well, in that case I'm in the same position as you."

"How can you compare yourself with me? You have your mother and your brother too; you have shops and land here as well, not to mention all your property at home. You're just staying here to be close to your relatives, not spending a cent of their money on anything, free to leave whenever you please. But I have nothing. Yet all I eat, wear and use, down to the least blade of grass or sheet of paper, is the same as their own girls get. Naturally those petty-minded people dislike me."

"It only means providing one extra dowry in future," Pao-chai chuckled. "And it's too early to worry about that yet."

Tai-yu flushed red. "I confide my troubles to you, thinking you'll take them seriously," she said, "but instead you make fun of me."

"I was only joking, but it's quite true. Don't worry. As long as I'm here I shall keep you company. Just tell me any complaints or troubles you have, and I'll help as far as I can. As for my brother, though, you know what *he*'s like. My only advantage over you is that I have a mother. Fellow-sufferers can sympathize with each other. Why should an intelligent girl like you lament your lack of a brother? Of course, you were right just now in saying that it's better not to put people to too much trouble. Tomorrow when I go home, I'll ask my mother for some of the bird's-nest I fancy we still have, and bring you a few ounces. You can get your maids to prepare some every day. It won't cost anything and you'll not be putting anybody out."

"It's a small thing, but I appreciate your kindness," said Tai-yu gratefully.

"It's not worth mentioning. I'm afraid I'm often lacking in

consideration. Well, you must be tired, I'll go now."

"Do drop in again this evening for a chat."

Pao-chai promised to do this and left.

Tai-yu sipped two mouthfuls of rice gruel, then lay down to rest again.

The weather changed unexpectedly before sunset and it began to drizzle. Autumn is a capricious season of many showers and as dusk fell it grew very dark, while the rain pattering on the bamboo leaves made the place seem unusually lonely. Knowing that Pao-chai would not come out in this weather, Tai-yu picked up a book at random under the lamp. It was an anthology of *Yueh-fu*, containing lyrics such as *Autumn Sorrow in a Girl's Chamber* and *The Pain of Parting*. Tai-yu was moved to write a poem about separation herself entitled *A Windy, Rainy Evening by the Autumn Window* in the style of *A Night of Flowers and Moonlight by the Spring River*. This was her poem:

> Sad the autumn flowers, sear the autumn grass,
> Autumn lamps flicker through the long autumn night;
> Unendurably desolate by the autumn window,
> In the wind and rain autumn seems infinite.
> The wind and rain speed autumn on its way,
> By the window shattering her autumn dream;
> And the girl with autumn in her heart cannot sleep
> But trims the candle by her autumn screen.
> Guttering on its stick, the candle sheds tears of wax,
> Evoking the grief of separation, its pain,
> As through each autumn courtyard gusts the wind
> And on each autumn window beats the rain.
> The autumn wind, through silken quilts strikes chill,
> Her water-clock the autumn rain spurs on.
> All night the pelting rain and soughing wind
> Accompany her tears for one now gone.
> Chill mist enwraps the court in loneliness,
> Bamboos drip by the lattice without pause;
> None can tell when the wind and rain will cease,
> But already tears have soaked her window's gauze.

Having read this through, she had just put down her brush and was about to go to bed when Pao-yu was announced. And in he walked, in a large hat of plaited bamboo leaves and a coir cape.

"Where does this fisherman come from?" she greet him laughing.

"Do you feel better today? Have you taken your medicine? How is your appetite?" As he made these inquiries he took off his cape and hat and picked up the lamp, shading it with one hand, to examine her face intently.

"You look a little better today," was his verdict.

She saw that he was wearing a red silk coat, no longer new, with a green girdle, green silk trousers embroidered with flowers, cotton socks embroidered with gold thread, and slippers with butterfly and flower designs.

"Why did you only protect your head and clothes from the rain, not your footwear?" she asked. "Not that your shoes and socks are dirty either."

"I've got a complete set of rain-wear," he told her gaily. "I came here in pyrus-wood pattens, which I left outside on the verandah."

She noticed then that his cape and hat were not the usual sort sold in the market, but extremely finely made.

"What plant are they woven of?" she asked. "You don't look like a hedgehog in that cape, for a wonder."

"These three things are all presents from the Prince of Pei-ching. When it's raining he wears a similar outfit at home. If you like them, I'll get you a set. The best thing is the hat as it's adjustable — the crown can be detached. So men or women alike can wear it in winter in the snow. I'll get you one for when it snows this winter."

"No thank you," Tai-yu chuckled. "If I wore one of those, I should look like the fisherman's wife in paintings and operas."

As these words left her lips she remembered with dismay that she had just greeted Pao-yu as a fisherman. She flushed scarlet and leaned forward over the table, coughing as if she could never stop. Pao-yu, however, appeared not to have noticed. Catching sight of the poem on the table, he picked it up, read it through, and exclaimed in involuntary admiration. Tai-yu hearing this instantly snatched the paper from him and burned it over the lamp.

"Too late! I know it by heart," he said cheerfully.

"I'm better now. Thank you for coming so often to see me, even in the rain," she said. "Now it's late and I'd like to sleep. Please go now. Come again tomorrow."

At this he took from his pocket a golden watch the size of a walnut. Its hands, he saw, showed that it was after nine. Replacing the watch he agreed:

"Yes, it's time to turn in. I've disturbed you too long again." He put on the cape and hat and took his leave, turning back at the door to ask, "What would you like to eat? Let me know and I'll tell the old lady first thing in the morning. I'm a better messenger than those old women."

"I'll think about it during the night, and let you know early tomorrow. Listen, how it's pouring outside. You'd better go quickly. Have you anyone with you?"

Two serving-women answered, "Yes, they're waiting outside with umbrellas and a lantern."

"A lantern? In this weather? ' she asked in surprise.

"That's all right," said Pao-yu. "It's a horn lantern, and it's rain-proof."

She took an ornate glass lantern from the bookcase, ordered a small candle to be lit in it, and handed it to him.

"This is brighter, just the thing to use in the rain."

"I have one like that too," he said. "I didn't bring it for fear they might slip and break it."

"Which is more valuable, lamp or man? You're not used to wearing pattens, so get them to carry the horn lantern in front and take this one yourself, since it's handy and bright and meant to be used in the rain. Wouldn't that be better? You can send it back later. And even if you drop it, it won't matter. What's come over you suddenly that you want to 'cut open your stomach to hide a pearl'?"

Pao-yu promptly took the lantern. Two serving-women led the way with an umbrella and the horn lantern, while two young maids with umbrellas followed behind. He made one of these hold the glass lantern and rested a hand on her shoulder.

Scarcely had he gone when a woman, also with an umbrella and a lantern, arrived to deliver a big package of the best quality bird's-nest and a packet of fine plum-petal snow-white sugar from Alpinia Park.

"This is better than any in the shops," she said. "Our young lady hopes you will use it, and when it's finished she'll send some more."

Tai-yu thanked her and asked her to sit down in the outer room to have some tea.

"I won't stay," the woman replied. "I've got other things to do."

"I know what keeps you busy," rejoined Tai-yu laughingly. "Now that it's turning cold and the nights are long, this is the time for evening gambling parties."

"I'll confess, miss, my luck has been very good this year," said the woman with a smile. "There are always a few of us on night duty, and we mustn't sleep during our watch; so gaming helps to keep us awake and pass the time pleasantly. Tonight it's my turn to be banker. Now that the Garden gates are closed it's time to start."

"Thank you very much for bringing these things in the rain. I'm sorry if I've kept you from making more money." She ordered her maids to give the woman a few hundred cash for wine to keep out the chill.

"Thank you, miss, for treating me again." The woman kowtowed and, having gone to the outer room to take the money, went off with her umbrella.

Tzu-chuan put away the packages, moved aside the lamp and lowered the curtains, then helped her mistress to bed.

Tai-yu's thoughts turned to Pao-chai as she lay on her pillow, and again she envied her for having a mother and a brother. Then she reflected that, good as Pao-yu was to her, there was still a certain distance between them. Moreover, the rain drumming steadily down on the bamboos and plantains outside

wafted a chill through her curtains and made her shed tears
again. Only towards the end of the fourth watch did she finally
fall asleep.

Chapter 18
Yuan-yang Vows Never to Marry

Hsi-feng received a mysterious summons from Lady Hsing and after hastily changing her clothes went off in her carriage to the east court.

Lady Hsing sent her maids away then confided to Hsi-feng, "The Elder Master has given me a difficult task, and I am at a loss, so I want your advice as to how to handle it. He's taken a fancy to the old lady's maid Yuan-yang and wants to make her his concubine. He's told *me* to go and ask the old lady for her. I know this is quite commonly done, but I'm afraid the old lady may not agree. What would you advise me to do?"

"If I were you, I wouldn't run my head against a brick wall," replied Hsi-feng promptly. "The old lady can't even eat without Yuan-yang; how could she part with her? Besides, when we're chatting I've often heard her remark that the Elder Master, at his advanced age, shouldn't be taking concubines left and right. For one thing, he's spoiling those girls' chances of marriage; for another, he's injuring his health and neglecting his official duties by spending all the time drinking with his concubines. You can judge from that, madam, that she's not particularly partial to the Elder Master. He'd do better to try to avoid offending her further instead of 'tickling the tiger's nose with a straw.' Please don't be annoyed, madam, but *I* haven't the courage to approach her. As far as I can see, it would be useless and just cause unpleasantness. The Elder Master's behaviour *is* rather unbecoming for a gentleman getting on in years; you should talk him out of it. It wouldn't matter if he were young;

but when a man has such a flock of younger brothers, nephews, children and grandchildren, doesn't it look bad to go on fooling around like this?"

"Other noble families often have three or four concubines, so why shouldn't we?" retorted Lady Hsing coldly. "I doubt if I can talk him out of it. Even if Yuan-yang is the old lady's favourite maid, when her elder son, a grey-bearded official wants her for his concubine his mother can hardly refuse him. I invited you over simply to ask your opinion, but at once you trot out all these reasons against it. Did you think I'd send *you* on this errand? I shall go myself, of course. You blame me for not dissuading him, but surely you know your father-in-law better than that. He'd ignore my advice and fly into a temper."

Hsi-feng knew that her mother-in-law was a stupid, weak-minded woman who, to save herself trouble, always humoured Chia Sheh, finding her sole pleasure in life in amassing property and money. All decisions great or small in their household she left to her husband; but when money passed through her hands she was extraordinarily tight-fisted, alleging that she had to economize to make up for *his* extravagance. Not one of her children or servants did she trust, nor would she listen to their advice. It would be futile to reason with her now, seeing that she was so stubborn.

So with a pleasant smile Hsi-feng replied, "You're quite right, madam. What can I know, young as I am? After all, she's his mother and would surely never refuse him the rarest treasure, not to say a maid. Whom else would she give her to if not the Elder Master? I was silly to take what she said in private so seriously. Even in Lien's case, for instance, the master and you may threaten to beat him to death when he displeases you, but the moment you see him your anger melts away and you still give him things you treasure. Of course, that's how the old lady will treat the Elder Master. As she's in high spirits today, it seems to me now's the time to make this request. Would you like me to go first to coax her into a good humour?

Then when you come I'll make some excuse to leave, taking everyone else there with me, so that you can broach the subject. If she agrees, so much the better. If she doesn't, no harm will be done as no one else will know."

Mollified by this, Lady Hsing told her, "My idea was not to approach the old lady first, for if she refused that would be the end of the matter. I was thinking of telling Yuan-yang first in private. She may be bashful, but when I've explained it all to her she naturally won't say anything. And that can be taken to mean consent. Then I'll go and ask the old lady, and she'll find it difficult to refuse even though she doesn't want to part with the girl. For as the proverb says, 'There's no holding someone who wants to leave.' It's sure to work out all right."

"After all, you know best, madam." Hsi-feng smiled. "This is bound to work. Every girl, not to mention Yuan-yang, wants to rise in the world and become someone of importance. Who would refuse to become a semi-mistress and remain in service instead, with no prospect but that of marrying some servant in the end?"

"That's what I think," agreed Lady Hsing. "Not to say Yuan-yang, even those senior maids in responsible positions would jump at the chance. All right, you go over first, but don't let a word leak out. I'll come over after dinner."

Meanwhile Hsi-feng had been thinking, "Yuan-yang is a sharp customer. Still she may refuse. If I go back first and Yuan-yang agrees, all right; but if she refuses my mother-in-law's so suspicious she's sure to think I told her and encouraged her to hold out. Seeing me proved right and herself made to look a fool, she may vent her temper on me and that would be no joke. Better if the two of us go over together, for then whether Yuan-yang agrees or not no suspicion can fall on me."

So she said cordially, "As I set out just now, my maternal uncle's house sent over two baskets of quails which I told the kitchen to have deep-fried and sent over for your dinner. And as I came through your main gate, I saw some pages carrying off your carriage for repairs — they said it was cracking up. Why don't you come back now, madam, with me in mine? Then we can go together."

Lady Hsing called for her maids to change her clothes, assisted by Hsi-feng, after which they both mounted the carriage.

Then Hsi-feng said, "If I accompany you to the old lady's place, madam, she may ask what I've come for and that would be awkward. Suppose you go first, and I follow after changing my clothes?"

Lady Hsing thought this reasonable, and went on first to call on the Lady Dowager. After chatting with her for a while, she left on the pretext of going to see Lady Wang. Instead, however, she slipped out through the back door to Yuan-yang's bedroom. The girl, who was sitting there doing some needlework, hastily rose to her feet at her approach.

Lady Hsing asked with a smile, "What are you making? Let me have a look. I'm sure you're doing finer work than ever." So saying she entered the room, inspected the embroidery and praised it loudly. Putting it down then, she subjected Yuan-yang to a careful scrutiny.

The maid was wearing a light purple silk tunic, none too new, a black satin sleeveless jacket with silk borders, and a pale green skirt. She had a supple wasp-waist, slender shoulders, an oval face, glossy black hair and a finely arched nose, while her cheeks were slightly freckled. This close inspection embarrassed and puzzled her.

"What brings you here at this hour, madam?" she asked with a smile.

Lady Hsing signed to her attendants to leave, then sat down and took Yuan-yang's hand. "I've come specially to congratulate you," she announced.

This gave Yuan-yang some inkling of what was afoot. She blushed and lowered her head without a word.

"You know, the Elder Master has no one reliable to wait on him," Lady Hsing continued. "He could buy a girl, of course, but those one gets through brokers aren't clean and there's no knowing what mayn't be wrong with them; besides, after two or three days they're liable to get up to monkey-tricks. So he's been trying to choose one in our household. At first there seemed to be no one suitable. One was ugly, another bad-tempered, and some had certain good points but other shortcomings. After keeping his eyes open for the past six months, he's decided that of all the girls here you're the best — pretty, well-behaved, dependable and sweet-tempered. So he wants to ask the old lady to let him take you into his chambers.

"Your position will be quite different from that of a girl bought from outside, for as soon as you enter our house we shall go through the ceremonies and give you the rank of a secondary wife, treated with all respect and honour. Besides, you're a girl with a will of your own. As the proverb says, 'True gold will find its price.' Now that the Elder Master has picked you, you'll be able to realize your highest ambitions, and this will stop the mouths of those who dislike you. So come along with me to tell the old lady."

She took Yuan-yang's hand to lead her out, but the girl coloured and shrank back.

"What's there to be so bashful about?" asked Lady Hsing, seeing how embarrassed she was. "You won't have to say a word. Just come with me."

Yuan-yang simply hung her head and would not budge.

"Don't tell me you're unwilling!" cried Lady Hsing. "You're a very silly girl if that's the case, turning down the chance to be a mistress and choosing to remain a maid instead. All you can look forward to then is marrying some servant in two or three years' time — you'll still be a slave. Far better come to us. You know I'm much too good-natured to be jealous, and the Elder Master will treat you well. In a year or so, when you give birth to a child, you'll be on the same footing as me with the whole household at your beck and call. If you let slip this chance to better yourself, you're going to regret it — but then it'll be too late."

Still Yuan-yang simply hung her head and said nothing.

"You've always been a straightforward girl," persisted Lady Hsing. "Why are you being so sticky about this? What's worrying you? Just tell me, and I'll see that your wishes are met."

Yuan-yang remained silent.

"I suppose you're too shy to say 'yes' yourself and would prefer to leave it to your parents." Lady Hsing smiled. "Quite right and proper too. I'll speak to them and get *them* to speak to you. You can be frank with them." This said, she went off to find Hsi-feng.

Hsi-feng had long since changed her clothes, and since no one else was in the room but Ping-erh she disclosed this news to her.

Ping-erh shook her head. "I don't see this working out," was her verdict. "From the way she's spoken when we were chatting on our own, she's not likely to consent. But we shall soon see."

"The mistress may bring Yuan-yang here to discuss it," said Hsi-feng. "If Yuan-yang's willing, all right; if not, she'll be feeling put out, and it would be embarrassing for her to have you others here. Tell the rest to go and deep-fry some quails and prepare a few other dishes to go with them. Then you can go off and amuse yourself somewhere else till you think she'll have gone."

Ping-erh passed on these instructions to the other servants, then sauntered off to enjoy herself in the Garden.

Meanwhile Yuan-yang had guessed that Lady Hsing would be going to discuss this business with Hsi-feng, and that other people were sure to come to sound her out again. Thinking it wisest to make herself scarce, she told Hu-po:

"If the old lady should ask for me, tell her I'm not feeling well and I had no breakfast. I've gone for a stroll in the Garden but shan't be long."

Hu-po agreed to this, and Yuan-yang went out. While walking in the Garden, to her surprise she met Ping-erh, who seeing that they were alone cried teasingly:

"Here comes the new concubine!"

Yuan-yang flushed scarlet. "So that's it!" she exclaimed. "You're all in league against me. Wait till I go and have this out with your mistress."

Ping-erh hearing this regretted her tactlessness. Drawing Yuan-yang over to sit on a rock under a maple, she told her frankly all that Hsi-feng had said since her return.

Still blushing, Yuan-yang answered bitterly, "What good friends we were, the dozen or so of us — Hsi-jen, Hu-po, Su-yun, Tzu-chuan, Tsai-hsia, Yu-chuan, Sheh-yueh, Tsui-mo, Tsui-lu who went with Miss Hsiang-yun, Ko-jen and Chin-chuan who've died, Chien-hsueh who's left, and the two of us. We worked together from the time we were young and never had any secrets from each other. Now that we've grown up we've gone our different ways, but I haven't changed — I don't hide anything from you. So I'll confide something to you, but mind you don't tell Madam Lien. Quite apart from the fact that the Elder Master only wants to make me his concubine, even if Lady Hsing had died and he sent matchmakers in style to make me his principal wife, I wouldn't agree to it."

Before Ping-erh could reply they heard laughter behind the rock.

"For shame!" someone cried. "Such talk's enough to set one's teeth on edge."

Startled, they jumped to their feet to see who was there. It was Hsi-jen, who emerged laughingly from behind the rockery.

"What's up?" she asked. "Let me into the secret."

The three of them sat down again and Ping-erh retold her story.

"Of course, we shouldn't say this, but what an old lecher the Elder Master is!" was Hsi-jen's comment. "He can't keep his hands off any girl who's not bad-looking."

"Since you're unwilling," said Ping-erh, "I'll tell you an easy way to fob him off."

"What's that?" asked Yuan-yang.

"Simply tell the old lady you've already given yourself to Master Lien." Ping-erh giggled. "The father can hardly take what belongs to his son."

Yuan-yang spat in disgust. "What rubbish! Your mistress was raving the other day. How can you go repeating that today?"

"If you don't want either of them," teased Hsi-jen, "get the old lady to tell Lord Sheh you're already promised to Pao-yu. Then he'll have to give up."

Frantic with rage and embarrassment, Yuan-yang swore, "You two bitches, you won't come to a good end! I turn to you in trouble, thinking you'll have the decency to help me, but instead you take it in turns to make fun of me. You think your own futures are assured and you'll both end up as secondary wives. I'm not so sure. In this world, things don't always turn out the way you want. So don't start counting your chickens before they're hatched."

Seeing how frantic she was, the two others did their best to soothe her.

"Don't take it the wrong way, dear sister," they cried. "We've been like real sisters since we were small and were only having a joke among ourselves. But, seriously, tell us your plan, so that we can stop worrying."

"Plan? What plan do I have? I just refuse to go."

Ping-erh shook her head. "Then he may not give up. You know what Lord Sheh's like. Though he won't dare do anything now while you're with the old lady, you won't be in her service all your life, will you? Some day you'll be leaving. If you fell into his clutches then, that would be worse."

"Pah! As long as the old lady lives, I shan't leave this house. If she passes away, he'll have to observe three years' mourning anyway: he can't take a concubine the moment his mother dies. And in those three years anything might happen. Time enough to worry then. If the worst comes to the worst, I can shave my hair off and become a nun. Failing that, I can kill myself. I don't care if I *never* get married. Then life would be simpler."

"What a shameless slut!" laughed Ping-erh. "The wild way

she runs on!"

"Things have gone too far for modesty," Yuan-yang retorted. "If you don't believe me, wait and see. Lady Hsing said just now she means to speak to my parents. She'll have to go to Nanking for that."

"Your father and mother are looking after properties in the south," said Ping-erh. "So even though they're not here, they can still be found. Besides, your elder brother and sister-in-law are here. It's too bad you're a house-born servant. It's worse for you than for us who are here on our own."

"What difference does it make? You can't force an ox to bend its head to drink. Would he kill my parents if I refuse?"

Just then they saw her sister-in-law approaching.

Hsi-jen remarked, "As your parents aren't on the spot, they must have spoken to your sister-in-law."

"That whore!" swore Yuan-yang. "She's a regular camel-dealer. She won't let slip this chance to suck up to them."

By now her sister-in-law had come up to her.

"I've been looking for you everywhere," she said smiling. "So this is where you'd run off to. Come with me. I want to have a word with you."

Ping-erh and Hsi-jen asked her to sit down.

"No thank you. Don't stir," said the woman. "I just want to have a word with my sister-in-law."

"What's the hurry?" they asked, pretending not to know. "We're guessing riddles here and making bets. We must hear her answer to this one before she goes."

"What do you want?" demanded Yuan-yang. "Out with it."

"Come with me," the other insisted. "I'll tell you over there. It's good news for you, anyway."

"You mean what Lady Hsing told you?"

"If you know, why keep putting me off? Come along, and I'll give you the details. It's simply the most wonderful piece of good fortune."

Yuan-yang sprang up and spat hard in her face. Pointing an

accusing finger at her she swore.

"Shut your foul mouth and clear off, if you know what's good for you. What's all this talk of 'good news' and 'good fortune'? No wonder, though. You've always envied those families who start throwing their weight about once their daughters are concubines, as if every one of them was a concubine too. You can't wait to pitch *me* into that fiery pit. Then if I get given face you can bully people outside, calling yourselves relatives of the Chia family; if I lose face and land in trouble, you turtles can shrink back into your shells and leave me to my fate."

She wept and stormed while Ping-erh and Hsi-jen restrained her and tried to calm her.

Her sister-in-law was goaded to retort, "Whether you're willing or not, you might at least explain properly instead of slinging mud at other people. The proverb says, 'One doesn't talk about midgets in front of dwarfs.' Your abuse of *me* I won't presume to answer. But these girls haven't offended you, why embarrass them with all this talk about concubines?"

"That's no way to speak," protested the other two. "She wasn't referring to us. *You're* the one trying to drag us into this. Which master or mistress has made us concubines? Besides, we've no parents or brother in service here who could make use of our position to bully others. There *are* people of that kind. Let her swear at them — it doesn't worry *us*."

"I put her to shame and she didn't know how to cover up," said Yuan-yang. "That's why she tried to provoke the two of you. It's a good thing you understand. Being carried away, I didn't choose my words carefully enough; then she saw her chance and grabbed it."

Her sister-in-law flounced off in a huff while Yuan-yang went on fulminating against her. When at last they had calmed her Ping-erh asked Hsi-jen:

"Why were you hiding there? We didn't see you."

"I went to Miss Hsi-chun's apartment to fetch Master Pao,

only to be told I'd just missed him — he'd gone back. I doubted that, for in that case I would have seen him. I decided to see if he was with Miss Lin, but I ran into some of her people who told me he wasn't there either. It had just occurred to me that he might have left the Garden, when you happened to come along. I dodged out of sight, and then Yuan-yang came along too. I slipped from behind that tree to behind this rockery; but you were so busy talking that even with two pairs of eyes you didn't see me."

"Even with two pairs of eyes they didn't see you?" Someone behind them laughed. "Even with *three* pairs of eyes you didn't see *me*!"

With a start they turned and saw Pao-yu approaching them.

"What a chase you've led me," Hsi-jen exclaimed with a smile. "Where have you been all this time?"

"After I left Hsi-chun, I spotted you coming and guessed you were looking for me, so I hid myself to tease you. I watched you sail straight past into the courtyard, then come out again and question everyone you met. I was laughing up my sleeve, ready to pop out and frighten you when you reached me. But then I saw you dodge into hiding too and knew you were playing a trick on someone else. I peeped out and saw these two. So I crept behind you, and after you came out I hid where you'd been hiding."

"We'd better go and have another look in case another couple's hiding there," proposed Ping-erh with a laugh.

"No, there's no one there now," he assured her.

Aware that Pao-yu must have overheard everything, Yuan-yang laid her head on her arms on the rock and pretended she was dozing off.

"It's cold on that stone. Come back to my place to rest," he suggested, nudging her.

Helping her up, he invited Ping-erh too for a cup of tea. Pressed by both Ping-erh and Hsi-jen, Yuan-yang acquiesced and the four of them went together to Happy Red Court. The conversation Pao-yu had overheard had naturally depressed him. He simply lay down quietly on his bed, leaving the three girls to chat in the outer room.

To return to Lady Hsing, she had learned from Hsi-feng that Yuan-yang's father Chin Tsai and his wife were acting as caretakers in Nanking and seldom came up to the capital. However, her elder brother Chin Wen-chiang was a buyer for the Lady Dowager, and her sister-in-law was chief laundress in her apartments.

Lady Hsing promptly sent for Wen-chiang's wife and told her what she proposed. Young Mrs. Chin was of course only too pleased and went off jubilantly to find Yuan-yang, sure that her mission would meet with instant success. Instead, she was denounced to her face by Yuan-yang and snubbed by Hsi-jen and Ping-erh into the bargain.

She returned, angry and discomfited, to report to Lady Hsing, "It's no use, she just swore at me." Since Hsi-feng was present she dared not mention Ping-erh, but she added, "Hsi-jen joined in her attack on me and talked a whole lot of other nonsense too, which doesn't bear repeating. You had better persuade Lord Sheh to buy another girl, madam. That little bitch isn't cut out for such great fortune, nor are we for such good luck."

"What has this to do with Hsi-jen?" asked Lady Hsing. "How did she come to hear of it? Who else was there?"

"Miss Ping-erh was there too."

Hsi-feng promptly interposed, "Why didn't you slap her face? Every time I go out, off she goes to amuse herself. When I got home today there was no sign of her. I suppose she took Yuan-yang's side too?"

"Miss Ping-erh wasn't there on the spot," replied Mrs. Chin. "It looked like her from a distance, but I may have been mistaken. That was just my guess."

Hsi-feng ordered a servant, "Go and fetch Ping-erh, quick. Tell her I'm back and Her Ladyship is here too. She's wanted for something."

Feng-erh hastily stepped forward to put in, "Miss Lin sent

a maid with a note several times to invite her over, so finally she went. As soon as you came back, madam, I went to fetch her, but Miss Lin asked me to tell you she'd like to keep her for a little, madam."

"Every day she seems to want her for something or other," remarked Hsi-feng, then let the matter drop.

As there was nothing more Lady Hsing could do, she went home after dinner and told her husband that evening what had happened. Chia Sheh thought the matter over, then summoned Chia Lien.

"We have other caretakers besides the Chins in Nanking," he said. "Send at once to have Chin Tsai recalled."

"According to the last letter from Nanking, Chin Tsai has had a stroke, sir," replied his son. "Money for his coffin has already been issued there, and for all we know he may already be dead. Even if he's still living he'll be in a coma, so it wouldn't be any use sending for him. And his old wife is deaf."

Chia Sheh swore. "You scurvy scoundrel!" he fumed. "Quite a know-all, aren't you? Get out!"

In consternation Chia Lien promptly withdrew. Soon he heard the order given to fetch Chin Wen-chiang. He himself remained on call in the outside study, daring neither to go home nor to confront his father.

Presently Wen-chiang arrived and some pages ushered him through the inner gate. He was with Lord Sheh for the space of five or six meals, and after he left Chia Lien did not venture to ask what had been said. Not until late that evening, having ascertained that his father was asleep, did he finally go home where Hsi-feng cleared up the whole mystery for him.

As for Yuan-yang, she passed a sleepless night. The next day her brother came and asked the Lady Dowager's permission to take her home for a rest. The old lady agreed and told her to go. This was not what Yuan-yang wanted, but she complied reluctantly in order not to arouse the old lady's suspicions. Her brother told her what Lord Sheh had said and what dignity she would have as his secondary wife. However, Yuan-yang refused to consider it. Unable to change her mind, he had to go back and report this to Chia Sheh.

Chia Sheh flew into a rage. "Tell your wife to tell her this from me," he fumed. "Tell her these are my own words. 'From of old, young nymphs have preferred youth to age. She must think me too old for her. I daresay she has set her heart on one of the young masters, most likely Pao-yu or possibly my son. If that's her scheme, tell her to forget it. For if she refuses me, who else will dare take her later? That's the first thing.

" 'The second is this: if she's counting on the old lady's partiality to her to find some decent husband outside, she'd better think again. For no matter whom she marries she'll still be within my reach, unless she dies or remains single all her life, in which case there is nothing I can do. Otherwise, the sooner she changes her mind the better for her.' "

Wen-chiang had expressed agreement after each sentence of this diatribe. Now Chia Sheh added:

"And don't you try to cheat me. Tomorrow I shall send the mistress to her again. If you've really told her and she still refuses, I won't hold you responsible. But if when we ask her again she agrees, you'll have to watch out for your head!"

Chin Wen-chiang agreed hastily and withdrew. Upon his arrival home, without waiting to get his wife to pass on this message he told Yuan-yang himself, reducing her to a state of speechless anger.

After some reflection she said, "Well, supposing I agree, you'll still have to take me back to report this to the old lady."

Her brother and his wife were overjoyed by this apparent change of heart. Her sister-in-law at once took her to the Lady Dowager, who happened to be chatting with Lady Wang, Aunt Hsueh, Li Wan, Hsi-feng, Pao-chai and the other girls, as well as a few of the chief stewards' wives, all of whom were doing their best to amuse the old lady.

Delighted by this opportunity, Yuan-yang drew her sister-in-law forward and threw herself on her knees before her mistress. Sobbing, she told the old lady what Lady Hsing had said to her, what her sister-in-law had told her in the Garden, and how her brother had threatened her today.

"Because I wouldn't agree, the Elder Master says I've set my heart on Pao-yu. He swears I'll never escape him, not even if I marry someone outside, no, not even if I go to the ends of the earth — he'll have his revenge in the end. Well, my mind's made up. Everybody here can bear witness. I shall never marry so long as I live, neither Pao-yu with his precious jade, nor someone born with silver or gold, not even a Heavenly King or Emperor!

"If Your Ladyship tries to force me, I'll kill myself rather than marry. If I'm lucky, I shall die before you, madam. Otherwise I mean to serve Your Ladyship till the end of your life; then, rather than go back to my parents or to my brother, I shall commit suicide or shave my head and become a nun. If you think I'm not in earnest and this is just empty talk which I'll go back on later, may Heaven, Earth, all the deities and the Sun and Moon who are my witnesses choke me with an ulcer in my throat so that I rot away into a pulp!"

Before coming in, she had hidden a pair of scissors in her sleeve, and while uttering this oath she let down her hair with her left hand and started cutting it with the scissors in her right. Maids and serving-women hurried over to stop her. She had cut off one lock already but, luckily, her hair being so thick, it was difficult to cut much. They lost no time in dressing it for her again.

The Lady Dowager was trembling with rage.

"The only girl left I can trust, and they want to get her away from me," she quavered. Her eye falling on Lady Wang beside her, she cried, "So you're all deceiving me, putting on a show of being dutiful but plotting against me in secret. Whenever I have anything good you come and demand it from me. And my best servants too. Now I've only this one girl left, and

儘磋跎人難免磋跎事
蕁鴦女竟化鴦鴦偶

seeing how partial I am to her naturally infuriates you. You're trying to get her away from me, so as to get me under your own thumb."

Lady Wang had risen to her feet but did not venture a word in self-defence. And Aunt Hsueh being her sister, could not try to shift the blame from her. Li Wan had quietly taken the girls outside when Yuan-yang began her story.

Tan-chun, however, had sense enough to see that it was not for Lady Wang to clear herself of these false charges, nor for Aunt Hsueh to defend her sister, nor for Pao-chai to defend her aunt, while Li Wan, Hsi-feng and Pao-yu were in no position to protest either. It was now up to one of the girls to speak. But Ying-chun was too naive, Hsi-chun too young. So after listening for a while outside the window, she entered the room with a smile.

"What has this to do with Her Ladyship?" she asked her grandmother. "Just think, madam, how could a younger sister-in-law know that her elder brother-in-law was going to get a concubine? Even if she did, could she say anything?"

At once the old lady chuckled. "I'm losing my wits with age," she exclaimed. "Don't laugh at me, Madam Hsueh. This elder sister of yours is a very good daughter-in-law, not like my elder son's wife who's so afraid of her husband she only makes a show of compliance to me. Yes, I was wrong to blame your sister."

Aunt Hsueh murmured agreement, then added, "I wonder if you're not, perhaps, rather partial to the wife of your younger son, madam?"

"No, I'm not partial," the old lady declared. She continued, "Pao-yu, why didn't you point out my mistake and prevent me from blaming your mother so unfairly?"

"How could I stick up for my mother at the expense of my elder uncle and aunt?" he countered. "Anyway, someone's done wrong; and if mother here won't take the blame, who will? I could have said it was *my* fault but I'm sure you wouldn't have believed me."

"Yes, that's right," chuckled the Lady Dowager. "Now kneel to your mother and ask her not to feel hurt, but to forgive me for your sake on account of my old age."

Pao-yu stepped forward and knelt to do as he was told, but his mother instantly stopped him.

"Get up," she cried with a smile. "This is absurd. How can you apologize for your grandmother?"

As Pao-yu rose to his feet the old lady said, "And Hsi-feng didn't pull me up either."

"I haven't said a word against you, madam," retorted Hsi-feng laughingly, "but now you're trying to put the blame on me."

All the others laughed and the old lady cried, "This is strange! Let's hear what you have to say against me."

"Who told you, madam, to train your girls so well? If you bring one up as fresh as a sprig of young parsley, you can't blame people for wanting her. It's lucky I'm a grandson's wife. If I were a grandson I'd have grabbed her long ago. I shouldn't have waited till now."

"So it's all my fault, is it?" the old lady chortled.

"Of course it is," agreed Hsi-feng.

"In that case I won't keep her. You can take her away."

"Wait till I've done enough good deeds in this life to be reborn as a man. Then I'll marry her."

"You can take her and give her to Lien. See if that shameless father-in-law of yours still wants her then or not."

"Lien doesn't deserve her," said Hsi-feng. "He'll have to make do with scarecrows like Ping-erh and me."

They were all laughing at this when Lady Hsing was announced.

Lady Wang hurried out to greet Lady Hsing who had come in the hope of news, unaware that the Lady Dowager knew all about her proposal to Yuan-yang. Only as she stepped into the courtyard was she quietly apprised of this by some serving-women; but it was too late to retreat now that her arrival had been announced and Lady Wang had come out to meet her.

She had no choice but to go in and pay her respects.

The old lady received her without a word, to her great mortification. Hsi-feng had already left on the pretext of some business, while Yuan-yang had retired to her room to sulk. Now Aunt Hsueh, Lady Wang and the others withdrew one by one to spare Lady Hsing embarrassment. She herself dared not leave, however.

Once they were alone the Lady Dowager sneered, "I hear you've been doing some matchmaking for your husband. Quite a model of wifely submission and virtue, aren't you? Only you carry this obedience too far. You have children and grand-children now, yet you're still afraid of him. Instead of giving him a little good advice you let him carry on just as he pleases."

Blushing all over her face Lady Hsing replied, "I *have* reasoned with him several times, but he pays no attention. You know how it is, madam. I had no choice."

"Would you commit murder too if he insisted? Have some sense! Your sister-in-law is a simple soul and, for all her poor health, she has to worry about high and low in this household. Though your daughter-in-law helps her, her work is never done. So I don't make too many demands on them, and when the two of them overlook certain things, that child Yuan-yang is thoughtful enough to attend to my wants. She sees I get what I need, and tells them in time what wants replenishing. If not for her, in all their press of business the pair of them would be bound to forget this or that. Do you expect *me* to see to everything? To work out every day what I need to ask for? She's the only maid left me who's not just a child and knows something of my ways and temperament. In the second place: she gets on well with the older and younger mistresses alike here, and never tries in my name to ask this mistress for clothes or that for money. So during the last few years the whole household old and young, starting with your sister-in-law and daughter-in-law, all trust her. It's not just that *I* rely on her, she saves them trouble too. As long as I've someone like her, I don't have to worry about going short of anything even if my daughters-in-law or my grandsons' wives forget it. But who would you give me in her place if she left now? Even if you managed to produce a girl of her size made of pearls but unable to talk she'd still be no use to me.

"I was just on the point of sending to tell your husband: I've money here for him if he wants to buy someone, and I don't care if it costs eight or even ten thousand taels; but he can't have *this* girl. If she can be left to wait on me for a few years, that'll be the same as him waiting on me day and night himself like a dutiful son. It's a good thing that you've come. It's more fitting that he should hear this from you."

When Lady Hsing gave her husband an abbreviated version of what the Lady Dowager had said, Chia Sheh felt at a loss and bitterly mortified too. After this, on the pretext of illness he stopped calling on his mother, being actually afraid to face her, sending his wife and son instead to pay their respects every day. None the less he made his men scout around and finally, for the sum of eight hundred taels, bought a seventeen-year-old girl called Yen-hung to be his concubine.

Chapter 19
A Spiteful Servant Imposes upon Her Young Mistress

No sooner was the bustle of New Year over than Hsi-feng had a miscarriage. She had to stop running the household for a month, and two or three doctors attended her every day; but overestimating her own strength, although staying indoors she continued mapping out plans for the household, which Ping-erh was sent to report to Lady Wang. All advice to rest she ignored.

Lady Wang felt as if she had lost her right arm, and simply had not the energy to cope. She decided important matters herself, entrusting lesser domestic affairs to Li Wan for the time being. But Li Wan, the widow of Chia Chu, being one of those people who have more virtue than ability, inevitably let the servants have their own way; so Lady Wang told Tan-chun to help her out for a month, until Hsi-feng was well enough to take over again.

One day, Lady Wang was invited to a feast in the house of the Marquis of Chinhsiang. Li Wan and Tan-chun rose early to attend her until she left, then went back to the hall. They were sipping tea there when Wu Hsin-teng's wife came in to inform them that Chao Kuo-chi, the brother of Concubine Chao, had died the previous day.

"I reported this yesterday to the mistress," she said. "She told me to let you ladies know."

She made no further comment after this, just stood by at respectful attention.

All the servants who had come to report on business were

eager to see how these two would handle the matter. If it was handled correctly they would respect them; if the least mistake was made, not only would they despise them, once out of the inner gate they would start gossiping and making fun of them. Mrs. Wu knew what should be done, and had she been dealing with Hsi-feng she would have made various suggestions to curry favour, quoting precedents for her to decide between. But as she looked down on Li Wan as a simpleton and Tan-chun as only a girl, she said no more, waiting to see what the two of them would do.

Tan-chun consulted Li Wan, who thought for a moment.

"The other day when Hsi-jen's mother died, I understand she was given forty taels," she said. "We can give the same amount."

Mrs. Wu promptly assented, took the tally and was about to go off when Tan-chun stopped her.

"Don't go for the money yet," said Tan-chun. "I've something to ask you. Some of those old concubines in the old lady's apartments came from outside, some from families serving here. There was a distinction. If a relative of one from our household died, how much was given? How much to one from outside? Give us a couple of examples."

When questioned like this, Mrs. Wu could not remember.

"It doesn't matter," she answered with a smile. "Whatever sum's given, who would dare to complain?"

"Nonsense!" retorted Tan-chun pleasantly. "I would just as soon give a *hundred* taels; but if I didn't go by the rules, not only would you laugh at me but I shouldn't be able to face the Second Mistress."

"In that case I'll go and look up the old accounts," offered Mrs. Wu. "I can't for the moment remember."

"You're an old hand at this," Tan-chun pointed out. "Yet you claim to have forgotten, so as to make things awkward for us. Do you have to go and look up the accounts when you report to the Second Mistress? If so, Hsi-feng would count as lenient, not as exacting. Fetch those accounts at once. One more day's delay, and instead of blaming you for negligence people will accuse us of incompetence."

Mrs. Wu flushed scarlet and hurried out, while the other stewards' wives stuck out their tongues in dismay. Then other matters were reported.

Soon Mrs. Wu came back with the old accounts. Tan-chun, taking them, found that two concubines who had been family servants had received twenty taels apiece, and two from outside forty. Two others from outside had received a hundred taels and sixty taels respectively; but it was recorded that this was because the first was allowed an extra sixty to have her parents' coffins moved to another province; the second was allowed an extra twenty to buy a burial ground.

Tan-chun showed these items to Li Wan.

"Give her twenty taels," she ordered Mrs. Wu.

"And leave these accounts here for us to go through carefully." Mrs. Wu assented and withdrew.

Suddenly Concubine Chao burst in. Li Wan and Tan-chun at once asked her to be seated.

"Everyone in this house tramples on my head," she stormed. "I should think *you* at least, miss, should take my side!" She began to sob and snivel as she was speaking.

"Whom are you accusing, madam?" asked Tan-chun. "I don't understand. Who's trampling on your head? If you'll tell me, I'll take your side."

"You're the one — so whom can I complain to?"

Tan-chun hastily rose to protest, "I wouldn't dare."

Li Wan also stood up to act as a peacemaker.

"Sit down, please, and listen to me!" cried the concubine. "I've been treated like dirt in this house all these years, though I've borne you and your brother, and now I rank even lower than Hsi-jen. What face have I got left? Not only me — this makes *you* lose face too."

"So that's it." Tan-chun smiled. "As if I dared take the law into my own hands!"

Sitting down again, she showed Concubine Chao the account

books and read out the items to her.

"These are the rules handed down by our ancestors," she declared. "We all have to abide by them — how could *I* change them? Hsi-jen isn't a special case. If Huan takes a concubine from outside later on, she'll naturally rank the same as Hsi-jen. This isn't a question of competing for status, it has nothing to do with face. If someone's in our mistress' service, I can only go by the rules. The sum's given thanks to the kindness of our ancestors and our mistress. If that someone thinks it unfair and is too stupid to know when she's well off, I can't stop her complaining. If our mistress were to give away the whole *house,* I'd get no face from it. If she didn't give a cent, it wouldn't make me lose face either.

"Take my advice and have a quiet rest while the mistress is out. Why work yourself up? The mistress is kindness itself to me, but you've grieved her more than once by the way you make trouble. If I were a boy, able to leave this house, I'd have gone long ago to make my own way in the world, for then of course I'd know what to do. It's too bad that I'm only a girl and mustn't say a word out of turn. The mistress fully understands, and thinks well enough of me to put me in charge; but before I've managed to be of any use you come and start picking on me. If she found out and relieved me of the job so as not to embarrass me, then I'd *really* lose face. And so would you as well." By this time she was sobbing bitterly.

The concubine having no other answer to this retorted, "If the mistress is partial to you, that's all the more reason to lend us a helping hand. But you've quite forgotten us in your eagerness to curry favour with *her.*"

"Who says I've forgotten you? How am I to lend a helping hand? You have to ask yourselves: Don't all mistresses like inferiors who make themselves useful? Good people don't need the kind offices of others."

Li Wan put in soothingly, "Don't be angry, madam. It's not her fault. She's only too eager to help you, but how can she say so?"

"Don't be ridiculous, sister-in-law!" cried Tan-chun. "Who do you mean I'm to help? Does the daughter of any house help servants? You should know what they are — their affairs are none of my business."

"Who asked you to help others?" fumed the concubine. "If you weren't in charge I wouldn't have come to you. Now if you say one it's one, if you say two it's two. If you gave an extra twenty or thirty taels for your uncle's funeral, why should the mistress object? Everyone knows how good she is — it's you people who are so stingy. It's too bad she has no chance to show her kindness. But don't worry, miss, it's not your own silver you're saving. I'd always hoped, after you married, you'd show more consideration to the Chao family; but now before your feathers have grown you've forgotten your roots, you're so keen to fly to the very top of the tree."

Before she had finished, Tan-chun's face was white with anger.

Nearly choking with sobs she demanded, "Who's my uncle? My uncle's just been appointed Military Inspector of Nine Provinces. What other uncles do I have? Is this my reward for always observing the rules of propriety — to have all these relatives foisted off on me? If what you say were true, why did Chao Kuo-chi have to stand up whenever Huan went out? Why follow him to school? Why didn't he behave like an uncle?

"Do you have to make such a scene? Everyone knows I'm a child by a concubine, yet you needs must bring it up every few months and rub it in, as if you had to make it plain for fear they didn't know. Who's making the other lose face? It's lucky I've sense enough to remember my manners, or you'd have driven me frantic long ago!"

Li Wan tried desperately to pacify them, but the concubine went on ranting. She did not stop until it was announced:

"Miss Ping-erh has come with a message from the Second Mistress."

Concubine Chao greeted Ping-erh with a smile and urged her to take a seat.

"Is your mistress better?" she asked. "I've been meaning to call on her but haven't yet found the time."

Li Wan asked Ping-erh her business.

"The Second Mistress thought you ladies might not know what the usual allowance would be in connection with the death of Concubine Chao's brother," answered Ping-erh. "The rule is to give only twenty taels, but it's up to you to decide. You can give more if you want."

"Why make an exception in this case?" retorted Tan-chun who had now dried her eyes. "Was he a prodigy who took twenty-four months to be born, or someone who saved his master's life in the army? How clever your mistress is, wanting me to break the rules while she gets the credit, buying herself goodwill at our mistress' expense! Tell her *I* don't dare to increase or cut down amounts for no good reason. If she wants to be charitable and add something, she'll have to wait till she's better."

Ping-erh had sensed as soon as she came in that something was wrong. After this tirade she grasped the situation. And since Tan-chun was glowering instead of replying with one of her usual jokes she waited there in a respectful silence.

At this point Pao-chai arrived too from Lady Wang's apartments. Tan-chun and the others rose to offer her a seat; but before they could enter into conversation another woman came in to make her report. And as Tan-chun's face was tear-stained, three or four young maids brought in a basin, towels and a mirror with a handle. One of them knelt before Tan-chun, who was cross-legged on the couch, and held the basin out to her while two others knelt beside her with the towels, mirror and cosmetics. Seeing that Tai-shu was not there to help, Ping-erh stepped forward to roll up Tan-chun's sleeves, take off her bracelets, and drape a large towel over the front of her clothes. Tan-chun had just dipped her hands into the basin when the woman who had come in announced:

"If you please, my ladies, the family school has sent for this year's allowance for Master Huan and Master Lan."

"What's the hurry?" scolded Ping-erh. "Can't you see the young lady is washing? You should wait outside, not come butting in like this. Would you be so impertinent to the Second Mistress? The young lady may be kind-hearted, but don't blame me if my mistress hears of this and your lack of respect gets you all into trouble."

"How stupid of me!" cried the woman in dismay, then hastily left the room.

Tan-chun, now powdering her face, smiled ironically at Ping-erh.

"You came just too late to see something still more ridiculous," she said. "Even an old hand like Mrs. Wu came without checking up on her facts in order to trip us up. When challenged, she'd the nerve to say she'd forgotten. I asked if that was the way she reported to the Second Mistress. I doubt whether that mistress of yours would put up with it."

"If she tried that just once, I can promise you she'd have her legs broken," replied Ping-erh. "You can't trust these people an inch, miss. They're trying to take advantage, because Madam Chu's a real Bodhisattva and you're such a gentle young lady." Turning towards the door she called to the women outside, "All right, just take all the liberties you like. Wait till Madam Lien's well again, and we'll settle scores with you!"

The matrons outside answered, "You're most understanding, miss. You know the saying: 'If a man does wrong, he alone must take the blame.' We'd never presume to deceive Miss Tan-chun. We'd deserve to die and go unburied if we provoked a delicate young lady like her."

"So long as you know that," replied Ping-erh scornfully. Then she turned with a smile to Tan-chun. "You know how busy Madam Lien was, miss. She couldn't cope with everything and is bound to have overlooked certain things. As the proverb says, 'The spectator sees most of the sport.' As a detached observer all these years, you may have noticed cases where she failed to make suitable cuts or additions. If you'll set these right, you'll first of all be helping the mistress in her work and showing your friendship for my lady as well. . . ."

"What a clever girl!" exclaimed Pao-chai and Li Wan, smiling, before Ping-erh could finish. "No wonder Hsi-feng is so attached to you. We'd no intention of making any changes, but after what you've said we shall reconsider one or two cases to show our appreciation."

"I was so furious I wanted to work off my feelings on her mistress." Tan-chun laughed. "But turning up and talking like this she has quite taken the wind out of my sails." She called in the woman who had just come and asked her, "What are these annual allowances for Master Huan and Master Lan for?"

"For a year's refreshments at school and the remainder for stationery," was the reply. "Each gets eight taels of silver a year."

"All the young masters' expenses are covered by the monthly allowances for the different apartments," countered Tan-chun. "Huan's two taels a month are given to Concubine Chao, Pao-yu's to the old lady's maid Hsi-jen; and Lan's to Madam Chu's maid. So why this extra eight taels for the school? Do they go to school for the sake of this eight taels? From now on this will be cancelled. Tell your mistress this from me, Ping-erh, when you go back. Say I think there's no need for it."

"This should have been cut long ago," said the maid with a smile. "Last year my mistress did speak of doing it, but with all the bustle over New Year she forgot."

Then the matron had to assent and take herself off.

Now servants from Grand View Garden brought lunch hampers, and Ping-erh set out the dishes on the small table put ready by Tai-shu and Su-yun.

"You can go and attend to your business now that you've had your say," Tan-chun told her. "You don't have to help out here."

"I'm free now," replied Ping-erh, smiling. "The Second Mistress sent me partly to give you that message, partly to help the girls wait on you if I found you short-handed."

"Where's Miss Pao-chai's lunch?" asked Tan-chun.

Some girls hurried out to notify the matrons, "Miss Pao-chai's lunching here too. Have her food brought over."

Hearing this Tan-chun said loudly, "Don't start ordering them about. They're all the wives of chief stewards, not people you can send to fetch rice and tea! Have you no manners? Ping-erh has nothing to do here. Let her go."

Ping-erh promptly agreed and went out.

The stewards' wives quietly drew her aside and said, "There's no need for you to go, miss. We've already sent someone." They dusted off the steps with their handkerchiefs and urged her to have a rest there in the sun after standing for so long.

As soon as she sat down, two women from the boiler house brought over a mattress.

"That stone's cold, miss," they said. "This is quite clean, do use it."

As she thanked them with a smile, someone else brought her a bowl of good freshly brewed tea.

"This isn't our usual tea but some for the young ladies," she whispered. "Do try it."

Ping-erh inclined her head and accepted it.

Then wagging a finger at them all she scolded, "You've really gone too far. She's only a girl and, quite properly, doesn't like to lose her temper; but that's no reason why you should be rude to her. If you really made her angry, at worst she could be blamed for flaring up but you'd get into big trouble. If she made a scene, even Lady Wang would have to humour her, and there's nothing the Second Mistress could do either. How have you the nerve to slight her in that way? It's like an egg dashing itself against a rock."

"How dare we?" they protested. "It was all Concubine Chao's fault."

"That's enough, my good women," whispered Ping-erh. " 'If a wall starts tottering, everyone gives it a shove.' Concubine Chao does tend to turn things upside down, I grant you, but when there's trouble you put all the blame on her. I've seen for myself these years the airs you give yourselves and the tricks you play. If the Second Mistress weren't so able, you fine ladies would have got the upper hand of her long ago. Every chance you get, you still try to land her in trouble. Several times she's only just missed falling into your traps.

"People say you're scared of her because she's such a terror," Ping-erh continued. "But I who know her best can tell you she's afraid of you too. Only the other day, we were saying things couldn't go on like this — there were bound to be a couple of rumpuses. Though Miss Tan-chun's an unmarried young lady, you've all misjudged her. She's the only one of the young ladies that my mistress is half afraid of; yet you think you can treat her any way you please!"

They were interrupted by Chiu-wen's arrival. All the matrons greeted her and urged her to rest for a while.

"They're having lunch inside," they explained. "You'd better not go in till they've finished."

"What time have I to wait?" retorted Chiu-wen. "I'm not like you."

She was walking in when Ping-erh called her back. At sight of her Chiu-wen smiled.

"What are *you* doing here? Acting as an extra bodyguard?" she asked, sitting down by her on the mattress.

"What business brings you here?" asked Ping-erh softly.

"We want to know when the monthly allowances for Pao-yu and the rest of us will be issued."

"Very important, I must say! Go back quickly and tell Hsi-jen from me not to try to settle any business today. Every single request you make will be refused."

Chiu-wen asked the reason and all of them promptly told her.

"They're looking for some big issues and someone who counts to make an example of as a warning to everyone," Ping-erh explained. "Why should you bump *your* head against this brick wall? If you go in now, they can hardly make an example of you, out of deference to Their Ladyships; but if they don't they may be accused of bias, of not daring to touch those backed by Their Ladyships and just picking on the weak instead. Wait and see. They're even countermanding a few of the Second Mistress' rulings too — that's their only way to stop gossip."

Chiu-wen stuck out her tongue in dismay.

"Thank goodness you came here, Sister Ping-erh!" she cried. "You've saved me from a snubbing. I'll go straight back and tell them." With that she left.

At this point Pao-chai's meal arrived and Ping-erh went in to serve her. Concubine Chao had now left and the three others were eating on the couch, Pao-chai facing south, Tan-chun west and Li Wan east. The matrons waited quietly outside on the verandah, none but personal serving-maids venturing to go in.

"We'd better watch our step and not try anything on," said the matrons softly. "Mrs. Wu was sent off with a flea in her ear, and do we have more face than she does?" They decided not to go in until lunch was over.

All was quiet now inside, with no clatter of bowls or chopsticks. Presently a maid raised the portière and two others carried out the table. Three girls from the boiler house had brought three basins of water, and as soon as the table was removed they went in, reappearing before long with the basins and rinse-bowls. Then Tai-shu, Su-yun and Ying-erh took in three covered bowls of tea on trays.

When these three came out again Tai-shu instructed the younger maids, "You must see to things here till we come back from our meal. Don't sneak off to have a rest."

Then, slowly, the matrons made their reports in turn, not presuming to behave with their previous impertinence.

Tan-chun was then somewhat mollified.

Chapter 20
Artful Tzu-chuan Tests Pao-yu's Feelings

One day Pao-yu went to call on Tai-yu. She was taking a siesta, and not wishing to disturb her he joined Tzu-chuan who was sewing on the verandah.

"Was her cough any better last night?" he asked.

"A little."

"Amida Buddha! I do hope she soon gets well."

"Really, this is news to me! Since when have you started invoking Buddha?" she teased.

" 'Men at death's door will turn in desperation to any doctor,' " he quipped.

Noticing that she was wearing a thin padded silk tunic with black dots under a lined blue silk sleeveless jacket, he reached out to feel her clothes.

"You shouldn't sit in the wind so lightly dressed," he remarked. "If *you* fall ill too in this treacherous early spring weather, it will be even worse."

"When we talk to each other in future kindly keep your hands to yourself," retorted Tzu-chuan. "You're growing up now and should want people to respect you, but you keep provoking those wretches to gossip behind your back. You're so careless, you still carry on like a little boy. Well, that won't do. Our young lady's warned us many a time not to joke with you. Haven't you noticed recently how she's been avoiding you?"

She got up then and took her needlework inside.

Pao-yu felt as if doused by a bucket of cold water. He was staring blankly at the bamboo grove when Mrs. Chu came to dig up some bamboo shoots and trim the bamboos. Then, stupefied, he went away. Presently, his wits wandering, not knowing what he did, he sank down in a daze on a rock and shed tears. For the time half a dozen meals would take he sat there brooding, but could not think what to do.

It so happened that Hsueh-yen passed here now on her way back from Lady Wang's quarters with some ginseng. Turning her head towards the rock below the peach tree she noticed someone sitting there lost in thought, his face propped on his hands. To her surprise she saw it was Pao-yu.

"What's he doing here all alone on such a chilly day?" she wondered. "Spring's a dangerous time for people in delicate health. Can his wits be wandering again?"

Going over she crouched down beside him.

"What are you doing here?" she asked.

"What do *you* want with me?" countered Pao-yu as soon as he saw who it was. "Aren't you a girl too? To prevent gossip she's ordered you to ignore me, but here you come seeking me out. If you're seen, there will be talk. Hurry up and go home."

Thinking Tai-yu had been scolding him again, Hsueh-yen had to go back to Bamboo Lodge where she gave Tzu-chuan the ginseng, as their mistress was still asleep.

"If our young lady's still asleep, who's been upsetting Pao-yu?" said Hsueh-yen. "He's sitting out there crying."

"Out where?"

"Under the peach-blossom behind Seeping Fragrance Pavilion."

At once Tzu-chuan laid down her needlework.

"Be ready if she calls," she told Hsueh-yen. "If she asks for me, tell her I'll be back in a minute." So saying she left Bamboo Lodge to look for Pao-yu.

Finding him, she told him gently, "I was only thinking of what's best for us all. Why take offence and rush over here to sit crying in the wind? Are you trying to scare me by risking your health like this?"

"I didn't take offence," he answered with a smile. "You were quite right. But if everyone feels the way you do, before long nobody will speak to me at all. The thought of *that* upset me."

Tzu-chuan sat down too then beside him.

"Just now we were talking face to face but you wouldn't stay," he pointed out. "Why are you sitting right beside me now?"

"You've probably forgotten, but a few days ago you and your cousin had just started talking about bird's-nest when Concubine Chao burst in. I've just heard that she's gone out, and that reminded me to come and ask you: what more did you mean to say if she hadn't interrupted you that day?"

"Oh, nothing much," said Pao-yu. "It simply occurred to me that now that she's taking bird's-nest and has to keep it up, it's not right to impose too much on Pao-chai who's only a visitor here. As it's no use asking my mother, I dropped a hint to the old lady, and I suspect she must have told Hsi-feng. That was what I started explaining. I understand an ounce of bird's-nest is being sent over to you every day now, so that's all right."

"So it was you who suggested that, was it?" said Tzu-chuan. "That was very good of you. We've been wondering what made the old lady suddenly start sending an ounce every day. So that's the reason."

"If she takes it regularly every day, after two or three years her health should be much better."

"She can have some every day here, but where will the money come from to continue the cure when she goes home next year?"

Pao-yu gave a start.

"Who's going to which home?" he demanded.

"Your cousin — back to Soochow."

"Nonsense!" Pao-yu chuckled. "Soochow may be her home town, but she came here because there was no one there to look after her after her parents' death. Whom could she go back to next year? No, you're obviously fibbing."

"What a poor opinion you have of other people!" Tzu-chuan snorted. "You Chias may be a big, wealthy family, but do other families have only a father and mother and no other relatives?

Our young lady was brought here for a few years while she was still only a child, because the old lady felt for her and didn't think her uncles could take the place of her parents. When she grows up to marriageable age, she's bound to be sent back to the Lin family.

"How can a daughter of the Lins stay all her life with you in your Chia family? Even if the Lins were desperately poor, for generations they've been a family of scholars and officials: they'd never expose themselves to ridicule by abandoning a daughter to relatives. So next spring or next autumn at the latest, even if your family doesn't send her back, the Lins are sure to send to fetch her.

"The other evening our young lady told me to ask you for all the little gifts and souvenirs she's given you since you were children. She means to return all yours to you as well."

Pao-yu was thunderstruck. Tzu-chuan waited for him to answer, but not a word could he utter. And just then Ching-wen came up.

"So here you are, Pao-yu!" she cried. "The old lady wants you."

"He's been inquiring after Miss Tai-yu's health, and I've been reassuring him," Tzu-chuan remarked. "But he won't believe me. You'd better take him away." With that she returned to her room.

Ching-wen noticed Pao-yu's distraught look, the hectic flush on his cheeks and the sweat on his forehead. She at once led him by the hand to Happy Red Court where his appearance horrified Hsi-jen, who imagined he must have caught a chill in the wind while overheated. A fever was not too alarming, but his eyes were fixed and staring, saliva was trickling from the corners of his lips, and he seemed in a state of stupe-faction. He would lie down if a pillow was put for him, would sit up if pulled, and drink tea if it was brought. His condition threw them all into a panic, but not daring to report this too hastily to the Lady Dowager they first sent for his old nurse, Nanny Li.

Nanny Li, arriving presently, examined Pao-yu carefully. When he made no answer to any of her questions she felt his pulse, then pinched his upper lip so hard that her fingers left deep imprints — yet he felt no pain. At that she gave a great cry of despair and, taking him in her arms, started weeping and wailing.

Hsi-jen frantically pulled her away.

"Is it serious, nanny?" she demanded. "Do tell us, so that we can let the old lady and the mistress know. Don't start carrying on like this."

Nanny Li beat the bed and pillows with her fists.

"He's done for," she wailed. "A life-time of care gone for nothing!"

Hsi-jen had asked the nurse to have a look because she respected her age and experience. So now her words carried conviction. They all started sobbing.

Ching-wen told Hsi-jen then what had just happened, whereupon Hsi-jen dashed off to Bamboo Lodge. There she found Tzu-chuan giving Tai-yu her medicine. Blind to everything else, Hsi-jen flew at her.

"What have you been saying to our Pao-yu?" she demanded. "Go and *see* the state he's in! You'll have to answer for this to the old lady. I wash my hands of it." So saying she threw herself into a chair.

Tai-yu was taken aback by Hsi-jen's furious, tear-stained face and this behaviour which was so unlike her.

"What's happened?" she asked.

Making an effort to calm herself Hsi-jen sobbed, "I don't know what your Miss Tzu-chuan's been telling him, but the silly boy's eyes are staring, his hands and feet are cold; he can't speak, and when Nanny Li pinched him he felt nothing. He's more dead than alive! Even Nanny Li says there's no hope and is weeping and wailing there. He may be dead by now for all I know."

Nanny Li was such an experienced old nurse that Tai-yu could not but believe her gloomy predictions. With a cry she threw up all the medicine she had just taken, and was racked by such dry coughing that her stomach burned and it seemed her lungs would burst. Red in the face, her hair tousled, her eyes distended, limp in every limb, she choked for breath and could

not lift up her head. Tzu-chuan made haste to massage her
back while she lay gasping on her pillow.

"Stop thumping me," cried Tai-yu at last, pushing her away.
"You'd far better fetch a rope to strangle me."

"I didn't say anything," the maid protested with tears. "Just
a few words in fun, which he took seriously."

"You should know how seriously the silly boy always takes
teasing," scolded Hsi-jen.

"Whatever you said, go and clear up the misunderstanding,
quick!" urged Tai-yu. "That may bring him back to his senses."

Tzu-chuan jumped up then and hurried off with Hsi-jen to
Happy Red Court, where the old lady and Lady Wang had
already arrived. At sight of Tzu-chuan the old lady's eyes
flashed.

"You bitch!" she stormed. "What did you say to him?"

"Nothing, madam. Nothing but a few words in fun."

At the sight of her Pao-yu cried out and burst into tears, to
the relief of everybody present. The Lady Dowager caught
Tzu-chuan's arm, thinking she had offended him, and urged him
to beat her. But Pao-yu seized hold of her and would not let
go.

"If you go," he shouted, "you must take me with you!"

No one could understand this till Tzu-chuan, when questioned,
explained her threat made in fun of going back to Soochow.

"Is that all?" exclaimed the Lady Dowager, the tears running
down her cheeks. "So it was because of a joke." She scolded
Tzu-chuan, "You're such a sensible girl normally, how could
you tease him like that when you know how credulous he is?"

"Pao-yu's always been too trusting," put in Aunt Hsueh soothingly. "And since Tai-yu came here as a child and they've
grown up together, they're particularly close. This sudden talk
of her leaving would have upset even a hard-hearted grown-up,
let alone such a simple, credulous boy. But this disorder isn't
serious; you ladies mustn't worry. One or two doses of
medicine will set him right."

Just then it was announced that the wives of Lin Chih-hsiao
and Shan Ta-liang had come to inquire after the young master.

"Show them in," said the old lady. "It's thoughtful of them."

But on hearing the name Lin, Pao-yu grew frantic again.

"No, no!" he shouted from his bed. "The Lins have come to fetch her. Drive them away!"

Hastily chiming in, "Drive them away!" his grandmother assured him, "They're not from the Lin family. All *those* Lins are dead. Nobody will ever come to fetch her. Don't you worry."

"Never mind who they are," stormed Pao-yu tearfully. "No one but Cousin Tai-yu should have the name Lin."

"There are no Lins here," repeated the old lady. "They've all been driven away." She ordered the attendants, "In future don't let Lin Chih-hsiao's wife into the Garden. And never mention the name Lin again. Mind you all do as I say like good children."

Suppressing their smiles at this, the others assented.

Pao-yu's eye now fell on a golden boat with an engine, a toy from the West, which was on his cabinet.

"Isn't that the boat coming to fetch them?" he shouted, pointing at it. "It's mooring there."

The Lady Dowager ordered its instant removal, and when Pao-yu reached out for it Hsi-jen gave it to him. He tucked it under his bedding.

"Now they won't be able to sail away," he laughed. Seizing tight hold of Tzu-chuan he refused to let her go.

At this point Doctor Wang was announced, and the old lady ordered him to be brought straight in. Lady Wang, Aunt Hsueh and Pao-chai withdrew to the inner room while the Lady Dowager seated herself by Pao-yu. When Doctor Wang found such a company assembled, he paid his respects to the Lady Dowager before taking Pao-yu's hand to feel his pulse, while Tzu-chuan had to stand there with lowered head, to the doctor's astonishment.

Presently the doctor rose and declared, "The trouble with our honourable brother is that some sharp distress has clouded his mind. According to the ancients, 'Disorders of the phlegm take different forms: indigestion owing to a weak constitution, derangement brought on by a sudden fit of anger, and obstruction caused by sudden distress.' This is a disorder of the third kind. It is only a temporary blockage, however, less serious than the other types."

"Just tell us if he's in danger or not," urged the Lady Dowager. "Who wants to hear this recital of medical lore?"

Doctor Wang bowed.

"He is in no danger, no."

"Is that really true?" she persisted.

"There is really no danger, madam, I give you my word."

"In that case, please take a seat in the outer room to make out your prescription. If you cure him, I shall prepare presents to show my gratitude and send him to kowtow to you in person. If you delay his recovery, though, I shall send to tear down the main hall of your Academy of Imperial Physicians!"

The doctor bowed again.

"You are too good, too good!"

For he had heard only the first part of her speech and not the jocular threat with which it concluded. He went on protesting his unworthiness until the old lady and all the rest burst out laughing.

When the medicine had been prepared according to the prescription and Pao-yu had taken it, he did indeed calm down a little. He still refused to let go of Tzu-chuan, however.

"If she leaves here, they'll go back to Soochow!" he cried.

The Lady Dowager and Lady Wang had perforce to let Tzu-chuan stay there. They dispatched Hu-po in her place to look after Tai-yu, who from time to time sent Hsueh-yen over to ask for news and was deeply moved when she learned all that had happened.

As everyone knew how cranky Pao-yu was, and how close he and Tai-yu had been since they were children, they took Tzu-chuan's joke as quite natural and his illness as nothing out of the way either, not suspecting anything else.

That evening, as Pao-yu was quieter, his grandmother and mother returned to their own quarters but sent several times during the night for reports from the sickroom. Nanny Li,

Mrs. Sung and some other matrons nursed the patient devotedly, while Tzu-chuan, Hsi-jen and Ching-wen watched day and night by his bedside. Whenever he slept he had nightmares, and would wake up crying that Tai-yu had gone or that people had come to fetch her. Each time this happened Tzu-chuan had to comfort him.

Now his grandmother had Pao-yu given all sorts of rare medicine — pills to dispel evil influences and powders to clear the mind. And the next day, after more of Doctor Wang's medicine, his condition gradually improved; but although he was in his right senses again, he pretended from time to time to be delirious in order to keep Tzu-chuan with him. As for her, thoroughly repenting the mischief she had caused she served him day and night without a murmur.

Hsi-jen, herself once more, told her, "As you're the one to blame for this, it's up to you to cure him. I've never seen such a simpleton as our young master, the way he catches at shadows. What's to become of him?" But enough of this.

By now Hsiang-yun was better, and she came every day to see Pao-yu. Finding that he had recovered his faculties she mimicked his crazy behaviour during his illness until, lying on his pillow, he had to laugh. Having no idea himself of what had passed, he could hardly believe what was told him.

When no one else was about but Tzu-chuan, he took her hand. "Why did you frighten me?" he asked.

"I only did it for fun," she replied. "But you took it seriously."

"You made it sound so convincing, how was I to know it was just a joke?" he retorted.

"Well, I made the whole thing up. There's really no one left in the Lin family except for some very distant relatives who no longer live in Soochow but are scattered in different provinces. Even if one of them asked for her, the old lady would never let her go."

"Even if the old lady would let her go, *I* wouldn't."

"*You* wouldn't!" Tzu-chuan laughed. "That's just talk, I'm

afraid. You're growing up now and already engaged; in a couple of years you'll be marrying, and then you'll forget other people."

"Who's engaged?" asked Pao-yu in dismay. "To whom?"

"Before New Year I heard the old lady say she wanted to engage Miss Pao-chin to you. Why else would she make such a favourite of her?"

He laughed.

"People may call me crazy, but you're even crazier! That was just a joke. She's already engaged to the son of Academician Mei. If I were engaged to her, would I be in this state? Didn't you plead with me and say I was mad when I swore that oath and wanted to smash that silly jade? Now you've come to provoke me again just as I'm getting better." Through clenched teeth he added, "I only wish I could die this very minute and tear out my heart to show you. Then all the rest of me, skin and bones, could be turned into ashes — no, ashes still have form — better be turned into smoke. But smoke still congeals and can be seen by men — it would have to be scattered in a flash, by a great wind, to the four quarters. *That* would be a good death." Tears were running down his cheeks as he spoke.

Tzu-chuan hastily put her hand to his mouth, then wiped away his tears.

"You needn't worry," she urged. "I was putting you to the test because *I* was worried."

"You worried? Why?" he asked in surprise.

"You know I don't belong to the Lin family. Like Hsi-jen and Yuan-yang, I was *given* to Miss Lin. And she couldn't have been kinder to me. She treats me ten times better than her own maids brought from Soochow; we don't like being parted for a single moment. I'm worried now because, if she leaves, I shall have to go with her; but my whole family's here. If I don't go, I'll be unworthy of all her goodness; if I do, I shall have to abandon my own people. That's why, in my dilemma, I told you that fib to see how you felt about it. How was I to know you'd take it so hard?"

"So that's what's worrying you," Pao-yu chuckled. "What a goose you are! Well, set your heart at rest. Let me just put it in a nutshell for you. If we live, we shall live together; and if we die, we shall turn into ashes and smoke together. What do you say to that?"

Tzu-chuan was turning this over in her mind when suddenly Chia Huan and Chia Lan were announced. They had called to ask after Pao-yu.

"Thank them for coming," he said. "But tell them I've just gone to bed and they needn't trouble to come in."

The woman who had brought the message assented and left.

"Now that you're better you should let me go back to see my own patient," said Tzu-chuan.

"I know," he replied. "I meant to send you yesterday, but then I forgot. Go along then, since I'm completely well again."

She set about bundling together her bedding and dressing-cases.

"I see several mirrors in your cases," he commented laughingly. "Will you leave me that small one? I can keep it by my pillow to use in bed, and it will come in handy when I go out."

Tzu-chuan had to do as he asked. Having sent her things on ahead, she took her leave of everyone and went back to Bamboo Lodge.

The news of Pao-yu's disorder had made Tai-yu suffer a relapse and brought on many bouts of weeping. Now she asked Tzu-chuan why she had returned and, learning that he was better, sent Hu-po back to wait on the Lady Dowager.

That night, when all was quiet and Tzu-chuan had undressed and lain down, she whispered to Tai-yu:

"Pao-yu's heart is really true to you. Fancy his falling ill like that when he heard we were leaving!"

Tai-yu made no answer to this.

Presently Tzu-chuan went on, half to herself, "Moving isn't as good as staying put. This is a good family anyway. It's the hardest thing in the world to find people who've grown up together and know each other's character and ways."

"Aren't you tired after the last few days?" scoffed Tai-yu. "Why don't you sleep instead of talking such nonsense?"

"It isn't nonsense. I was thinking of you. I've felt worried for you all these years with no father, mother or brothers to care for you. The important thing is to settle the main affair of your life in good time, while the old lady's still clear-headed and healthy. The proverb says, 'The healthiest old people last as long as a chilly spring or a hot autumn.' If anything should happen to the old lady your marriage might be delayed, or else not turn out in the way you hoped.

"There's no lack of young lordlings, but they all want three wives and five concubines and their affections change from one day to the next. They may bring home a wife as lovely as a fairy, yet after four or five nights they cast her off, treating her like an enemy for the sake of a concubine or a slave girl. If her family's large and powerful, that's not so bad; and for someone like you, miss, so long as the old lady lives you'll be all right. Once she's gone, you'll have to put up with ill treatment. So it's important to make up your mind. You've sense enough to understand the saying, 'Ten thousand taels of gold are easier come by than an understanding heart.'"

"The girl's crazy!" exclaimed Tai-yu. "A few days away, and you've suddenly changed into a different person. Tomorrow I shall ask the old lady to take you back. *I* no longer dare keep you."

"I meant well," was the smiling answer. "I just wanted you to look out for yourself, not to do anything wrong. What good will it do if you report me to the old lady and get me into trouble?" With that Tzu-chuan closed her eyes.

Although Tai-yu had spoken so sharply, this talk had distressed her. After Tzu-chuan went to sleep she wept all night, not dozing off until dawn.

Chapter 21
Girls Feast at Night to Celebrate Pao-yu's Birthday

By now Pao-yu's birthday had come round.

Pao-you told Hsi-jen, "We mustn't stand on ceremony tonight but drink and enjoy our-selves. Let them know in good time what dishes we want so that they'll have them ready."

"Don't worry," she replied. "Ching-wen, Sheh-yueh, Chiu-wen and I have contributed half a tael of silver each, which makes two taels; and Fang-kuan, Pi-heng, Hsiao-yen and Ssu-erh have each given thirty cents. So, apart from those who are away, we've raised three taels and twenty cents which we've already given to Mrs. Liu, who's preparing forty dishes. I've also arranged with Ping-erh to have a vat of good Shaohsing wine smuggled in. The eight of us are going to throw a birthday party for you."

Pao-yu was delighted but demurred, "How can they afford it? You shouldn't have made them chip in."

Ching-wen demanded, "Do we have money and not they? All of us are just showing our feeling. Never mind whether they can afford it. Even if they steal the money, just you accept it."

"That's right," said Pao-yu.

"It seems that you can't be satisfied unless she gives you a few digs every day," chuckled Hsi-jen.

"Now you're learning bad ways too," shot back Ching-wen. "Always goading others on to stir up trouble!"

At that all three laughed, after which Pao-yu proposed locking the courtyard gate. But Hsi-jen objected:

"No wonder people say you're for ever making a great ado about nothing. If we lock the gate now that will arouse suspicion. Better wait a bit."

Pao-yu nodded.

Now, as the time came to light the lamps, they heard people approaching the courtyard gate and when they peeped through the window saw Mrs. Lin with a few other stewards' wives, the one in front carrying a big lantern.

"They're making their nightly check-up of those on duty," whispered Ching-wen. "Once they've gone we can close the gate."

All the servants on night duty in Happy Red Court had gone out to meet these women. After checking that they were all present Mrs. Lin warned them:

"No gambling or drinking now, and no sleeping till morning! If I hear of such goings-on I'll have something to say."

"Which of us would dare?" they answered laughingly.

Then Mrs. Lin asked, "Is Master Pao in bed yet?"

As they replied that they did not know, Hsi-jen nudged Pao-yu, who put on slippers to go out to greet them.

"No, I'm not in bed yet," he called. "Come in and sit down." Looking towards the house, he ordered: "Serve tea, Hsi-jen."

Mrs. Lin entered then, smiling.

"Still up!" she exclaimed. "Now the days are long, the nights short, you should go to bed early so as to get up early tomorrow. Otherwise you may oversleep, and people will jeer that you don't behave like a scholarly young gentleman but like a common coolie." Having said this she laughed.

Pao-yu promptly agreed, "You're right, nanny. I do generally go to bed early, so that I don't know when you come every evening because I'm already asleep. But today after eating noodles I was afraid of getting indigestion; that's why I've stayed up a bit."

Mrs. Lin advised Hsi-jen and Ching-wen to brew him some

puerh tea.

"We've made him some *nuerh* tea[1] and he's drunk two bowls. Won't you try some, madam?" they answered. "It's already brewed."

As Ching-wen poured a bowl Mrs. Lin observed, "Recently I've noticed that the Second Master always calls you girls by your names. Though you're working here you belong to Their Ladyships, so he should show more respect. If once in a while he happens to use your names, that doesn't matter; but if this becomes a habit then his cousins and nephews may follow suit, and then people will laugh at us and say we've no respect for elders in our household."

"You're right, nanny," agreed Pao-yu again. "Actually I only do that once in a while."

The two girls put in, "You must be fair to him. Even now he still refers to us as 'elder sisters,' only using our names occasionally in fun. In front of others he always addresses us as he did before."

"That's good," approved Mrs. Lin. "That's how someone with education and good manners ought to behave. The more modest you are, the more respected you'll be. Not to say members of the staff of long standing or those transferred from Their Ladyships' apartments, but even the dogs and cats from there mustn't be badly treated. That's the way a well brought up young gentleman should behave." She then drank up her tea and said, "We must be off now. I'll wish you a good night."

Pao-yu pressed them to stay, but Mrs. Lin had already led her party off to finish making their rounds. At once Ching-wen and others ordered the gate to be locked, and coming back Ching-wen said:

---

[1] *Puerh* tea, a green tea from Yunnan, is good for the digestion. *Nuerh* tea is not really tea but brewed from tender *wutung* leaves grown in the Taishan Mountains.

"That grandame must have been drinking, gabbing away and nagging at us like that."

"She means well anyway," remarked Sheh-yueh as she started to lay the table. "She has to remind us from time to time to be on our guard and not overstep the limits."

"We don't need that high table," put in Hsi-jen. "Let's put that round low pear-wood one on the *kang*. There's room for all of us at it, and it's more convenient."

So they carried the table over, after which Sheh-yueh and Ssu-erh fetched the dishes, making four or five trips with two big trays while two old women squatting outside by the brazier warmed the wine.

"It's so hot, let's take off our outer clothes," Pao-yu suggested.

"You can if you want to," said the girls, "but we have to take it in turns to offer toasts."

"If you do that it'll take all night," he objected. "You know how much I dislike those vulgar conventions. We may have to observe them in front of outsiders, but if *you* provoke me like that it won't be nice."

"We'll do as you say," they agreed.

Hsi-jen and the rest poured wine for each.

Hsi-jen held the first cup to her lips and took a sip, to be followed by the others, after which all sat down in a circle. As there was insufficient room on the *kang*, Hsiao-yen and Ssu-erh set two chairs beside it. The forty white *Ting* ware dishes no bigger than saucers held all manner of sweetmeats and delicacies of land and sea, fresh or preserved, from every part of the country and from abroad. And now Pao-yu proposed playing some drinking games.

"Something quiet, not too rowdy," advised Hsi-jen. "We don't want people to hear us. And nothing too literary either, as we're no scholars."

"How about the dice game 'Grabbing the Red'?" said Sheh-yueh.

"That's no fun," objected Pao-yu. "Better play the 'Flower

Game.' "

"Yes, do let's!" cried Ching-wen. "I've always wanted to play that."

"It's a good game," agreed Hsi-jen, "but no fun for just a few people."

"I've an idea," put in Hsiao-yen. "Let's quietly invite Miss Pao-chai and Miss Tai-yu over to play for a short time. It won't matter if we go on till the second watch."

"If we go around knocking different people up, we may run into some night-watchers," Hsi-jen pointed out.

"Don't be afraid," said Pao-yu. "My Third Sister likes drinking too; we should count her in. Hurry up and invite them."

Hsiao-yen and Ssu-erh, who had been awaiting this order, immediately called for the gate to be unlocked and went off to the different apartments.

"They may not be able to get Miss Pao-chai and Miss Tai-yu," predicted the senior maids. "We'll have to go and drag them here by main force." So, telling an old woman to bring a lantern, Hsi-jen and Ching-wen went off as well.

Sure enough, Pao-chai objected that it was too late while Tai-yu pleaded poor health, but the two maids begged them:

"Do give us a little face. Just go and sit there for a while."

As for Tan-chun, she was eager to come but felt that if Li Wan were left out and came to hear of it later that wouldn't be good; so she told Tsui-mo and Hsiao-yen to insist that Li Wan should be invited. Presently they all arrived, one by one, at Happy Red Court. Another table had to be put on the *kang* before they could all sit down.

"Cousin Tai-yu feels the cold," said Pao-yu. "Come and sit by the partition."

She was given a cushion for her back while Hsi-jen and the other maids fetched chairs and seated themselves beside the *kang*.

Leaning against her back-rest some way from the table, Tai-yu teased Pao-chai, Li Wan and Tan-chun, "You're always accusing people of drinking and gambling at night, and now that's just what *we're* doing. How can we blame others in future?"

"It doesn't matter," replied Li Wan, "if we only do this on birthdays or festivals, not every night. There's nothing to be afraid of."

As she was speaking, Ching-wen brought in a carved bamboo container filled with ivory slips bearing the names of flowers. Having shaken this she put it down in the middle. Next she brought the dice-box and shook it, and upon opening the box saw that the number on the dice was five. She counted, starting from herself, and Pao-chai being the fifth was the one who should start.

"I'll draw," said Pao-chai. "I wonder what I shall get."

She shook the container and took out a slip on which they saw the picture of a peony with the words "Beauty surpassing all flowers." Inscribed in smaller characters beneath was the line of Tang poetry, "Though heartless she has charm." The instructions read, "All the feasters must drink a cup by way of congratulations, for this is the queen of the flowers. She can order anyone to compose a poem or tell a joke to enliven the drinking."

"What a coincidence!" all exclaimed laughingly. "A peony is just the flower for you." With that they drank a cup each.

Pao-yu, holding the slip of ivory, had been softly repeating to himself, "Though heartless she has charm," lost in thought. Now Hsiang-yun snatched the slip from him and gave it to Pao-chai who threw sixteen, which made it Tan-chun's turn.

"I wonder what I'll get," she said with a smile.

But having drawn a slip out and seen what it was, she threw it down.

"We shouldn't play this game," she declared with a blush. "It's a game for those men outside, a whole lot of silly nonsense."

The others were wondering what she meant when Hsi-jen picked up the slip for all to see. Under the picture of an apricot-blossom were the words in red "Fairy flower from paradise" and the verse "A red apricot by the sun grows in the clouds." The directions were: "Whoever draws this will have a noble husband. All must drink to her, then drink another cup together."

"Is that all?" they laughed. "This is a game for the inner apartments. Apart from a couple of slips with mottoes like these, there's nothing improper; so what does it matter? Our family already has one Imperial Consort; are you going to be another? Congratulations!"

They all raised their cups, but Tan-chun would not drink this toast until compelled to by Hsiang-yun, and Li Wan.

When she protested, "Let's give up this game and play another," they would not agree, and Hsiang-yun held her hand, forcing her to throw the dice. The number nineteen coming up, it was Li Wan's turn. She shook the container, took out a slip, and smiled when she saw what it was. "Excellent!" she crowed. "Just see what I've got. This is fun."

They saw the picture of an old plum-tree with the motto "Cold beauty in frosty dawn" and the line of verse "Content to stay by the bamboo fence and thatched hut." The instructions were: "Whoever draws this lot must drink a cup, then the one whose turn comes next must throw the dice."

"That's fine," said Li Wan. "You go on dicing while I just drink one cup without worrying how the rest of you get on."

She drained her cup and passed the dice to Tai-yu, who threw eighteen, making it Hsiang-yun's turn. Hsiang-yun rolled up her sleeves to draw her lot, a picture of crab-apple-blossom with the motto "Deep in a fragrant dream" and the line "So late at night the flower may fall asleep."

They read the instructions, "As she is deep in a fragrant sleep and cannot drink, the two next to her must each drink a cup instead."

Hsiang-yun clapped her hands.

"Amida Buddha!" she cried. "This is really a lucky dip!"

It so happened that Tai-yu and Pao-yu were on either side of her, so they both filled their cups. Hsiang-yun then threw a nine, which made it Sheh-yueh's turn. On the lot she drew they saw a rose with the motto "Flower of final splendour" and the line "When the rose blooms, spring flowers fade." Below was written, "All at the feast should drink three cups each to farewell the spring."

When Sheh-yueh asked what was written there, Pao-yu frowned and hid the slip, saying, "We must all drink." So they took three sips each to symbolize three cups.

Now it came to Tai-yu's turn. "I hope I get something good," she thought while drawing a lot. It showed a hibiscus flower with the motto "Quiet and sad in wind and dew" and the line "Blame not the east wind but yourself." The instruction was: "Both hibiscus and peony must drink a cup."

"Fine!" cried the others. "She's the only one here fit to be compared to a hibiscus."

Tai-yu smiled too as she drank, then threw a twenty which made it Hsi-jen's turn.

Hsi-jen drew a picture of peach-blossom with the motto "Exotic scene at Wuling" and the line "Another spring returns and the peach blooms red." The instructions were, "The apricot-blossom, as well as those born in the same year, on the same day and those with the same surname must drink one cup."

"This one is lively and good fun," cried the rest.

They worked it out that Ching-wen and Pao-chai were the same age as Hsi-jen, while Tai-yu's birthday fell on the same day.

As they filled their cups Tai-yu remarked to Tan-chun, "You're the apricot-blossom destined to have a noble husband. So drink up quickly and we'll follow suit."

"Stop talking nonsense!" retorted Tan-chun. "Sister-in-law, give her a slap."

"She hasn't got a noble husband and now you want me to beat her," teased Li Wan. "No, I can't bring myself to do it."

At that they all laughed.

Hsi-jen was about to throw the dice when they heard someone at the gate. An old woman went to see who was there and found it was a maid sent by Aunt Hsueh to fetch Tai-yu back.

"What time is it?" everyone asked.

"After the second watch," the maid informed them. "The clock's just struck eleven."

Pao-yu could not believe it was so late, but when he called for his watch and looked at the time it was ten past eleven.

"I can't stay up any longer," said Tai-yu getting up. "I have to take medicine too after I go back."

All agreed that it was time to disperse, so when Hsi-jen and Pao-yu tried to keep them Li Wan and Pao-chai demurred:

"It doesn't look right being so late. We've already made an exception to our rule."

"In that case," said Hsi-jen, "let's each have one final cup."

Ching-wen and the others filled the cups, and after drinking them they called for lanterns. Hsi-jen and the rest, having seen the visitors past Seeping Fragrance Pavilion to the other side of the stream, came back and locked the gate.

Chapter 22
A Hen-Pecked Young Profligate Takes
a Concubine in Secret

One day, some servants from the Eastern Mansion came rushing up frantically. "The old master's ascended to Heaven!" they announced.

Everybody was consternated.

"He wasn't even ill, how could he pass away so suddenly?" they exclaimed.

The servants explained, "His Lordship took elixirs every day; now he must have achieved his aim and become an immortal."

Madam Yu was most worried by this news; for as her husband Chia Chen, their son Chia Jung, and Chia Lien too were all away, there was no man at home to take charge. She hurriedly took off her finery and sent a steward to Mysterious Truth Temple to have all the Taoist priests there locked up until her husband came back to question them. Then she hastily went by carriage out of the city with the wives of Lai Sheng and some other stewards, having also sent for doctors to see what illness her father-in-law had succumbed to.

As Chia Ching was dead it was no use for the doctors to feel his pulse. They knew, however, that for years he had been practising absurd Taoist breathing exercises. As for his yoga, worship of the stars, keeping vigil on certain nights, taking sulphide of mercury and wearing himself out with his senseless striving for immortality — these were what had carried him off. His belly after death was hard as iron, the skin of his face and lips parched, cracked and purple. They reported to the serving-women that he had died of excessive heat as a result of taking Taoist drugs.

The Taoist priests in their panic confessed, "His Lordship had just concocted a new elixir with some secret formula, and that was his undoing. We'd warned him not to take such things before achieving a certain potency; but last night, during his vigil, unknown to us he took some and became an immortal. Doubtless he has attained immortality owing to his piety, leaving this sea of woe and sloughing his earthly integument to fare forth at will."

Madam Yu, shutting her ears to this, ordered them to be immured until Chia Chen's return. And she sent messengers posthaste to take the news. Seeing that the temple was too cramped for the coffin to be left there, and as it could not be taken into the city, she had the corpse shrouded and conveyed by sedan-chair to Iron Threshold Temple. She reckoned that her husband could not be back for another fortnight at least, and as the weather was too hot for the funeral to be delayed she decided to get an astrologer to choose a day for it. As the coffin had been prepared many years ago, and kept ever since in the temple, the funeral was easily managed. Three days later a mourning service was held and further masses were performed while waiting for Chia Chen. Since Hsi-feng of the Jung Mansion could not leave home and Li Wan had to look after the girls, while Pao-yu knew nothing of practical affairs, the work outside was entrusted to a few second-rank stewards. Chia Pien, Chia Kuang, Chia Heng, Chia Ying, Chia Chang and Chia Ling also had their different assignments. Madam Yu, being unable to go home, invited her step-mother old Mrs. Yu to come and keep an eye on things in the Ning Mansion. And Mrs. Yu, to be easy in her mind, had to bring her two unmarried daughters with her.

Chia Lien had long heard of Madam Yu's lovely step-sisters and longed to meet them. Recently, with Chia Ching's coffin in the house, he had been seeing Second Sister and Third Sister every day so that he was on familiar terms with them and had designs on them too. Knowing how free and easy both girls were with Chia Chen and Chia Jung, he tried in a hundred ways to convey his own feelings, casting arch glances at them. Third Sister only treated him coolly, however, while Second Sister appeared very interested; but since there were so many people about he could not make any advances. Fear of arousing Chia Chen's jealousy also kept him from acting too rashly. So the two of them had to be content with a secret understanding.

After the funeral, however, there were few people left in Chia Chen's house. The main quarters were occupied only by old Mrs. Yu and her two daughters attended by a few of the maids and serving-women who did the rough work, all the senior maids and concubines having gone to the temple. As for the female servants who lived outside, they simply kept watch at night and minded the gate in the daytime, and would not go inside unless they had business. So Chia Lien was eager to make good use of this chance. He spent the nights in the temple too, on the pretext of keeping Chia Chen company; but he often slipped back to the Ning Mansion to inveigle Second Sister, telling Chia Chen that he was going to see to the family affairs for him.

One day the young steward Yu Lu came to report to Chia Chen, "The funeral sheds, mourning clothes and blue uniforms for attendants and carriers cost a thousand taels in all, of which we've paid five hundred; so we're still five hundred short, and the tradesmen have sent to ask for payment. That's why I've come for your instructions, sir."

"Just get the money from the treasury. Why come and ask me for it?" said Chia Chen.

"I did go to the treasury yesterday," Yu Lu replied. "But since His Lordship's demise there have been all sorts of expenses, and the money on hand is being kept for the hundred days' masses and for use in the temple; so for the moment they can't issue me any. That's why I've come specially to report to you. Perhaps this sum could be taken from the inner treasury for the time being, or raised some other way. Just give me your orders and I'll carry them out."

"Do you think this is like the old days when we had silver

lying idle?" retorted Chia Chen. "Go and borrow some for the time being, I don't care from where."

Yu Lu smiled.

"I can probably raise a couple of hundred taels somewhere," he said. "But how can I get hold of four or five hundred so fast?"

Chia Chen thought it over, then instructed Chia Jung, "Go and ask your mother for this sum. After the funeral the Chen family in the south sent us five hundred taels for a sacrifice. That money arrived yesterday, and we haven't sent it to the treasury yet. Get that first and give it to him."

Chia Jung assented and went over to tell his mother, coming back to report:

"We've already spent two hundred of the five that arrived yesterday. The remaining three hundred were sent home today to be kept by granny."

"In that case, take Yu Lu along and get it from her. You can also make sure that all's well at home and ask after your two aunts. Yu Lu can borrow the rest."

Chia Jung and Yu Lu agreed and were just starting out when Chia Lien came in. Yu Lu stepped forward to pay his respects. Chia Lien asked what he had come for, and Chia Chen told him. At once Chia Lien thought, "This is a chance for me to go to the Ning Mansion and see Second Sister."

"This is a small sum," he said. "Why borrow from others? Yesterday I received some silver which I haven't spent yet. Better give him that for this payment to save trouble."

"Fine," said Chia Chen. "Send Jung along and tell him how to get it."

"I shall have to get it myself," said Chia Lien hastily. "Besides, I haven't been home these last few days; I ought to go and pay my respects to the old lady and my other elders. Then I'll go to your place to make sure that the servants aren't making trouble, and call on old Mrs. Yu as well."

"I don't like putting you to so much trouble," objected Chia Chen.

"What does it matter between cousins?" Chia Lien answered.

So Chia Chen told his son, "Go with your uncle, and mind you go too to pay your respects to the old lady, master and mistresses of the other house. Give them our regards and ask if the old lady is better now or still taking medicine."

Chia Jung assented and went off with Chia Lien. Taking a few pages with them, they mounted their horses and rode back to the city, chatting idly on the way.

Then Chia Lien deliberately mentioned Second Sister Yu, praising her for her good looks and modest behaviour, her lady-like ways and gentle speech, as if she were a paragon admired and loved by all.

"Everyone praises your Aunt Hsi-feng," he said, "but to my mind she can't stand comparison with your Second Aunt."

Chia Jung, knowing his game, rejoined, "If you've taken such a fancy to her, uncle, I'll act as your go-between to make her your secondary wife. How about that?"

"That would be fine!" Chia Lien beamed. "I'm only afraid your Aunt Hsi-feng wouldn't agree, and neither might your grandmother. Besides, I heard that your Second Aunt is already engaged."

"That doesn't matter," Chia Jung assured him. "My second and third aunts aren't my grandfather's daughters but only step-daughters. I've been told that while old Mrs. Yu was in the other family she promised her second daughter, before the child was born, to the Chang family who managed the Imperial Farm. Later the Changs were ruined by a lawsuit, and she herself married again into the Yu family. Now, for the last ten years or so, the two families have lost touch completely. Old Mrs. Yu often complains that she'd like to break off the engagement, and my father also wants to find Second Aunt a different husband. As soon as they've picked a suitable family, all they need do is send someone to find the Changs, pay them a dozen or so taels of silver, and have a deed written breaking off the betrothal. The Changs are so hard up that when they see the silver they're bound to agree; on top of which they'll know that in dealing with a family like ours they can't do anything else. If a gentleman like you, uncle, wants her as a secondary wife, I guarantee both her mother and my father will be willing. The only problem is my Aunt Hsi-feng."

At this Chia Lien was too overjoyed to speak and could only grin foolishly.

After a little reflection Chia Jung continued, "If you have the nerve to do as I say, uncle, I guarantee it will be all right. It will simply mean spending a little extra money."

"What's your plan? Out with it quick! Of course I'll agree."

"Don't let on a word about this when you go home. Wait till I've told my father and settled it with my grandmother; then we'll buy a house and the furnishings for it somewhere near the back of our mansion, and install a couple of our servants and their wives there. That done, we'll choose a day and you can get married on the sly. We'll forbid the servants to tell anyone about it. As Aunt Hsi-feng lives tucked away inside the big mansion, how can she possibly get to know of it? Then you'll have *two* homes, uncle. After a year or so, if word does get out, at most you'll get reprimanded by your father; but you can say that as my aunt had no son you arranged this in secret outside, in the hope of having descendants. When Aunt Hsi-feng sees that the rice is already cooked, she'll have to put up with it; and if you ask the old lady then to put in a word for you, the whole thing will blow over."

As the old proverb says, "Lust befuddles the mind." Chia Lien was so infatuated by Second Sister's beauty that he felt Chia Jung's plan was foolproof, completely forgetting that he was in mourning and how inappropriate it was to have a concubine outside when he had a stern father and jealous wife at home.

As for Chia Jung, he had ulterior motives. He was attached to both his young aunts, but his father's presence at home cramped his style. If Chia Lien married Second Sister he would have to have a separate establishment outside, where Chia Jung could go to fool about in his absence.

Of course none of this occurred to Chia Lien, who thanked him saying, "Good nephew, if you fix this up I'll buy you two really ravishing maids."

By now they had reached the Ning Mansion and Chia Jung said, "Uncle, while you go in to get the silver from my grandmother and give it to Yu Lu, I'll go on ahead to call on the old lady."

Chia Lien nodded, then said with a smile, "Don't tell the old lady that I've come with you."

"I know." Chia Jung whispered then into his ear, "If you see Second Aunt today, don't act too rashly. If there's any trouble now, it will make things more difficult in future."

"Don't talk rot," chuckled Chia Lien. "Go on. I'll wait for you here."

Chia Jung accordingly went to pay his respects to the Lady Dowager.

When Chia Lien entered the Ning Mansion, some of the stewards stepped forward with other servants to pay their respects and followed him to the hall. Chia Lien questioned them briefly for appearance's sake, then dismissed them and went in alone. As he and Chia Chen were cousins and on a close footing, he was not subject to any restrictions here and did not need to wait to be announced. He went straight to the main apartment. The old woman on duty in the corridor lifted the portière as soon as she saw him; and on entering the room he saw Second Sister sewing with two maids on the couch on the south side, but of old Mrs. Yu and Third Sister there was no sign. Chia Lien went forward to greet Second Sister, who asked him to take a seat, and he sat down with his back to the east partition.

After an exchange of civilities he asked, "Where are your mother and Third Sister? Why aren't they here?"

"They just went to the back for something; they'll be here soon," she told him.

As the maids had gone to fetch tea and there was no one else present, Chia Lien kept darting smiling glances at Second Sister, who lowered her head to hide a smile but did not respond, and he dared not make any further advances. Seeing that she was toying with the handkerchief to which her pouch was fastened, he felt his waist as if groping for his own pouch.

"I've forgotten to bring my pouch of betel-nuts," he said. "Will you let me try one of yours, sister?"

"I have some, but I never give mine away."

Smiling, he approached her to take one; and afraid this would look bad if someone came in, she laughingly tossed him her pouch. Having caught it he emptied it out, chose one half-eaten nut which he popped into his mouth, then pocketed all the others. He was about to return the pouch when the two maids came back with the tea. As Chia Lien sipped his tea, he surreptitiously took off a Han-Dynasty jade pendant carved with nine dragons and tied this to her handkerchief. And when both maids were looking the other way, he tossed the handkerchief back. Second Sister just let it lie and went on drinking her tea, as if she had not noticed. Then the portière behind them swished and in came old Mrs. Yu and Third Sister with two young maids. With a wink Chia Lien signalled to Second Sister to pick up the handkerchief, but she simply paid no attention; and not knowing what she meant by this he felt frantic. He had to step forward to greet the newcomers. As he did so, he glanced back at Second Sister, who was still smiling as if nothing had happened. But looking again he noticed with relief that the handkerchief had vanished. They all sat down now and chatted for a while.

"My sister-in-law says she gave you some silver the other day to keep for her, madam," said Chia Lien. "Today they have to settle an account, so Cousin Chen sent me to fetch it and to see if everything is all right at home."

On hearing this old Mrs. Yu immediately sent Second Sister to fetch the key and get the silver.

Chia Lien went on, "I wanted to come anyway to pay my respects to you and see both the young ladies. It's good of you to have come here, madam, but we're sorry to be putting our two cousins to such trouble too."

"What way is that for close relatives to talk!" she protested. "We've made ourselves at home here. The truth is, sir, that since my husband died we've found it hard to make ends meet, and we've only managed thanks to my son-in-law's help. Now that they have their hands full, we can't help in any other way but at least we can keep an eye on things here for them — how can you talk of putting us to trouble?"

By now Second Sister had brought the silver and given it to her mother, who passed it to Chia Lien. He sent a young maid to fetch a serving-woman.

"Give this to Yu Lu," he ordered her. "Tell him to take it back to the other house and wait for me there."

As the old woman assented and left, they heard Chia Jung's voice in the courtyard; and presently in he came to pay his respects to the ladies.

"Just now His Lordship your father was asking about you, uncle," he said. "He has some business he wants you to see to and was going to send to the temple to fetch you, but I told him you'd be coming presently. His Lordship told me, if I met you, to ask you to hurry."

As Chia Lien rose to leave he heard Chia Jung tell old Mrs. Yu, "The young man I told you about the other day, grandmother, the one my father has in mind for Second Aunt, has much the same features and build as this uncle of mine. How does he strike you, madam?"

As he said this he pointed slyly at Chia Lien and motioned with his lips at Second Sister. She was too embarrassed to say anything, but her sister scolded:

"What a devilish monkey you are! Have you nothing else to talk about? Just wait, I'm going to pull out that tongue of yours."

She ran towards him but Chia Jung had slipped out, laughing, and now Chia Lien took his leave of them with a smile. In the hall he cautioned the servants not to gamble and drink, then secretly urged Chia Jung to hurry back and take the matter up with his father. Next he took Yu Lu over to the other house to make up the sum of silver needed; and while the steward went off with this he paid his respects to his father ánd the Lady Dowager.

To return to Chia Jung, when he saw that Yu Lu and Chia Lien had gone for the money and he had nothing to do, he went in again to fool around with his two aunts before leaving.

It was evening by the time he got back to the temple and reported to his father, "The money's been given to Yu Lu. The old lady's much better now and has stopped taking medicine." He then took this opportunity to describe how Chia Lien had told him on the road of his wish to make Second Sister Yu his secondary wife and set up house outside, so that Hsi-feng should know nothing about it.

"This is just because he's worried at having no son," Chia Jung explained. "And as he's seen Second Aunt, who's already related to our family, marrying her would be better than getting some girl from a family about which we know nothing. So uncle repeatedly begged me to propose this to you, father." He omitted to say that this idea had originated with him.

Chia Chen thought it over.

"Actually, it would be just as well," he said finally. "But we don't know whether your Second Aunt would be willing. Go and talk it over first with your old granny tomorrow. Get her to make sure your Second Aunt agrees before we make any decision."

Then, having given his son some further instructions, he went to broach the matter to his wife. Madam Yu, knowing that this would be improper, did her best to dissuade him; but as Chia Chen had already made up his mind and she was in the habit of falling in with his wishes, and as Second Sister was only her step-sister and she was therefore not so responsible for her, she had to let them go ahead with this preposterous scheme.

Accordingly, the first thing the next day, Chia Jung went back to the city to see old Mrs. Yu and tell her his father's proposal. In addition, he expatiated on Chia Lien's good qualities and declared that Hsi-feng was mortally ill and, if they bought a house to live in outside for the time being, after a year or so when Hsi-feng died his Second Aunt could move in as the proper wife. He also described the betrothal presents his father would give, and the wedding ceremony Chia Lien would arrange.

"They'll take you in to live in comfort in your old age, madam," he assured her. "And later they'll see to Third Aunt's marriage too."

He painted such a glowing picture that naturally old Mrs. Yu agreed. Besides, she was wholly dependent on Chia Chen for money, and now that he had proposed this match she would not have to provide any dowry. Furthermore, Chia Lien was a young gentleman from a noble family, ten times better than the wretched Chang family. So she went straight to discuss it with her second daughter.

Second Sister was a coquette. She had already had an affair with Chia Chen, and it was her constant regret that her betrothal to Chang Hua prevented her from making a better marriage. Now that Chia Lien had taken a fancy to her and her brother-in-law himself had proposed the match, of course she was only too willing. She nodded in assent, and this was at once reported to Chia Jung, who went back to inform his father.

The next day they sent to invite Chia Lien to the temple. When Chia Chen told him that old Mrs. Yu had given her consent, he was so overjoyed that he could not thank Chia Chen and Chia Jung enough. They made plans then to send stewards to find a house, have trinkets made and the bride's trousseau prepared, as well as the bed, curtains and other furnishings for the bridal chamber.

Within a few days everything was ready. The house they bought was in Flower Sprig Lane about two *li* behind the Ning and Jung Street. It had over twenty rooms. They also bought two young maids. In addition, Chia Chen installed his own servant Pao Erh and his wife there to wait on Second Sister after she moved in. He then sent for Chang Hua and his father and ordered them to write a deed cancelling the betrothal for old Mrs. Yu.

Now Chang Hua's grandfather had been in charge of the Imperial Farm. After his death Chang Hua's father had taken his place, and as he was a good friend of old Mrs. Yu's first husband, Chang Hua and Second Sister Yu had been engaged to each other before they were born. Later the Changs became involved in a lawsuit which ruined their family, leaving them too poor to feed and clothe themselves well, to say nothing of bringing home a bride for their son. And as old Mrs. Yu had left her first husband's home, the two families had lost touch for more than ten years. When the Chia family's stewards summoned Chang Hua and ordered him to renounce his betrothal to Second Sister Yu, although unwilling he had to agree for fear of the power which Chia Chen and the others wielded. He accordingly wrote a deed cancelling the engagement, and old Mrs. Yu gave him ten taels of silver, after which the matter was settled.

When Chia Lien saw that all preparations were ready, he chose the third of the next month, an auspicious day, for the wedding.

On the second of the month, old Mrs. Yu and Third Sister were escorted first to the new house. Old Mrs. Yu saw at a glance that it was not as grand as Chia Jung had claimed; still, it appeared quite respectable, and she and her daughter were both satisfied. Pao Erh and his wife gave them an effusive welcome, assiduously addressing old Mrs. Yu as "Old Madam" or "Old Lady" and Third Sister as "Third Aunt" or "Third Young Mistress".

The next day at dawn when Second Sister was brought over in a white sedan-chair, all the incense, candles and sacrificial paper as well as fine bedding, wine and food were ready. Presently Chia Lien, dressed in mourning, arrived in a small sedan-chair, after which they bowed to Heaven and Earth and burned sacrificial paper. And old Mrs. Yu was most gratified to see Second Sister's new finery, so unlike the trinkets and clothes she had worn at home. The bride was helped into the bridal chamber, where that night she and Chia Lien enjoyed the transports of love.

Chia Lien, more enamoured than ever of his new bride, did all in his power to please her in every way. He forbade Pao Ërh and the other servants to refer to her as "Second Mistress". They must all call her the mistress just as he did, as if Hsi-feng had been blotted out of existence. Whenever he went home he merely claimed to have been detained by business in the East Mansion; and Hsi-feng, knowing how close he and Chia Chen were, thought it natural for them to talk things over together and never suspected the truth. As for the domestics, they never interfered in affairs of this kind. In fact, the idlers among them who made a point of learning all the gossip tried to profit by the situation, seizing this chance to make up to Chia Lien; thus none of them was willing to expose him. So Chia Lien's gratitude to Chia Chen knew no bounds.

Every month Chia Lien paid five taels of silver to defray the daily expenses of this new establishment. In his absence, the mother and two daughters ate together; if he came, husband and wife had their meal alone while old Mrs. Yu and Third Sister retired to their own room to eat. Chia Lien also made over to Second Sister the savings he had put aside in the last few years, and when in bed told her freely all about Hsi-feng and her behaviour, promising to take her into the family as soon as Hsi-feng died. This, of course, was what Second Sister hoped for. So their household of a dozen or so people managed very comfortably.

Chapter 23
A Wanton Girl Mends Her Ways and
Picks Herself a Husband

Two months passed in a flash. One evening when Chia Chen came home from Iron Threshold Temple, he decided to pay a visit to the two sisters whom he had not seen for so long. First he sent a page to find out whether Chia Lien was there, and was delighted when the boy reported that he was not. Having dismissed his attendants except for two trusted boys to lead his horse, he went straight to the new house. It was already lighting-up time when he slipped quietly in. The two pages tethered the horse in the stable, then went to the servants' quarters to await further orders.

When Chia Chen entered the house the lamps had just been lit. He first met old Mrs. Yu and Third Sister; then Second Sister came out to greet him, and he addressed her as before as Second Cousin. They sipped tea together and chatted.

"Well, how is the marriage I arranged for you?" asked Chia Chen with a smile. "If you'd missed this chance, you couldn't have found another such man, not even if you'd searched with a lantern! Your elder sister will be coming to call one of these days with presents."

Second Sister ordered wine and food to be prepared. And as they were members of one family now they closed the door and chatted without constraint until Pao Erh came in to pay his respects.

Chia Chen told him, "It's because you're an honest fellow that I sent you here to work. In future I shall give you more important jobs. Don't get drunk outside or make trouble, and

I shall reward you well. Your Second Master Lien is busy and there are all sorts of people about in his place, so if you're short of anything here just let me know. After all, we're cousins — it's not as if I were an outsider."

"Yes, sir, I understand," answered Pao Erh. "If I don't do my best, you can cut off my head."

Chia Chen nodded.

"I just want you to understand."

The four of them drank together until Second Sister, sizing up the situation, said to her mother, "I'm afraid to go out alone. Will you come with me?"

Old Mrs. Yu took the hint and withdrew with her, leaving only two young maids there. Then Chia Chen and Third Sister nestled up to each other and flirted so outrageously that the maids were shocked and slipped out, leaving them to amuse themselves however they pleased.

Chia Chen's pages were drinking in the kitchen with Pao Erh, while his wife attended to the cooking, when the two maids burst in, giggling, and asked for drinks.

But as they were enjoying themselves they heard a sudden knocking on the gate; and when Pao Erh's wife hurried out to open it, she saw Chia Lien dismounting from his horse. He asked if all was well.

She quietly told him, "The Elder Master is here, in the west courtyard."

When Chia Lien heard that he went to his bedroom and found Second Sister there with her mother. At sight of him, they looked a little put out, but he pretended not to notice.

"Bring some wine, quick," he ordered. "After a couple of drinks we can go to bed. I'm tired out."

Second Sister at once stepped forward with a smile to take his outer garments and offer him tea, then asked about this and that. Chia Lien was so pleased that he itched to make love to her. Soon Pao Erh's wife brought in wine which the two of them drank, while his mother-in-law went back to her room, sending one of the young maids to wait on them.

When Chia Lien's trusted page Lung-erh went to stable the horse he discovered another there and, looking closely, recognized it as Chia Chen's. Understanding the situation, he too went to the kitchen where he found Hsi-erh and Shou-erh sitting drinking. At sight of him, they exchanged knowing glances.

"You've come just at the right time," they chortled. "We couldn't overtake the master's horse, and as we were afraid of being caught out after curfew, we came here to spend the night."

Lung-erh chuckled, "Well, there's plenty of room on the *kang*, just lie down as you like. Second Master sent me to bring the monthly allowance to the mistress, so I shan't be going back either."

"We've drunk too much," said Hsi-erh. "You must have a cup now."

But as Lung-erh sat down and raised his cup, they heard a sudden commotion in the stable where the two horses, unwilling to be tethered together, had started kicking each other. Lung-erh hastily put down his cup and rushed out to soothe them, coming back after he had managed to tie Chia Lien's horse up elsewhere.

The commotion made by the horses had alarmed Second Sister, who tried to distract Chia Lien with conversation. After a few cups, feeling randy, he ordered the maids to clear away the wine and dishes, then closed the door to undress. Second Sister was wearing nothing but a scarlet jacket. With her hair hanging loose, her cheeks flushed, she looked even lovelier than in the daytime.

Throwing his arms around her, Chia Lien declared, "Everyone calls that shrew of mine good-looking, but to me she isn't fit even to pick up your shoes."

"I may have good looks but I've got a bad name," she answered. "So it seems not to be good-looking would be better."

"Why do you say that?" he asked. "I don't understand."

"You all think me silly," she told him, shedding tears. "But I have my wits about me. Now I've been your wife for two months, and already in that short time I've learned that you're no fool either. I'll be yours dead or alive. Being married to you, I'll depend on you all my life, so of course I won't keep any secrets from you. *I'm* provided for, but what about my sister? Seems to me things can't go on the way they are now. We must think of some long-term plan."

"Don't worry," chuckled Chia Lien. "I'm not the jealous type. I know all that happened in the past, you don't have to be afraid. As your brother-in-law is my cousin, you naturally don't like to broach the subject. It would be better for me to make the proposal."

So he went to the west courtyard and saw through the window that the room was brightly lit and Chia Chen and Third Sister were drinking and enjoying themselves inside. Chia Lien opened the door and went in.

"So you're here, sir," he said with a smile. "I've come to pay my respects."

Chia Chen, too embarrassed to speak, simply stood up and waved him to a seat.

Chia Lien laughed. "Why look so worried? As cousins we've always been on the closest terms. I can't thank you enough for all you've done for me. If you take offence now, I shall be most upset. Please behave just as you did before. Otherwise I shall never dare come here again, not even if it means having no son." He made as if to kneel down.

Chia Chen hastily raised him.

"I'll do whatever you say, cousin," he assured him.

Then Chia Lien called for wine, saying, "I'll have a couple of drinks with Elder Cousin." Taking Third Sister by the hand he added, "Come and drink a cup with me too."

Chia Chen laughed.

"What a character you are! I shall have to empty this cup." And he tossed it off.

Third Sister jumped on to the *kang* then and pointed at Chia Lien.

"Don't try to get round me with your glib tongue!" she cried. "We'd better keep clear of each other. I've seen plenty of

310

shadow-plays in my time; anyway don't tear the screen to show
what's behind the scenes. You must be befuddled if you think
we don't know what goes on in your house. Now after spending
a bit of your stinking money, you two figure you can amuse
yourselves with us as if we were prostitutes! Well, you're out
in your calculations.

"I know your wife's such a termagant that you tricked my
sister into coming here to be your second wife; but you can't
beat a stolen gong. And I've a good mind to call on this Madam
Hsi-feng, to see what sort of prodigy she is. If everyone treats
us right we can all live at peace. But if anyone takes the least
liberties, I'm quite capable of tearing out both your stinking
guts, then fighting it out with that shrew. If I don't, I'm not
Third Mistress Yu! Who's afraid of drinking? Let's go ahead
and drink."

She picked up the wine-pot to fill a cup and drank half of this
herself, then throwing one arm round Chia Lien's neck started
pouring the rest down his throat.

"I've already drunk with your cousin," she said. "Now let's
us play at being sweethearts."

This gave Chia Lien such a scare that he sobered up. Chia
Chen, for his part, had never dreamed that Third Sister could
act so brazenly. The two cousins, for all their experience of
loose women, now found themselves struck dumb by this chit
of a girl.

Then Third Sister cried out, "Ask my sister in! If you want
fun, let's all *four* of us have fun together. As the saying goes,
'Perks should be kept inside the family.' You're cousins, we're
sisters; none of us are outsiders — come on!"

Second Sister who had joined them began to feel embarrassed,
and Chia Chen wanted to sneak away, but Third Sister would
not let him. By now Chia Chen regretted having come. He
had had no idea that Third Sister would behave like this, making it impossible for him and Chia Lien to have their way with
her.

Now Third Sister wound her hair in a loose knot, her scarlet jacket, half unbuttoned, disclosing her leek-green bodice and snow-white skin. Below she was wearing green trousers and red slippers, and she now kicked her dainty feet against each other, now stretched them out side by side — never still for a moment — while her pendant eardrops swung this way and that. Under the lamplight her willowy eyebrows curved enticingly, her fragrant lips glowed red as cinnabar, and her eyes, bright as autumn pools, sparkled even more seductively after drinking. To Chia Chen and Chia Lien it seemed that not only did she surpass her elder sister but that none of the girls they had ever seen, whether high or low, noble or humble, had possessed such bewitching charm. Both were too dazed and too intoxicated even to lift a finger. Her wanton coquetting had deprived them of speech.

Gesticulating and making eyes at them, Third Sister Yu had not put herself out to excite them, yet already the two men were at a loss to know which way to look, and had not so much as a word to say for themselves, so befuddled were they both by wine and lust. Holding forth loudly and freely, she heaped abuse on them, taunting and teasing them just as she pleased, as if *they* were prostitutes called in by her instead of men who had wanted to seduce her. Finally, sated with wine, having worked off her high spirits she drove them out, closed the door behind them, and retired to bed.

After this, whenever the maids were remiss in any way, Third Sister would loose a flood of abuse against Chia Chen, Chia Lien and Chia Jung, accusing them of cheating a widow and her two fatherless daughters. Thereafter, Chia Chen hardly dared to come back unless Third Sister happened to be in the mood to send a page boy secretly to fetch him. And when he arrived he had to let her have her way.

Third Sister was in fact a born eccentric. Being good-looking and romantic, she liked to dress strikingly and behave more lasciviously and seductively than all other girls to infatuate men until they were fairly drooling, unable either to approach her or stay away. She delighted in keeping them on a string like this.

Her mother and sister tried in vain to dissuade her.

"How silly you are, sister," she would retort. "Why let those two reincarnated apes defile our precious bodies? Why act so helpless? Besides, that wife of his is a real terror. As long as this is kept from her, we're all right. If she comes to hear of it one day, she won't take it lying down and there's bound to be a big row. Who knows which of you will survive? If I don't have some fun now treating them like dirt, by the time this breaks it'll be too late to regret it — I'll be left with nothing then but a bad name."

They realized then it was no use trying to persuade her, and gave up.

And now Third Sister started demanding the best of everything, whether food or clothing. When silver trinkets were made for her she wanted gold as well; when pearls were given her she asked for gems; if a fat goose was served her she demanded duck, and unless humoured would overturn the table. If her clothes were not just as she wanted, regardless of whether they were silk or satin, new or old, she would cut them up, swearing as she tore them to shreds. So not for a day did Chia Chen have any satisfaction. Instead, he squandered large sums of money for nothing.

Chia Lien when he went there just stayed in Second Sister's rooms, and he was beginning to regret this set-up. But Second Sister had an affectionate disposition. To her, Chia Lien was her lord and master for life, she doted on him. As regards gentleness and obedience, she was ten times better than Hsi-feng, for she would consult him on everything and never dared make any decisions herself or trust to her own better judgement. As regards her looks, conversation and behaviour, she was superior too. Yet although she had now reformed, because of her previous slip-ups she had been labelled a wanton, and so her other good qualities counted for nothing.

However, Chia Lien said, "Who's perfect? If you recognize your mistakes and correct them, that's all right." Thus he never mentioned her loose living in the past, content to dwell on her present goodness. And he stuck to her like glue, like a fish to water, vowing from his heart to be true to her his whole life long, having lost all interest in Hsi-feng and Ping-erh.

When they shared the same pillow and quilt, Second Sister often urged him, "Why not talk it over with your cousin Chen, and choose some man you know to marry my sister? It's no good keeping her here indefinitely, because sooner or later there's bound to be trouble, and then what shall we do?"

"I did mention this to him the other day," said Chia Lien. "But he can't bear the idea of giving her up. I pointed out, 'What's the good of fat mutton if it's too hot to eat? The rose is lovely but prickly. How can we control her? We'd better find someone and marry her off.' He just hemmed and hawed, then changed the subject. So what do you expect me to do?"

"Don't worry," said Second Sister. "Tomorrow we'll first tackle my sister. If she's willing, we'll let her go on making rows until he has no choice but to marry her off."

"That's the idea," agreed Chia Lien.

The next day Second Sister prepared a feast and Chia Lien stayed in. At noon, they invited Third Sister and her mother over and made them take the seats of honour. Third Sister guessed their intention, and when their cups had been filled three times, without waiting for her sister to speak she said tearfully:

"You must have invited me today, sister, for some important reason. I'm no fool, and there's no need to harp on my shameful conduct in the past. I'm aware of it; it's no use talking about it. You've found yourself a good niche now, and so has mother, and it's only right and proper that I should look for a home of my own too. But marriage is a serious business; it's for life, not a joking matter. I've had a change of heart and mean to turn over a new leaf, but I must find someone congenial before I'll marry. If your choice, no matter how rich, talented and handsome, wasn't a man after my own heart then my whole life would be wasted."

"That's no problem," said Chia Lien. "You can make your

own choice. And we'll provide the whole dowry, so that mother needn't worry about that either."

"Sister knows who I mean," sobbed Third Sister. "I don't have to name him."

"Who is he?" Chia Lien asked Second Sister, but she could not think who it could be.

While the others were wondering, Chia Lien, sure that he had guessed, clapped his hands.

"I know who it is! He's certainly not bad. You've made a good choice."

"Who is it?" asked Second Sister.

"It must be Pao-yu," he chuckled. "No one else would do for her."

Second Sister and old Mrs. Yu thought he had guessed right, but Third Sister spat in disgust.

"If there were ten of us sisters, would we all have to marry your brothers and cousins?" she asked. "Are there no men outside your family?"

This puzzled them all. Who else could it be? they wondered.

"Forget about the present, sister," said Third Sister. "Just think back five years and you'll know."

As they were talking, Chia Lien's trusted page Hsing-erh came in to report, "The old master wants you to go over at once, sir. I told him you'd gone to see your uncle, then came straight to fetch you."

"Did they ask about me at home yesterday?" demanded Chia Lien hastily.

"I told Madam that you were at the family temple making plans for the hundredth day sacrifice with Lord Chen, so you probably couldn't come home."

Chia Lien promptly called for his horse and rode off, accompanied by Lung-erh, leaving Hsing-erh behind to attend to other things.

Second Sister ordered the gate to be closed and they turned in early, but she spent most of the night questioning her sister.

The next day it was after noon before Chia Lien arrived.

"Why be in such a hurry to come when you've other important business?" Second Sister asked him. "You mustn't delay your journey on my account."

"It's not all that important," he told her. "The nuisance is I've got to make a long trip, starting early next month, and I shan't be back for a fortnight."

"Well, just go with an easy mind. You needn't worry about anything here. My sister's not the type that keeps changing her mind. She says she's going to turn over a new leaf, and she'll be as good as her word. She's already made her choice of a man. All you need do is to fall in with her wishes."

"Who is he?" asked Chia Lien.

"He's not here now, and there's no knowing when he'll come back. But she's made an intelligent choice. If he stays away for a year, she'll wait for a year, she says. If he doesn't return for ten years, she'll wait for ten years. If he's dead and never comes back, she'll gladly shave off her hair and become a nun, fasting and chanting sutras all her life."

"Who can the fellow be that has won her heart so completely?"

"It's a long story," said Second Sister with a smile. "Five years ago, when it was our grandmother's birthday, my mother took us there to offer congratulations. They'd invited a troupe of amateur actors, among them a certain Liu Hsiang-lien who liked to play the young hero's part in operas. She took such a fancy to him, she now declares he's the only man for her. Last year we heard that he'd got into trouble and run away. We don't know whether he has ever come back."

"Well, I never!" exclaimed Chia Lien. "So that's who it is. I was wondering what sort of fellow he could be. Yes, she's made a good choice. But you know this Second Master Liu, for all he's so handsome, is cold and stand-offish. He has no time for most people but happens to get on splendidly with Pao-yu. Last year after he beat up that fool Hsueh Pan he left, feeling too embarrassed to see us, and we don't know

賈二舍偸娶尤二姨
尤三姐思嫁柳二郎

where he's gone. Some people say he's returned. I suppose we can ask Pao-yu's pages to find out. If he hasn't come back and is still drifting about, Heaven knows how many years he may stay away. Your sister may wait in vain."

"No, my sister's always as good as her word," she assured him. "Just let her have her way."

At this point Third Sister joined them.

"Believe me, brother-in-law, I'm not one of those who don't say what they think," she declared. "I mean what I say. If Mr. Liu comes I'll marry him. Until then I'll fast, chant sutras and look after my mother while waiting for him to come and marry me, even if I have to wait a hundred years. If he never comes, I'll go and become a nun." Drawing a jade pin from her hair she broke it in two, exclaiming, "If I've said a single word that isn't true, may I end up like this pin!"

This said, she went back to her room. And after that she was, indeed, most correct in her speech and behaviour.

There was nothing Chia Lien could do. Having discussed some family business with Second Sister, he went home to tell Hsi-feng about his trip, then sent to ask Ming-yen whether Liu Hsiang-lien had returned or not.

"I don't know," said Ming-yen. "Probably not. Otherwise I would have heard."

And Liu's neighbours when questioned said he had never come back. So Chia Lien had to pass on this information to Second Sister.

Chapter 24
A Cold-Hearted Man Repents and
Turns to Religion

Chia Lien left the city early in the morning and took the highway to Pinganchou. He travelled all day, stopping only to refresh himself when he was hungry or thirsty, staying in inns at night, and he had been three days on the way when a caravan of pack-horses came towards him escorted by a dozen or so men on horseback. As they drew near he saw to his astonishment that among them were Hsueh Pan and Liu Hsiang-lien. At once he spurred his horse forward to meet them, and after exchanging the usual courtesies they chose an inn in which to rest and chat.

Chia Lien said, "After the two of you fell out we were very eager to patch it up between you, but Brother Liu had vanished without a trace. How come you're together today?"

"Wonders never cease," said Hsueh Pan. "I and my assistants bought some goods and started back to the capital this spring. All went well till the other day when we reached Pinganchou and a band of brigands seized everything we had. Then along came Brother Liu in the nick of time to drive the brigands away, rescue our goods and save our lives into the bargain. When he wouldn't accept anything for his help, we became sworn brothers and have been travelling together. From now on we shall be like real blood-brothers. But we shall part company at the crossroad in front, as he has to go two hundred *li* farther south to visit an aunt of his. I shall go to the capital first to finish my business, then find a house for him and a suitable wife, so that we can all settle down there."

"If that's the case," exclaimed Chia Lien, "we've been

worrying needlessly for several days." As Hsueh Pan had spoken of finding a wife for Hsiang-lien, he hastened to continue, "I've got the very bride for him, a splendid match for Brother Liu." He went on to explain how he had married Second Sister Yu and now wanted to find a husband for her younger sister, omitting only to add that Liu was Third Sister's own choice. He then cautioned Hsueh Pan, "Mind you don't tell the family. Just wait until she has a son, then of course they'll have to know."

Hsueh Pan was delighted.

"You should have done that long ago," he said. "It serves Cousin Hsi-feng right."

"You're talking nonsense again," put in Hsiang-lien with a smile. "You'd better shut up."

"In that case," said Hsueh Pan, changing the subject, "we must fix up this match."

"It's been my intention all along," Hsiang-lien told them, "to marry only an outstanding beauty. But as this proposal comes from my honourable elder brothers, I shan't insist on that. I'll agree to whatever you suggest."

"Words don't carry conviction," Chia Lien rejoined. "But once you see her, Brother Liu, you'll realize that this sister-in-law of mine is a matchless beauty."

Hsiang-lien was overjoyed by this assurance.

"If that's so," he said, "when I've called on my aunt, in less than a fortnight I'll come to the capital and we can settle everything then. How's that?"

"We're both men of our word," replied Chia Lien. "But you're such a rolling stone, always on the move, I don't like leaving it undecided. If you drift away now and don't come back, what's to become of her? You'd better let me have some betrothal token."

"A true man never goes back on his word. I'm not rich and I'm in the middle of a journey, so where would I get a betrothal token?"

"I've something suitable," Hsueh Pan cut in. "Just take it, Second Brother."

"I don't want gold or silk," said Chia Lien. "What I have in mind is one of Brother Liu's personal possessions; it doesn't have to be anything valuable. I'll just take it as a pledge."

"Very well, then," agreed Hsiang-lien. "The only things I have with me, apart from this sword which I need in self-defence, are a pair of 'duck and drake' swords in my luggage — they're a family heirloom which I never use but always keep with me. You can take them as a pledge. However much of a wanderer I am, I'd never give up these swords."

After that they drank a few more cups, then mounted their horses, took their leave of each other and went their different ways.

Truly:

> Generals, not dismounting from their horses,
> Gallop off to their destinations.

After Chia Lien reached Pinganchou he called on the governor to settle his business, and was told to come back again before the tenth month. The very next day he hurriedly started back, and as soon as he got home went to see Second Sister.

Since his departure Second Sister had been running her household most prudently, staying in every day behind closed doors and taking no interest in outside affairs. And Third Sister had proved her iron resolution: apart from waiting on her mother and sister she had kept to herself, doing her share of work every day and sleeping alone at night on her lonely pillow. Although unaccustomed to such a solitary life she avoided all company, simply longing for Liu Hsiang-lien's early return, so that the main affair of her life could be settled.

When Chia Lien saw how things were, he was very pleased with Second Sister's virtuous conduct. After the usual civilities had been exchanged, he described his encounter with Liu Hsiang-lien on the road and taking out the pair of swords passed them to Third Sister. She looked at the dragon and serpent designs on the sheath which was studded with bright pearls and jewels, then drew out the two swords, identical in size, one engraved with the word "duck," the other "drake." The blades had the cold gleam of two autumn streams. Overjoyed, she hastily took them to her chamber to hang them on the wall over her bed. Every day she would feast her eyes on them, happy that her future was provided for.

After Chia Lien had spent two days there, he went to report on his mission to his father, then returned home to see his family. By now Hsi-feng was well enough to attend to affairs and get about again. When Chia Lien told Chia Chen about Third Sister's engagement his cousin showed little interest, as he had recently found himself a new mistress and given up calling on the Yu sisters. He was willing to let Chia Lien do as he pleased. But suspecting that the latter might be unable to defray all the expenses, he gave him thirty taels of silver which Chia Lien passed on to Second Sister to prepare her sister's trousseau.

Liu Hsiang-lien did not come to the capital till the eighth month. When he called on Aunt Hsueh and Hsueh Ko he learned that Hsueh Pan, being unaccustomed to the rigours of travel and a different climate, had fallen ill as soon as he arrived home and was still being treated by doctors. Hearing of Hsiang-lien's arrival, he invited him into his bedroom.

Full of gratitude for the good turn Hsiang-lien had done them, Aunt Hsueh let bygones be bygones, both she and her son thanking him most profusely. They went on to speak of the wedding, all the preparations for which were complete except for the choice of an auspicious day. Hsiang-lien, in turn, was loud in his thanks.

The next day he called on Pao-yu, and meeting again they felt so at home with each other that Hsiang-lien asked for more details about Chia Lien's secret marriage to a second wife.

"I only heard about it from Ming-yen and the others," Pao-yu told him. "And it wasn't my business to interfere. I also heard from Ming-yen that Cousin Lien was very anxious to find you — I don't know what for."

Hsiang-lien explained all that had happened on the road.

"Congratulations!" cried Pao-yu. "You'd be hard put to it to find a lovelier girl. She's really ravishing, just the right match for you."

"If she's so lovely she ought to have lots of suitors; why should he single me out? It's not as if the two of us were close friends or he has any special concern for me. In our brief meeting on the road he kept pressing me to agree to this engagement. Why should the girl's family be in such a hurry? I couldn't help having misgivings, and soon started regretting having given him my swords as a pledge. That's why I thought of asking you just what's behind this."

"You're a smart fellow," answered Pao-yu. "Once you've given your pledge how can you start having second thoughts? You always said you wanted a ravishing beauty, and now you've got one. Isn't that good enough? Why be so suspicious?"

"If you didn't know about Chia Lien's secret marriage, how do you know that she's so beautiful?"

"She's one of the two daughters of Madam Yu's step-mother, old Mrs. Yu, by her first marriage. I saw a lot of them for a couple of months, so of course I know. She and her sister are really a pair of beauties."

Hsiang-lien stamped his foot.

"That's no good then! I can't go through with it. The only clean things in that East Mansion of yours are those two stone lions at the gate. Even the cats and dogs there are unclean. I don't want to be a cuckold and take someone else's leavings."

Pao-yu blushed. And Hsiang-lien, regretting his tactlessness, made haste to bow.

"I deserve death for talking such nonsense. But do at any rate tell me what her character's like."

"If you know so much already, why ask *me*? I may not be clean myself either."

"I forgot myself just now," said Hsiang-lien with a smile. "Please don't make such an issue of it."

"Why mention it again?" retorted Pao-yu. "This makes it

seem that you take it seriously."

Hsiang-lien took his leave then with a bow and left. He thought of going to see Hsueh Pan, but reflected that as the latter was unwell and so irascible at the best of times he had better go and get his pledge back instead. This decision reached, he went to find Chia Lien.

Chia Lien was in the new house. When he heard that Hsiang-lien had come he was overjoyed and hurried out to welcome him, then ushered him into the inner room and introduced him to old Mrs. Yu. To his astonishment, instead of kneeling to her as his future mother-in-law, Hsiang-lien simply bowed and addressed her as "aunt," referring to himself as "your nephew".

And as they were sipping tea he said, "During my journey, as it happened, I was overhasty, not knowing that my aunt had arranged a match for me in the fourth month, making it impossible for me to retract. It wouldn't be right would it, brother, for me to accept your proposal and refuse my aunt's. If I'd given the usual gifts of money and silk, I wouldn't venture to ask to have them back; but those swords were left me by my grandfather, so I must beg you to return them."

Chia Lien was very put out when he heard this.

"A pledge is a pledge," he argued. "And a pledge is given to stop a man from going back on his word. Can you cancel an engagement so casually? Pray reconsider the matter."

"In spite of what you say," replied Hsiang-lien, "I'm willing to accept any penalty, but on this matter I definitely cannot obey your order."

Chia Lien was about to reply when Hsiang-lien stood up.

"Let's discuss this outside," he proposed. "It's not convenient here."

Third Sister had heard all this clearly from her room. She had been waiting and waiting for Liu Hsiang-lien's arrival, but now he had suddenly broken the engagement. It was clear to her that he must have heard some gossip in the Chia mansions which led him to believe her a shameless wanton, not fit to be his wife. If she let the two men go out now to discuss it, she foresaw that Chia Lien would fail to win him round and she would be utterly humiliated. So as soon as Chia Lien agreed to his proposal she took down the swords, concealing the "duck" behind her elbow, and went out to intercept them.

"There's no need for you to go out to discuss this further," she told them. "Here's your pledge, I'm returning it."

Her tears falling like rain, with her left hand she passed the sheath with one sword in it to Hsiang-lien, and with her right cut her throat with the other blade. Alas!

> The jade hill crumbles, never to rise again;
> Peach-blossom, trampled, stains the ground with red.
> Her fragrant spirit is lost in the infinite —
> None knows whither it has fled.

All present were consternated and tried in vain to revive her. Old Mrs. Yu sobbing with horror cursed Hsiang-lien, while Chia Lien seized hold of him, calling servants to tie him up and drag him to court.

Second Sister dried her tears then to urge her husband, "Let him be! He didn't threaten her, she took her own life. So what use would it be to take him to court? That would only cause a worse scandal. You'd better let him go, to save further trouble."

Then Chia Lien, not knowing what else to do, let go of Hsiang-lien and told him to get out. However, he did not move but burst into tears.

"I never knew this intended wife of mine was so chaste, such a magnificent girl!" he exclaimed.

Prostrating himself over her corpse he gave way to a storm of weeping. And when a coffin was brought and her body laid in it, he clasped it and lamented bitterly before finally leaving them.

Once outside the gate he did not know where to go, dazed and sunk in gloom as he recalled what had just happened. "So she was so lovely and chaste," he reflected, torn by remorse.

He wandered aimlessly on until one of Hsueh Pan's pages appeared and asked him to go back. The boy took him to a

magnificent bridal chamber. He heard the tinkling of pendants, and in came Third Sister, in one hand the "duck and drake" swords, in the other a book. With tears she told him:

"Your devoted handmaid waited five years for you, my lord, not knowing you would prove so cold-hearted. I have paid with my life now for my infatuation. Today, at the order of the Goddess of Disenchantment, I am going to the Illusory Land of the Great Void to register all the amorous spirits in this case. But I couldn't bear to go away without bidding you farewell, for from this day on we shall never meet again." This said, she turned to leave.

Hsiang-lien could not bear to let her go and quickly stepped forward to stop her and question her.

"We came from the Heaven of Love and we must return there from the Earth of Love," she told him. "I was deluded by love in my last life, but as I have repented of it and awakened, from now on I shall have nothing to do with you, sir."

As her voice died away, a fragrant wind sprang up and she vanished into thin air.

Hsiang-lien woke with a start, wondering if he had been dreaming. When he opened his eyes and looked round, there was no sign of the Hsuehs' page boy or of the bridal chamber. He was in a tumble-down temple, and beside him a lame Taoist priest was sitting catching lice. Hsiang-lien rose to his feet, then bowed to the ground.

"Where are we, holy master?" he asked the priest. "And what is your immortal name?"

The priest chuckled, "I myself don't know where we are or who I am. I'm simply putting up here for the time being."

At this Liu Hsiang-lien shuddered with cold, as if the marrow of his bones had frozen. He drew the "drake" sword and with one stroke cut off his hair, then went away with the priest, no one knows where.

Chapter 25
Hsi-feng Questions a Page Boy and Hatches a Plot

Hsi-jen left by the Garden gate and went straight to Hsi-feng's place.

Hsi-feng and Ping-erh were discussing Chia Lien's secret marriage. As Hsi-jen was a rare visitor and they did not know her errand, they broke off their conversation on her arrival.

After Ping-erh had seen Hsi-jen out, Hsi-feng called her back to cross-examine her further. The more she heard, the more furious she became.

"You say you heard from the pages at the inner gate that your Second Master had secretly married another wife outside. Who told you that?"

"Lai Wang."

At once Hsi-feng sent for him.

"Did you know that your Second Master had bought a house and married a concubine outside?" she demanded.

"I'm on duty all day long at the inner gate," stammered Lai Wang. "How could I know about the Second Master's business? I heard this from Hsing-erh."

"When did Hsing-erh tell you?"

"Before the master left on that trip."

"Where is Hsing-erh now?"

"He's working in the new mistress' house."

In a furious temper Hsi-feng spat at him.

"You contemptible son of an ape," she swore. "Who are you to talk about a new mistress or an old mistress? How dare *you* confer the title of mistress on her. The nonsense you talk, you deserve to be slapped." Then she asked, "Isn't Hsing-erh supposed to wait on the Second Master? Why didn't he go with him?"

"He was specially left here to look after Second Sister Yu; that's why."

Hsi-feng at once ordered him to fetch Hsing-erh.

Lai Wang rushed off on this errand and, when he found Hsing-erh fooling about with some other pages outside he simply told him that Hsi-feng wanted him. When Hsing-erh heard this, without asking why he was wanted, he hurried with Lai Wang to the inner gate, where he announced his business and was admitted. Having bowed to Hsi-feng he stood respectfully to one side. At sight of him she glared.

"What fine goings-on have you, master and slave, been up to outside?" she snapped. "Did you take me for a fool who wouldn't know? As Second Master's personal attendant, you must know the whole story. I want the true facts from you. Any attempt to cover up or lie, and I'll have you beaten till your legs are broken!"

Hsing-erh fell on his knees to kowtow.

"What goings-on are these, madam, that you're asking about?"

"How dare you stall, you little bastard! I'm asking how your master fixed things up outside with Second Sister Yu. How did he buy the house and furnish it? How did the marriage take place? Tell me all these things clearly, you dog, and I may spare your life."

Hearing these explicit questions Hsing-erh reflected: Both mansions know about this business; the only ones kept in the dark were the old lady, Lord Sheh, Lady Hsing and Madam Lien. As the truth's bound to come out in the end, why should I try to cover it up? I may as well come clean to get off a beating and worse punishment. For one thing, I'm too young to be expected to know how serious this was; for another, I've always known that Madam's such a firebrand that even Master Lien's half afraid of her; and, besides, this business was arranged by Master Lien, Lord Chen and Master Jung between them — it had nothing to do with *me*.

His mind made up, he screwed up his courage.

"Have mercy on me, madam!" he begged on his knees. "I'll tell you everything. It started during our mourning for the Elder Master of the East Mansion. Second Master happened to meet Second Sister Yu there a few times, and I suppose he took a fancy to her and wanted to make her his concubine. So he first discussed it with Master Jung, asking him to act as go-between and arrange the match, and promising him presents if he pulled it off. Master Jung agreed readily and told Lord Chen, who broached it to Madam Yu and old Mrs. Yu.

"Old Mrs. Yu was quite willing but she said, 'Second Sister was engaged as a child to the son of the Chang family; so how can I marry her to Master Lien? If the Changs hear of it there may be trouble.'

" 'That's nothing serious,' said Lord Chen. 'Leave it to me. That fellow Chang's family has been beggared. If we just give him a few extra taels of silver, we can make him write a document cancelling the engagement and there'll be no further trouble.'

"Later they did fetch that man Chang and put it to him. When he'd written the document they paid him and off he went. Then Second Master felt safe enough to go boldly ahead. Only, for fear lest this came to your ears, madam, and you stopped him, he bought and furnished a small house outside at the back, then took her over. And Lord Chen gave him a married couple to work there.

"Often, when he says he has business to attend to for Lord Sheh or Lord Chen, that's a lie — an excuse for him to stay outside there.

"Originally the mother and the two sisters lived there, and they wanted to arrange a match for Third Sister Yu too, promising to give her a handsome dowry; but now Third Sister Yu's dead, so there's only old Mrs. Yu keeping Second Sister

Yu company.

"All this is the truth, I haven't dared hide a thing." With that he kowtowed again.

This account had left Hsi-feng transfixed with rage, her face livid, her almond eyes squinting. For a while she trembled convulsively, unable to get a word out for stupefaction. Then, looking down suddenly, she saw that Hsing-erh was still kneeling there.

"You're not the one most to blame for this," she said. "But when Second Master carried on like that outside you ought to have told me about it earlier. For not doing that you fully deserve a beating. Still, since you've told me honestly now, without lying, I'll let you off this time."

"I deserve death, madam, for not telling you before." Again he thumped his head hard on the ground.

"Be off now."

As he rose to leave she added, "Next time I send for you, mind you come at once. Don't go far away."

Assenting repeatedly, Hsing-erh withdrew. Once outside he stuck out his tongue in dismay.

"That was touch and go!" he exclaimed. "I only just escaped a good beating." He regretted having passed on the news to Lai Wang, and was scared stiff for worrying what to say when Chia Lien returned. But no more of this.

After the page had left, Hsi-feng turned to Ping-erh and asked, "Did you hear what Hsing-erh said?"

"Yes, I heard it all."

"How can there be such a shameless man in the world? Guzzling what's in the bowl, he has his eyes on what's in the pan. He wants every woman he sees, the greedy dog. Talk about off with the old love and on with the new! It's a pity to give a lecher like him the insignia of the fifth or sixth rank. He may believe in the saying that the flowers at home aren't as sweet as flowers growing wild; but if he thinks that, he's making a big mistake. Sooner or later he'll cause such a scandal outside, he won't be able to face relatives and friends;

and then only will he give up."

To mollify her Ping-erh said, "Of course you're right to be angry; but you've only just got over your illness, madam, you shouldn't let yourself be carried away. After that affair with Pao Erh's wife, the master seemed to be restraining himself and behaving much better. So why is he having affairs of this sort again? It must be Lord Chen's fault."

"Of course Lord Chen's to blame too. Still, it's because our master is so debauched that it's easy for people to tempt him. As the proverb says, 'If an ox doesn't want to drink, you can't force it to.' "

"Lord Chen's wife ought to have stopped him from doing such a thing."

"Exactly. How could Madam Yu let her sister be betrothed to two different families? First the Changs, then the Chias. Have all the other men in the world died out? Must all girls marry into our Chia family? Are we so well off, or what? It's lucky that slut Third Sister Yu had sense enough to kill herself first; otherwise they'd have married her to Pao-yu or Huan.

"Madam Yu doesn't seem to have cared about saving her sister's face — how could she ever have held up her head in future? But she wouldn't worry about that, as after all Second Sister was only her half-sister and, by all accounts, a loose-living, shameless bitch. But Cousin Chen's wife is a lady of rank; shouldn't she feel ashamed of having such a flighty sister at home? Yet instead of trying to keep her away she blatantly brings her here to carry on in that shocking way, not caring if people laugh.

"Besides, Lord Chen's an official. He may not know all the rules of propriety, but surely he knows that it's taboo for a man in mourning to marry, or to spurn his wife and take another woman. What I'm wondering is this: did he fix this up as a favour for his cousin or to harm him?"

"Yes, Lord Chen is too short-sighted," said Ping-erh. "He just wanted to please his cousin without worrying about the consequences."

"Please his cousin?" Hsi-feng snorted sarcastically. "No, this was giving him poison. Of all our cousins, he's the oldest and most experienced; but instead of setting the others a good example he teaches them bad ways to spoil their reputation. And when there's a public scandal he'll just stand aside watching the fun. Honestly, I can't find words strong enough to damn him. The scandalous goings-on in that East Mansion of his don't bear speaking of. And to cover up his own debauchery he must needs make his cousin follow his example. Is this the way an elder brother should behave? He should have drowned himself in his own piss and died in place of his father, for what's his life worth? Look how virtuous Lord Ching of the East Mansion was, fasting, chanting sutras and doing so many good deeds. How could he beget a son and grandson like these? I suppose all the family's good luck, generated by the auspicious geomancy of the ancestral tombs, was used up by the old man."

"That does seem to be the case. How else could they be so lacking in decency?"

"It's lucky the old lady, Lord Sheh and Lady Hsing haven't heard of it. If it came to their ears, not only would our good-for-nothing master get beaten and cursed, even Lord Chen and Madam Yu would certainly be made to smart for it."

Hsi-feng went on cursing and raging, refusing to go over for lunch on the excuse that her head ached. Seeing that she was working herself up into a greater fury, Ping-erh urged:

"You'd better calm down, madam. The thing's done, so there's no hurry. There'll be plenty of time to talk it over again after Second Master's return."

Hsi-feng gave a couple of snorts.

"After his return? No, that would be too late."

Ping-erh knelt down to reason with her and comfort her, till at length Hsi-feng calmed down enough to sip some tea. Then, after taking some deep breaths, she asked for her pillow and lay down on the bed, her eyes closed as she considered what to do. When Ping-erh saw that she was resting, she withdrew. And when some people ignorant of what had happened arrived to report on their business, they were sent packing by Feng-erh. Then Ma-nao was sent by the Lady Dowager to ask:

"Why hasn't the Second Mistress gone over for lunch? The old lady's worried and sent me to see what's wrong."

As it was the Lady Dowager who had sent to inquire, Hsi-feng forced herself to get up.

"I've a bit of a headache, nothing serious," she said. "Tell the old lady not to worry. After lying down for a while I'm feeling better." With that she sent the maid back.

She then thought the whole business over carefully once more, and hit on a cunning plan to kill several birds with one stone, working out the safest measures to achieve this. This done, instead of disclosing her plan to Ping-erh, she behaved as cheerfully as if nothing had happened, giving no sign of her fury and jealousy.

Chapter 26
Unhappy Second Sister Yu Is Decoyed into Grand View Garden

When Chia Lien left on his mission, it so happened that the Governor of Pinganchou was away for a month inspecting border areas. To get a definite reply, Chia Lien had to wait in the hostel for his return. Thus by the time the governor came back, received him and settled the matter, nearly two months had passed.

Hsi-feng's plans were already laid. As soon as Chia Lien left she ordered workmen to fix up the three rooms on the eastern side, decorating and furnishing them just like her own. On the fourteenth, she reported to the Lady Dowager and Lady Wang that she wanted to go to the nunnery to offer incense the next morning, taking only Ping-erh, Feng-erh and the wives of Chou Jui and Lai Wang. Before setting out she disclosed her true purpose to them and ordered them all to wear mourning.

Then they set off, Hsing-erh leading the way, to the house where Second Sister Yu lived. He knocked at the gate, which was opened by Pao Erh's wife.

Hsing-erh announced with a grin, "Tell the Second Mistress that Madam Lien is here. Quick!"

Frightened out of her wits, Pao Erh's wife flew in to report this. Second Sister Yu, too, was taken aback; but since Hsi-feng had come she had no choice but to receive her with befitting respect. She hastily straightened her clothes and went out to meet her as Hsi-feng dismounted from her carriage and stepped through the gate.

Second Sister Yu saw that Hsi-feng had nothing but silver trinkets in her hair and was wearing a pale blue satin jacket, black satin cape and white silk skirt. Under eyebrows arched like willow leaves her almond eyes were as bright as those of a phoenix; she was pretty as peach-blossom in spring, simple and austere as chrysanthemums in autumn. As the wives of Chou Jui and Lai Wang helped her into the courtyard, Second Sister Yu stepped forward with a smile to curtsey to her, addressing her as "elder sister."

"I wasn't expecting the honour of this visit, so I didn't come out to meet you," she apologized. "Please overlook my negligence, elder sister." Again she curtseyed.

Smiling, Hsi-feng returned her greeting and hand in hand they entered the house, where Hsi-feng took the seat of honour while Second Sister ordered her maid to bring a cushion, then knelt to pay her respects.

"Your slave is young," she said. "Since coming here, I've left all decisions to my mother and my step-sister. Now that I've had the good fortune to meet you, elder sister, if you don't consider me too far beneath you I'd like to ask for your advice and instructions. I'll bare my heart to you, too, and wait upon you." She bowed low.

Hsi-feng left her seat to return the courtesy.

"This all comes of my behaving like a silly woman," she answered, "for ever advising my husband to take good care of his health and keep away from brothels, to spare his parents worry. We're both fond, foolish women. But he seems to have misunderstood me. If he'd taken a mistress outside and hidden it from me, that wouldn't have signified; but now he's taken you as his second wife, and that's an important matter, in accordance with the rules of propriety, yet he never told me about it.

"Actually, I'd advised him to take another wife, because if he begets a son I, too, shall have someone to rely on in future. But he seems to have thought me the jealous type, and so he took this important step in secret. That was really wronging me! And to whom can I complain but to Heaven and Earth?

"This came to my ears about ten days ago, but for fear of vexing my husband I didn't venture to take it up with him. Now that he happens to have gone on a long journey, I've come to call on you in person. I do hope you'll understand how much I take this to heart and agree to move into our house so that we can live together as sisters, both of one mind, to advise Second Master to pay careful attention to his business and to look after his health. This is only right and proper.

"Foolish and lowly as I am, and unworthy of your company, if we live in separate establishments like this, how do you suppose I can set my mind at rest? Besides, once outsiders know, it will reflect badly on both of our reputations. Not that gossip about *us* is so serious — it's Second Master's reputation that really counts. Besides, it's entirely up to you to save me from getting a bad name.

"I daresay you've heard talk about me from servants who think I run the household too strictly and most likely exaggerate behind my back. But how can someone as intelligent and broad-minded as you believe such disgruntled talk? If I were really so impossible, why have three generations of my seniors as well as all my cousins and in-laws — and don't forget that the Chias are a well-known old family — put up with me all this time? Anyone else would have been angry at his marrying you in secret like this outside, but I actually consider it a blessing which shows that the gods and Buddhas of Heaven and Earth don't want me to be defamed by those low creatures' slander.

"I've come today to beg you to move in and live with me, on the same footing, share and share alike to serve our father and mother-in-law and advise our husband together, and share the same griefs and joys like real sisters. Then those low types will be sorry they sized me up wrongly; and when Second Master comes back and sees this, he as our husband will regret his mistake. So, sister, you'll have become my benefactress, redeeming my reputation.

"If you won't agree to coming back with me, I'll gladly move out to live with you here and wait on you like a younger sister. All I beg of you is to put in a few good words for me to Second Master, so that he'll allow me somewhere to stay. Then I shall die content."

With that she started sobbing and weeping, moving Second Sister to tears too.

After this exchange they resumed their seats, and now Ping-erh came in to pay her respects. As she was unusually well-dressed and looked a cut above the other maids, Second Sister Yu realized who she was and hastily laid a restraining hand on her arm.

"Don't do that, sister!" she exclaimed. "You and I are of the same rank."

Hsi-feng rose with a smile to protest, "Don't overrate her — that would spoil what little good fortune she may have! Just let her pay her respects, sister. She's after all our maid. There's no need to stand on ceremony with her."

She then ordered Chou Jui's wife to unwrap four rolls of fine silk and four pairs of jewelled trinkets set in gold as her gift to Second Sister Yu at this first meeting, and these were accepted with thanks. Then, sipping tea, they spoke of what had happened.

"It was all my fault," Hsi-feng kept reiterating. "No one else is to blame. But do be good to me."

Second Sister, quite taken in by her protestations, thought it was only natural for disgruntled servants to run down their mistress. So she replied very frankly, treating Hsi-feng as a trusted friend. Moreover, Mrs. Chou and the other serving-women there praised Hsi-feng for her goodness, saying it was her being honest to a fault which had given rise to resentment. They announced too that the house had been made ready, as the new mistress would see for herself when she moved in. Second Sister had always thought it would be better for her to live in the Chia mansion, and hearing all this she naturally agreed.

"I ought to accompany you, sister," she said. "But what about this household here?"

"That's no problem," Hsi-feng assured her. "Just get the

servants to take over your personal belongings. The furniture here won't be needed. You can assign anyone you think fit to stay here so as to keep an eye on it."

"Since I've met you today, elder sister, I'll leave all the arrangements for the removal to you. I haven't been here long, and never having run a house before I'm too inexperienced to make decisions. These few cases can be taken. I've really nothing else here of my own, the other things belong to Second Master."

Hsi-feng ordered Chou Jui's wife to make a note of these cases and see to it that they were carried carefully to the eastern rooms. Then she urged Second Sister to put on her jewels and they went out hand in hand to mount the carriage, in which they sat side by side.

"Our family rules are strict," Hsi-feng now told her confidentially. "So far the old lady knows nothing about this business. If they learned that the Second Master married you while still in mourning, they'd have him beaten to death! So we can't present you yet to Their Ladyships. We have a very big garden where the girls of our family live, but other people hardly ever go there. Now that you're moving over, you can stay in the Garden for a couple of days till I've found some way to break this news, and then it will be all right to pay your respects."

"Do exactly as you think best, elder sister," acquiesced Second Sister.

As the pages accompanying the carriage had received their orders in advance, instead of entering the main gate they went straight to the one at the back; and as soon as the ladies alighted, everyone in the neighbourhood was chased away. Then Hsi-feng led Second Sister through the back gate of Grand View Garden to see Li Wan.

By this time most of the inmates of the Garden had heard the news. Now that they saw Hsi-feng bringing Second Sister in, they flocked over to see her and she greeted each in turn. Not one but was very favourably impressed by her beauty and her charm.

"Don't let word of this get out," Hsi-feng warned them all. "If it comes to the ears of Their Ladyships, I'll kill the lot of you!"

The matrons and maids in the Garden were all afraid of Hsi-feng. And as Chia Lien had taken this second wife while observing state mourning and family mourning too, they knew it was a most serious offence and took care not to speak of the matter.

Hsi-feng quietly asked Li Wan to put up the new arrival for a few days.

"Once this business is straightened out," she said, "of course she'll move over with me."

Knowing that rooms had been made ready in Chia Lien's quarters and that it would not be fitting to announce this marriage during the period of mourning, Li Wan agreed.

Hsi-feng then dismissed all Second Sister's maids, assigning some of her own to wait on her, and ordered the women in the Garden to look after her well.

"If she disappears or runs away, you'll have to answer for it!" she threatened them, after which she went off to make other secret arrangements.

Everyone in the household was amazed to see how benevolent Hsi-feng had become. As for Second Sister, now that she had found this niche and all the girls in the Garden treated her well, she was quite contented and happy, thinking her future assured.

After three days, however, Shan-chieh, the maid assigned to her, started showing signs of insubordination.

"There's no hair-oil left," Second Sister told her. "Go and ask Madam Lien for some."

"How can you be so inconsiderate, madam?" Shan-chieh retorted. "Madam Lien has to look after the old lady every day, as well as the mistresses of both mansions and all the young ladies. At the same time she has to give orders to several hundred men-servants and women-servants all told. Not a day goes by but she has ten or twenty important matters to attend to, besides dozens of minor ones. Outside, she has to see to sending gifts and returning the courtesies of so many noble families from Her Imperial Highness down to princess and marquises; on top of which she has to cope with countless relatives and friends, as well as receiving or sending out thousands of taels of silver every day. How can you trouble her with trifles like this? I wouldn't be so demanding if I were you. Yours isn't a proper marriage. She's treating you well because she's so exceptionally kind and generous. If not for that, hearing the way you talk, she could well storm at you and kick you out. And then what could you do? You'd really be stranded."

This harangue made Second Sister hang her head. She saw she would just have to stomach such slights. And things went from bad to worse: Shan-chieh even stopped fetching her meals, or served them unpunctually, bringing nothing but scraps. If Second Sister complained, the maid started screaming at her; but for fear others might scoff that she didn't know her place, she had to put up with it. Every week or so when she happened to see Hsi-feng, the latter was all smiles and sweetness, for ever addressing her as "my dear sister".

"If any servants are remiss and you can't control them, just let me know and I'll have them beaten," promised Hsi-feng. Then she scolded the maids and matrons, "I know the way you take advantage of those who are kind and fear only those who are hard on you. Once my back's turned you're not afraid of anyone. If I hear one word of complaint from the second mistress, I'll have your lives for it!"

Second Sister was taken in by this show of kindness.

"With her taking my side like this, I'd better not make any fuss," she reflected. "Some servants have no sense, that's only natural. If I report them and get them into trouble, I'm the one people will blame." So she covered up for the maids instead.

Meanwhile Hsi-feng had sent Lai Wang out to make detailed inquiries, and had now ascertained that Second Sister had indeed been engaged before to a certain Chang Hua now nineteen, a wastrel and loafer who spent his time gambling and whoring and had squandered his family's money. Having been driven out by his father, he now stayed in a gambling den. And his father, without telling him, had accepted ten taels of silver from old Mrs. Yu for cancelling the engagement.

After Hsi-feng had learned all these particulars, she gave Lai Wang a packet of twenty taels of silver and secretly ordered him to get Chang Hua to stay with him and bring a suit against Chia Lien. He was to accuse him of marrying during a period of state and family mourning, against Imperial decree and unknown to his parents; of relying on his wealth and power to force Chang Hua to renounce his engagement; and of taking a second wife without the consent of his first.

Chang Hua, however, only too well aware of the danger involved, dared not bring such a charge. When Lai Wang reported this to Hsi-feng she fumed:

"Damn him for a mangy cur that won't let itself be helped over a wall! Go and explain to him that it doesn't matter even if he accuses our family of *high treason*. I just want him to make a row so that everyone loses face. If big trouble comes of it, I can always smooth things over."

Lai Wang carried out her orders and explained this to Chang Hua.

Hsi-feng also instructed Lai Wang, "Get him to implicate *you*, then you can confront him in court — I'll tell you just what to say — and I guarantee everything will be all right."

When Lai Wang saw that he had Hsi-feng's backing, he told Chang Hua to include his name in his charge.

"Just accuse me of acting as the middleman and of putting Second Master up to this," he said.

Chang Hua, given this cue, acted on Lai Wang's advice and wrote out his plaint, taking it the next morning to the Court of Censors. When the judge took his seat in the court and saw that this charge against Chia Lien involved his servant Lai Wang, he had no choice but to send for the latter to answer the charge. The runners, not daring to enter the Chia mansion, meant to order a servant to deliver the summons. But Lai Wang had reckoned on their coming, and was already waiting out in the street. When he saw the runners he approached them with a smile.

"Sorry to have put you to this trouble, brothers," he said. "I must have done wrong. All right, put the chains round my neck."

Not venturing to do this, they replied, "Please just come quietly, sir, and stop joking."

Then Lai Wang went to the court and knelt down before the judge, who showed him the charge. He pretended to read it through and then kowtowed.

"I was in the know about this," he admitted. "My master did this all right. But this fellow Chang Hua has a grudge against me, that's why he's accused me of being the middleman. Actually, it was someone else. I beg Your Honour to make investigations."

Chang Hua, kowtowing too, said, "That's true; but it's someone I dared not mention, that's why I accused the servant instead."

"Silly fool!" Lai Wang made a show of desperation. "Hurry up and come clean. This is a government court. You must name him even if he's a gentleman."

Then Chang Hua named Chia Jung. And the judge had to have him served with a summons.

Hsi-feng had secretly sent Ching-erh to find out when this summons was issued. Now she promptly called for Wang Hsin, explained what had happened, and told him to go and bribe the judge with three hundred taels just to make a display of severity in order to frighten the culprits.

That evening Wang Hsin went to the judge's house and fixed things up. The judge, knowing the situation, accepted the bribe and the next day announced in court that Chang Hua was a scoundrel who had trumped up this charge against innocent people because he was in debt to the Chia family. For as this judge was on good terms with Wang Tzu-teng, after a word in private from Wang Hsin he was all for settling the matter without making trouble for the Chias. He therefore said no more, simply detained the plaintiff and the accused and summoned Chia Jung to court.

Chapter 27
Jealous Hsi-feng Makes a Scene in the Ning Mansion

Chia Jung was seeing to some business for Chia Chen when someone brought him word of this charge against him and urged him to think of a way out at once. He made haste to report this to Chia Chen.

"I was prepared for this; but that fellow certainly has a nerve!" said Chia Chen.

At once he sealed two hundred taels in a packet to be sent to the judge, and ordered a servant to go and answer the charge. As they were discussing their next step, the arrival of Madam Lien from the West Mansion was announced. Both men started and wanted to slip away into hiding, but it was too late — Hsi-feng had already entered.

"A fine elder brother you are!" she cried. "A fine thing you got your younger brother to do!"

Chia Jung hastily stepped forward to pay his respects. Hsi-feng simply caught hold of him and went on in.

"Entertain your aunt well," said Chia Chen. "Order a good meal for her." He then called for his horse and made off.

Hsi-feng marched Chia Jung towards the inner rooms and Madam Yu came out to meet her.

"What's the matter?" she asked, seeing how furious she looked. "Why this hurry?"

Hsi-feng spat in her face.

"Couldn't you find husbands for the girls of your Yu family that you had to smuggle them into the Chia family?" she

苦尤娘
赚入大观园
酸凤姐大闹宁国府

demanded. "Are all men of the Chias so wonderful? Have all the other men in the world died out? Even if you want to pawn off your sisters, there's a proper procedure for marriage and it should be announced in a decent way. Have you taken leave of your senses? How could you send her over during a time of state and family mourning? And now that someone's brought a charge against us, I'm all in a flurry. Even the court thinks me a jealous shrew and has summoned me to stand trial. My name will be mud! And I shall be divorced!

"What wrong have I done you since I've come to this house that you treat me so cruelly? Or did Their Ladyships tip you a hint to trap me like this so as to get rid of me? Let's go to face the judge now, both of us, to clear this up. Then we can put the case before the whole clan. If they give me a bill of divorce, I'll leave."

Sobbing and storming she caught hold of Madam Yu, insisting on going to court. Chia Jung knelt in desperation and kowtowed, begging her not to be angry.

"May lightning blast your skull!" she swore at him. "May five devils tear you apart, you heartless wretch! You fear nothing in heaven or on earth, playing such dirty tricks all the time and doing such shameless, lawless things to ruin our family. Even your dead mother's spirit will disown you, so will all our ancestors. How dare you appeal to me?"

After this tearful tirade she raised her hand to strike him. Chia Jung thumped his head on the ground again.

"Don't be angry, aunt!" he cried. "'Don't hurt your hand — let me slap myself instead. Please don't be angry, auntie."

He raised his hands and slapped himself on both cheeks.

"Will you meddle in that thoughtless way again?" he asked himself. "Just listen to your uncle and not to your aunt?"

All present, repressing smiles, begged him to stop.

And now Hsi-feng threw herself into Madam Yu's arms to weep and wail, calling on Heaven and Earth.

"I wouldn't mind you finding another wife for your brother-in-law," she sobbed. "But why make him flout the Imperial decree and keep it secret from his parents? Why give *me* a bad name? We must go to find the judge before he sends police and runners to arrest me. After that we must go and see Their Ladyships and call the whole clan together to discuss this. If I've acted so badly, refusing to let my husband take a second wife or another concubine, just give me a bill of divorce and I'll leave at once.

"Actually, I've fetched your sister here myself, but didn't venture to report it to Their Ladyships for fear they'd be angry. She has maids in the Garden to wait on her hand and foot, and I've prepared rooms for her in our place exactly like my own, where I meant to take her as soon as the old lady knew. We could all have settled down then, minding our own business, and I'd have let bygones be bygones. How was I to know that she was engaged to another man before? How was I to know what you'd been up to?

"Yesterday, hearing that her betrothed had brought a charge against me, I was so desperate that I had to take five hundred taels of the mistress' silver to use as a bribe; because if I were summoned to court your Chia family would lose face. And my servant is still locked up by the police."

She went on storming and wailing, sobbingly invoking their ancestors and her parents, then tried to dash out her brains and kill herself. Madam Yu, reduced to a squelch, her clothes covered with tears and snot, could only round on Chia Jung.

"You degenerate!" she scolded. "You and your father are to blame for this. I warned you against it."

Hsi-feng let out another wail, clasping Madam Yu's face between both hands.

"Were you crazy?" she demanded. "Was your mouth stuffed with eggplant or with a bit and curb, that you couldn't let me know? If you had, I wouldn't be in such a fix, with this business so out of hand it's been taken to court. Yet you're still trying to shift the blame to *them*! As the saying goes, 'A good wife keeps her husband out of trouble — a sound woman counts for more than a sound man.' If you were any good, how could they do such things? You're as stupid and dumb as a gourd with its tip sawn off. All you care about, you fool, is getting a *name* for goodness. So they're not afraid of you and won't listen to what you say." She spat again and again in disgust.

"That's how it was, really," sobbed Madam Yu. "If you don't believe me, ask the servants. Of course I tried to stop them — they just wouldn't listen. So what could I do? I don't blame you for being angry, sister, but I simply couldn't help it."

The concubines and maids kneeling fearfully round them now pleaded with Hsi-feng, "You're so wise and understanding, madam, even if our mistress did wrong you've got even with her now. Usually, in front of us slaves, you're both on the best of terms. So please leave her some face!"

They brought Hsi-feng some tea, but she smashed the cup. However, she stopped crying and smoothed her hair.

"Fetch your father here!" she ordered Chia Jung. "I want to ask him why, with still a fortnight to go before the mourning for the uncle was over, he let the nephew take a wife. I've never heard of such a thing! I must learn the rules of propriety from him so as to pass them on later to the young people."

Still on his knees, Chia Jung kowtowed and protested, "This had nothing to do with my parents. It was I who put my uncle up to it — I must have eaten some shit. My father knew nothing about it. He's gone now to prepare for the funeral procession. If you make a scene, aunt, it will be the death of me. Whatever punishment you impose I'll accept it, but for pity's sake settle this court case — it's too serious for me to handle. You're so intelligent you know the saying: 'If your arm is broken, hide it in your sleeve.' I was an utter fool. As I've done such a despicable thing, I'm just like a cat or a dog. Now that you've given me this lesson, auntie, do please do your best to settle this with the court. Though I've been so undutiful and wronged you, aunt, by causing all this trouble, what else can I do but beg you to take pity on me!" He went on kowtowing as if he would never stop.

The behaviour of mother and son made it hard for Hsi-feng to go on storming at them. She had to adopt a different attitude now.

Apologizing to Madam Yu she said, "I'm too young and inexperienced. When I heard the case had been taken to court, I was frightened out of my wits. How could I have been so rude to you just now, sister! Still, Jung is right: 'If your arm is broken, hide it in your sleeve.' You must forgive me. And please ask Cousin Chen to lose no time in settling this lawsuit."

"Don't worry," Madam Yu and Chia Jung assured her.

"Uncle won't be involved at all," added Chia Jung. "You said just now you'd spent five hundred taels, aunt. Of course we'll get together that sum and send it over to make it up to you. How can we make you out of pocket over us? That would be even more outrageous. But one thing, aunt, will you help see to it that no word of this reaches Their Ladyships?"

Hsi-feng smiled sarcastically at Madam Yu.

"First you stab me in the back and now you ask me to hush it up for you! I may be a fool but I'm not all *that* foolish. Your cousin happens to be my husband, sister. If you were worried because he had no son, wouldn't I be still more worried? I look on your younger sister as my own sister. When I heard about this I was too excited to sleep and made my people get ready rooms at once, to fetch her in to live with us. Actually the servants had more sense: they said, 'You're too kind-hearted, madam. It seems to us it would be better to wait till you've reported this to Their Ladyships and see what they have to say.' That made me rage at them, so they said no more.

"But nothing worked out as I wanted. Like a slap in the face or a bolt from the blue came this suit brought by Chang Hua. I had to beg people to find out who this Chang Hua was, that he had such a nerve; and two days later I was told he was a rascally beggar. Being young and ignorant, I laughed and asked what he'd accused us of. The servants told me, 'The new mistress was engaged to him. Now he's desperate, liable to starve or freeze to death anyway, so he's seized on this chance. Even if he dies for it, it's a better bet than dying of hunger and cold; so how can you blame him? After all, the master acted too hastily and was guilty of two offences by marrying during state mourning and family mourning. He was wrong, too, to keep it a secret from his parents and to take a new wife without his wife's consent. As the proverb says, "One who will risk being sliced to pieces dare unsaddle the Emperor." A man so desperately poor will go to any lengths. He's in the right too, so why not make an indictment?'

"So you see, sister, even if I'd been as wise as Han Hsin[1] or Chang Liang,[2] such talk would have frightened me out of my wits. Besides, with my husband away, I had no one to consult; I could only try to patch things up with money. Yet the more I gave him, the more I was at his mercy and the more he blackmailed me. But how much can he squeeze out of *me*? No more than from a pimple on a rat's tail. That's why I panicked and flew into such a rage that I came looking for you. . . ."

Not waiting for her to finish, Madam Yu and her son said, "Don't worry. We'll see to it."

Chia Jung added, "It's Chang Hua's poverty that's made him so reckless he's risked his life to indict us. I know what to do. Promise him some money and get him to admit that he brought a false accusation; then we can settle the business.

---

[1] Han Hsin, a native of Huaiyin, was so poor in his early days that he asked a washerwoman to share her meal with him. He later helped Liu Pang defeat Hsiang Yu and was entitled Prince of Chi, but then he was killed for plotting against Liu Pang.

[2] Chang Liang (?-189 B.C.), one of the advisors and generals of Liu Pang, the founding emperor of the Han Dynasty, laid siege to Hsiang Yu, the Conqueror of Chu, at Kaihsia (present-day Linpi, Anhwei). Chang Liang made his men play iron flutes and sing Chu folksongs every night, making the Chu troops so homesick that their morale was undermined and they were finally defeated by the Han troops.

When he comes out, we'll give him some more silver and that will be that."

"What a clever boy!" said Hsi-feng derisively. "No wonder that you did this thing with no thought of the consequences. How stupid you are! Suppose he agreed to what you proposed and got money from us after the case was settled, of course that would be that — for the time being. But as such people are rascals, as soon as that silver was spent he'd start black-mailing us again. If he made further trouble what should we do? We may not be afraid of him, still it's something to worry about. And he can always say if we hadn't wronged him why should we give him money?"

Chia Jung had sense enough to understand this.

He said with a smile, "Well, I have another plan. Since I caused the trouble it's up to me to fix it. I'll go and sound Chang Hua out. Does he want her back, or will he give her up and settle for money with which he can marry another girl? If he insists on having her, I'll go and persuade my second aunt to leave here and marry him; if he wants money, we shall have to give him some."

"That's all very well," said Hsi-feng hastily. "I certainly don't want her to leave us, and I certainly won't let her. If you've any feeling for me, nephew, just give him a bigger sum in settlement."

Chia Jung knew very well that in spite of Hsi-feng's prot-estations she really wanted to get rid of Second Sister and was only posing as broad-minded. He had to agree, however, to whatever she said, at which she looked delighted.

"The problem outside is easy to handle, but what about the arrangement at home?" Hsi-feng now asked. "You must come back with me to report this."

This threw Madam Yu into another panic. She begged Hsi-feng to make up some story for her.

"If you can't talk your way out, why do this in the first place?" asked Hsi-feng sarcastically. "I've no patience with the way you're carrying on. But it wouldn't be like me to refuse to find a way out for you, as I'm so soft-hearted that even when people trick me I still act like a fool. All right then, I'll see to this. Both of you keep out of it.

"I'll take your sister to pay her respects to Their Ladyships, and tell them that I took a fancy to her, and because I have no son I was thinking of buying a couple of concubines. Finding your sister so charming, and as we're relatives too, I wanted her to be Lien's second wife. But because her parents and sister had died recently and she was finding it hard to manage, with no home of her own, how could she possibly wait till after the full hundred days' mourning? So I decided to bring her into our house, and I've made the side rooms ready for her to stay in for the time being. Once the mourning is over she can live with my husband.

"I shall brazen it out somehow in my shameless way. If anyone is blamed it won't be *you*. What do you think of this plan?"

Madam Yu and Chia Jung responded, "It's most generous and kind of you. How clever you are! Once it's settled, we'll certainly both come to thank you."

Madam Yu ordered her maids to help Hsi-feng wash her face and comb her hair. Then the table was spread and she herself served the wine and food. Before long, however, Hsi-feng rose to go.

She went to the Garden and told Second Sister what had happened, explaining how worried she had been, how she had ascertained the facts, and what would have to be done to keep them all out of trouble. She promised to get them out of the dilemma.

Chapter 28
Crafty Hsi-feng Kills Her Rival by Proxy

Unable to express all her gratitude, Second Sister went off with Hsi-feng. And propriety required Madam Yu to accompany them to report to the old lady.

"You needn't say anything," Hsi-feng assured her. "Leave all the talking to me."

"Of course," agreed Madam Yu. "If there's any blame we'll let you take it."

They went first to the Lady Dowager's room where she was chatting and laughing with the girls from the Garden. At sight of the pretty young woman Hsi-feng had brought in, the old lady looked at her searchingly. "Whose child is this?" she asked. "So charming!"

Hsi-feng stepped forward and said with a smile, "Take a good look, Old Ancestress. Isn't she sweet?" Pulling Second Sister forward too, she told her, "This is grandmother-in-law. Hurry up and kowtow to her."

At once Second Sister prostrated herself to pay her respects. Then Hsi-feng introduced the girls to her one by one.

"Now you know them," she said. "After the old lady's through with inspecting you, you can pay your respects to each other."

Second Sister pretended that this was the first time she had met them, then stood there with lowered head while the Lady Dowager looked her up and down.

"What is your name?" she inquired. "How old are you?"

"Never mind about that, Old Ancestress," Hsi-feng chuckled. "Just say, is she prettier than me?"

The old lady put on her spectacles, telling Yuan-yang and Hu-po, "Bring the child closer. I want to look at her skin."

Amid suppressed laughter, Second Sister was pushed forward and subjected to a carefully scrutiny. Then the Lady Dowager made Hu-po hold out her hands for inspection. Yuan-yang lifted Second Sister's skirt as well to show her feet. Her examination at an end, the old lady took off her spectacles.

"Perfect!" she pronounced. "She's even prettier than you."

Smiling, Hsi-feng promptly knelt down to relate in detail the story she had made up in Madam Yu's room. "Do take pity on her, Old Ancestress," she pleaded. "Let her move in now, and after a year they can be formally married."

"That's quite in order," the old lady conceded. "I'm glad you're so understanding and tolerant. But she mustn't live with Lien for a year."

Hsi-feng kowtowed, then got up and requested that two maids be sent to present Second Sister to Lady Hsing and Lady Wang and tell them this was the old lady's decision. The Lady Dowager agreed and this was done. Lady Wang had been worried because of Hsi-feng's bad name. Now that she was taking in a second wife for her husband, she was naturally pleased. So from now on Second Sister could come into the open, and she moved to Hsi-feng's side rooms.

Hsi-feng meanwhile sent a messenger in secret to urge Chang Hua to insist on claiming his bride, promising that in addition to a generous dowry he would be given money to set up house. For Chang Hua himself was too spineless to dare sue the Chia family.

Then Chia Jung sent a man to court to contend, "It was Chang Hua who first gave up the engagement. Being related to the Yu family we did, it is true, invite her to stay in our house; but there was no talk of marriage. Because Chang Hua owed us money and could not pay it, he trumped up this charge against our master."

As the judges were all connected with the Chia and Wang

families and had in addition accepted bribes from them, they condemned Chang Hua as a rascal whom poverty had driven to blackmail. His plea rejected, he was beaten and thrown out of court. But Ching-erh outside had fixed it with the runners not to beat him severely.

And now Ching-erh told Chang Hua, "As you were engaged to the girl first, if you demand her the court will have to give her to you."

Thereupon Chang Hua brought a new suit; but again Wang Hsin took a message to the judge, and the court's verdict was: "Chang Hua's debt to the Chia family must be repaid in full by a specified date. As for his betrothed, he can marry her when he has the means."

Chang Hua's father, summoned to court to hear this verdict after having been told the situation by Ching-erh, exulted that now he would get both the money and the girl. He went to the Chia mansion to fetch Second Sister.

Hsi-feng with a great show of alarm reported this to the Lady Dowager.

"This muddle is all my Sister-in-Law Chen's fault!" she complained. "Apparently the engagement was never really cancelled. That's why the Changs took the case to court, and now this decision's been made."

The old lady sent at once for Madam Yu.

"Because your sister was promised from childhood to the Chang family, and they never broke the engagement, they've brought this charge against us now," she scolded.

"But they took the money," protested Madam Yu. "How can they still claim her?"

Hsi-feng put in, "According to Chang Hua, he never saw any money, and no one contacted him. According to his father, Second Sister's mother did make such an offer but they turned it down; and after her mother died you took her in as a secondary wife. As we've no proof to the contrary, he can talk any nonsense he pleases. It's lucky Second Master Lien isn't at home and they haven't been formally married. Still, as she's already here, how can we send her back? Wouldn't that make us lose face?"

The old lady said, "They're not married yet, and it wouldn't look good to seize someone promised to another man. That would damage our reputation. We'd better send her back. It'll be easy enough to find some other nice girl."

When Second Sister heard this she exclaimed, "My mother really *did* give them ten taels of silver to cancel the engagement. Now in desperation because he's poor, he denies it. My sister did nothing wrong."

"That shows how troublesome such rascals are," said the Lady Dowager. "Well, I leave it to you, Hsi-feng, to sort this out."

Hsi-feng had to comply. On her return she sent for Chia Jung, who knew perfectly what she was aiming at. He realized what a great loss of face it would be if Second Sister were to be reclaimed by the Changs, so he reported this to Chia Chen and secretly sent Chang Hua the message: Now that you've got so much money, why must you have the girl back? If you insist, the gentlemen may get angry and find a way to kill you where no one will bury you. With money, you can go home and find a good bride. If you do that, we'll help with your travelling expenses.

Chang Hua on reflection thought this a good idea. He discussed it with his father, and they reckoned they were now the richer by about a hundred taels. So the next day at dawn, father and son started home.

When Chia Jung heard this he told the Lady Dowager and Hsi-feng, "Chang Hua and his father have fled for fear of being punished for bringing a false charge. The court knows of this but has decided to let the matter drop. The whole business is over!"

Hsi-feng reflected, "If I make Chang Hua reclaim Second Sister, Lien on his return will most likely offer more money to get her back, and Chang Hua's bound to agree. So I'd better keep her here with me until I've made other plans. The only snag is we don't know where Chang Hua will go, and whether he'll spread this story or come back later to re-open this case. If he does, I'll have cut my own throat! I should never have given other people this handle against me." She bitterly regretted what she had done.

Then she hit on another plan. She quietly ordered Lai Wang to send men to find Chang Hua, then either hale him to court on a charge of theft and have him done to death, or send assassins to kill him secretly. In this way the root of the trouble would be removed and her reputation assured.

Lai Wang went home and thought over these instructions.

"Since the man's gone and the matter's dropped, why do anything so drastic?" he asked himself. "Taking someone's life is a serious crime, no joke. I'll fool her into thinking it's done instead."

He lay low outside for a few days, then returned to report that Chang Hua, travelling with a fair amount of silver had been beaten and killed at dawn one day by some highwaymen in the Chingkou district, and his father had died of fright in the inn. A post-mortem had been held there and the bodies buried.

Hsi-feng did not believe him.

"If I find you've been lying, I'll knock out your teeth!" she threatened. But there the matter rested.

Meanwhile Hsi-feng and Second Sister were on the best of terms, to all appearances closer even than sisters.

When Chia Lien finally came home after completing his business, he went straight to the new house. But it was locked up and deserted, with only an old caretaker there who told him all that had happened. Chia Lien stamped his foot in the stirrup, then went to report on his mission to his parents. Chia Sheh, very pleased, praised his competence and rewarded him with a hundred taels of silver as well as a new concubine — a seventeen-year-old maid of his named Chiu-tung. Chia Lien kowtowed his thanks and left in high spirits. Having paid his respects to the Lady Dowager and other members of the family he went home somewhat sheepishly to see Hsi-feng, but found her less stern than usual. She came out with Second

Sister to welcome him and ask after his health. Then Chia
Lien, telling her of his father's gift, could not help looking
pleased and proud. Hsi-feng immediately sent two serving-
women to fetch Chiu-tung by carriage. Before she had rid
herself of one thorn in her side, here — out of the blue — was
another! However, she had to watch her tongue and hide her
anger by a show of complaisance, ordering a feast of welcome,
then taking Chiu-tung to present her to the Lady Dowager and
Lady Wang, much to her husband's amazement.

On the Double Twelfth, Chia Chen rose early to sacrifice to
the ancestors, then took his leave of the Lady Dowager and
other ladies of the family. Most of the men saw him off to
the Pavilion of Tearful Parting, only Chia Lien and Chia Jung
accompanying him all the way to the temple and back, a trip
taking three days and three nights. On the road, Chia Chen
admonished them on the need to run their households well,
and they gave him the appropriate assurances — there is no
need to dwell on their conversation.

To return to Hsi-feng at home. Outwardly, it goes without
saying, she treated Second Sister well; but inwardly she plotted
to destroy her.

When the two of them were alone she told Second Sister,
"You have such a bad name, sister, even the old lady and
the mistresses have heard about it. They say that while still
a girl you were unchaste and intimate with your brother-in-
law. 'You've picked someone nobody else wanted,' they scold
me. 'Why not get rid of her and choose someone better.' Talk
like that makes me furious. I've tried to find out who started
this, but I can't. If this goes on, how are we to hold up our
heads in front of these slaves? I seem to have landed myself
in a foul mess." Having said this a couple of times, she pretended to fall ill with anger, refusing to eat or drink.

All the maids and servants, with the exception of Ping-erh,
kept gossiping, making sarcastic remarks, and casting asper-
sions at Second Sister. As for Chiu-tung, having been given
to Chia Lien by his father, she felt superior to everyone else

including even Hsi-feng and Ping-erh, not to say a discarded
wanton who had been Chia Lien's mistress before she became
his wife. "How can she take precedence of *me*!" she thought.
So she treated her with contempt. Hsi-feng was secretly
pleased at this, and Second Sister had to swallow her indignation.

As Hsi-feng was shamming sickness she stopped having her
meals with Second Sister, just ordering the servants to take
food to her room every day — and the rice and dishes were
always of the worst. Ping-erh took pity on her. She would
spend her own money on extra dishes for her, or take her
sometimes for a stroll in the Garden, getting special soups made
for her in the kitchen there. No one else dared report this to
Hsi-feng; but Chiu-tung, happening to find out, went to tell
her.

"Ping-erh's spoiling your reputation, madam," she said. "The
good dishes we have here are wasted on her — she won't eat
them. Instead, she scrounges food in the Garden."

Hsi-feng swore at Ping-erh, "Other people's cats catch mice
for them, but mine just steals my chickens!"

Ping-erh did not venture to talk back. After that she had
to keep at a distance from Second Sister, and she bore Chiu-
tung a grudge but could not speak out.

Li Wan, Ying-chun and Hsi-chun in the Garden thought
Hsi-feng was uncommonly good to Second Sister. Others like
Pao-yu and Tai-yu were worried for her, but did not like to
meddle in their affairs. Second Sister looked so pathetic when
she called that they sympathized with her, and when they were
talking alone she would shed tears, but she never breathed a
word against Hsi-feng who had shown her nothing of her
vicious side.

When Chia Lien came home and observed Hsi-feng's irre-
proachable behaviour to Second Sister, he did not give the
matter a second thought. Besides, he had long had designs
on many of his father's concubines and young maids, including
Chiu-tung, who for their part were disgusted because their
senile old master, still lecherous, was virtually impotent. Why,

then, should he keep them all there? So apart from a few with some sense of propriety, the rest played about with the pages at the inner gate or even made eyes at Chia Lien, who was only too ready to flirt with them but for fear of his father dared go no further than that.

Although Chiu-tung had been interested in Chia Lien, they had never had an affair. Now that as luck would have it she had been given to him, it was truly like throwing a dry faggot on a blazing fire. They clung to each other like glue, Chia Lien so enamoured of his new concubine that he never left her side. Little by little his affection for Second Sister lessened. Chiu-tung was the only one he cared for.

Hsi-feng, though hating Chiu-tung, was eager to use her first to rid herself of Second Sister by "killing with a borrowed sword" and "watching from a hilltop while two tigers fought". For once Chiu-tung had killed Second Sister, she could do this new concubine in. Her mind made up, when they were alone she often advised Chiu-tung:

"You're young and inexperienced. She's now the second mistress, your master's favourite. Even *I* have to yield to her to some extent, yet you keep provoking her. You're just looking for trouble."

Inflamed by such talk, Chiu-tung took to cursing and storming every day, "The mistress is too soft and weak; I haven't that kind of forbearance. What's happened to her? She used to be such a terror. Well, the mistress may be broad-minded, but I'm not going to put up with a mote in my eye. Just let me have it out with that bitch — then she'll see!"

Hsi-feng in her room pretended to be too frightened to say a word. Second Sister in her room wept for rage and could not eat, but she dared not tell Chia Lien. And the next day when the Lady Dowager asked why her eyes were so red and swollen, she dared not explain.

Chiu-tung seized every chance to score off her. She secretly told the old lady and Lady Wang, "She keeps making trouble, complaining and whining all day for no reason at all, besides cursing madam and me behind our backs. She hopes we'll both die early, so that she can live with Second Master and do just as she pleases."

"Imagine!" exclaimed the old lady. "When a girl's too pretty, she is bound to be jealous. Hsi-feng's been kind to her all along, yet she repays her by treating her like a rival! This shows she's a worthless creature."

Little by little she took a dislike to Second Sister. And when the others saw that she had lost favour with the old lady, they naturally bullied her too. Second Sister was in such a miserable dilemma, she could neither die nor live. Ping-erh was the only one who tried, behind Hsi-feng's back, to help her and divert her mind from her troubles.

How could Second Sister, fragile as snow, delicate as a flower, stand up to such cruel treatment? After suppressing her anger for just a month, she fell ill and lost her appetite. Too listless to move, she grew daily thinner and paler. One night when she closed her eyes, she saw her younger sister approaching, the duck-and-drake swords in her hands.

"You've always been too naive and soft-hearted," Third Sister told her. "That's why you're in trouble now. Don't trust that shrew's honeyed talk or her show of being such a virtuous wife — at heart she's crafty and cruel. She's made up her mind to kill you. If I'd been alive, I'd never have let you move into their house; even if you had, I'd not let her treat you like this. Still, we brought this on ourselves by our worthless lives and wanton ways, corrupting men and upsetting family relations. So this is just retribution. Now take my advice and kill that shrew with this sword, then go together to the Goddess of Disenchantment for her to decide the case. Otherwise you will die in vain and no one will pity you."

Second Sister sobbed, "I've already got a bad name, sister. As I deserve my present fate, why should I add to my crimes by killing her? Let me just put up with it. If Heaven takes pity on me, I may recover. Wouldn't that be better?"

"Still so naive, sister?" the other scoffed. "No one, since time immemorial, has escaped Heaven's far-flung net. The Way of Providence is retribution. Although you've repented and mended your ways, you've already made father, son and cousins guilty of incest; so how can Providence allow you to live at peace?"

"If I can't live at peace, that's only just," said Second Sister tearfully. "I bear no resentment."

Hearing this, Third Sister heaved a long sigh and withdrew. Second Sister woke with a start to find it was only a dream.

When Chia Lien came to see her, as no one else was about she told him with tears, "I shan't get over this illness. I've been with you for half a year and I'm with child, but don't know whether it will be a boy or a girl. If Heaven has pity and the child is born, well and good. Otherwise, I shan't be able to save myself, let alone the child."

"Don't you worry," Chia Lien, in tears himself, reassured her. "I'll get a good doctor for you."

He immediately went out to send for the doctor. However, Doctor Wang was busy manoeuvring to get a post in the army in order to acquire a noble title for his offspring. In his absence the servants fetched Doctor Hu Chun-jung. His diagnosis was that her menstruation was irregular and some tonic would set her right. When Chia Lien told him that she had missed three periods and was often sick, so it looked like a pregnancy, Hu Chun-jung asked the serving-women to show him the lady's hand, and Second Sister stretched out her hand from behind the curtains. After feeling the pulse for some time he declared:

"If it were a pregnancy, the liver humour should be strong. But the wood is in the ascendant, and that engenders the fire element which causes irregular menstruation. May I make so bold as to ask to have a glimpse of the lady's face, so that I can see how she looks before venturing to make out a prescription."

Chia Lien had to order the curtain to be raised. But the sight of Second Sister robbed Hu Chun-jung of his senses. He was too dazed to know what he was doing. Then the curtain was lowered and Chia Lien escorted him out. Asked what the trouble was he said:

"It's not a pregnancy, just congestion of the blood. To make her periods normal, we must get rid of the congestion." He then wrote a prescription and took his leave.

Chia Lien ordered servants to send over the doctor's fee and buy and prepare the medicine for the patient.

In the middle of the night, Second Sister had such a pain in her stomach that she miscarried — the foetus was male — and bled so copiously that she fainted. Chia Lien hearing this cursed Hu Chun-jung and had another doctor fetched at once. He also sent men to go and beat up Hu; but the latter heard of this in time to bundle together his things and run away.

The newly summoned doctor said, "She had a weak constitution to begin with, and after conceiving she seems to have been bottling up some resentment. That other gentleman made the mistake of using potent drugs which have undermined the lady's health completely. We cannot look for a speedy recovery. She will have to take both potions and pills, and must pay no attention to any malicious gossip; then we can only hope she may get well." This said, he left.

In a frenzy, Chia Lien asked who it was that had fetched that fellow Hu and had the man beaten within an inch of his life.

Hsi-feng showing ten times more anxiety exclaimed, "We seem fated to have no son! After going to such trouble to beget one, we come up against this bungling quack." She offered incense and kowtowed to Heaven and Earth, praying earnestly, "Let me fall ill if only Sister Yu can recover, conceive again and give birth to a boy. Then I'll gladly fast and chant sutras for the rest of my life."

Chia Lien and the others, seeing this, could not but praise her.

While Chia Lien stayed with Chiu-tung, Hsi-feng prepared soup and broth for the invalid.

She also berated Ping-erh, "You're just as luckless as me with my illness, because you're not ill, just barren! It must be our bad luck that's brought the Second Mistress to this pass — or may be someone's horoscope clashes with hers."

Thereupon she sent out to consult fortune-tellers, who returned the reply that the trouble had been caused by a woman born in the year of the rabbit. They checked, and as Chiu-tung was the only one in their household born in that year they laid the blame at her door.

Chiu-tung's jealousy had already been aroused by the care Chia Lien lavished on Second Sister, fetching doctors, giving her medicine, and having the servant who had blundered beaten. Now *she* was told that she was the one to blame, and Hsi-feng advised her to move out for a few months and make herself scarce.

Chiu-tung wept and stormed, "What's all this senseless talk from that blind rascal? I kept as clear of her as well water and river water. How could *my* horoscope clash with hers? She had all sorts of contacts outside, the slut. Why does the jinx have to be found here? Which of all those fine fellows she knew got her with child? It's only this credulous master of ours who's taken in by her. Even if she had a child, we wouldn't know whether its name should be Chang or Wang. *You* may treasure her bastard, madam, but not I! Who can't have a child? If I have one a year or so from now, at least there'll be no doubt who fathered it."

The maids were amused by this tirade but dared not laugh outright. And just then Lady Hsing called.

Chiu-tung told her, "The Second Master and Second Mistress want to throw me out. I've nowhere to go. Please take pity on me, madam!"

Lady Hsing first scolded Hsi-feng, then said sternly to Chia Lien:

"You ungrateful cur! Whatever her faults, she was given you by your father. How can you throw her out for the sake of a woman you brought in from outside? Have you no respect for your father? If you want to get rid of her, you can at least return her to him." She then left in a temper.

Emboldened by this, Chiu-tung went to Second Sister's window to scream abuse at her, making her feel even more wretched.

Chia Lien spent that night in Chiu-tung's room. And after Hsi-feng had gone to bed Ping-erh slipped in to see Second Sister and comfort her, advising her to rest well and not trouble about that bitch.

Second Sister took her hand and said through tears, "How good you've been to me, sister, since I came here! *You've* suffered a lot too on my account. If I come out of this alive, I'll repay your kindness. I'm afraid I'm done for, though, and can only pay you back in my next life."

Ping-erh was reduced to tears too.

"It was all *my* fault," she confessed. "I was too naive. I never kept anything from her, so when I heard of your marriage outside I felt I had to tell her. I had no idea such trouble would come of it."

"No, you're wrong," protested Second Sister. "If you hadn't told, she'd have found out anyway. You just happened to tell her first. At any rate, I *wanted* to move in for appearances' sake. So you're in no way to blame."

They both wept again and presently, after a few more words of advice, Ping-erh saw that it was late and went back to rest.

Left to herself Second Sister thought, "I'm so ill, and getting worse every day, I see no hope of recovery. And now that I've miscarried and haven't the child to worry about, why should I go on putting up with such taunts? Better die and be done with it! They say swallowing gold will kill you. Wouldn't that be a cleaner death than hanging myself or cutting my own throat?"

She struggled out of bed and opened her case, from which she took a piece of gold of a fair size. Weeping and cursing her fate, she put it in her mouth and after several desperate attempts succeeded in swallowing it. Then she hastily dressed herself neatly and put on her trinkets, after which she lay down on the *kang*. Not a soul had any suspicion of what she had done.

The next morning when she failed to call for her maids, they attended cheerfully to their own toilets while Hsi-feng

弄小巧因借剑殺人

覺大浪吞生金自遜

and Chiu-tung went off to pay their respects to the senior mistresses.

Ping-erh was shocked by this and scolded the maids, "Don't be so heartless! You only obey harsh people who beat or curse you — and that's the treatment you deserve. Have you no pity at all for someone so ill? You might at least behave decently, instead of taking advantage of her good nature and kicking her when she's down."

The maids opened Second Sister's door then. At sight of her lying — neatly dressed — dead on her bed, they screamed with fright. Ping-erh running in wept bitterly when she saw this. And the maids, remembering now how gentle Second Sister had been and how much kinder to them than Hsi-feng, shed tears over her death as well, but took care to hide their grief from their dreaded mistress.

The news spread at once through the whole mansion. Chia Lien came in, clasped the corpse and wept without stop.

Hsi-feng put on a show of sobbing, "How cruel of you, sister, to leave me alone like this! What a poor return for my kindness!"

Madam Yu and Chia Jung also came to mourn and console Chia Lien. Then he reported the matter to Lady Wang, and obtained permission to leave the corpse for five days in Pear Fragrance Court before its removal to Iron Threshold Temple. Hasty orders were given to have the court gate opened and the three main rooms cleared for the coffin's resting place. Since it would be unbecoming to carry the bier through the back gate, Chia Lien had a new gate leading to the street made through the main wall facing Pear Fragrance Court; booths were set up on either side of this and an altar was erected for Buddhist masses. And there Second Sister was carried on a soft couch with a silken mattress and a coverlet shrouding her body. Eight pages and a few matrons escorted the bier from the inner wall to Pear Fragrance Court, where they had an astrologer waiting.

When Chia Lien lifted the coverlet and saw Second Sister

lying there as if alive, yet even lovelier than in life, he threw his arms around her.

"Wife, your death is a mystery," he wailed. "But I brought it on you."

Chia Jung hastily stepped forward to console him.

"Don't give way to such grief, uncle. This aunt of mine was ill-starred." As he spoke he pointed south at the wall of Grand View Garden.

Chia Lien caught his meaning and softly stamped his foot.

"Yes, I know. I shall get to the bottom of it and avenge you!"

The astrologer reported that as the lady had died at five in the morning she could not be carried to the temple on the fifth, but the third or the seventh would be appropriate, and the body should be coffined at three the next morning — an auspicious hour.

"The third won't do," said Chia Lien. "We'll make it the seventh. As my uncle and cousin are away, we mustn't leave her here too long as this is a minor funeral. After the coffin has been placed in the temple for five weeks, we'll have a big mass and then close the mourning shrine. Next year it can be taken south for burial."

The astrologer approved this and left after writing out the obituary. Pao-yu had already come to mourn, and now other members of the clan arrived. Chia Lien hurried back then to ask Hsi-feng for money for the coffin and funeral rites.

Meanwhile, after seeing the body carried away, Hsi-feng had shammed illness again and claimed that Their Ladyships would not let her attend any ceremonies while unwell. She did not put on mourning either. Going instead to the Garden, past the rockeries to the wall at the north end, she eavesdropped on her husband outside, then came back to report the few remarks she had caught to the Lady Dowager.

"Don't listen to his nonsense," said the old lady. "Girls who die of consumption are cremated, aren't they, and their ashes scattered? Why should she have a formal funeral and burial? Still, as she was a secondary wife, let her body be kept for five weeks in the temple before being carried out to be burnt or buried in some common graveyard."

Hsi-feng smiled.

"That's exactly what I think, but I dare not urge him to do that."

A maid came then to ask Hsi-feng to go back as Chia Lien had gone home to get some money from her, and so she had to return.

"What money do we have?" she asked him. "Don't you know how tight things have been here recently? We couldn't distribute each month's allowance on time. It's been like hens eating up next year's grain. Yesterday I pawned a gold necklace for three hundred taels, and that may have given you ideas; but now only about two dozen taels are left. If you want that you can have it."

She told Ping-erh to fetch this and gave it to Chia Lien, then went off again on the excuse that the old lady wanted her.

Chia Lien, swallowing his resentment, had to resort to opening Second Sister's cases to look for any savings; but all he found were some broken trinkets, soiled artificial flowers and some of her half worn silk clothes, the sight of which reduced him to tears again. He wrapped them up in a cloth and, not asking the maids or pages to carry the bundle, started out to burn it himself. Ping-erh, both touched and amused, filched a packet of loose silver — about two hundred taels — and going to the eastern rooms gave him this, warning him to keep it a secret.

"If you must cry, can't you cry as much as you want outside?" she scolded him. "Why do it here, attracting attention?"

"You're right," said Chia Lien as he took the silver. He then gave a skirt to Ping-erh saying, "This is one she was fond of wearing. Keep it for me as a memento."

Ping-erh accepted it and put it away.

Having taken the silver, Chia Lien came out with some others and ordered men to buy wood for the coffin. The best timber was expensive, but nothing inferior would satisfy him; so he mounted his horse and went to make the choice himself. By evening some good timber had been delivered — as it cost five hundred taels, he had to buy it on credit. He had the coffin made immediately, at the same time assigning mourners to keep vigil, and he did not go home that night, but watched by the coffin.

Chapter 29
The Loss of Pao-yu's Jade of Spiritual
Understanding Heralds Trouble

Pao-yu had been resting at home that day, wearing a fur-lined gown, when he noticed that the crab-apples had blossomed and went out to look at them, sighing with admiration. So enchanted with them was he that he became quite wrapped up in their flowers, which evoked in him mixed feelings of grief and joy. At the sudden news that the old lady was coming, he changed into a fox-fur archer's jacket and black fox-fur coat, then went out so hurriedly to welcome her that he omitted to put on his Precious Jade of Spiritual Understanding. Not till the old lady had left and he had changed back into a gown did Hsi-jen see that the pendant which usually hung around his neck was missing.

"Where is your jade?" she asked.

"When I changed just now in such a hurry, I took it off and put it on the small table on the *kang* instead of wearing it."

Hsi-jen could not see it on the small table. She searched the whole room, but there was no trace of it. Dismay made her break out into a cold sweat.

"Don't worry," said Pao-yu. "It's bound to be somewhere here. Ask the others. They must know."

It occurred to Hsi-jen that one of the other girls must have hidden it to tease her. "You bitches!" she said playfully to Sheh-yueh and the rest. "What sort of joke is this to play? Where have you hidden it? If it really got lost that would be the end of us all!"

"What are you talking about?" they answered seriously.

"Joking is all very well, but this is no joking matter. Don't talk nonsense. You must be crazy! Better think back to where you put it instead of accusing *us*."

"Heavens!" cried Hsi-jen anxiously, seeing them so much in earnest. "Where exactly did you put it, Master Pao?"

"I remember quite clearly putting it on that table," he assured her. "Make a good search for it."

Not daring to let outsiders know, Hsi-jen, Sheh-yueh, Chiu-wen and the other girls quietly searched the whole place. They hunted around for hours, even turning out cases and crates — but all in vain. When the jade was nowhere to be found, they wondered if one of their visitors that day could have taken it.

But Hsi-jen said, "All of them know how precious this jade is. Who'd dare take it? You mustn't, for goodness' sake, let word of this get out, but go and make inquiries at different households. If one of the other girls took it to play a trick on us, kowtow to her and beg her to return it. And if you find out that one of the little maids stole it, don't report it to the mistresses but give her something in exchange for it. This isn't just anything! If it's really lost, that's more serious than losing Master Pao!"

As Sheh-yueh and Chiu-wen were leaving, she hurried after them with a final warning: "Don't start by asking those who came to the feast. Because then, if you can't find it, that will cause more trouble and make matters worse."

Sheh-yueh and Chiu-wen agreed and went off separately to make inquiries; but nobody had seen the jade, and they were all alarmed. The two of them hurried back to eye each other blankly in consternation. By now Pao-yu was alarmed too, while Hsi-jen could only sob in desperation. The jade had vanished, and they dared not report it. All the inmates of Happy Red Court were petrified.

While they were in this state of stupefaction, along came some people who had heard of their loss. Tan-chun ordered the Garden gate to be closed and sent an old serving-woman with two young maids to make another comprehensive search, promising a handsome reward to anyone who found the jade. Eagerness to clear themselves and receive a reward made everyone search frantically high and low — they even scoured the privies. But it was like looking for a needle in a haystack. They searched all day in vain.

"This is no laughing matter," said Li Wan in desperation. "I've a blunt proposal to make."

"What is it?" the others asked.

"Things have come to such a pass, we can't be too nice. Now apart from Pao-yu all the others in the Garden are women. I'm going to ask all you girls, as well as the maids you brought with you, to take off your clothes to be searched. If the jade isn't found, we'll tell the maids to search the serving-women and the maids doing the rough work. What do you say?"

"That's an idea," they agreed. "With such a crowd of us here we're a mixed lot, and this would be a way to clear ourselves."

Only Tan-chun made no comment.

As the maids also wanted to clear themselves of suspicion, Ping-erh volunteered to be the first to be searched. Then the others stripped too, and Li Wan searched them in turn.

"Sister-in-law!" snapped Tan-chun. "Where did you learn to behave in this scandalous way? If anyone stole it she wouldn't keep it on her, would she? Besides, this jade may be treasured here but to outsiders not in the know it's quite useless, so why should anyone steal it? I'm sure that someone is up to monkey tricks."

When they heard this and noticed Huan's absence — though earlier on he had been running all over the place — they suspected him but were unwilling to say so.

"Huan's the only one who'd play such a trick," Tan-chun continued. "Send somebody to fetch him quietly and persuade him to return it; then give him a scare to make him keep his mouth shut, and that will be that."

The others nodded approval.

Li Wan told Ping-erh, "You're the only one who can get the truth out of him."

Ping-erh agreed to try and hurried off, coming back before

long with Chia Huan. The rest pretended that nothing was amiss and told maids to serve him tea in the inner room. Then they excused themselves, leaving him to Ping-erh.

"Your Brother Pao has lost his jade," she told him with a smile. "Have you seen it?"

Chia Huan flushed scarlet and glared.

"When he loses something, why suspect *me*?" he protested. "Am I a convicted thief?"

He looked so worked up that Ping-erh dared not press him. "I didn't mean that," she explained with a smile. "I thought you might have taken it to scare them; that's why I simply asked if you'd seen it or not, to help them find it."

"He was the one wearing the jade, so he's the one you should ask instead of me. You all make so much of him! When there's something good going, you don't ask me to share it; but when anything's lost, I'm the one you ask about it!" He got up and marched out, and they could not stop him.

"All this trouble's due to that silly thing!" burst out Pao-yu. "I don't want it, so you needn't make such a fuss. When Huan gets back he's bound to tell everyone and raise a fearful rumpus."

Weeping in desperation Hsi-jen said, "*You* may not care that the jade's lost, Little Ancestor, but if this comes to the mistresses' ears it'll be the death of us!" She broke down and sobbed.

Now that it was clear that this could not be hushed up, feeling even more worried they discussed how best to report it to the old lady and other mistresses.

"There's no need to discuss it," expostulated Pao-yu. "Just say I've smashed it."

"How casually you're taking it, sir!" rejoined Ping-erh. "Suppose they ask why you smashed it? These girls will still be the ones to take the blame. And suppose they ask to see the broken bits?"

"Well then, say I lost it outside."

That sounded more plausible, until they remembered that Pao-yu had not been to school for a couple of days or paid any visits outside. They pointed this out.

"That's not true," he remonstrated. "Three days ago I went to see the opera in the Duke of Linan's mansion. Just say I lost it that day."

"That won't do," countered Tan-chun. "If you lost it then, why didn't you report it at the time?"

They were racking their brains to think up some good story when they heard sobbing and wailing — it was Concubine Chao approaching.

"You lose something, yet instead of looking for it you torture my Huan behind my back!" she screamed. "I've brought him here to hand him over to you arse-lickers. You can kill him or slice him to pieces just as you please!" With that she shoved Huan forward. "You're a thief!" she cried. "Own up, quick."

Then Huan started crying too from mortification.

Before Li Wan could placate them a maid announced, "Here comes the mistress!"

Hsi-jen and the other maids wished the earth would swallow them up, but they had to hurry out with Pao-yu to meet her. Concubine Chao went with them, afraid to say any more for the time being. And when Lady Wang saw the panic they were in, she realized that the news she had heard was true.

"Is the jade really lost?" she demanded.

No one dared answer.

Lady Wang went inside and sat down, then called for Hsi-jen, who fell on her knees in confusion, tears in her eyes, preparing to make her report.

"Get up," ordered Lady Wang. "Have another careful search made. It's no use losing your heads."

Hsi-jen sobbed, unable to speak.

For fear she might tell the truth Pao-yu put in, "This has nothing to do with Hsi-jen, madam. I lost it on the road the other day when I went to the duke's mansion to see the opera."

"Why didn't you look for it then?"

"I was afraid to let on, so I didn't tell them. Instead I asked Pei-ming and the rest to hunt for it outside."

"Nonsense!" his mother exclaimed. "Don't Hsi-jen and the other girls help you off with your clothes? Whenever you come back from outside, if so much as a handkerchief or pouch is missing they have to look into it, not to mention that jade! They would certainly have asked about it."

This silenced Pao-yu but pleased Concubine Chao.

"If he lost it outside why should they accuse Huan..." she began.

Before she could finish Lady Wang rapped out, "We're talking about the jade. Stop drivelling!"

With Concubine Chao crushed, Li Wan and Tan-chun told Lady Wang all that had happened, making her shed tears in dismay. She decided to report this to the old lady so that she could send people to question those members of Lady Hsing's household who had come with her to Happy Red Court that morning.

Just then, however, along came Hsi-feng, having heard about the loss of Pao-yu's jade and Lady Wang's visit to the Garden. Although still an invalid, feeling unable to hold aloof she now arrived leaning on Feng-erh's arm, just as Lady Wang was about to leave.

"How are you, madam?" she faltered.

Pao-yu and the others went over and greeted her.

"So you've heard too?" said Lady Wang. "Isn't it odd? It just vanished all of a sudden and can't be found. Think now: which of the maids from the old lady's place down to your Ping-erh is unreliable and a mischief-maker? I shall have to report this to the old lady and organize a thorough-going search. Otherwise, Pao-yu's life may be cut short!"

"Our household's so big, it's a mixed lot," Hsi-feng answered. "As the proverb says, you can't judge by appearances, madam. Who can guarantee that everyone here is honest? But if we raise a hue and cry so that this becomes public knowledge, the thief will realize that if you find him out — or her, as the case may be — he will have to pay for it with his life, and in desperation he may smash the jade to destroy the evidence. Then what shall we do? In my foolish opinion, we'd better say that Pao-yu never liked it and its loss is of no consequence, so long as we all keep this secret and don't let the old lady and the master know. At the same time, we can secretly send people to search high and low and trick the thief into producing it. Once we have the jade back, we can punish the culprit. What do you think of this, madam?"

After some thought Lady Wang answered, "You're right of course, but how are we to keep this from the master?" She called Huan over and told him, "Your brother's jade is lost. Why should you raise such a row when simply asked a question? If you spread the news and the thief smashes the jade, I can't see you living it down!"

In his terror Huan sobbed, "I won't breathe a word about it!"

And Concubine Chao was too cowed to say any more.

Lady Wang now told the others, "There must be places you haven't searched. It was here all right, so how could it fly away? But the thing is to keep this quiet. I give you three days, Hsi-jen, to find it for me. If you still haven't recovered it by then, I'm afraid we shan't be able to hush it up and there will be no peace for anyone!" She told Hsi-feng to go with her to Lady Hsing's house to discuss plans for a search.

Li Wan and the others talked it over again, then summoned the servants in charge of the Garden and made them lock the gates. Next they sent for Lin Chih-hsiao's wife and told her to order the gatekeepers both at the front and the back not to let out any domestics, whether male or female, for the next three days. All were to remain in the Garden until something missing had been found again.

"Very well," said Mrs. Lin.

"When I was down south," said Hsiu-yen. "I heard that Miao-yu was able to divine by writing on sand. Why don't we consult *her*? Besides, this jade is said to be supernatural, so the oracle should disclose its whereabouts."

The others rejoined in surprise, "We often see her but never heard tell of this."

"I doubt if she'll agree if we others ask her, miss," said Sheh-yueh to Hsiu-yen. "So let me kowtow to you and beg you to take this errand on yourself. If she clears up this mystery, we shall never forget your kindness as long as we live!"

She knelt down to kowtow but Hsiu-yen stopped her, while Tai-yu and the other girls also urged her to go straight to Green Lattice Nunnery.

Now Hsiu-yen on reaching Green Lattice Nunnery, as soon as she saw Miao-yu had asked her — without any preliminaries — to consult an oracle for them by writing on sand. Miao-yu laughed disdainfully.

"I've treated you as my friend," she said, "because you're not one of the vulgar herd. Why trouble me like this today on the base of some rumour? Besides, I know nothing about 'writing on sand'. " And, this said, she ignored her.

Knowing the young nun's temperament, Hsiu-yen regretted having come. Still she reflected, "After telling the others, I can hardly go back empty-handed." Since she could not very well argue with Miao-yu and affirm that she could use a planchette, she explained to her with a conciliatory smile that the lives of Hsi-jen and the other maids depended on this. When she saw her wavering, she got up and curtseyed to her several times.

Miao-yu sighed, "Why should you put yourself out for others? No one's known, since I came to the capital, that I can consult oracles. If I make an exception for you today, I'm afraid I shall have a lot of trouble in future."

"I couldn't help blurting it out, counting on your kindness," said Hsiu-yen. "If you're pestered in future, it's up to you whether you agree or not — who'd dare to force you?"

Miao-yu smiled and told the old deaconess to burn some incense, then from her case she took out a sand-board and stand and wrote an incantation. Hsiu-yen, after bowing and praying on her instructions, got up to help hold the planchette. Presently the wand wrote swiftly:

> Ah! Come and gone without a trace
> By the ancient pine at the foot of Blue Ridge Peak.

To seek it, cross myriads of mountains:
Entering my gate with a smile you will meet again.

This written, the wand stopped.

"Which deity did you invoke?" Hsiu-yen asked.

"Saint Li the Cripple."

Hsiu-yen wrote down the oracle, then begged Miao-yu to explain it.

"I can't," was the answer. "I don't understand it myself. Hurry up and take it back. You have plenty of clever people over there."

Hsiu-yen went back, and as soon as she entered the court-yard the others all wanted to know how she had fared. With-out giving them the details, she handed Li Wan the oracle she had transcribed. The girls and Pao-yu crowded round to read it and took it to mean that the jade could not be found quickly, but it would turn up some time when they were not looking.

"But where is this Blue Ridge Peak?" they asked.

"That must be some divine riddle," said Li Wan. "We've no such peak here, have we? I expect the thief has thrown it under some rockery with pine trees on it, for fear of detection. But it says 'entering my gate' — whose gate would that be?"

Tai-yu remarked, "I wonder whom she invoked."

"Saint Li the Cripple," Hsiu-yen told her.

"If it's an immortal's gate, that won't be easy to enter!" exclaimed Tan-chun.

Hsi-jen hunted frantically round, clutching at shadows and searching under each rock, but there was no trace of the jade. When she came back, Pao-yu smiled foolishly instead of asking whether she had found it.

"Little Ancestor!" cried Sheh-yueh in desperation. "Where exactly did you lose it? If you tell us, even if we suffer for it, we shall have something to go on."

"When I said I lost it outside, you wouldn't have it," he reminded her. "Now how can I answer your question?"

Li Wan and Tan-chun interposed, "We've been in a flurry ever since this morning, and now it's nearly midnight. Look, Cousin Lin's already left — she couldn't last out any longer.

We ought to get some rest too: we'll have our hands full tomorrow."

They all dispersed then, and Pao-yu went to bed. But poor Hsi-jen and the other maids wept and racked their brains all night, unable to sleep.

Early the next day, Lady Wang sent to make inquiries at various pawnshops, and Hsi-feng also had a search made in secret. This went on for several days, but to no effect. Luckily the old lady and Chia Cheng did not know this. Hsi-jen and the other maids were on tenterhooks every day, while Pao-yu stayed away from school looking dazed and dejected, saying not a word. However, his mother did not take this to heart, attributing it to the loss of his jade.

Then one day Chia Cheng burst in, tears streaming down his cheeks.

"Quick!" he panted. "Go and ask the old lady to go at once to the Palace! You can escort her there — no need for too many people. Her Highness has suddenly fallen ill. A eunuch is waiting outside. According to him, the Imperial physicians say she's had a stroke and there's no hope!"

Lady Wang at once gave way to a storm of weeping.

"This is no time for crying," he interposed. "Hurry up and fetch the old lady. But break it to her gently. Don't frighten the old soul." He then left to tell the servants to make preparations.

His wife, holding back her tears, went to tell the Lady Dowager that Yuan-chun was ill and they were to call to pay their respects to her.

Invoking Buddha the old lady exclaimed, "Is she unwell again? Last time I had a bad fright till we heard it was just a rumour. Let's hope this proves to be a false report too."

Lady Wang concurred and urged Yuan-yang and others to open the chests at once and get out the old lady's ceremonial costume. She then hurried back to her room to change herself before returning to wait on the old lady. Presently they went out and were carried by sedan-chairs to the Palace.

Now Yuan-chun, highly favoured by the sagacious sovereign since her installation as Imperial Concubine in Phoenix Palace, had grown too plump to exert herself — the least fatigue made her liable to apoplexy. A few days before this, on her way back from waiting on the Emperor at a feast, she had caught a chill which had brought on her former trouble. And this time it was serious: phlegm blocked her wind-pipe, her limbs were numb and cold. This was reported to the Emperor, and Imperial physicians were summoned. However, she was unable to take any medicine, nor could they clear up the congestion. In their anxiety the Palace officials asked permission to prepare for her death, which was why the Lady Dowager had been sent for.

Entering the Palace in response to the Imperial summons, she and Lady Wang found Yuan-chun unable to speak. At sight of her grandmother she showed signs of distress but had no tears to shed, while the old lady stepped forward to pay her respects and offer condolences. Soon the cards of Chia Cheng and the rest were sent in and presented by maids-in-waiting; but Yuan-chun's sight had failed and the colour was slowly ebbing from her face. The Palace officials and eunuchs had to report this to the Emperor and, anticipating that other Imperial concubines would be sent to see her, in which case it would not be fitting for her relatives to remain there, they asked them to wait outside. The old lady and Lady Wang could hardly bear to leave, but they had to conform to court etiquette and withdraw with aching hearts, not even daring to weep.

News was sent to the officials at the Palace gate, and presently a eunuch came out to summon the Imperial Astrologer. The old lady knew what this foreboded, but did not venture to move. Very soon a younger eunuch came out to announce: "The Imperial Consort Chia has passed away."

As the Beginning of Spring fell on the eighteenth of the twelfth lunar month that year, and Yuan-chun had died on the nineteenth, it was already the first solar month of the next year and so her age was reckoned as forty-three.

Nursing her grief, the old lady rose to leave the Palace and go home by sedan-chair. Chia Cheng and the others, having also received the news, made their way sadly back. When they reached home, Lady Hsing, Li Wan, Hsi-feng, Pao-yu and the rest were ranged on both sides in front of the hall to meet them. After paying their respects to the Lady Dowager, then to Chia Cheng and Lady Wang, they all gave way to weeping.

Early the next day, those with official titles went to the Palace to mourn beside the coffin as etiquette prescribed.

Since the loss of his jade Pao-yu had grown thoroughly listless and talked nonsense. When told that the old lady was back and he should go to pay his respects, he went; if not prompted, he made no move. Hsi-jen and his other maids felt deep misgivings yet dared not take him to task for fear of his anger. When his meals were set before him he would eat; otherwise he never asked for anything. Hsi-jen suspected that he was not sulking but ill.

Pao-yu grew more deranged from day to day. He had no fever or pain but could neither eat nor sleep properly and even grew incoherent in his speech. Hsi-jen and Sheh-yueh in their alarm reported this more than once to Hsi-feng, who came over from time to time. At first she thought he was sulking because the jade had not been found; then she realized that he was losing his mind and had doctors fetched to attend him every day. Although they prescribed various medicines, his condition only grew worse. Asked whether he felt any pain, he would not answer.

Chapter 30
Hsi-feng Withholds Information and
Lays a Cunning Plan

That year the records of officials in the capital were examined, and the Ministry of Works ranked Chia Cheng as first class. In the second month, the Minister of Civil Affairs took him to an audience at court and the Emperor, in recognition of his frugality and circumspection, appointed him Grain Commissioner of Kiangsi. That same day, giving thanks for this favour, he reported to the throne the date of his departure. Kinsmen and friends came to offer congratulations, but disturbed as he was by his domestic problems Chia Cheng was in no mood to entertain them. Still he dared not postpone his journey.

He was in a quandary when he received a summons from the old lady and, hastening to her room, found his wife there too in spite of her illness. He paid his respects to his mother, who told him to take a seat.

"You will soon be going to your new post," she said tearfully. "There is much I want to say to you, but will you listen?"

Chia Cheng promptly rose to his feet.

"Just give me your orders, madam. How dare your son disobey them?"

"I'm eighty-one this year, yet you're going to a post in the provinces," she sobbed. "You can't ask for compassionate leave either, as you have an elder brother at home to take care of me. Once you're gone, there'll be only Pao-yu here that I care for, but the poor boy's losing his mind and we don't know what will become of him! Yesterday I sent Lai Sheng's wife to get someone to tell Pao-yu's fortune. She found a very clever fortune-teller who said, 'He must marry a bride with gold in her stars to help counteract his bad luck; otherwise there'll probably be no saving him.' I know you don't believe in such things, so I've asked you here to consult you. Your wife is here too, so the two of you can talk it over. Should we try to save Pao-yu? Or let things take their course?"

Chia Cheng answered submissively, "You were so good to your son, madam, do you think I don't love my son too? It's only because Pao-yu made so little progress that I was often exasperated with him — just a case of wanting to 'turn iron into steel'. If you wish him to take a wife, as is right and proper, how could I disobey you and show no concern for him? I am worried too by his illness. Since you kept him away from me I dared not object; but can I not see for myself just how ill he is?"

Lady Wang saw that the rims of his eyes had reddened and knew how distressed he was. She therefore told Hsi-jen to bring Pao-yu in. When the boy saw his father, prompted by Hsi-jen he paid his respects; but with his emaciated face and his lack-lustre eyes he looked like a moron. Chia Cheng told them to take him back.

He reflected, "I'm nearing sixty, and now I'm posted to the provinces with no knowing when I shall come back. If this child really doesn't recover, I shall be left heirless in my old age; for my grandson, after all, is another generation removed. Besides, Pao-yu is the old lady's favourite: if anything happens to him, I shall be guilty of a greater crime." He saw from his wife's tears how this must affect her too.

Rising to his feet he said, "Old as you are, madam, you show such concern for your grandson, how can I, your son, disobey you? I shall fall in with whatever you think best. But will Aunt Hsueh agree to this, I wonder?"

"She gave her consent some time ago," Lady Wang told him. "We haven't spoken of it yet simply because Pan's business still isn't settled."

"This is the first problem," he answered. "With her brother in jail, how can his sister get married? In the second place, although an Imperial Consort's death does not preclude marriages, Pao-yu should mourn for nine months for a married sister, and this is hardly the time for him to take a wife. Furthermore, the date of my departure has already been reported to the throne, and I cannot postpone it. How are we to arrange a wedding in these few days?"

The old lady thought, "He's right. But if we wait till these are no longer problems, Pao-yu's father will be gone, and what shall we do if his illness gets steadily worse? We shall just have to disregard certain rules of etiquette."

Her mind made up she said, "If you're willing, I know of a way to get round these obstacles. I shall go myself with your wife to ask Aunt Hsueh's consent. As for Pan, I'll get Ko to tell him that we have to do this to save Pao-yu's life, and then he's bound to agree. Of course it wouldn't do to have a real marriage while in mourning, and Pao-yu is too ill for that anyway — we just want a happy event to ward off evil. As both our families agree and there was that prediction about the young people's 'gold' and 'jade', there's no need to compare their horoscopes; we'll just select a good date to exchange gifts according to our family status. Then we'll choose a day for the wedding, not engaging musicians but following the example of the Palace, fetching the bride over in a sedan-chair with eight bearers and twelve pairs of lanterns. They can bow to each other as is done in the south, then sit down on the bed and let down the curtains, and won't that count as a wedding?

"Pao-chai's so intelligent, we don't have to worry. Besides, he has Hsi-jen in his chambers as well, and so much the better, as she's another reliable, sensible girl who knows how to reason with him. She and Pao-chai get on well too.

"Another thing. Aunt Hsueh once told me, 'A monk said that Pao-chai with her golden locket is destined to marry someone with jade.' So for all we know, once she marries into our household her gold locket may bring the jade back. Then he should get steadily better, and wouldn't that be a blessing for us all?

"All that needs to be done straight away is to get their rooms ready and furnished — it's for you to assign them a place. We won't give any feasts, but wait till Pao-yu's better and out of mourning before inviting relatives and friends. In this way we can manage everything in time, and you can leave with an easy mind, having seen the young couple settled."

Chia Cheng though averse to this could not gainsay his mother. Forcing a smile he said, "You have thought it out well and that would be most fitting, madam. We must order the servants, though, not to noise this abroad or we should be censured for it. I'm only afraid Aunt Hsueh's family may not agree. If they really do, we must manage it your way."

"Just leave Aunt Hsueh to me," she said, then dismissed him.

Chia Cheng withdrew feeling thoroughly uneasy. He had so much to do before going to his post, what with fetching credentials from the ministry, receiving relatives and friends who came with recommendations and entertaining a host of other people, that he left the arrangements for Pao-yu's wedding to his mother, wife and Hsi-feng. All he did was to assign his son a side-court with more than twenty rooms in it, adjacent to Lady Wang's house behind the Hall of Glorious Felicity. When the old lady sent him word of some decision, he simply replied, "Very good." But this is anticipating.

After Pao-yu had seen his father, Hsi-jen helped him back to the *kang* in the inner room. Since Chia Cheng was outside, no one ventured to speak to Pao-yu, who dozed off and thus heard nothing of the conversation in the outer room. However, Hsi-jen, keeping quiet, heard it clearly. Talk of this had reached her before, though only as hearsay, yet she tended to believe it in view of the fact that Pao-chai's visits had stopped. This confirmation today delighted her.

"The mistresses certainly have good judgement," she thought. "This is just the match for him. And what luck for me too! If she comes, my load will be ever so much lighter. But he's set his heart on Miss Lin, so it's a blessing that he didn't hear this. If he had, Heaven knows how wildly he'd carry on!" This set her worrying.

"What shall I do?" she wondered. "Their Ladyships have no idea of their feelings for each other. They may be so pleased that they tell him, in the hope of curing him. Then suppose he acts the way he did when he first met Miss Lin and tried to smash his jade; or that summer in the Garden, when he mistook me for her and poured out his love; or when Tzu-chuan teased him later, and he nearly cried himself to death? If they tell him now that he's to have not Miss Lin but Miss Pao-chai, it may not matter if his wits are wandering; but if he's fairly lucid, far from curing his madness it may hasten his death. Unless I explain this to them I may ruin three lives!"

Having reached this resolve she waited till Chia Cheng had gone, then leaving Pao-yu in the care of Chiu-wen she slipped out and quietly asked Lady Wang to go with her to the back room. The Lady Dowager paid little attention, assuming that there was something Pao-yu wanted, and went on considering the gifts and arrangements for the wedding.

Once in the back room with Lady Wang, Hsi-jen threw herself on her knees and burst into tears.

Lady Wang pulled her up and asked in surprise, "What's come over you? What's the trouble? Get up and tell me."

"This is something a slave shouldn't say, but I see no other way out!"

"Well, take your time and tell me."

"Your Ladyships have decided to marry Miss Pao-chai to Pao-yu, and of course nothing could be better. All I'm wondering, madam, is this: which of the two, Miss Pao-chai and Miss Lin, do you think Pao-yu prefers?"

"As he and Miss Lin were together as children, he's slightly fonder of her."

"Not just 'slightly fonder'," Hsi-jen demurred, going on to cite examples of their behaviour. "Except for the avowal he made that summer, which I've never dared tell anyone, you saw the other instances yourself, madam," she concluded.

Holding Hsi-jen's hand Lady Wang answered, "I did have some inkling from what I saw. Now you've clinched it. But he must have heard what the master said just now. Did you notice his reaction?"

"Nowadays when people talk to him he smiles; if no one talks to him he goes to sleep. So he didn't hear what was said."

"Then what's to be done?"

"I've made bold to tell you this, madam. It's for you to tell the old lady and think of some really safe plan."

"In that case, get back to your work. I won't mention it now — there are too many people there. I'll wait for a chance to tell her later on, and then we shall see."

She rejoined the Lady Dowager who was discussing Pao-yu's marriage with Hsi-feng.

"What did Hsi-jen want that she looked so secretive?" the old lady asked.

Lady Wang took this opening to give her a detailed account of Pao-yu's feeling for Tai-yu. For a while the old lady said nothing, and Lady Wang and Hsi-feng kept silent too.

"Nothing else really matters," the old lady sighed at last. "We needn't worry about Tai-yu. But if Pao-yu is really so infatuated, it's going to be difficult!"

"Not too difficult," said Hsi-feng after some thought. "I've an idea, but don't know whether Aunt Hsueh will agree to it or not."

"If you have a plan, tell the old lady," said Lady Wang. "We can discuss it together."

"To my mind," said Hsi-feng, "the only way is to 'palm off a dummy' on him."

"Palm off what dummy?" the old lady asked.

"Never mind whether Pao-yu is in his right mind or not, we must all drum it into his head that on the master's orders he is to marry Miss Lin, and see how he takes it. If he doesn't care either way, we needn't trick him. If he's pleased, we'll have to do things more deviously."

"Well, assuming he's pleased, what then?" asked Lady Wang.

Hsi-feng went over to whisper something into her ear, at which she nodded and smiled.

"That should work," she said.

"Tell me what you two are plotting," urged the old lady.

瞞消息鳳姐設奇謀
洩機關顰卿迷本性

In order not to give away the secret, Hsi-feng whispered in her ear too. As she had anticipated, the old lady did not understand at first and Hsi-feng, smiling, had to explain more fully.

"That's all right," agreed the old lady. "Rather hard on Pao-chai, though. And if word gets out, what about Tai-yu?"

"We'll just tell Pao-yu and forbid any mention of this outside, then how could she hear?"

Chapter 31
Disclosure of a Secret Deranges Tai-yu

One morning after breakfast, Tai-yu set off to call on her grandmother to pay her respects and also by way of diversion. They had not gone far from Bamboo Lodge when she found that she had forgotten her handkerchief. She told Tzu-chuan to go back for one then catch her up — she would be walking on slowly. She had passed Seeping Fragrance Bridge and reached the rocks behind which she and Pao-yu had buried blossom, when she suddenly heard sobbing. She stopped to listen, but could not tell who was lamenting there or hear what she was saying. Very puzzled, she strolled over and found that the one crying there was an under-maid with thick eyebrows and big eyes.

Tai-yu had expected to see one of the upper-maids come here to vent some grief which she could not confide to others. But when she saw this girl she thought with amusement, "A stupid creature like this can't have been crossed in love. She's one of those doing rough work who must have got scolded by the senior maids." She looked hard at the girl but could not recognize her.

When Tai-yu appeared, the maid dared not go on crying but stood up and wiped her eyes.

"Why are you weeping here? What's come over you?" Tai-yu asked.

That set the maid off again. "Judge for yourself, Miss Lin!" she sobbed. "They knew something, but I wasn't in on it; so even if I made a slip of the tongue, sister had no call to slap me."

Tai-yu could not make head or tail of this.

"Which sister do you mean?" she asked with a smile.

"Sister Chen-chu."

Knowing from this that she worked for the old lady, Tai-yu asked again, "What's your name?"

"They call me Numskull."

"Why did she slap you? What did you say wrong?"

"Why? Just because of the marriage of our Master Pao to Miss Pao-chai."

Tai-yu felt thunderstruck. Her heart beat wildly. Composing herself a little she said, "Come with me."

Numskull accompanied her to the quiet spot where she had buried the peach-blossom. Then Tai-yu asked, "Why should she slap you because Master Pao is marrying Miss Pao-chai?"

"Their Ladyships have settled it with Madam Lien. Because His Lordship's going to leave so soon, they're fixing up hurriedly with Aunt Hsueh to have Miss Pao-chai brought over before he goes. This will counter Master Pao's bad luck with good. And after that . . ." — she beamed at Tai-yu — "after his wedding they'll fix up a match for *you*, miss."

Tai-yu listened, half stupefied, as the maid rattled on, "I don't know how they settled this, but they won't let anybody talk about it for fear of embarrassing Miss Pao-chai if she heard. All I did was to remark to Sister Hsi-jen — the one who works for Master Pao, 'Things are going to be livelier here with Miss Pao-chai becoming Second Mistress Pao — how ought we to address her?' Tell me, Miss Lin, why should that annoy Sister Chen-chu? Yet she marched over and slapped my face, saying I was talking nonsense and should be thrown out for not obeying orders! How was I to know the mistresses didn't want this talked about? They never tell me anything, yet slap me!" She started sobbing again.

Tai-yu felt as if her heart were filled with a mixture of oil, soy, sugar and vinegar — so sweet, bitter, painful and sharp that she could not put her sensations into words.

After a pause, in a trembling voice she said, "Don't talk such nonsense. If they heard, they'd give you another slapping.

Be off with you now."

She turned to go back to Bamboo Lodge. But there seemed to be a mill-stone round her neck and her legs were as limp, her steps as faltering, as if treading on cotton-wool. It seemed a long way to Seeping Fragrance Bridge, she was walking so slowly and so shakily; and moreover she added two bowshots to the distance by wandering about at random in a daze. When at last she reached the bridge, she inadvertently started back along the dyke.

When Tzu-chuan brought the handkerchief Tai-yu had gone. Looking round for her, she saw her white-faced, her eyes fixed in a vacant stare, wandering unsteadily this way and that. She also glimpsed a maid walking off in front, but too far away to make out which it was. In shocked surprise she ran over.

"Why are you going back, miss?" she asked gently. "Where do you want to go?"

Hearing her as if in a dream, Tai-yu answered without thinking, "To ask Pao-yu what this means."

Tzu-chuan, nonplussed as she was, had to help her to the Lady Dowager's quarters. When Tai-yu reached the door, her mind seemed to clear. Turning to her maid who was supporting her, she stopped to ask:

"Why have *you* come?"

"To bring your handkerchief," was the smiling answer. "Just now I saw you by the bridge, but when I accosted you you paid no attention."

"I thought you'd come to see Master Pao," Tai-yu laughed. "Why else should you come this way?"

Tzu-chuan saw that her wits were wandering, and knew that she must have heard something from that maid. She could only nod and smile. However, this visit to Pao-yu unnerved her, for he was already demented and now Tai-yu was bemused too — what if they said something improper?

But for all this, she had to do as she was told and help her young mistress inside.

Strange to say, Tai-yu was no longer as limp as before. Lifting the portière herself instead of waiting for Tzu-chuan, she stepped in. All was quiet, for the old lady was having a nap, and her maids had either slipped out to play or were nodding drowsily or attending her. The clack of the portière alerted Hsi-jen, who came out from the inner room.

"Please come in and take a seat, miss," she invited when she saw who it was.

"Is Master Pao in?" Tai-yu asked with a smile.

Hsi-jen, being in the dark, was about to answer when Tzu-chuan signalled to her from behind Tai-yu and, pointing at her young mistress, waved her hand warningly. Hsi-jen was too puzzled by this to say any more. Tai-yu, disregarding her, went on into the inner room where Pao-yu was sitting. Instead of rising to offer her a seat, he simply stared at her with a foolish grin. Tai-yu sat down and gazed back at him with a smile. They exchanged neither greetings nor civilities, just simpered at each other without a word.

Hsi-jen, at a complete loss, did not know what to do.

"Pao-yu," said Tai-yu abruptly. "Why are you ill?"

"Because of Miss Lin," he answered with a smirk.

Hsi-jen and Tzu-chuan turned pale with fright and at once tried to change the subject; but the other two ignored them, still smiling foolishly. It dawned on Hsi-jen that Tai-yu was now deranged too, exactly like Pao-yu.

She whispered to Tzu-chuan, "Your young lady's just over her illness. I'll get Sister Chiu-wen to help you take her back to rest." She turned to tell Chiu-wen, "Go with Sister Tzu-chuan to see Miss Lin back. Mind you don't say anything foolish."

Chiu-wen complied readily. In silence she and Tzu-chuan helped Tai-yu to her feet. She kept her eyes on Pao-yu, smiling and nodding.

"Go home and rest, miss," Tzu-chuan urged her.

"Of course!" said Tai-yu. "It's time for me to go now."

She turned and went out, still smiling, without their assistance and walking much faster than usual. The two maids hurried after her as once out of her grandmother's compound she forged straight ahead.

"This way, miss!" cried Tzu-chuan, catching hold of her arm.

Tai-yu allowed herself to be led back and soon they approached the gate of Bamboo Lodge.

"Gracious Buddha!" sighed Tzu-chuan in relief. "Home at last!"

But the words were still on her lips when Tai-yu staggered and fell, vomiting blood. The two maids were just able to catch her as she was collapsing and carry her inside; then Chiu-wen left Tzu-chuan and Hsueh-yen to attend to her.

After a while, Tai-yu regained consciousness and saw that her maids were crying. She asked them the reason.

In relief Tzu-chuan answered, "You seemed unwell just now, miss, when you left the old lady's place, and we didn't know what to do — we cried for fright."

"Oh, I'm not going to die as easily as all that," retorted Tai-yu, panting as she spoke.

The news of Pao-yu's impending wedding to Pao-chai, a prospect which Tai-yu had dreaded for years, had so enraged her that she had lost her senses. After the hemorrhage her mind gradually cleared, but she had completely forgotten what Numskull had said. Tzu-chuan's tears brought it back to her vaguely. Instead of grieving, however, she just longed to die quickly and be done with it. Her maids felt constrained to stay with her although they wanted to go and report her condition, for they were afraid Hsi-feng would scold them again for raising a false alarm.

However, Chiu-wen had gone back panic-stricken. The old lady, just up from her nap, saw her agitation and asked her what had happened. Chiu-wen's fearful description of what she had seen made the Lady Dowager exclaim in horror and send at once for Lady Wang and Hsi-feng to communicate this bad news.

"I ordered all the maids to keep quiet," said Hsi-feng. "Who could have blabbed? This makes things more difficult."

"Never mind about that now," said the old lady. "Let's go and see how she is."

The three of them went to Bamboo Lodge and found Tai-yu deathly pale. She seemed comatose and her breathing was very weak. Presently she had another fit of coughing. Her maids brought over the spittoon and to their consternation her sputum was streaked with blood. Her eyelids fluttered then, and she saw the old lady by her.

"Madam," she gasped, "your love for me has been wasted."

Her heart aching, her grandmother said, "Don't be afraid, dear child. You must rest well."

Tai-yu smiled faintly, closing her eyes again as a maid came in to report the doctor's arrival to Hsi-feng. Thereupon the ladies withdrew, and Doctor Wang was led in by Chia Lien to feel the patient's pulse.

"She will be all right," he observed. "Pent-up anger has drained her liver of blood, resulting in nervous disorders. Some medicine to regulate the blood will set her right again."

This said, he went out with Chia Lien to write out his prescription and fetch medicine.

The Lady Dowager had seen that Tai-yu's state was critical. After leaving her she said to Hsi-feng, "It's not that I want to put a jinx on her but it doesn't look to me, I'm afraid, as if the child will recover. You must get ready after-life things to counter her bad luck. If she gets over this illness, that'll be a great weight off our minds. And if it comes to the worst, you won't be caught unprepared at the last minute. We've that other business to attend to these days."

When Hsi-feng had acquiesced, the old lady questioned Tzu-chuan; but the maid did not know who had told Tai-yu the news.

Dubiously, the old lady went on, "It's natural for young people who've played together as children to be partial to each other; but now that they're big enough to know the facts of life they should keep at a distance. That's how a girl should behave if she wants me to love her. To get other ideas into her head would be most improper, and all my love for her would be thrown away. I'm quite upset by what you've been telling me."

On her return to her own quarters, she called in Hsi-jen to interrogate her. Hsi-jen repeated what she had told Lady Wang, then described Tai-yu's behaviour earlier that day.

"She didn't look deranged when I saw her just now," commented the old lady. "I simply can't understand this. In a family like ours, of course there can't be any carryings-on, but even *thinking* such thoughts is taboo! If that's not the root of her illness, I'm willing to spend any sum to cure her. If it *is*, I doubt if it can be cured and I don't care!"

Hsi-feng put in, "Don't worry about Cousin Lin, madam. Lien will take the doctor to see her every day anyway. It's the other business that matters. I heard this morning that the rooms are practically ready. Why don't you and Her Ladyship call on Aunt Hsueh to discuss it with her? I'll go with you. The only snag is that with Cousin Pao-chai there it will be difficult to talk. Suppose we ask Aunt Hsueh over for a consultation here this evening? Then we can settle everything tonight."

"You're right," Their Ladyships agreed. "But it's too late today. We'll go over there tomorrow after breakfast."

As the old lady had finished her supper by now, Hsi-feng and Lady Wang went back to their own apartments.

Chapter 32
Pao-chai Goes Through Her Wedding Ceremony

The next day, Hsi-feng came over after breakfast and went in to sound out Pao-yu.

"Congratulations, Cousin Pao!" she greeted him gaily. "The master has chosen a lucky day for your wedding. Doesn't that make you happy?"

Pao-yu just grinned at her and nodded imperceptibly.

"Your bride will be Cousin Lin. Are you glad?"

He simply burst out laughing, and she was unclear about his mental state.

"The master says you can marry her if you're better, not if you go on acting the fool," she warned.

"If anyone's a fool, it's you — not me!" he retorted seriously, then stood up and announced, "I'm going to see Cousin Lin to reassure her."

Hsi-feng promptly barred his way.

"She knows it already," she said. "As she's to marry you, she'll naturally feel too shy to see you."

"Will she see me after the wedding?"

Amused and perturbed Hsi-feng thought, "Hsi-jen was right. At the mention of Tai-yu, though he still raves his mind seems clearer. If he really comes to his senses and finds out that it isn't Tai-yu but we've played a trick on him, then the fat will be in the fire!"

Suppressing a smile she said, "If you're better she'll see you, not if you act crazily."

"I've given her my heart. When she comes, she's bound to

bring it and put it back in my breast."

As he was raving, Hsi-feng came out and smiled at the old lady, who had been both amused and upset by their conversation.

"I heard," she said. "We can ignore him for now and leave Hsi-jen to calm him down. Let's go."

For by then Lady Wang had come too, and together they called on Aunt Hsueh, ostensibly to see how her family was faring. Aunt Hsueh was most grateful and gave them news of Hsueh Pan. When tea had been served she wanted to send for Pao-chai, but Hsi-feng stopped her.

"You needn't summon her, aunty," she said with a smile. "The old lady came partly to see how you are and partly because there's some important business which she'd like to discuss with you in our place."

Aunt Hsueh nodded and agreed to this, and after a little more idle talk they left.

That evening Aunt Hsueh came over. Having paid her respects to the old lady she called on Lady Wang.

"Just now in the old lady's place, Pao-yu came out to pay his respects," remarked Aunt Hsueh. "He looked all right, simply a little thinner. Why do you speak as if it were so serious?"

"Actually it's nothing much," replied Hsi-feng. "But the old lady is worried. Now the master is going to a provincial post and may not be back for some years. Her idea is to have Pao-yu's wedding while he's still here. Firstly, to set his father's mind at rest; and secondly, in the hope that Cousin Pao-chai's golden locket will bring Pao-yu good luck, overcoming the evil influence so that he recovers."

Aunt Hsueh wanted the match but feared Pao-chai might feel herself wronged. "That's all right," she replied, "but we must think it out more carefully."

Lady Wang told her Hsi-feng's plan, adding, "As your son is away from home now, you need not give any dowry. Tomorrow send Ko to tell Pan that while we have the wedding here we'll find some way to settle his lawsuit for him." Omitting to mention that Pao-yu had lost his heart to Tai-yu, she concluded,

"Since you agree to it, the sooner the bride comes the better — the sooner we'll all feel easier in our minds."

At this point Yuan-yang arrived, sent by the old lady to hear what they had decided. Though this was treating Pao-chai shabbily, Aunt Hsueh could hardly refuse as they were so pressing. She consented with a show of readiness. Yuan-yang went back to report this to the old lady, who in elation sent her back to urge Aunt Hsueh to explain the situation to Pao-chai so that she would not feel unfairly treated. Aunt Hsueh agreed to this. Having decided that Hsi-feng and her husband should act as go-betweens, the others left. Then Lady Wang and her sister sat up half the night talking.

The next day Aunt Hsueh went home and told Pao-chai in detail all these arrangements to which she had agreed. Pao-chai lowered her head in silence, and presently shed tears. Her mother did her best to comfort her, explaining the matter at length; and when Pao-chai went back to her room Pao-chin went with her to try to cheer her up. Aunt Hsueh also told Hsueh Ko, urging him to leave the following day to find out what sentence had been passed and to give Hsueh Pan this news, then to come back immediately.

Four days later Hsueh Ko returned.

"Regarding Cousin Pan's business," he reported, "the judge has approved a verdict of accidental manslaughter, which will be pronounced at the next session; and we must have silver ready by way of compensation. As for his sister's wedding, Pan says your decision was a good one, and rushing it through will save a good deal of money. He says you shouldn't wait for his return but do as you think fit."

This news reassured Aunt Hsueh that her son would be released and her daughter's wedding could be carried through, although she could see that Pao-chai looked rather unwilling. "Still," she thought, "she's a girl who's always been submissive and a model of propriety. Knowing that I've agreed, she won't raise any objections."

She told Hsueh Ko, "Get a gilded card and write her horoscope on it, then have it sent at once to Second Master Lien and ask the date for the exchange of gifts, so that you can make preparations. We don't mean to notify relatives and friends because, as you've said, all Pan's friends are a bad lot and our only relatives are the Chia and Wang families. Now the Chias are the bridegroom's family and the Wangs have no one in the capital. When Miss Shih was engaged her family didn't invite us, so we needn't put them out either. But we must ask Chang Teh-hui here to help see to things as he's elderly and experienced."

Hsueh Ko, acting on her instructions, had a card sent to the Chia family. And the next day Chia Lien called to pay his respects to Aunt Hsueh.

"Tomorrow is a very auspicious day," he said. "So I've come to propose that we exchange gifts tomorrow. We only hope you won't think us too niggardly, aunt." He handed her the card on which was written the date of the wedding, and when she had made a polite rejoinder and nodded her consent he hurried back to report this to Chia Cheng.

"Let the old lady know," said Chia Cheng. "Suggest that as we're not notifying friends and relatives, we may as well keep everything rather simple. Regarding the gifts, just ask her to approve them; no need to refer to me."

Chia Lien assented and went off on this errand. Lady Wang told Hsi-feng to take all the gifts to the old lady for her inspection, and to get Hsi-jen to let Pao-yu know as well.

"Why go to all this bother?" Pao-yu chuckled. "We send things to the Garden, then they send them back here again — our own people doing the sending and the accepting!"

Their Ladyships hearing this remarked cheerfully, "We say he's weak in the head, but today he's talking sense."

Yuan-yang and the other maids could not suppress smiles either as they showed the gifts one by one to the old lady.

"This is a gold necklet," they said. "Here are gold and pearl trinkets, eighty of them in all. There are forty rolls of serpent-patterned brocade, a hundred and twenty rolls of coloured silk and satin and a hundred and twenty garments for all four seasons. As no sheep and wine have been prepared, here is the equivalent in silver."

When the old lady had approved these gifts she quietly instructed Hsi-feng, "Go and tell Aunt Hsueh not to stand on ceremony. Ask her to wait till Pan is released to return gifts for his sister in his own good time. We here will prepare the bedding for the happy occasion."

Hsi-feng assented and left to send Chia Lien to Aunt Hsueh's place. She then instructed Chou Jui and Lai Wang, "Don't take the presents through the main gate but by that old side-gate in the Garden. I'll be coming over myself presently. That gate is a good distance from Bamboo Lodge. If people from other households notice you, warn them not to mention this to anyone there."

The stewards went off to carry out these orders.

In the happy belief that he was to marry Tai-yu, Pao-yu's health improved, though he still talked foolishly. The stewards sending the presents named no names when they came back; and though most of the household knew where they had been, in view of Hsi-feng's instructions they dared not disclose it.

Now Tai-yu, although taking medicine, was sinking steadily. Tzu-chuan and her other maids pleaded hard with her.

"Things have come to such a pass, miss, we must speak out," they said. "We know what's in your heart. But nothing unforeseen can possibly happen. If you don't believe us, just think of Pao-yu's health — he's so ill, how could he get married? Don't listen to silly rumours, miss, but rest quietly till you're better."

Tai-yu smiled faintly without a word, then started coughing again and brought up more and more blood. Her maids saw that she was dying, and nothing they could say would save her. They remained at her bedside weeping, though sending three or four times a day to report to the old lady. But as Yuan-yang had noticed that recently Tai-yu had lost favour in her grandmother's eyes, she often neglected to pass on their messages. And as the old lady was occupied with preparations for the approaching wedding, when she had no news of Tai-yu she asked no questions. All her maids could do was send for the doctor to see her.

During Tai-yu's previous illnesses, everyone from the old lady herself down to the maids of her cousins had come to ask after her health. But now not one relative or servant came, not even sending inquiries, and when she opened her eyes there was nobody but Tzu-chuan in the room. She knew there was not the least reason for her to live on.

"Sister, you're the one closest to me," she murmured with an effort. "Ever since you were assigned to me by the old lady, I've always looked on you as my own sister. . . ." Here she had to stop for breath.

Tzu-chuan's heart ached. She was sobbing too much to speak.

"Sister Tzu-chuan!" panted Tai-yu after a while. "I feel uncomfortable lying down. Please help me to sit up."

"But you're not well, miss. If you sit up you may catch cold."

Tai-yu closed her eyes without a word but presently struggled to sit up and Tzu-chuan and Hsueh-yen had to help her, propping her up with soft pillows on either side while Tzu-chuan sat by her supporting her. Though she was so weak that she felt the bed beneath her painfully hard, she stuck it out.

"My poems . . ." she gasped to Hsueh-yen.

Hsueh-yen guessed that she wanted her manuscript book which she had been going through a few days ago. She found it and gave it to her. Tai-yu nodded, then glanced up at the case on a shelf; but this time the maid could not read her thoughts. Tai-yu's eyes dilated with exasperation till a fresh fit of coughing made her bring up more blood. Hsueh-yen hastily fetched her water to rinse out her mouth over the spittoon, then Tzu-chuan wiped her lips with a handkerchief. Taking it, Tai-yu pointed at the case, gasping for breath again so that she could not speak. Her eyes had closed.

"Better lie down, miss," urged Tzu-chuan.

When Tai-yu shook her head, Tzu-chuan realized that she

must want a handkerchief and told Hsueh-yen to fetch a white silk one from the case. But at sight of it, Tai-yu put it aside.

"The one with writing . . ." she managed to whisper.

Then it dawned on Tzu-chuan that she wanted Pao-yu's old handkerchief on which she had written verses. She made Hsueh-yen get it out and passed it to her.

"For pity's sake, rest, miss!" she begged her. "Why tire yourself out? You can look at it when you're better."

But not even glancing at the poems, Tai-yu tried with all her might to tear up the handkerchief. However, her trembling fingers lacked the strength. Although Tzu-chuan knew how incensed she was by Pao-yu, she dared not disclose this.

"Don't wear yourself out again, miss, being angry!" she pleaded.

Tai-yu nodded weakly and stuffed the handkerchief up her sleeve.

"Light the lamp," she ordered.

Hsueh-yen hastily complied. After glancing at the lamp Tai-yu closed her eyes again and sat there breathing hard.

"Bring the brazier," she murmured presently.

Thinking she was cold Tzu-chuan urged, "You'd better lie down, miss, and put on more bedding. Charcoal fumes might be bad for you."

As Tai-yu shook her head, Hsueh-yen had to light the brazier and put it on its stand on the floor. At a sign that Tai-yu wanted it on the *kang*, she moved it there, then went out to fetch a low table.

Tai-yu bent forward, supported by Tzu-chuan's two hands. She pulled out the handkerchief, looked at the fire and nodded, then dropped the handkerchief on it. This shocked Tzu-chuan, who wanted to snatch it off but could not let go of her mistress, as Hsueh-yen was still outside fetching the low table. By now the handkerchief was burning.

"Miss!" protested Tzu-chuan. "Why do such a thing?"

Turning a deaf ear, Tai-yu picked up her manuscript book and after glancing at it put it down. For fear she might burn this too, Tzu-chuan hastily leaned against her to support her, thereby freeing one of her own hands. But Tai-yu forestalled her by dropping the book on the fire out of her reach.

Hsueh-yen coming in with the table saw Tai-yu toss something on the fire and made a grab for it; but the inflammable paper was already smouldering. Not caring whether she burned her hands or not, Hsueh-yen snatched the book from the fire, threw it on the ground and trampled it with her feet. Too late — there was nothing but a charred remnant left.

Tai-yu closed her eyes and sank back, nearly knocking over Tzu-chuan who, her heart palpitating, hastily asked Hsueh-yen to help lay her down. It was too late to fetch help; yet what if they called no-one and their young mistress should die during the night with only herself, Hsueh-yen, Ying-ko and a few young maids in attendance? They sat up apprehensively till dawn, when Tai-yu seemed a little better. But after breakfast she had a sudden relapse, coughing and retching again.

Fearing the worst, Tzu-chuan left Hsueh-yen and the others in charge while she hurried to report this to the old lady. However, she found the place quiet and deserted, except for a few old nurses and some young maids of all work left there to mind the house. Asked where the old lady was, they returned evasive answers. In surprise, Tzu-chuan went into Pao-yu's room and found it empty too. The young maids there also denied any knowledge of his whereabouts.

By then Tzu-chuan had a good inkling of the truth. "How cruel these people are!" she thought to herself, remembering that not a soul had called on Tai-yu during the last few days. The more she dwelt on it, the more bitter she felt. In her indignation she turned and left abruptly.

"I'd like to see how Pao-yu looks today," she fumed. "Wouldn't the sight of me shame him? That year when I told him a fib he fell ill, he was so frantic; but today he blatantly does a thing like this. It shows that all men's hearts are as cold as ice — they really make you gnash your teeth!"

As she walked on brooding over this, she soon reached Happy Red Court. The gate was closed and all inside was quiet. It occurred to her then, "If he is getting married, he must have new bridal chambers. I wonder where they are?"

She was looking around when Mo-yu came flying along and she called to him to stop. The page walked over, grinning broadly.

"What brings you here, sister?" he asked.

"I heard Master Pao's getting married so I came to watch the fun, but apparently the wedding's not here. When exactly is it to be?"

"I'll tell you in strict confidence, sister," he whispered. "But don't let Hsueh-yen know. Our orders are not even to let *you* know. The wedding will take place this evening. Of course it won't be here. His Lordship made Second Master Lien fix up new quarters for them. Well, is there anything you want me to do?"

"No, nothing. Off you go."

Mo-yu darted off.

Tzu-chuan remained lost in thought until she remembered Tai-yu — was she still alive?

"Pao-yu!" she swore through clenched teeth, her eyes swimming with tears. "If she dies tomorrow, you'll get out of seeing her. But after you've had your pleasure, how are you going to brazen it out with *me*?"

She walked on in tears towards Bamboo Lodge and saw two young maids at the gate looking out for her.

At sight of her one cried, "Here comes Sister Tzu-chuan!"

With a sinking heart she signalled to them to keep quiet. Hurrying to Tai-yu's bedside, she found her feverish, her cheeks hectically flushed. Knowing that this was a bad sign, Tzu-chuan called for Tai-yu's old nurse Nanny Wang, who took one look then started sobbing and wailing.

Tzu-chuan had hoped that old Nanny Wang with her experience would lend her courage; but the nurse's reaction threw her into a tizzy till she bethought herself of someone else and sent a young maid quickly in search of her. Do you know who this was? Li Wan. As a widow, it was out of the question for her to attend Pao-yu's wedding; besides, she was the one ·in charge in the Garden. So Tzu-chuan sent to ask her over.

Li Wan was correcting a poem for Lan when a young maid burst in.

"Madam!" she cried. "It looks as if Miss Lin's done for! They're all weeping and wailing there."

Li Wan was horrified. Not stopping to ask any questions she sprang up and hurried out, followed by Su-yun and Pi-yueh. And on the way she reflected tearfully, "We've been as close as sisters here. Her looks and talents are truly so outstanding, one can only compare her to some goddess in heaven. But poor girl, fated to die so young and be buried far from home! I didn't like to visit her all because of Hsi-feng's underhand plan to fob off a different bride on Pao-yu — so I've let my cousin down. How tragic this is!"

Now, reaching the gate of Bamboo Lodge, she was unnerved not to hear a sound inside. "Perhaps she's already dead and they've finished lamenting her," she thought as she hurried inside. "I wonder if they had clothes, bedding and shroud ready."

A young maid by the door of the inner room at sight of her announced, "Here's Madam Chu!"

Tzu-chuan hastily came out as Li Wan walked in.

"How is she?" she asked urgently.

Tzu-chuan choked with sobs and could not get a word out. Her tears falling like pearls from a broken string, she could only point at Tai-yu.

The maid's grief distressed Li Wan even more. Asking no further questions she went over to look at the dying girl, already past speaking. She called her softly twice. Tai-yu opened her eyes slowly and seemed to recognize her. She was still breathing faintly, but though her eyelids fluttered and her lips quivered, she could not utter a single word or shed a single tear.

Turning away, Li Wan saw that Tzu-chuan had vanished and asked Hsueh-yen where she was.

"In the outer room," was the answer.

Li Wan hurried out and found her lying on the divan there,

her face pale, tears flowing so fast from her closed eyes that a big patch of the silk-bordered flowered mattress was wet with tears and mucus. At Li Wan's call she opened her eyes slowly and got up.

"Silly creature!" scolded Li Wan. "This is no time for weeping. Hurry up and get Miss Lin's clothes ready. How long will you wait to change her? Are you going to expose an unmarried girl to set out naked to the other world?"

At this, Tzu-chuan broke down and sobbed bitterly. Li Wan though weeping too was impatient as well. Wiping her own eyes, she patted the maid on the shoulder.

"Good child, your crying is driving me distracted! Prepare her things quickly before it's too late," she urged.

She was startled just then by someone rushing in. It was Ping-erh. Bursting in on this scene she stood rooted to the spot, speechless.

"Why aren't you over there now? What brings you here?" asked Li Wan as Lin Chih-hsiao's wife also joined them.

Ping-erh said, "Our mistress was worried and sent me to have a look. But as *you're* here, madam, I shall tell her that she need only attend to affairs over there."

Li Wan nodded.

"I'll go in to see Miss Lin too," added Ping-erh, already in tears as she entered the inner room.

"You've come in the nick of time," Li Wan told Mrs. Lin. "Go out quickly and get some steward to prepare Miss Lin's after-life things. When everything's ready he's to report to me — there's no need to go over there."

Mrs. Lin assented but made no move.

"Do you have other business?" Li Wan asked.

"Just now Madam Lien consulted the old lady and they want to have Miss Tzu-chuan to help out there."

Before Li Wan could answer, Tzu-chuan interposed, "Please don't wait for me, Mrs. Lin. When she's dead, of course we'll leave her. They needn't be in such a hurry...." Embarrassed by this outburst she went on more mildly, "Besides, nursing an invalid here I'm not clean. Miss Lin is still breathing and wants me from time to time."

Li Wan helped her out by explaining, "It's true. The affinity between Miss Lin and this girl must have been predestined. Though Hsueh-yen's the one she brought with her from the south, she doesn't care for her much. I can see that Tzu-chuan is the only one who can't leave her for a second."

Mrs. Lin had been put out by Tzu-chuan's reply, but she was unable to rebut Li Wan. Seeing Tzu-chuan dissolved in tears, she smiled at her faintly.

"It's all very well for Miss Tzu-chuan to talk like that," she rejoined. "But what am I to say to the old lady? And how can I repeat this to Madam Lien?"

At these words, Ping-erh came out wiping her eyes.

"Repeat what to Madam Lien?" she wanted to know.

Mrs. Lin explained the situation, and Ping-erh lowered her head to think it over.

"In that case," she suggested, "let Hsueh-yen go instead."

"Will she be suitable?" Li Wan inquired.

Ping-erh stepped closer to whisper something to her, at which she nodded.

"Very well, then. Sending Hsueh-yen will do just as well."

Mrs. Lin asked Ping-erh if she agreed, and the answer was: "Yes, it's the same."

"Then please tell her to come with me immediately. I'll report to the old lady and Madam Lien that this was your idea, madam, and Miss Ping-erh's too. Later you can explain to Madam Lien yourself, miss."

"All right," said Li Wan. "But why should someone of your seniority be scared to answer for such a little thing?"

"It's not that." Mrs. Lin smiled. "But we can't be sure what plan the old lady and Madam Lien have; and besides you and Miss Ping-erh are here, madam."

Ping-erh had already called out Hsueh-yen, who had been holding aloof these last few days as the others had been taunting her as a careless child; and in any case she would never dream of ignoring a summons from the Lady Dowager and Madam Lien. She hastily smoothed her hair and on Ping-erh's instructions changed into colourful clothes, then went off with Mrs. Lin. Li Wan, after a brief discussion with Ping-erh, sent her to tell Mrs. Lin to urge her husband to get a coffin ready without delay.

Ping-erh left to attend to this and, rounding a bend, saw Mrs. Lin walking ahead of her with Hsueh-yen. She called to them to stop.

"I'll take her there," she said. "You go first to tell your husband to get Miss Lin's things ready. I'll report this for you to my mistress."

Mrs. Lin agreed and went off, while Ping-erh took Hsueh-yen to the bridal chambers and, having made her report, left to see to her own business.

Now that things had come to such a pass, Hsueh-yen could not but grieve for Tai-yu, though she dared not show her feelings to the old lady and Hsi-feng. "What do they want me for?" she wondered. "I'll wait and see. Pao-yu used to be so devoted to our young lady, why doesn't he come out? Is he really ill or just shamming? He may be trying to put her off by pretending to have lost his jade and to be out of his mind, so that she'll lose interest in him and he can marry Miss Pao-chai. I'll slip in and see whether he's really crazy or not. He can hardly be shamming today."

She tiptoed to the door of the inner room and peeped in.

Now though the loss of his jade had deranged Pao-yu, the news that he was to marry Tai-yu seemed to him the most wonderful thing that had ever happened, and at once his health had improved, though he seemed less quick in the uptake than before. So Hsi-feng's cunning scheme had succeeded completely. He could hardly wait to see Tai-yu and go through with his wedding today. Beside himself with joy, although he sometimes talked nonsense he behaved quite differently from when he was demented. Hsueh-yen saw this with indignation and distress, not knowing what was in his heart, then she slipped away.

Pao-yu, seated in Lady Wang's room, was pressing Hsi-jen to help him into his wedding clothes and watching busy Hsi-feng and Madam Yu as he longed for the auspicious hour to arrive.

"Cousin Lin's only coming from the Garden," he said to Hsi-jen. "Why should it take so long?"

Suppressing a smile she answered, "She has to wait for the appointed hour."

Then he heard Hsi-feng say to Lady Wang, "Although we're in mourning and won't have musicians outside, according to us southerners' rule they must bow to each other and utter silence won't do. So I've ordered our troupe of house musicians to play some tunes and liven things up a little."

"Very well," said Lady Wang, nodding.

Presently a big sedan-chair entered the courtyard and the family musicians went out to meet the bride, while in filed twelve pairs of maids in two rows with Palace lanterns — a novel and distinctive sight. The Master of Ceremonies invited the bride to alight from the chair, and Pao-yu saw a maid with a red sash help her out — her face was veiled. And who do you think the other maid assisting the bride was? No other than Hsueh-yen!

"Why Hsueh-yen and not Tzu-chuan?" he wondered, then told himself, "Of course. She brought Hsueh-yen with her from her home down south. Tzu-chuan is one of *our* household; so naturally she needn't bring her." Reasoning like this, he felt as jubilant as if seeing Tai-yu herself.

The Master of Ceremonies announced the procedure. Bride and bridegroom paid their respects to Heaven and Earth, then invited the old lady to come out and receive four bows from them, after which they bowed to Chia Cheng and Lady Wang. Next they ascended the hall and paid their respects to each other before being ushered into the bridal chamber where they went through other ceremonies such as "sitting on the bed" and "letting down the bed curtains", in accordance with the old rules of Chinling.

Chia Cheng had never believed that this wedding could

cure Pao-yu, but he had to go along with his mother's decision. Today, however, he was pleased because Pao-yu looked as if he had really recovered.

After the bride sat down on the bridal bed, she had to be unveiled. To be on the safe side, Hsi-feng had asked the old lady and Lady Wang there to keep an eye on things. Pao-yu fatuously stepped over to the bride.

"Are you better, Cousin Lin?" he asked. "It's so long since I've seen you! Why keep your face covered with that rag?"

He reached out to take off the veil, making the old lady break out in a cold sweat. But then Pao-yu reflected, "Cousin Lin's very sensitive; I mustn't offend her." So he waited till he felt he could wait no longer, then stepped forward and removed the veil, which the bridesmaid whisked away. At the same time Hsueh-yen withdrew, and Ying-erh came in to wait upon her young mistress.

Pao-yu looked at his bride and could not believe his eyes — she seemed to be Pao-chai. He shone the lamp on her face and rubbed his eyes. There was no doubt about it — it was Pao-chai! Splendidly dressed, soft and plump, her hair slightly dishevelled, fluttering her eyelashes and holding her breath she looked as alluring as lotus dripping with dew, as bashful as apricot blossom moistened by mist.

Pao-yu was stupefied by the realization that Hsueh-yen had disappeared and Ying-erh had taken her place. At a loss, he thought he must be dreaming and stood there in a daze till they took the lamp from his hand and made him sit down. Staring vacantly, he uttered not a word. The old lady, afraid he had lost his senses again, took charge of him herself while Hsi-feng and Madam Yu led Pao-chai to the inner room to rest. She, of course, remained silent too, lowering her head.

Soon Pao-yu calmed down sufficiently to notice the presence of his grandmother and mother.

"Where am I?" he whispered to Hsi-jen. "Is this a dream?"

"This is your wedding day," she answered. "Don't let the master hear you talking such nonsense. He's just outside."

林黛玉焚稿斷痴情
薛寶釵出閨成大禮

"Who's that beautiful girl sitting there?" he asked, pointing inside.

Hsi-jen put a hand to her mouth to hide her laughter, so amused that she could not speak.

"That's the new Second Young Mistress," she finally told him.

The others also turned their heads away, unable to keep from smiling.

"Don't be silly!" cried Pao-yu. "What Second Young Mistress do you mean?"

"Miss Pao-chai."

"Then where is Miss Lin?"

"It was the master's decision that you should marry Miss Pao-chai, so why ask in that foolish way about Miss Lin?"

"But I saw her just now, and Hsueh-yen too. How can you say they're not here? What game are you all playing?"

Hsi-feng stepped forward to whisper, "Miss Pao-chai is sitting in the inner room; so don't talk foolishly. If you annoy her, the old lady won't like it."

This bewildered Pao-yu still more. Already deranged, after the mysterious apparitions and vanishings of this evening he knew even less what to think. Ignoring all else he just clamoured to go and find Cousin Lin. The ladies did their best to pacify him, but he would not listen to reason; and as Pao-chai was inside they could not speak out plainly. Indeed, they knew that explanations were useless now that his wits were wandering again. They lit benzoin incense to calm him and made him lie down. No one made a sound and presently, to the old lady's relief, he fell into a lethargic sleep. She decided to sit up with him till dawn and sent Hsi-feng to urge Pao-chai to rest too. Pao-chai, behaving as if she had heard nothing, lay down then fully dressed in the inner room.

Chapter 33
Unhappy Vermilion Pearl's Spirit
Return in Sorrow to Heaven

On the day of Pao-yu's wedding Tai-yu lay in a coma, her life hanging by a thread, while Li Wan and Tzu-chuan wept as if their hearts would break. That evening she recovered consciousness and feebly opened her eyes. She seemed to want something to drink. As Hsueh-yen had gone, leaving only Li Wan and Tzu-chuan there, the latter brought her a bowl of pear juice and dried-longan syrup and gave her two or three sips with a small silver spoon, after which Tai-yu closed her eyes to rest again. Li Wan knew that this lucid interval and slight rallying were the prelude to the end, but thinking that still a few hours away she went back to Paddy-Sweet Cottage to see to some business.

Meanwhile Tai-yu opened her eyes and saw only Tzu-chuan, her old nanny and some young maids. Clasping Tzu-chuan's hand she addressed her with an effort.

"I'm done for! You've served me for several years, and I'd hoped that the two of us could always stay together. But now. . . ." Stopping to catch her breath, she closed her eyes in exhaustion.

Tzu-chuan, whose hand she was still gripping, dared not move. Because Tai-yu seemed better than earlier on she was still hoping for her recovery, and so these words struck chill into her heart.

"Sister!" continued Tai-yu presently. "I have no dear one here, I have lived chastely. . . . Get them to send me home!"

Closing her eyes again, she clasped Tzu-chuan's hand even

more tightly as she panted silently, breathing out more than she breathed in — at her last gasp.

Tzu-chuan was frantically sending to fetch Li Wan when luckily Tan-chun arrived.

"Look at Miss Lin, miss!" whispered Tzu-chuan, her tears falling like rain.

Tan-chun came over and felt Tai-yu's hand — it was chill and her eyes were glazed. Weeping, they called for water with which to wash her. Then Li Wan hurried in. The three of them had no time for civilities. They were washing Tai-yu when she raised a sudden cry:

"Pao-yu, Pao-yu! How. . . ."

Those were her last words. She broke out in a cold sweat. Tzu-chuan and the others, holding her as she sweated, felt her body grow colder and colder. Tan-chun and Li Wan bade her maids dress her hair and change her clothes. But her eyes turned up — alas!

> Her sweet soul gone with the wind,
> They sorrow at midnight, lost in fragrant dreams.

It was in the very same hour in which Pao-yu and Pao-chai were married that Tai-yu breathed her last. Tzu-chuan and the other maids wept bitterly while Li Wan and Tan-chun, recalling her lovable ways, lamented her fate and sobbed too with distress. As Bamboo Lodge was far from the bridal chambers, their wailing could not be heard there. Presently they caught the sound of distant music, but as soon as they pricked up their ears it vanished. When Li Wan and Tan-chun stepped into the courtyard to listen, they saw only the wind-tossed bamboos and the shifting moonlight on the wall — a scene of loneliness and desolation.

They sent for Lin Chih-hsiao's wife, had Tai-yu laid out and assigned maids to watch by her corpse, not notifying Hsi-feng till the next morning.

As Their Ladyships were so busy with Chia Cheng leaving home that morning and Pao-yu's increased derangement making the whole household frantic, Hsi-feng decided not to report

Tai-yu's death for fear Their Ladyships would fall ill under this fresh burden of grief. So she went herself to the Garden. On reaching Bamboo Lodge, she could not hold back her tears. Then she was told by Li Wan and Tan-chun that all preparations had been made for the funeral.

"Well done," she said. "But why didn't you let me know before to save me worrying?"

Tan-chun answered, "How could we, when seeing the master off?"

"At least the two of you took pity on her," commented Hsi-feng. "Very well then, I must go back to cope with the lovesick one over there. What a to-do! Not to report it today would be wrong; but if I report it I'm afraid it may be too much for the old lady."

"Do as you think fit," said Li Wan. "If possible, you should report it."

Nodding, Hsi-feng hurried away.

When she reached Pao-yu's quarters and heard that the doctor had pronounced him out of danger, to Their Ladyships' relief, she broke the news to them about Tai-yu without letting Pao-yu know. The old lady and Lady Wang were consternated.

"I have her death on my conscience," sobbed the old lady. "But the child was really too foolish!"

She was in a dilemma, wanting to go to the Garden to mourn Tai-yu, yet reluctant to leave Pao-yu. Lady Wang, suppressing her own grief, persuaded her to remain to look after her health, and the old lady agreed to her going instead.

"Tell her spirit for me," she instructed, "it's not because I'm heartless that I'm not coming to see you off, but there's someone closer here whom I have to see to. As my daughter's daughter you are dear to me; but Pao-yu is closer to me even than you. If any harm comes to *him*, how am I to face his father?" She wept again.

"You were very good to her, madam," said Lady Wang soothingly. "But each one's span of life is fixed by Heaven, and now that she's dead there's nothing we can do except give her the best funeral possible. That will show our feeling for her, and her mother's spirit and hers can rest in peace."

This made the old lady weep still more bitterly. And not wanting her to grieve too much, as Pao-yu was still bemused Hsi-feng quietly sent someone with the trumped-up message, "Pao-yu is asking for you, madam."

"Has anything happened?" she asked, no longer weeping.

"No, nothing," Hsi-feng assured her. "I expect he just wants to see you."

The old lady hurried out attended by Chen-chu and followed by Hsi-feng. Half-way there they met Lady Wang, whose report on her visit to Bamboo Lodge naturally caused the old lady fresh distress; but she swallowed back her tears because she was going to see Pao-yu.

"As all the preparations are made, I won't go over for the time being," she said. "Do as you think fit. Seeing her would make my heart ache. But mind you give her a handsome funeral."

When Lady Wang and Hsi-feng had agreed to this, she went on to see Pao-yu and asked what he wanted her for.

"Last night I saw Cousin Lin," he said with a smile. "She wants to go back south. I'm sure you're the only one who can keep her here for me, madam. Don't let her go!"

"All right. Don't worry," she answered.

Then Hsi-jen made Pao-yu lie down again.

After leaving him the old lady went in to see Pao-chai, who having been married less than a week behaved shyly in company. She noticed that the old lady's face was tear-stained. After she had served tea, she was told to take a seat and perched respectfully on the edge of a chair.

"I heard that Cousin Lin was unwell," she remarked. "Is she any better?"

Bursting into tears the Lady Dowager answered, "I'll tell you, child, but don't let Pao-yu know. It's all because of your Cousin Lin that you've been so unfairly treated. Now that you're married I can tell you the truth: your Cousin Lin died a couple of days ago — at the very hour of your wedding. This illness Pao-yu has is because of her. You used to live together in the Garden, so I'm sure you know what I mean."

Pao-chai blushed, then shed tears at the thought of Tai-yu's death. And after chatting with her a little longer, the Lady Dowager left.

After this, Pao-chai weighed the pros and cons carefully before hitting on a plan; but not wanting to act rashly she had waited till after her visit home on the ninth day after their wedding before breaking the news to Pao-yu. And now that, sure enough, he was on the mend, they no longer had to keep things secret from him.

But though Pao-yu was recovering steadily, he had not overcome his infatuation and he insisted on going to mourn for Tai-yu. Knowing that the cause of his illness was not yet uprooted, his grandmother forbade him to give way to foolish fancies, but that only deepened his gloom and brought on a relapse. The doctor, however, saw that he was ill with long-ing and advised them to allow him to vent his feelings, for then the medicine would be more efficacious. Hearing this, Pao-yu at once clamoured to go to Bamboo Lodge. They had to send for a bamboo chair and help him on to it, after which they set off, the old lady and Lady Wang leading the way.

The sight of Tai-yu's coffin in Bamboo Lodge made the old lady weep till she had no more tears to shed and was out of breath. Hsi-feng and the others urged her to desist. Meanwhile Lady Wang had wept too. And they shed tears anew even after Li Wan invited them to rest in the inner room.

Pao-yu on his arrival thought back to his visits here before his illness. Now the lodge remained but its young mistress was gone. He gave way to a storm of grief. How close they had been, yet today they were parted by death! He felt his heart would break. Alarmed by his frenzied anguish, all tried to comfort him, but already he had almost fainted away. They helped him out to rest. Pao-chai and the others who had come with him also mourned bitterly.

Now Pao-yu insisted on seeing Tzu-chuan to ask her what Tai-yu's dying words had been. Tzu-chuan had a deep grudge against him, but his misery softened her heart and in the presence of Their Ladyships she dared take no liberties. So she reported in detail how her young mistress had fallen ill again, how she had burned his handkerchief and her poems, and what her last words had been. Pao-yu wailed again until he was hoarse and breathless, and Tan-chun seized this chance to repeat Tai-yu's dying request to have her coffin taken back to the south, reducing Their Ladyships to tears again. It was Hsi-feng with her persuasive tongue who succeeded in consoling them a little and urged them to go back. When Pao-yu refused, his grandmother had to override his wishes.

Because the Lady Dowager was old and had been on tenterhooks day and night ever since Pao-yu fell ill, this fresh access of grief made her so dizzy and feverish that although still worried about him she had to retire to her room to lie down. Lady Wang went back too in even greater anguish, leaving Tsai-yun to help Hsi-jen, with the instructions:

"If Pao-yu breaks down again, send us word at once."

Knowing that his grief must run its course, instead of trying to console him Pao-chai made some cutting remarks; and suspecting that she was jealous he swallowed back his tears. So the night passed without mishap.

The next morning when others came to see how he was, they found him debilitated but less distracted. They nursed him devotedly till he slowly recovered.

Chapter 34
Imperial Guards Raid the Ning Mansion

Chia Cheng was entertaining his guests in the Hall of Glorious Felicity when in burst Lai Ta.

"Commissioner Chao of the Imperial Guards and several of his officers are here to see you, sir," he announced. "When I asked for their cards the commissioner said, 'No need: we are old friends.' He dismounted from his carriage and came straight in. Please make haste to meet them, sir, with the young gentlemen."

Chia Cheng, who had had no dealings with Commissioner Chao, could not understand why he should have come uninvited. As he had guests he could hardly entertain him, yet not to ask him in would be discourteous.

He was thinking it over when Chia Lien urged, "Better go at once, uncle, before they all come in."

That same moment a servant from the inner gate announced, "Commissioner Chao has entered the inner gate."

Chia Cheng and others hastily went to meet him. The commissioner, smiling, said not a word as he walked straight into the hall. Behind him were five or six of his officers, only a few of whom they recognized, but none of these answered their greetings. At a loss, Chia Cheng had to offer them seats. Certain of the guests knew Commissioner Chao, yet with his head in the air he ignored them all, simply taking Chia Cheng's hand as he made a few conventional remarks. This looked so ominous that some of the guests slipped into the inner room while all the rest stood at respectful attention.

Chia Cheng, forcing a smile, was about to make conversation when a flustered servant announced the Prince of Hsiping. Before he could hasten to meet him the prince had entered.

Commissioner Chao stepped forward at once to salute him, then ordered his officers, "Since His Highness has arrived, you gentlemen can take runners to guard the front and back gates."

His officers assented and went out. Chia Cheng, knowing that this spelt trouble, fell on his knees to welcome the prince, who helped him to his feet with a smile.

"We wouldn't presume to intrude without special reason," he said. "We have come to announce an Imperial decree to Lord Sheh. You have many feasters here, which is somewhat inopportune, so I'll ask your relatives and friends to disperse, leaving only your own household to hear the decree."

Commissioner Chao put in, "Your Highness is very gracious, but the prince officiating at the East Mansion takes his duties so seriously that the gates are doubtless already sealed up."

Hearing that both mansions were involved, the guests were desperate to extricate themselves.

"These gentlemen are free to go," the prince said affably. "Have attendants see them out and notify your guards that there is no need to search them as they are all guests. Let them leave at once."

Then those relatives and friends streaked off like lightning, leaving Chia Cheng, Chia Sheh and their households livid and trembling with fear. Meanwhile runners had swarmed in to guard all the doors, so that no one — whether master or man — could stir a foot from his place.

Commissioner Chao turned to request the prince, "Please read the decree, Your Highness, then we can start the search."

The runners hitched up their tunics and rolled up their sleeves, ready to go into action.

The Prince of Hsiping proclaimed slowly, "His Majesty has ordered me to bring Chao Chuan of the Imperial Guards to search Chia Sheh's property."

Chia Sheh and the rest prostrated themselves on the ground.

The prince, standing on the dais, continued, "Hear the Imperial decree: Chia Sheh has intrigued with provincial officials and abused his power to molest the weak, showing himself unworthy of Our favour and sullying his ancestors' good name. His hereditary rank is hereby abolished."

Commissioner Chao thundered, "Arrest Chia Sheh! Keep guard over the others."

At that time, all the men of both Chia Mansions were in the hall except for Pao-yu, who had slipped off to join the old lady on the pretext of indisposition, and Chia Huan who was seldom presented to guests. So all the rest were now under surveillance.

Commissioner Chao told his men to dispatch officers and runners to search the different apartments and draw up an inventory. This order made Chia Cheng's household exchange consternated glances, while the runners gleefully rubbed their hands, eager to ransack the place.

The prince interposed, "We hear that Lord Sheh and Lord Cheng keep separate accounts, and according to the decree we are to search the former's property. The rest is to be sealed up pending further orders."

Commissioner Chao rose to his feet. "May it please Your Highness," he said, "Chia Sheh and Chia Cheng have not divided the family property, and we hear that Chia Cheng has put his nephew Chia Lien in charge of his household affairs. We shall therefore have to search the whole premises." When the prince made no comment he added, "I must go in person with my officers to search the houses of Chia Sheh and Chia Lien."

"There is no hurry," demurred the prince. "Send word first so that the ladies inside may withdraw before you start to search."

But already the commissioner's attendants and runners, making the Chias' servants show them the way, had set off in different directions to ransack both mansions.

"No disorder now!" called the prince sternly. "I shall come in person to supervise the search!" Then getting up slowly he ordered, "None of those who came with me are to move. Wait here. Later we shall check up on the property and make an inventory."

Just then a guard came in and knelt to report, "In the inner apartments we have found some clothes from the Palace and other forbidden things which we haven't presumed to touch. I have come, Your Highness, to ask for your orders."

Presently another group gathered round the prince to report, "In Chia Lien's house we have found two cases of title-deeds and one of promissory notes — all at illegally exorbitant rates of interest."

"Good!" cried Commissioner Chao. "So they are usurers too. All their property should certainly be confiscated! Please rest here, Your Highness, while I supervise the search before coming back for your instructions."

Just then, however, the prince's steward announced, "The guards at the gate say that His Majesty has sent the Prince of Peiching to proclaim another decree and they ask the commissioner to receive him."

As Commissioner Chao started out to meet the Prince of Peiching he told himself, "I was out of luck having that crabbed prince foisted on me. Now, with this other one here, I should be able to crack down on them hard!"

The Prince of Peiching had already entered the hall. Standing facing the doorway he announced, "Here is a decree. Let Chao Chuan, Commissioner of the Imperial Guards, pay heed." He then proclaimed, "The commissioner's sole task is to arrest Chia Sheh for trial. The Prince of Hsiping will determine what other measures to take according to the earlier decree."

Elated by this, the Prince of Hsiping seated himself beside the Prince of Peiching and sent the commissioner back to his yamen with Chia Sheh. This development disappointed all his officers and runners, who had come out on hearing of the second prince's arrival. They had to stand there awaiting Their Highnesses' orders. The Prince of Peiching selected two honest officers and a dozen of the older runners, sending away the rest.

The Prince of Hsiping told him, "I was just losing patience with Old Chao. If you hadn't brought that decree in the nick of time, sir, they'd have been really hard hit here."

"When I heard at court that Your Highness had been sent to search the Chia Mansions I was relieved, knowing you would let them off more lightly," the Prince of Peiching replied. "I never thought Old Chao was such a scoundrel. But where are Chia Cheng and Pao-yu now? And how much damage has been done inside?"

His men reported, "Chia Cheng and the rest are under guard in the servants' quarters, and the whole place has been turned upside-down."

At the Prince of Peiching's orders, the officers fetched Chia Cheng for questioning. He fell on his knees before Their Highnesses and with tears in his eyes begged for mercy. The prince helped him up and urged him not to worry, then informed him of the terms of the new decree. With tears of gratitude, Chia Cheng kowtowed towards the north to thank the Emperor then turned back for further instructions.

The prince said, "When Old Chao was here just now, Your Lordship, his runners reported finding various articles for Imperial use and some promissory notes for usurious loans — this we cannot cover up. Regarding those forbidden articles, as they were for Her Imperial Highness' use it will do no harm to report them. But we must find some way to explain those IOU's. Now I want you, sir, to take the officers and honestly hand over to them all your brother's property, to end the matter. Don't on any account conceal anything, or you will be asking for trouble."

"I would never dare," answered Chia Cheng. "But we never divided up our ancestral estate, simply considering the things in our two houses as our own property."

"Very well," they said. "Just hand over everything in Lord Sheh's house." They sent the two officers off with orders to attend only to this and nothing else.

Let us return now to the ladies' feast in the Lady Dowager's quarters. Lady Wang had just warned Pao-yu that unless he went out to join the gentlemen his father might be angry.

Hsi-feng, still unwell, said faintly, "I don't think Pao-yu's afraid of meeting them, but he knows there are plenty of people there to entertain the guests, so he's waiting on us here instead. If it occurs to the master that they need more people there to look after the guests, you can trot out Pao-yu, madam. How about that?"

"This minx Hsi-feng!" the old lady chuckled. "She still has the gift of the gab for all she's so ill!"

The fun was at its height when one of Lady Hsing's maids came rushing in crying, "Your Ladyships! We're done for! A whole lot of robbers have come, all in boots and official caps.... They're opening cases, overturning crates, ransacking the whole place!..."

The old lady and the others had not recovered from this shock when Ping-erh, her hair hanging loose, dashed in with Chiao-chieh.

"We're ruined!" she wailed. "I was having lunch with Chiao-chieh when Lai Wang appeared, in chains, and told me to lose no time in warning you ladies to keep out of the way, as some prince has come to raid our house! I nearly died of fright! Before I could go in to fetch any valuables, a band of men drove me out. You'd better make haste to get together the clothes and things you need."

Lady Hsing and Lady Wang were completely flummoxed, frightened out of their wits. Hsi-feng who had listened wide-eyed now collapsed in a faint. The old lady was crying with terror, unable to utter a word.

Pandemonium reigned as the maids tried to attend to their mistresses. Then they heard shouts, "The women inside must make themselves scarce! The prince is coming!"

Pao-chai and Pao-yu looked on helplessly as the maids and nurses attempted desperately to hustle the ladies out. Then in ran Chia Lien.

"It's all right now!" he panted. "Thank goodness the prince has come to our rescue!"

Before they could question him, he saw Hsi-feng lying as if dead on the floor and gave a cry of alarm. Then the sight of the old lady, terror-stricken and gasping for breath, made him even more frantic. Luckily Ping-erh and others managed to revive Hsi-feng and help her up. The old lady recovered consciousness too, but lay back dizzily on the couch sobbing and choking for breath, while Li Wan did her best to soothe her.

Taking a grip on himself, Chia Lien explained to them how kindly the two princes had intervened. But fearing that the news of Chia Sheh's arrest might make the old lady and Lady Hsing die of fright, he withheld it for the time being and went back to his own quarters.

Once over the threshold, he saw that all their cases and wardrobes had been opened and rifled. He stood speechless in consternation, shedding tears, till he heard his name called and had to go out. Chia Cheng was there with two officers drawing up an inventory, which one of the officers read out as follows:

> One hundred and twenty-three gold trinkets set with jewels; thirteen strings of pearls; two pale gold plates; two pairs of gold bowls; two gilded bowls; forty gold spoons; eighty big silver bowls and twenty silver plates; two pairs of ivory chopsticks inlaid with gold; four gilded pots; three pairs of gilded cups; two tea-trays; seventy-six silver saucers; thirty-six silver cups; eighteen black fox furs; six deep-grey fox furs; thirty-six sable furs; thirty yellow fox furs; twelve ermine furs; three grey fox furs; sixty marten furs; forty grey fox-leg furs; twenty brown sheep-skins; two raccoon furs; two bundles of yellow fox-leg furs; twenty pieces of white fox fur; thirty lengths of Western worsted; twenty-three lengths of serge; twelve lengths of velveteen; twenty musk-rat furs; four pieces of spotted squirrel fur; one bolt of velvet; one piece of plum-deer skin; two fox furs with ornamental cloud patterns; a roll of badger-cub skin; seven bundles of platypus fur; a hundred and sixty squirrel furs; eight male wolf-skins; six tiger-skins; three seal-skins; sixteen otter furs; forty bundles of grey sheep-skins; sixty-three black sheep-skins; ten sets of red fox-fur hat material; twelve sets of black fox-fur hat material; two sets of sable-fur hat material; sixteen small fox furs; two beaver-skins; two otter-skins; thirty-five civet-cat furs; twelve lengths of Japanese silk; one hundred and thirty bolts of satin; one hundred and eighty-one bolts of gauze; thirty-two bolts of crepe; thirty bolts of Tibetan serge; eight bolts of satin with serpent designs; three bales of hemp-cloth; three bales of different kinds of cloth; one hundred fur coats; thirty-two Tibetan serge garments; three hundred and forty padded and unpadded garments; thirty-two jade articles; nine jade buckles; over five

hundred utensils of copper and tin; eighteen clocks and watches; nine chaplets; thirty-two lengths of different kinds of satin with serpent designs; three satin cushions with serpent designs for Imperial use; eight costumes for Palace ladies; one white jade belt; twelve bolts of yellow satin; seven thousand and two hundred taels of silver; fifty taels of gold; seven thousand strings of cash.

Separate lists were made of all the furnishings and the mansions conferred on the Duke of Jungkuo. The title-deeds of houses and land and the bonds of the family slaves were also sealed up.

Chia Lien, listening at one side, was puzzled not to hear his own property listed.

Then the two princes said, "Among the property confiscated are some IOU's which are definitely usurious. Whose are they? Your Lordship must tell the truth."

Chia Cheng knelt down and kowtowed. "I am guilty of never having managed the household affairs and that is the truth," he said. "I know nothing about such transactions. Your Highnesses will have to ask my nephew Chia Lien."

Chia Lien hastily stepped forward and knelt to report, "Since those documents were found in my humble house, how can I deny knowledge of them? I only beg Your Highnesses to be lenient to my uncle who knew nothing about this."

The two princes said, "As your father has already been found guilty, your cases can be dealt with together. You did right to admit this. Very well then, let a guard be kept over Chia Lien; the rest of the household can return to their different quarters. Lord Cheng, you must wait prudently for a further decree. We shall go now to report to His Majesty, leaving officers and runners here to keep watch."

They mounted their sedan-chairs, Chia Cheng and the others kneeling at the inner gate to see them off. The Prince of Peiching, on leaving, stretched out one hand with a look of compassion and said, "Please set your minds at rest."

By now Chia Cheng felt slightly calmer, although still dazed.

Chia Lan suggested, "Grandfather, won't you go in to see the old lady first? Then we can send for news of the East

Mansion."

Chia Cheng hastily did so, and found serving-women from different apartments all milling about in confusion. In no mood to check what they were doing he entered his mother's room, where one and all were in tears. Lady Wang, Pao-yu and others had gathered silently around the old lady, tears streaming down their cheeks. Lady Hsing was shaken by sobs. At his arrival they exclaimed in relief.

"The master has come back safely," they told the old lady. "Don't worry any more, madam."

The Lady Dowager, apparently at her last gasp, feebly opened her eyes and quavered, "My son, I never thought to see you again!"

She burst out weeping and all the others joined in until Chia Cheng, fearing these transports of grief might be too much for his mother, held back his tears.

"Set your heart at rest, madam," he urged. "It is a serious matter, but His Gracious Majesty and the two princes have shown us the kindest consideration. The Elder Master has been taken into custody for the time being; but once the matter is cleared up the Emperor will show more clemency. And our property is not being confiscated."

Chia Sheh's arrest distressed the old lady anew, and Chia Cheng did his best to comfort her.

Lady Hsing was the only one who ventured to leave, going back to her apartments. She found the doors sealed up and locked, the serving-women confined in a few rooms. Unable to get in she burst out wailing, then made her way back to Hsi-feng's apartments. The side-gate there was also sealed, but Hsi-feng's room was open and from it came the sound of continuous sobbing. Entering, she saw Hsi-feng lying with closed eyes, her face ashen-pale, while Ping-erh wept beside her. Thinking her dead, Lady Hsing started sobbing too.

"Don't cry, madam," said Ping-erh, stepping forward to greet her. "We carried her back just now in a dead faint, but presently she came to and cried a little. Now she is quieter. Please calm down, madam. How is the old lady now?"

Lady Hsing made no answer but went to rejoin the Lady Dowager. The only people there were members of Chia Cheng's household, and she could not hold back her grief at the thought that both her husband and son had been arrested, her daughter-in-law was at death's door, and her daughter was ill-treated by her husband, so that she had nowhere to turn. The others tried to console her. Li Wan told servants to clear out some rooms for her for the time being, and Lady Wang assigned maids to look after her.

As Chia Cheng was waiting impatiently for news from court, Hsueh Ko came running in. "What a time I had getting in here!" he panted. "Where is uncle?"

"Thank Heaven you've come!" Chia Cheng exclaimed. "How did you gain admittance?"

"By pleading hard and promising them money."

Chia Cheng described the raid to him and asked him to make inquiries. "I can't very well send messages to other relatives and friends now that we're under fire," he explained. "But you can deliver messages for me."

"It never occurred to me that you'd have trouble here, sir; but I've heard something about the East Mansion's business."

"What exactly are the charges against them?"

"Today I went to the yamen to find out what Cousin Pan's sentence is, and I heard that two censors have accused Cousin Chen of corrupting young nobles by getting them to gamble — that isn't so serious. The more serious charge is of abducting the wife of an honest citizen, who was forced to kill herself rather than submit. To bring this charge home, the censors got our man Pao Erh and a fellow called Chang as witnesses. This may involve the Court of Censors too, as that fellow Chang had brought a suit before."

Chia Cheng stamped his foot. "Terrible! We're done for!" he sighed, tears streaming down his cheeks.

Hsueh Ko tried to reassure him then went off to find out more news, returning a few hours later.

"It looks bad," he informed him. "When I asked at the Board of Punishments, I didn't hear the result of the two princes' report but was told that this morning Censor Li brought another charge against the prefect of Pingan, accusing him of pandering to an official in the capital and oppressing the people to please his superior — there were several serious charges."

"Never mind about other people," said Chia Cheng impatiently. "What did you hear about *us*?"

"That charge against the prefect of Pingan involves us too, sir. The official in the capital referred to by the censor was Lord Sheh, who's accused of tampering with lawsuits. This adds fuel to the flames! All your colleagues are trying hard to keep out of this, so who would send you word? Even those relatives and friends at your feast either went home or are keeping well away until they know the upshot. Some clansmen of yours — confound them! — have been saying openly, 'Their ancestors left them property and titles. Now that they're in trouble who knows whom the title may go to. We all ought to take steps....'"

Without hearing him out Chia Cheng stamped his foot again. "What a fool my brother is!" he groaned. "It's a scandal, too, the way they've carried on in the East Mansion! For all we know this may be the death of the old lady and Lien's wife! Go and see what more you can find out while I look in on the old lady. If there's any news, the sooner we know it the better."

Just then a great commotion broke out inside and they heard cries of "The old lady's dying!" Chia Cheng hurried anxiously in.

Chapter 35
The Lady Dowager Prays to Heaven to Avert Disaster

The Lady Dowager had in fact fainted from shock, but Lady Wang, Yuan-yang and the rest had revived her and given her a sedative which had gradually restored her, though she was still crying for grief.

In the hope of soothing her he said, "Your unfilial sons have brought this trouble upon our family, alarming you, madam. If you will take comfort, we can still handle the situation outside; but if you fall ill our guilt will be even greater!"

"I'm four score years and more," was her reply. "Ever since my girlhood when I married your father, thanks to our ancestors I've lived in the lap of luxury and never even heard tell of a nightmare like this. Now, in my old age, seeing you come to grief — it's too bad! I wish I could die and be done with worrying about you!" She broke down again.

Chia Cheng was at his wit's end when a servant outside announced a messenger from the court. He went out at once and saw that it was the Prince of Peiching's chamberlain.

"Good news, sir!" were the chamberlain's first words.

Chia Cheng thanked him and offered him a seat. "What instructions has His Highness for me?" he asked.

"Our master and the Prince of Hsiping reported to the Emperor your trepidation, sir, and your gratitude for His Majesty's magnanimity. As it is not long since the Imperial Consort's passing, His Majesty, being most merciful, cannot bring himself to condemn you. You are to retain your post in the Ministry of Works. Regarding the family property, only Chia Sheh's share is to be confiscated; the rest will be restored to you and you are enjoined to work well. As for those promissory notes, our master has been ordered to examine them. All those at usurious, illegal rates of interest are to be confiscated according to regulations. Those on which the standard rates are charged are to be returned to you, together with your title-deeds. Chia Lien is dismissed from his post, but will be released without further punishment."

Chia Cheng rose to kowtow his thanks to the Emperor, then bowed his thanks to the prince.

"I beg you, sir, to report my gratitude now," he said. "Tomorrow I shall go to court to express my thanks, then go to your mansion to kowtow to His Highness."

Soon after the chamberlain had left the Imperial edict arrived and was put into force by the officers in charge, who confiscated certain things, returning the rest. Chia Lien was released, while all Chia Sheh's men and women bondservants were registered and sequestrated.

Unhappy Chia Lien had lost virtually all his possessions apart from some furnishings and those legitimate promissory notes which were returned to him. For though the rest of his property was not confiscated, the runners during their raid had carried it off. He had dreaded being punished and rejoiced at his release, but the loss overnight of all his savings as well as Hsi-feng's money — seventy or eighty thousand taels at least — was naturally galling; on top of which he was afflicted by his father's imprisonment by the Imperial Guards and Hsi-feng's critical condition. And now Chia Cheng reproached him with tears in his eyes.

"Because of my official duties, I turned over the supervision of our family affairs to you and your wife," he said. "Of course you could hardly keep a check on your father, but who is responsible for this usury? Such conduct is most unbefitting a family like ours. Now that those notes of yours have been confiscated, the financial loss is of secondary importance, but think of the damage to our reputation!"

Chia Lien fell on his knees to reply, "In running the household I never presumed to act on selfish interests. All our

income and expenditure were entered in the accounts by Lai
Ta, Wu Hsin-teng and Tai Liang, and you can check on them
by asking them, sir. In the last few years, our expenditure has
exceeded our income; and as I haven't made good the difference
there are certain deficits in the accounts. If you ask the mistress,
sir, she will confirm this. As for those loans, I myself have no
idea where the money came from. We shall have to find out
from Chou Jui and Lai Wang."

"According to you, you don't know even what is going on
in your own apartments, to say nothing about family affairs!
Well, I won't cross-examine you now. You've got off lightly
yourself, but shouldn't you go to find out about the cases of
your father and Cousin Chen?"

Wronged as he felt, Chia Lien assented with tears and went
away.

Heaving sigh after sigh Chia Cheng thought, "My ancestors
spared no pains in his sovereign's service, winning fame and
two hereditary titles; but now that both our houses have got
into trouble these titles have been lost. As far as I can see,
none of our sons or nephews amounts to anything. Merciful
Heaven! Why should our Chia family be ruined like this?
Though His Gracious Majesty has shown extraordinary compassion by restoring my property, how am I — alone — to meet
our two households' expenses? Chia Lien's admission just now
was even more shocking: it seems that not only is our treasury
empty but there are deficits in the accounts, so we've made a
mere show of affluence all these years, and I can only blame
myself for being such a fool! If my son Chu were alive he
would have been my right hand. Pao-yu, though he's grown
up, is a useless creature." By now tears had stained his clothes,
and he reflected, "My mother is so old yet not for a single
day have we, her sons, provided for her out of our own earnings.
Instead of that we've made her faint for terror. How can I
shirk the blame for all these misdeeds?"

He was sunk in self-abasement when a servant announced
some relatives and friends who had called to condole with
him. Chia Cheng thanked each in turn.

As they were talking Hsueh Ko brought back the news, "Commissioner Chao of the Imperial Guards insists on pressing the charges made by the censors. I'm afraid things look black for the Elder Master and for Master Chen."

"You must go and beg the princes to intervene, sir," Chia Cheng's friends urged him. "Otherwise both your families will be ruined."

He agreed and thanked them, after which they dispersed.

It was already time to light the lamps. Chia Cheng went inside to pay his respects to his mother and found her better. Returning to his own quarters, he brooded resentfully over the folly of Chia Lien and his wife, whose usuary — now that it had come to light — had landed the whole family in trouble. He was most put out by this disclosure of Hsi-feng's misdoings. But since she was so ill and must be distraught too by the loss of all her possessions, he could hardly reprimand them for the time being. Thus the night passed without further incident.

The next morning Chia Cheng went to court to express his gratitude for the Imperial favour, then called on both princes to kowtow his thanks and beg them to intervene on behalf of his brother and nephew. After they had agreed to do this, he went to enlist the help of other colleagues.

Let us return to Chia Lien. Unable to extricate his father and cousin from the straits they were in, he returned home. He found Ping-erh sitting weeping by Hsi-feng, who was being abused by Chiu-tung in the side-room. Chia Lien walked over to Hsi-feng, but as she seemed at her last gasp he had to hold back his reproaches.

"What's done is done," sobbed Ping-erh. "We can't get back what we've lost. But the mistress is so ill, you must send for a doctor for her."

"Pah!" spat out Chia Lien. "My own life is still at stake; why should I care about *her*?"

At this Hsi-feng opened her eyes and, without a word, shed tears. As soon as Chia Lien had left she said to Ping-erh, "Stop being so dense. Now that things have come to this pass, why worry about me?

I only wish I could die this very minute! If you have any feeling for me, just bring up my daughter Chiao-chieh after my death and I shall be grateful to you in the nether regions!"

This only made Ping-erh sob more bitterly.

"You've sense enough to see," Hsi-feng continued, "that even if they haven't come to complain he must hold me to blame. Though the trouble was sparked off outside, if I hadn't been greedy for money I'd have been in the clear. Now after scheming so hard and trying all my life to get ahead, I've ended up worse off than anyone else! If only I hadn't trusted the wrong people! I heard something vaguely too about Master Chen's trouble and how he abducted the wife of an honest citizen named Chang to be his concubine, forcing her to kill herself rather than submit. Well, we know, don't we, who that fellow Chang was? If that business comes out, Master Lien will be involved too and I shall lose face completely. I'd like to die this instant, but I haven't the courage to swallow gold or take poison. And here you are talking of getting a doctor for me! That's not doing me a kindness but a bad turn."

This upset Ping-erh even more. She was at her wit's end. For fear that Hsi-feng might try to take her own life, she kept a close watch over her.

Luckily the Lady Dowager was ignorant of these developments. Now that her health was improving, she was relieved that Chia Cheng had kept out of trouble and Pao-yu and Pao-chai stayed by her side every day. As Hsi-feng had been her favourite she told Yuan-yang, "Give some of my things to Hsi-feng, and take Ping-erh some money so that she can look after her well. Once she's better I'll see what else can be done for her." She also told Lady Wang to help Lady Hsing.

Since the whole estate of the Ning Mansion had been confiscated, all its bondservants' registered and taken away, the Lady Dowager sent carriages to fetch Madam Yu and her daughter-in-law over. Alas for the Ning Mansion, once so grand! All that remained of it was these two ladies and the concubines Pei-feng and Hsieh-luan, without a single servant. The old lady placed at their disposal a house next to Hsi-chun's, sent four women-servants and two maids to wait on them, had food prepared for them by the main kitchen, and provided them with clothing and other necessities. She also allotted them the same monthly allowances as were issued by the accountants' office to members of the Jung Mansion.

As for the expenses incurred by Chia Sheh, Chia Chen and Chia Jung in prison, the accountants' office was quite unable to meet them. Hsi-feng had no property left; Chia Lien was heavily in debt; while Chia Cheng who had no head for affairs simply said:

"I have asked friends to see that they are looked after."

Chia Lien in desperation thought of appealing to their relatives; but Aunt Hsueh's family was bankrupt, Wang Tzu-teng was dead, and none of the rest was in a position to help. All he could do was send some stewards in secret to raise a few thousand taels by selling certain country estates to defray the prison expenses. As soon as he did this, however, the servants realized that the family was on the rocks and seized this chance for hanky-panky, filching money from the rents of the eastern manors too.

To revert to the old lady, she had not a moment's peace of mind but kept weeping as she wondered what was to become of them all. Their hereditary titles had been abolished, one of her sons and two younger kinsmen were in jail awaiting trial, Lady Hsing and Madam Yu were disconsolate, and Hsi-feng was at death's door. Though Pao-yu and Pao-chai kept her company to console her, they could not share her worries.

One evening, after sending Pao-yu away, she struggled to sit up and told Yuan-yang and the other maids to burn incense in the various shrines and then to light a censerful in her courtyard. Leaning on her cane she went out there. Hu-po, knowing that she meant to worship Buddha, had placed a red felt cushion on the ground. The old lady offered incense and knelt down to kowtow and invoke Buddha several times.

She prayed to Heaven then with tears in her eyes, "Born a Shih, I married into the Chia family, and I earnestly implore holy Buddha in Heaven to have mercy on us! For generations our Chia family has never dared transgress or abuse our power. A devoted wife and mother, though unable to do much good I have never done anything wicked. But some of the Chia descendants must have offended Heaven by their arrogance and dissipation; thus our family has been raided, its property confiscated. Now my son and grandsons are in jail and fortune is frowning on them. I alone am responsible for these misfortunes because I failed to give them the proper training. Now I entreat Heaven to save us, turning the sorrow of those in jail to joy, and curing those who are ill. Even if the whole family has sinned, let me alone take the blame! Spare my sons and grandsons! Have pity, Heaven, on a pious woman! Grant me an early death, but spare my children and grandchildren!" Her voice faltered here from distress and she burst out sobbing. Yuan-yang and Chen-chu as they helped her back inside did their best to comfort her.

Chapter 36
Chia Cheng's Hereditary Title Is Restored by Imperial Favour

One day Chia Cheng was thinking things over in his study when one of his men rushed in. "Your Lordship, you are wanted at once at court for questioning!" he announced.

He found the whole Privy Council as well as the princes assembled in the Palace.

The Prince of Peiching announced, "We have summoned you today on His Majesty's orders for an interrogation."

Chia Cheng at once fell on his knees.

"Your elder brother connived with provincial officials to oppress the weak, and allowed his son to organize gambling parties and abduct another man's wife, who took her own life rather than submit. Were you cognizant of these facts?" the ministers asked him.

"After my term of office as Chief Examiner by His Majesty's favour, I inspected famine relief," replied Chia Cheng. "I returned home at the end of winter the year before last and was sent to inspect some works, after which I served as Grain Commissioner of Kiangsi until I was impeached and came back to the capital to my old post in the Ministry of Works. Never, day or night, did I neglect my duties. But in my folly I paid insufficient attention to household affairs and failed to train my sons and nephews correctly. I have proved unworthy of the Imperial favour and beg His Majesty for severe punishment."

The Prince of Peiching reported this to the Emperor, who soon issued an edict which the prince proclaimed:

We have ordered a strict investigation of Chia Sheh, who has been impeached by the censors for conniving with local officials to oppress the weak and, in league with the prefect of Pingan, subverting the law. Chia Sheh admits that he and the prefect were connected by marriage but denies intervening in a lawsuit, and the censors have no evidence of this. It is true that he took advantage of his power to extort antique fans from the Stone Idiot; but fans are mere trifles and this offence is less serious than robbery with violence. Though the Stone Idiot committed suicide, it was because he was deranged, not because he was hounded to death. Chia Sheh is to be shown lenity and sent to the frontier to expiate his crime.

As for the charge that Chia Chen abducted another man's wife and she killed herself rather than be his concubine, a study of the censorate's original report reveals that Second Sister Yu was betrothed to Chang Hua but he, being poor, consented to break the engagement, and her mother agreed to marry her to Chia Chen's younger cousin as his concubine. This was not a case of abduction. Regarding the charge that Third Sister Yu's suicide and burial were not reported to the authorities, it transpires that she was the sister of Chia Chen's wife and they engaged her to a man who demanded the betrothal gifts back because of talk of her loose morals. She killed herself for shame; Chia Chen did not hound her to death.

However, Chia Chen deserves harsh punishment because, although he inherited a title, he flouted the law by a clandestine burial; but in view of his descent from a meritorious minister We will forbear from inflicting punishment and in Our clemency will revoke his hereditary title and send him to serve at the coast to expiate his crime. Chia Jung, being young and not involved, is to be released. Since Chia Cheng has undeniably worked diligently and prudently for many years outside the capital, his reprehensible mismanagement of his household is condoned.

Chia Cheng, moved to tears of gratitude, had kowtowed repeatedly while listening to this edict. He now begged the Prince of Peiching to petition the Emperor for him.

"You should kowtow your thanks for the Imperial favour," replied the prince. "What other petition have you?"

"Although I am guilty, His Majesty in His great favour has not punished me severely and my property has been returned to me. Overwhelmed with shame as I am, I would like to make over to the state my ancestral estate, emoluments and savings."

"His Majesty, ever merciful to His subjects, disciplines them with perspicacity, meting out unerring rewards and punishments," replied the prince. "Since you have been shown such clemency and had your property restored, it would be inappropriate to present any further petition."

The other ministers also dissuaded him. Then Chia Cheng kowtowed his gratitude and having thanked Their Highnesses withdrew, hurrying home to reassure his mother.

All the men and women, high and low, in the Jung Mansion had been wondering what this summons to the Palace meant and had sent out for news. Chia Cheng's return relieved them but none dared question him. He hastened to the old lady's side to explain to her all the details of his pardon; but although this set her mind at rest, she could not help grieving over the loss of the two hereditary titles and the banishment of Chia Sheh and Chia Chen to such distant regions. As for Lady Hsing and Madam Yu, this news reduced them to tears.

"Don't worry, madam," said Chia Cheng, hoping to comfort his mother. "Though Elder Brother is going to serve at the frontier, he will be working for the government too and isn't likely to undergo any hardships. Provided he handles matters well, he may be reinstated. Chen is young, it is only right for him to work hard; otherwise he won't be able for long to enjoy the fortune left us by our ancestors."

The old lady had never been too fond of Chia Sheh, while Chia Chen being of the East Mansion was not one of her descendants. Only Lady Hsing and Madam Yu were sobbing as if they would never stop.

Lady Hsing was thinking, "We've lost everything and my husband is going so far away in his old age. Though I still have my son Lien, he always listens to his Second Uncle, and now that we have to live on him naturally Lien and his wife will take their side. What's to become of me left all on my own?"

Madam Yu had been in sole charge of household affairs in the Ning Mansion, second only to Chia Chen, and they were a well-matched couple. Now he was to be banished in disgrace, all their property had been confiscated, and she would have to live in the Jung Mansion where, though the old lady was fond of her, she would be a poor dependent saddled with Pei-feng and Hsieh-luan into the bargain; for her son Jung and his wife were in no position to restore the family's fortunes.

She thought, "Lien was the one to blame for my two sisters' deaths; yet he's in no trouble now, not parted from his own wife, while we're left stranded. How are we to cope?" These reflections made her sob.

The old lady's heart ached for them. She asked Chia Cheng, "Can't your elder brother and Chen come home now that they've been sentenced? And as Jung is not involved, shouldn't he be released as well?"

"According to the rules, elder brother can't come home," he told her. "But I've asked people to put in a word so that he and Chen can come back to get their luggage together, and the ministry has agreed. I expect Jung will return with his grand-uncle and father. Please don't worry, madam. I shall see to this."

"These years I've grown so old and useless that I haven't checked up on our family affairs," she said. "Now the East Mansion has been confiscated. Not only the house either, but your elder brother and Lien have lost all their property too. Do you know how much is left in our West Mansion's treasury? And how much land in our eastern estates? You must give them a few thousand taels for their journeys."

Chia Cheng was in a dilemma. He reflected, "If I tell her the truth she may be very worried; but if I don't, how am I to manage now — to say nothing of the future?"

Accordingly he answered, "If you hadn't questioned me, madam, I wouldn't have ventured to report this. But since you ask — and Lien is here too — I must tell you that yesterday I investigated. Our treasury is empty. Not only is all the silver gone but we have debts outside too. Now that elder brother is in this predicament, if we don't bribe people to help, then in spite of His Majesty's kindness they may be hard put to it. But I can't think where the money is to come from. We've already used up next year's rent from our eastern estates, so can't raise any sums there for the time being. We shall just have to sell those clothes and trinkets which thanks to Imperial favour weren't confiscated, to cover the travelling expenses of elder brother and Chen. As to what to live on ourselves, we can worry about that later."

The old lady shed tears in her consternation.

"Is our family reduced to this?" she exclaimed. "I didn't see it for myself, but in the old days my family was ten times richer than this one, yet after a few years of keeping up appearances — though we were never raided like this — it went downhill and in less than two years was done for! Do you mean to say we shan't be able to manage even for a couple of years?"

"If we'd kept those two hereditary stipends we could still manoeuvre outside. But whom can we expect to help us now?" In tears he continued, "All those relatives whom we helped before are poor, and the others we didn't help won't be willing to come to our rescue. I didn't investigate too carefully yesterday, but simply looked at the register of our servants. Quite apart from the fact that we can't meet our own expenses, we can't afford to feed such a large staff."

The old lady was distraught with anxiety when Chia Sheh, Chia Chen and Chia Jung came in together to pay their respects to her. At sight of them she clasped Chia Sheh with one hand, Chia Chen with the other, and sobbed. Her grief made them blush for shame and fall to their knees.

"We are reprobates who have forfeited the honours accorded to our ancestors and brought you grief, madam," they said tearfully. "We don't even deserve a piece of ground in which to bury our bones after death!"

All present seeing this gave way to weeping.

Chia Cheng interposed, "The first thing to do is make ready for their journey. The authorities will probably not agree to their staying at home for more than a couple of days."

Holding back her tears the old lady dismissed Chia Sheh and Chia Chen to see their wives. Then she told Chia Cheng, "There's no time to be lost! I'm afraid it's no use trying to raise money outside, and it will be bad if they fail to leave by the appointed time. So I had better settle this for you. But the household is topsy-turvy — this won't do!" She sent Yuan-yang off to restore order.

After Chia Sheh and Chia Chen had withdrawn with Chia Cheng, weeping again they deplored their past excesses and spoke of their grief at parting. Then they went to lament with their wives. Chia Sheh being old did not mind leaving Lady Hsing; but Chia Chen and Madam Yu could not bear to be parted, and Chia Lien and Chia Jung wept beside their fathers. For though their banishment was less harsh than service in the army, the exiles might never again see their families. However, since things had come to such a pass they had to make the best of the situation.

The old lady made Lady Hsing, Lady Wang, Yuan-yang and the others open up her cases and take out all the things she had stored away since coming here as a bride. Then she summoned Chia Sheh, Chia Cheng and Chia Chen to share out her belongings.

Chia Sheh received three thousand taels of silver with the instructions, "Take two thousand for your journey and leave your wife one thousand."

"This three thousand is for Chen," the old lady continued. "You are only to take one thousand, leaving your wife two thousand. She and your concubines can go on as before, sharing the same house but eating separately; and I shall see to Hsi-chun's marriage in future. Poor Hsi-feng has put herself out for us all these years yet now she has nothing left; so I shall give her three thousand too, on condition that she keeps it herself and doesn't let Lien use it. As she's still only half-conscious, tell Ping-erh to come and take it. And here are clothes left by your grandfather and costumes and trinkets I wore when I was young, which I have no further use for. The Elder Master, Chen, Lien and Jung can divide his clothes between them; the rest are to be shared out by the Elder Mistress, Chen's wife and Hsi-feng. This five hundred taels of silver is for Lien, for when he takes Tai-yu's coffin back south next year."

Having made this apportionment she told Chia Cheng, "You spoke of debts outside; well, they must be cleared. Take this gold to settle them. It's the others' fault that I have to part with all my possessions like this; but you're my son too, and I can't show favouritism. Pao-yu is already married. The gold, silver and other things which I have left must be worth a few thousand taels, and that will go to him. Chu's wife has always been dutiful to me, and Lan's a good lad, so I'll give them something too. This is all that I can do."

Impressed by her sound judgement and fair treatment, Chia Cheng and the rest knelt down and said with tears, "You are so advanced in years, Old Ancestress, and your sons and grandsons have failed in their duty to you. Your goodness to us makes us doubly ashamed!"

"Stop talking nonsense," she answered. "If not for this trouble I'd have kept everything to myself. But our household is too large now, with only the Second Master holding a post, so we can manage with just a few servants. Tell the stewards to summon them all and make the necessary retrenchment. Provided each house has someone, that's enough. What should we have done, anyway, if they'd all been sequestrated? The maids should be re-assigned too, and some of them married off, some given their freedom. And though this mansion of ours wasn't taken over by the authorities, you should at least give up the Garden. As for our other estates, let Lien investigate to see which should be sold and which kept up. We must stop putting on an empty show. I can speak bluntly: the Chen family down south still has some money in the Elder Mistress' keeping, which she should send back. Because if any other trouble should happen to us in future, wouldn't they be 'out of the frying-pan into the fire'?"

Chia Cheng had no head for family affairs and readily agreed to all her proposals. "The old lady certainly is a good manager!" he reflected. "It's her worthless sons who have ruined the family." Then, as his mother looked tired, he urged her to go and rest.

"I haven't much else," she continued. "What there is can be spent on my funeral, and anything left over can go to my maids."

Distressed to hear her talk like this, Chia Cheng and the others knelt down again and pleaded, "Don't take it so hard, madam! Sharing in your good fortune, we can hope later on for more marks of Imperial favour; and then we shall exert ourselves to set our house in order, and atone for our faults by caring for you until you are a hundred."

"I certainly hope it turns out like that, so that I can face our ancestors after death. But you mustn't imagine I'm someone who enjoys riches and rank and can't endure poverty. These last few years you seemed to be doing fine, so I didn't interfere, content to laugh and chat and nurse my health, never dreaming that our family was doomed to ruin like this! I knew all along that we were putting on an empty show, but everyone in the household was so used to luxury that we couldn't cut down expenses all of a sudden. Well, here's a good chance to retrench, to keep the family going, if we don't want to become a laughing-stock. You expected me to be worried to death on hearing that we're bankrupt. But in fact I was upset because, recalling the honours conferred on our ancestors for their splendid services to the state, I kept wishing that you might do even better, or at least manage to keep what you'd inherited. Who knows what dirty business they got up to, uncle and nephew!"

As she was haranguing them like this, a flustered Feng-erh ran in to tell Lady Wang, "This morning our mistress cried and cried when she learned about our trouble. Now she's at her last gasp. Ping-erh sent me to report this to you, madam."

Before she could finish the old lady asked, "Just how is she?"

"Not too well, they say," Lady Wang replied for Feng-erh.

"Ah!" exclaimed the old lady rising to her feet. "These wretched children won't give me a moment's peace!" She told maids to help her over to see Hsi-feng, but Chia Cheng barred the way.

"Madam, you've been so upset and attended to so much business, you ought to rest now. If your grandson's wife is unwell, your daughter-in-law can go and see to her; there's no need to go yourself. If you were to be upset again and fall ill, how could your sons bear it?"

"You're all to leave now and come back presently — I've more to say to you."

Not venturing to raise any further objections, Chia Cheng went to help prepare for his brother's and nephew's journeys, instructing Chia Lien to choose servants to accompany them.

Meanwhile the old lady made Yuan-yang and the others go over with her to see Hsi-feng, taking her gifts for her. Hsi-feng's breath was coming in gasps, and Ping-erh's eyes and cheeks were red from weeping. When Their Ladyships were announced, Ping-erh hurried out to meet them.

"How is she now?" asked the old lady.

Not wanting to alarm her Ping-erh said, "She's a little better. Since you're here, madam, please step in and see for yourself."

She followed them inside, then darted over and quietly raised the bed-curtains. Hsi-feng, opening her eyes, was overcome with shame at sight of the old lady, for she had assumed that the Lady Dowager must be angry with her erstwhile favourite and would leave her to die — she had never expected this visit. . Relief eased her choking sensation and she struggled to sit up; but the old lady made Ping-erh hold her down.

"Don't move," she said. "Are you feeling a bit better?"

"Yes, madam," answered Hsi-feng with tears in her eyes. "Since I came here as a girl, Your Ladyships have been so good to me! But it was my misfortune to be driven out of my mind by evil spirits so that I couldn't serve you dutifully and win my father- and mother-in-law's approval. You treated me so well, letting me help run the household; and after turning everything upside-down how can I look you in the face again?" Here she broke down and sobbed, "Now Your Ladyships have come in person to see me, quite overwhelming me! Even if I had another three days to live, I deserve to have two days docked!"

"That trouble started outside," said the old lady. "It had nothing to do with you. And even though you were robbed it doesn't matter. I've brought you a whole lot of things, to do just as you like with." She told the maids to show Hsi-feng her gifts.

Hsi-feng was insatiably acquisitive. The loss of all her possessions had naturally cut her to the quick, in addition to which she had dreaded being held to blame and felt life was not worth living. Now it seemed she was still in the old lady's good books, and Lady Wang instead of reproaching her had come to comfort her, while she knew that Chia Lien had kept out of trouble too. In relief she kowtowed to the old lady from her pillow.

"Please don't worry, madam," she said. "If I recover thanks to your good fortune, I'll gladly be your menial and serve Your Ladyships with all my heart!"

Her obvious distress made the Lady Dowager give way to tears. Pao-yu was accustomed to comfort and enjoyment, and had never known genuine anxiety. This was his first experience of disaster. Now that sobbing and wailing assailed him wherever he turned, his mind became more unhinged and when others wept he joined in.

All of them seemed so upset that Hsi-feng raised her head from the pillow and made an effort to comfort the old lady. "Please go back, Your Ladyships," she urged. "When I'm a bit better I'll come to kowtow my thanks."

The old lady told Ping-erh, "Mind you look after her well. If you're short of anything, come to me for it."

On her way back with Lady Wang, they heard weeping in several apartments. Once home, unable to check her grief any longer, the old lady dismissed Lady Wang and sent Pao-yu to see off his uncle and cousin. She then lay down on her couch and burst into tears. Luckily Yuan-yang and the other maids finally succeeded in consoling her, so that she fell asleep.

Chia Sheh and Chia Chen were by no means the only ones to be distressed at leaving. None of the servants escorting them wanted to go. Simmering with resentment they cursed their fate, for separation in life is harder to bear than separation by death, and saddest of all were the people seeing them off. The once splendid Jung Mansion resounded with lamentations.

Chia Cheng, a model of propriety with a strong sense of moral obligation, clasped his brother's hand in farewell then rode ahead out of the city to offer them wine at the Pavilion of

Parting and wish them a good journey. He reminded them of the government's concern for meritorious ministers, and exhorted them to work hard to repay this compassion. Shedding tears then, Chia Sheh and Chia Chen went their different ways.

When Chia Cheng returned with Pao-yu, they found messengers outside their gate clamouring that an Imperial edict had just been issued bestowing the title of Duke of Jungkuo on Chia Cheng. These men wanted largesse for bringing such good tidings.

The gatemen argued, "This is a hereditary title which our master already possesses; so how can you claim to be bringing us good tidings?"

The messengers retorted, "Hereditary titles are a great honour, harder to come by than an official appointment. Your Elder Master has lost his and will never get it back. But now His Sagacious Majesty has shown kindness greater than Heaven and restored this title to your Second Master — such a thing only happens once in a thousand years. So why don't you tip us for bringing the good news?"

Chia Cheng arrived in the middle of this dispute. When the gatemen reported the news to him he was pleased, although this reminded him of his brother's offence. Shedding tears of gratitude he hurried in to report this to the old lady. She was naturally delighted and, taking him by the hand, urged him to work diligently to repay the Emperor's kindness. Lady Wang, arriving just then to comfort the old lady, rejoiced too at this news. Lady Hsing and Madam Yu, the only ones sick at heart, had to hide their feelings.

Those relatives and friends outside who had fawned on the Chias when they were powerful had steered clear of them since hearing of their disgrace. Now that Chia Cheng had inherited the title and apparently still enjoyed the Emperor's favour, they hurried over to offer congratulations. To their surprise, Chia Cheng felt genuine embarrassment at inheriting his brother's title, despite his gratitude to the Emperor. The next day he went to court to offer thanks, and asked permission to make over to the state the houses and Garden which had been returned to him. When an edict declared this petition unwarranted, he went home in relief and continued to work steadily at his post.

But the family was now impoverished, its income falling short of its expenditure, and Chia Cheng was unable to take advantage of his social connections. The servants knew that though he was a worthy man, while Hsi-feng was too ill to run the household Chia Lien was piling up debts from day to day which forced him to mortgage houses and sell land. The wealthier of the stewards were afraid Chia Lien might appeal to them for help, and therefore made a pretence of poverty or kept out of his way. Some even asked for leave and did not return, for each was looking around for a new master.

The old lady's improved spirits these last two days had made her overeat, and that evening she was out of sorts. The next day her chest felt constricted; however, she would not let Yuan-yang report this to Chia Cheng.

"I've been rather greedy these two days and had too much to eat," she said. "Missing a meal will set me right. Don't make a fuss about it." So Yuan-yang and the others kept quiet.

After this the Lady Dowager fasted for two days, yet the congestion of her chest persisted and she had dizzy spells and fits of coughing. When Lady Hsing, Lady Wang and Hsi-feng came to pay their respects and saw that she looked quite cheerful, they simply sent to notify Chia Cheng, who immediately came over. On leaving, he sent for a doctor to examine her. Before long the doctor arrived and felt her pulses. He diagnosed that the old lady had caught a chill as a result of not eating regularly, but some medicine to help the digestion and expel the cold would cure her. He wrote out a prescription. Chia Cheng, noting that the ingredients were ordinary medicines, told servants to prepare this for his mother.

The Lady Dowager's illness grew daily worse, no medicine proving effective, and later she developed diarrhoea too. Worried because she was not likely to recover, Chia Cheng sent to ask leave from his yamen and he and his wife attended her day and night.

The Lady Dowager, failing from day to day, longed to see her grand-daughters and nieces. Her thoughts turned to Hsiang-yun and she sent to fetch her. The servant on her return slipped in to find Yuan-yang, but could not enter the old lady's room where Yuan-yang happened to be with Lady Wang and others. Instead she went to the back where she found Hu-po.

"The old lady wanted to see Miss Shih and sent us to ask her to come," she told her. "But we found her crying her heart out, because her husband's desperately ill, and the doctors say he's not likely to recover unless it turns into consumption — in which case he may drag on for another four or five years. So Miss Shih is frantic. She knows the old lady is ill, but she can't come. She told me, too, not to mention this to her grand-aunt. If the old lady asks, she hopes you'll make up some excuse for her." Hu-po exclaimed in dismay but did not answer. After some time she told the other to go. Not liking to report this, she decided to tell Yuan-yang and ask her to make up some story. She went to the old lady's bedside then and found her in a critical condition. As there were many people standing round murmuring that it seemed there was no hope, Hu-po had to hold her tongue.

Chia Cheng quietly drew Chia Lien aside and whispered some instructions to which he assented softly. He then went out to summon all the stewards at home.

"The old lady's sinking fast," he said. "You're to send at once to make the necessary preparations. First, get out the coffin and have it lined. Then get the measurements of the whole household and order tailors to make mourning for them. The funeral retinue must be arranged too, and more hands will be needed to help in the kitchen."

Lai Ta told him, "You needn't worry, Second Master. We've got it all figured out. But where is the money to come from?"

"You needn't raise money outside," replied Chia Lien. "The old lady has kept a sum in readiness. Just now the master told me that it must be handsomely done — we want a good show."

The stewards assented and went off to see to these matters while he returned to his own quarters.

"How is your mistress today?" he asked Ping-erh.

Ping-erh pouted towards the inner room. "Go in and see her."

He did so and found Hsi-feng, exhausted by dressing, leaning against the small table on the *kang*.

"I'm afraid you can't rest now," he told her. "The old lady will be gone by tomorrow at the latest, so you can't keep out of it. Hurry up and get somebody to clear up here, then make the effort to go over there. If it comes to the worst, we shan't be able to come back today."

"What is there here to clear up?" retorted Hsi-feng. "We've only these few things left, so what does it matter? You go first; the master may want you. I'll come when I've changed my clothes."

Chia Lien went ahead to the old lady's place and whispered to Chia Cheng that all the preparations had been made. Chia Cheng nodded. Then the doctor was announced. Chia Lien invited him in to feel the old lady's pulse. After some time he withdrew and quietly told Chia Lien, "The old lady's pulse is very weak. Be prepared. . . ."

Chia Lien understood and told Lady Wang, who signalled to Yuan-yang and, when she came over, sent her off to make ready the garments in which to lay out the old lady. At this point the Lady Dowager opened her eyes and asked for some tea. Lady Hsing gave her a cup of ginseng broth but after tasting it she said:

"Not this. Give me a cup of tea."

Forced to humour her, they brought it immediately. She took two sips, then said, "I want to sit up."

"If you want something, madam, just tell us," urged Chia Cheng. "There is no need to sit up."

"After a little drink I feel better," she answered. "Prop me up on the pillow so that I can talk to you."

Sitting up the old lady said, "I've lived in your family sixty years and more, from girlhood to old age, and had more than my share of good fortune. Reckoning from your father down, all my sons and grandsons are good. But Pao-yu whom I've been so fond of...." She broke off here and looked round. Lady Wang pushed Pao-yu to her bedside and the old lady reaching out one hand from the quilt took his hand.

"You must make good, child!" she exhorted him.

"Yes, madam." He felt a pang but dared not cry, simply standing there while his grandmother continued, "I shall be content if I can see another great-grandson born. Where is my Lan?"

As Li Wan pushed him forward, the old lady let go of Pao-yu and took Lan's hand.

"You must be a dutiful son," she said. "Make your mother feel proud of you when you grow up! Where is Hsi-feng?"

Hsi-feng, standing near the bed, stepped forward saying, "Here I am."

"You're too clever, child; you must do more good works. I haven't done many myself, simply letting others take advantage of me. I never went in much for fasting or chanting Buddhist scriptures, except that year when I had all those copies of the *Diamond Sutra* made. Have they all been distributed?"

"Not yet," was Hsi-feng's reply.

"Then hurry up and have them all given away. Our Elder Master and Chen are enjoying themselves outside, but the most heartless one of all is that little wretch Hsiang-yun who still hasn't come to see me!"

Yuan-yang and those who knew the reason said nothing. Next the old lady looked at Pao-chai and sighed. Her face was flushed now, a sign as Chia Cheng knew that the end was near. He offered her some ginseng broth, but already her jaws were locked and her eyes closed. She opened them, however, for a last look round the room. Lady Wang and Pao-chai stepped forward and gently propped her up, while Lady Hsing and Hsi-feng changed her clothes. Meanwhile serving-women had prepared the bier and spread bedding over it. Now they heard a rattling in her throat, and a smile overspread her face as she breathed her last — at the age of eighty-three.

Chapter 37
Pao-yu, His Divine Jade Recovered, Attains Understanding in the Illusory Realm

When Pao-yu and Pao-chai heard that Hsi-feng was mortally ill, they hastily got up and the maids brought in candles to wait on them. They were on the point of leaving when some of Lady Wang's servants arrived to report, "Madam Lien is in a bad way, but not yet at her last gasp. The second master and mistress had better not go there just yet. There is something very strange about her illness, for she has been delirious since midnight, calling for a boat and sedan-chair so that she can hurry back to Chinling to fill in some register. Nobody knows what she means, and she keeps on crying and wailing. So Master Lien has had to order a paper boat and paper chair for her. They haven't been delivered yet, and Madam Lien is still waiting, panting for breath. Her Ladyship sent us to tell you not to go over till she has passed away."

"That's odd!" exclaimed Pao-yu. "Why should she go to Chinling?"

Hsi-jen reminded him softly, "I seem to remember you had a dream one year about some registers, didn't you? Perhaps that's where she's going."

He nodded. "That's right. It's a pity I can't remember what was written there. It goes to show that all mortals' fates are predestined. But where can Cousin Lin have gone, I wonder? Now that you've reminded me, I feel I have an inkling. If I ever have that dream again I must read those registers carefully so as to be able to foretell the future."

"You're impossible to talk to!" protested Hsi-jen. "How can you take a casual remark of mine so seriously? Even if you were able to foresee the future, what could you do about it?"

Pao-yu was about to dispute this when Lady Wang sent a maid to announce, "Madam Lien has breathed her last and everyone's gone over there. Her Ladyship wants the young master and young mistress to go too now."

Hearing this Pao-yu stamped his foot, on the verge of tears. Pao-chai although upset too tried to restrain him.

"Why mourn here?" she demurred. "We'd better go over."

They went straight to Hsi-feng's quarters, and found many mourners assembled there. When Pao-chai saw Hsi-feng already laid out, she gave way to loud weeping. Pao-yu, taking Chia Lien's hand, sobbed bitterly; and Chia Lien too wailed again. As there was no one else present to remonstrate, Ping-erh stepped forward sadly to urge them to desist; but still they went on lamenting.

Chia Lien, unable to cope, summoned Lai Ta and told him to see to the funeral, then reported this to Chia Cheng and obtained his approval. But having little money in hand, he was hard put to it. The thought of Hsi-feng's help in the past increased his wretchedness; and the sight of Chiao-chieh beside herself with grief made his heart ache even more.

One day, Lady Wang went to Pao-chai's apartments. Horrified to find Pao-yu out of his mind, she reprimanded Hsi-jen, "How careless you all are! Why didn't you tell me that Pao-yu was ill again?"

"This illness of his is chronic," replied Hsi-jen. "He gets better for a while, then has a relapse. He's been going to pay his respects to you every day, with nothing wrong with him, madam, and it's only today that his wits have wandered again. Madam Pao was just thinking of letting you know, but was afraid you might scold us for raising a false alarm."

When Pao-yu heard his mother rebuking them, his mind cleared for a moment and to defend them he said, "Don't worry, madam. There's nothing wrong with me except that I feel rather gloomy."

"This is an old trouble of yours. You should tell me as soon as you feel unwell, so that we can get a doctor to prescribe medicine. What an ado there'd be if you had another bad relapse like that time when you lost your jade!"

"If you're worried, madam, you can send for a doctor and I'll take some medicine," he answered.

Lady Wang despatched maids to see to this and, not returning to her own quarters until the doctor had come and made out a prescription.

A few days later Pao-yu was more feeble-minded and, to everyone's consternation, he would not eat.

On the day that they returned from terminating the mourning, Lady Wang came to see Pao-yu. He was unconscious, and the whole household was frantic.

Weeping she told Chia Cheng, "The doctor refuses to prescribe any medicine. All we can do is prepare for the last rites."

Sighing bitterly Chia Cheng went over in person, and when he saw that Pao-yu was indeed dying he told Chia Lien to have preparations made. Chia Lien had to pass on his orders, but lacking money he was in a dilemma.

Just at this juncture a servant rushed in crying, "More trouble, Master Lien!"

Staggered, staring at the servant, Chia Lien demanded, "What now?"

"A monk has come to our gate bringing the jade which Master Pao lost. He's asking for a reward of ten thousand taels."

Chia Lien spat in the fellow's face. "Is that any reason to panic? Don't you know last time it was a fraud? Even if this is genuine, Pao-yu is dying, so what good will the jade do him?"

"I told the monk that. But he says if we give him the silver Master Pao will recover."

Just then they heard shouts outside, "This monk has run amuck! He rushed in and no one could stop him."

"Preposterous!" cried Chia Lien. "Throw him out, quick!"

They heard another commotion, and Chia Cheng was wondering what to do when a wailing went up inside, "Master Pao is dying!"

Feeling still more distraught, he heard the monk shouting,

"If you want him to live, give me the money!"

He thought, "Last time it was a monk who cured Pao-yu; now another has turned up who may be able to save him. But even if it's the genuine jade, how are we to raise so much money?" On second thoughts he decided, "Never mind. We can worry about that if Pao-yu really recovers." He was sending for the monk when in the man came and, without so much as paying his respects or saying a word, ran towards the inner apartments.

Chia Lien grabbed his arm protesting, "There are ladies inside; how can you charge in so wildly?"

"Any delay and I'll be too late to save him!"

Then Chia Lien went over yelling, "Stop crying, everyone inside! A monk is coming in!"

Lady Wang and the others were sobbing too bitterly to pay any attention. As Chia Lien entered, still shouting, they turned to see a hulking monk. Although terrified, they had no time to hide as the monk marched straight to Pao-yu's *kang*. Pao-chai slipped away then, but Hsi-jen dared not move as Lady Wang had remained standing there.

"Benefactresses," cried the monk, "I've brought the jade." Holding it up he added, "Hurry up and bring out the silver, then I'll save him."

Panic-stricken Lady Wang could not tell whether it was genuine or not. "Provided you save his life, you'll get the silver," she promised.

"Hand it over then!" the monk insisted.

"Don't worry. We can raise that much silver anyway," Lady Wang assured him.

The monk roared with laughter and, holding the jade, lent over the *kang* to cry, "Pao-yu, Pao-yu! Your precious jade has come back."

Lady Wang and the rest saw Pao-yu open his eyes, at which Hsi-jen cried out for joy.

"Where is it?" Pao-yu asked.

The monk placed it in his hand and he grasped it tightly, then slowly held it up to examine it closely. "Ah!" he exclaimed.   "At last!"

All there invoked Buddha in elation, even Pao-chai forgetting the monk's presence.

Chia Lien coming over too now saw that Pao-yu had indeed regained consciousness.   Although delighted he made off hastily. The monk, however, overtook and grabbed him without a word, and Chia Lien had to go with him to the front of the house where he lost no time in reporting this to Chia Cheng.   Overjoyed, Chia Cheng bowed his thanks to the monk, who bowed in return then sat down, making Chia Lien suspect that he would not leave until he received his reward.   Chia Cheng, looking closely at him, saw that this was not the same monk as last time.

He asked, "Where is your monastery, and what is your name in religion?   Where did you find this jade?   How is it that the sight of it restored my son to life?"

"That I don't know," answered the monk with a smile.   "All I want is ten thousand taels of silver."

He looked so boorish that Chia Cheng dared not offend him and simply replied, "You shall have it."

"If you have it, hurry up and bring it.   I must be going."

"Please wait a little while I go inside to have a look."

"Go on then.   Don't be long about it."

Chia Cheng went inside without having himself announced and walked to Pao-yu's bedside.   At sight of him his son wanted to sit up but was too weak to do so, and Lady Wang made him lie down, telling him not to move.

With a smile Pao-yu showed his father the jade and said, "The precious jade has come back."

Chia Cheng glanced at it but did not examine it closely, knowing there must be some mystery about it.   "Now that Pao-yu has recovered," he said to his wife, "how are we to raise the reward?"

"We must just give the monk all we possess," she answered.

"I can't believe this monk came for the money, did he?" asked Pao-yu.

Chia Cheng nodded.   "I find it strange too, yet he keeps demanding silver."

Lady Wang suggested, "Go and entertain him first, sir."

After his father had left, Pao-yu said he was hungry. He finished a bowl of congee then asked for rice, and the serving-women brought him a bowl. His mother did not want him to eat too much, but he assured her, "It's all right, I'm better now." He propped himself up to finish the bowl, and very soon felt well enough to sit up.

Sheh-yueh helped him gently up, and in her jubilation remarked tactlessly, "This really is a treasure! Just the sight of it cured him. How lucky it wasn't smashed that time before!"

Reminded of his quarrel with Tai-yu, Pao-yu changed colour, let fall the jade and toppled over backwards and fainted away again. Lady Wang and the others cried out in consternation, and although they did not reproach her Sheh-yueh knew that her ill-considered comment was to blame. Weeping, she resolved that if Pao-yu died she would follow him to the grave. When the others failed to revive him, his mother sent to ask the monk to save him; but when Chia Cheng looked for him, the monk had disappeared. Taken aback and hearing a fresh commotion from the inner apartments, he hurried in and found Pao-yu once more in a coma. His teeth were clenched and his pulse had stopped, though when they felt his heart it was still warm. In desperation Chia Cheng summoned a doctor to administer medicine and restore him to life.

By then Pao-yu's spirit had taken flight. Do you think he was really dead? As if in a dream he sped to the front hall where he paid his respects to the monk who was seated there. The monk at once rose to his feet and led him away. Pao-yu felt as light as a leaf floating through the air, and somehow without passing through the main gate they left the mansion.

After a while they came to a desolate region with a distant archway which struck Pao-yu as familiar; but before he could ask the monk their whereabouts, the nebulous figure of a woman approached them. "How could there be such a beauty in a wilderness like this?" he wondered. "She must be a goddess come down to earth." Going closer and gazing at her more intently, he thought he knew her yet could not identify her. The woman greeted the monk, then disappeared, and as she did so he realized that it was Third Sister Yu. Marvelling at her presence there, he was again about to question the monk when the latter pulled him through the archway. On it was inscribed in large characters "Happy Land of Truth" flanked by the couplet:

> When false gives way to true, true surpasses false.
> Though nothingness exists, being differs from nothingness.

Once through the archway they came to a palace gate, on its lintel the inscription "Fortune for the Good, Calamity for the Licentious." Another couplet on the two sides read:

> Even sages cannot change the past and future;
> Causes and effects tear the closest kin apart.

Having read this, Pao-yu thought, "So here is my chance to find out about karma, past and future." At this point he saw Yuan-yang standing there beckoning to him. "Apparently after coming all this way I'm still in the Garden," he mused. "But why is it so changed?" He wanted to accost her, but to his astonishment in a flash she was gone. Going over towards where she had stood, he saw a row of side courts with tablets over their gates. In no mood to read their inscriptions, he hurried to the place where Yuan-yang had vanished. The gate of this court was ajar, but not liking to intrude he decided to ask permission from the monk. When he turned round, however, the monk was nowhere to be seen. He gazed abstractedly at the magnificent hall which he had certainly never seen in the Garden, and halted to look up at the inscription "Enlightenment for the Infatuated". The couplet on both sides read:

> Joy and sorrow alike are false;
> Desire and longing are folly.

Pao-yu nodded to himself, sighing, and wanted to go in to ask Yuan-yang what this place was. Then realizing that it looked familiar he summoned up courage to open the gate and step in. Yuan-yang was nowhere in sight and the whole building was so eerily dark that he was about to slip away when his eye fell on a dozen or so large cabinets, their doors half open. It suddenly occurred to him, "When I was young, I dreamed that I came to a place like this. What a stroke of luck my coming here again today!"

In a daze he forgot his search for Yuan-yang and boldly opened the first cabinet, in which he found several albums. Elatedly he told himself, "Most people think dreams are false, but this one was based on fact! I never expected to have the same dream again, yet today I've recaptured it. I wonder whether these albums are the same as those I saw last time?"

He took the topmost album entitled *First Register of Twelve Beauties of Chinling*. Holding it he thought, "I have a faint recollection of this; it's too bad that I can't remember clearly." He opened it at the first page and saw a picture, too blurred to make out distinctly. On the back were a few lines of indistinct writing, but by straining his eyes he deciphered a few words about a jade belt, and over these what seemed to be the word *lin*. "Could this refer to Cousin Lin?" he wondered, then read about a golden hairpin in the snow and marvelled at the resemblance to Pao-chai's name. But when he reread the four lines consecutively, he could make no sense of them except that they seemed to suggest Tai-yu and Pao-chai, which in itself was nothing extraordinary. Only the words "pity" and "sighing" were ominous. How to interpret this? Then he rebuked himself, "I'm doing this on the sly. If I rack my brains too long and somebody comes, I shan't be able to read the rest." So he leafed through the register without paying much attention to the pictures, and finally found the lines:

> When Hare and Tiger meet,
> From this Great Dream of life she must depart.

At that, the truth dawned on him. "Right! This prediction came true! It must mean Sister Yuan-chun. If all the others were equally clear and I could copy them down to study them, I'd be able to find out the life-spans and fortunes of all these girls. When I went back I'd keep it secret, but knowing in advance would save me worrying so much for nothing."

He looked round but could see no writing-brush or ink, and

for fear of being disturbed he read rapidly on. One of the pictures showed a shadowy figure flying a kite, but he did not trouble to examine it carefully. Instead he read hastily through all the twelve verses. Some he understood at a glance, some after reflection; others baffled him and he tried to memorize them. Then, sighing, he picked up the third register of the beauties of Chinling. At first he did not understand the lines:

> This prize is borne off by an actor,
> And luck passes the young master by.

But when he saw the picture of flowers and a mat, he wept in consternation.

Before he could read on he heard someone calling, "You're playing the fool again. Your Cousin Lin wants you."

It sounded like Yuan-yang's voice, yet when he turned he could see no one. While he was vacillating she suddenly beckoned to him from outside the gate and he hurried joyfully over. Yuan-yang's shadowy figure walked ahead so fast that he could not overtake her.

"Good sister, wait for me!" he cried.

She paid no attention, continuing on her way, so that Pao-yu was forced to put on a spurt. Then he saw another fairyland with high pavilions, stately mansions with hanging eaves, and among them the indistinct figures of palace maids. As he feasted his eyes on this scene he forgot Yuan-yang and his legs carried him through a palace gate. Inside were all manner of exotic flowers and herbs unknown to him, while in a flower-bed surrounded by a white stone balustrade grew a green plant, the tips of its leaves a light red. He wondered what rare plant this could be that it was so specially treasured, observing that the faintest breeze set it swaying incessantly, and that though it was so small and had no blossoms its delicate grace was utterly enchanting.

He was looking on raptly when someone beside him demanded, "Where did this oaf come from to spy on our fairy plant?"

He swung round in dismay to see a fairy maid and explained to her with a bow, "While looking for Sister Yuan-yang I blundered into this fairy realm.   Please pardon my presumption! May I ask what place this is? Why did Sister Yuan-yang come here to tell me that Cousin Lin wants me? I beg you to enlighten me."

"Who knows your cousins?" the fairy maid retorted.   "I am keeping watch over this fairy plant, and no mortals are allowed to loiter here."

Reluctant to leave, he pleaded, "Sister Fairy, if you are in charge of these fairy plants you must be the Goddess of Flowers. Do tell me what makes this plant unique!"

"That's a long story," she answered.   "This plant, Vermilion Pearl, used to dwell on the shore of the Sacred River and was withering away until it was revived by being watered every day with sweet dew by the attendant Shen Ying.   Because of this, it went down to the world of men to repay Shen Ying's kindness.   Now that it has returned to the realm of truth, the Goddess of Disenchantment has ordered me to watch over it and not let butterflies or bees molest it."

Pao-yu could not fathom this.   Convinced that he had met the Goddess of Flowers and determined not to let slip this chance, he persisted, "If you are in charge of this plant, Sister Fairy, there must be others in charge of those countless rare flowers. I won't trouble you to tell me who all of them are, but which fairy is in charge of the hibiscus?"

"That I can't tell you, but my mistress may know."

"Who is your mistress, sister?"

"The Queen of Tear-stained Bamboos."

"That's it!"   Pao-yu exclaimed.   "The Queen of Bamboos, I'd have you know, is my cousin Lin Tai-yu."

"Nonsense! This is the celestial abode of goddesses.   Even if you call your cousin the Queen of Bamboos she's no Ngo-huang or Nu-ying[1] — how could *my* mistress be related to mortals? If you go on talking so wildly, I'll call guards to drive you out!"

---

[1] Legendary figures, said to be wives of King Shun.   When King Shun died, they were broken-hearted and shed so many tears on bamboos that thereafter the stems became speckled.

In abashed dismay Pao-yu was just withdrawing when a messenger arrived to announce, "The attendant Shen Ying is invited to enter."

The fairy maid said, "I've been waiting all this time, but he hasn't put in an appearance. So how can I send him in?"

"Isn't that him leaving now?"

Then the fairy maid hurried out calling, "Please come back, Shen Ying!"

Pao-yu, thinking it was somebody else she wanted and afraid of being driven away, made off as fast as he could.

Suddenly his way was barred by a sword and he was ordered to halt. In panic he looked up and saw Third Sister Yu. Slightly reassured he pleaded, "Sister, why should you threaten me too?"

"All the men of your house are a bad lot, spoiling people's reputations and breaking up marriages! Now that you're here I'm not going to let you off!"

Reduced to despair by this threat, Pao-yu heard a voice behind him call, "Sister, stop him! Don't let him get away!"

"On my mistress' orders," Third Sister Yu told Pao-yu, "I've been waiting for a long time. Now that we've met, with one stroke of my sword I'm to cut through your involvements in the mundane world!"

This made Pao-yu even more frantic, not that he fully understood her meaning. Turning to run, he found Ching-wen, his close maid, behind him and torn between sorrow and joy appealed to her, "I've lost my way all on my own, and run into enemies. I want to go back but have none of you with me. Thank goodness you're here, Sister Ching-wen! Do take me home at once."

"Don't be so alarmed, sir," she said. "I'm not Ching-wen but have come on our Queen's orders to take you to her. No one is going to harm you."

Nonplussed he replied, "You say your Queen wants to see me. Who is she?"

"This is no time to ask questions. You'll know when you meet."

潯通靈幻境悟仙緣送慈故故枢鄉孝全道

Pao-yu had no choice but to follow her, and watching her carefully he felt certain she was Ching-wen. "No doubt about it, that's her face and her voice," he told himself. "So why should she deny it? Well, I'm too confused to bother about that now. When I see her mistress I'll beg her to forgive me for anything I've done wrong. After all, women are so kind-hearted, she's bound to excuse my presumption."

By now they had reached a fine palace blazing with colour, with a clump of bamboos in the courtyard, outside the door several pines. Under the eaves stood maids dressed like palace attendants who at sight of him murmured, "Is this the attendant Shen Ying?"

The maid who had brought him there said, "Yes, it is. Go in quickly to announce him."

One of the waiting-maids beckoned Pao-yu with a smile, and he followed her through several buildings to the main apartment which had a pearl curtain over its lofty door.

"Wait here till you're sent for," she told him, and in abject silence he did so while she went in, reappearing soon to say, "You may go in to pay your respects."

Another maid rolled up the portière, and Pao-yu saw a garlanded young lady in embroidered robes seated inside. Raising his eyes to her face he saw it was Tai-yu.

"So here you are, cousin!" he blurted out. "How I've been longing for you!"

The waiting-maids outside expostulated, "This attendant has no manners! Out you go, quick!" One of them lowered the portière again.

Pao-yu longed to go in but dared not, yet was reluctant to leave. He wanted to question the waiting-maids, but none of them knew him and they drove him out. Ching-wen, when he looked round for her, was nowhere to be seen. Filled with misgivings he left disconsolately, still with no one to guide him, unable to find the way by which he had come. He was in a quandary when he caught sight of Hsi-feng under the eaves of a house beckoning to him.

"Thank goodness!" he exclaimed. "I'm home again! What

flummoxed me so just now?" He ran towards her crying, "So this is where you are, sister. The people here have been plaguing me, and Cousin Lin refused to see me, I don't know why."

As he reached her he saw it was not Hsi-feng but Chin Ko-ching, the first wife of Chia Jung. He halted and asked where Hsi-feng was. Instead of answering, Ko-ching went inside.

Not venturing to follow her, he stood there woodenly in a daze and sighed, "What have I done wrong to make them all cut me like this?" He burst out crying.

At once guards in yellow turbans with whips in their hands bore down on him demanding, "Where is this fellow from that he dares intrude into this fairy realm of bliss! Off you go!"

Afraid to protest, Pao-yu was trying to find a way out when in the distance he saw a group of girls approaching, chatting and laughing. He was pleased to see that one of them looked like Ying-chun.

"I've lost my way," he called to her. "Come to my rescue!"

At once the guards behind gave chase, and as he dashed off headlong the girls changed into demons too and joined in the pursuit.

Pao-yu was desperate when along came the monk who had returned his jade. Holding up a mirror he declared, "I have come on orders from the Imperial Consort to save you."

The demons instantly vanished — all left was the desolate plain.

Seizing the monk by the arm, Pao-yu implored him, "I remember you were the one to bring me here, but then you disappeared. I met many people dear to me, but they all ignored me and suddenly turned into demons. Was that a dream or did it really happen? Please explain this to me, father."

"Did you pry into any secrets here?" asked the monk.

Pao-yu thought, "Since he brought me to this fairy realm, he himself must be an immortal; so how can I hide anything from him? Besides, I want him to elucidate this." He therefore answered, "Yes, I saw some registers."

"There you are! After reading them can't you understand? All earthly ties of affection are bewitchments. Just bear what has happened carefully in mind, and I shall explain it to you later on." He gave him a violent shove. "Now go back!" Pao-yu lost his balance and fell with a cry of dismay.

His whole household was in tears when Pao-yu regained consciousness. At once they called out to him. He opened his eyes to find himself on the *kang* and, seeing that the eyes of Lady Wang, Pao-chai and the rest were red and swollen from weeping, he calmed himself and thought, "Why, I must have died and come to life again!" Recalling all that had befallen his spirit, and pleased that he could still remember it, he laughed aloud and exclaimed, "That's it, that's it!"

His mother summoned a doctor, thinking he was deranged again, at the same time sending maids to report to Chia Cheng that their son had recovered from his heart attack and now that he could talk there was no need to prepare for the last rites. At this, Chia Cheng hurried over and saw that Pao-yu had indeed regained consciousness.

"You luckless fool!" he cried. "Trying to frighten us to death!" All unwittingly he shed tears. Then, sighing, he called in the doctor to examine Pao-yu's pulse and administer medicine.

Sheh-yueh, who had been thinking of suicide, was equally relieved by his recovery. Lady Wang sent for a longan cordial, and when he had taken a few sips he felt calmer. In the general relief no one blamed Sheh-yueh, but Lady Wang had the jade given to Pao-chai to hang on Pao-yu's neck.

"I wonder where that monk found the jade," she remarked. "It's odd the way one moment he was asking for silver and the next he vanished. Could he be an immortal?"

Pao-chai said, "Judging by the way he came and left, he can't have *found* the jade. When it was lost before, it must have been this monk who took it away."

"But it was here in our house," objected Lady Wang. "How could he have taken it?"

"If he could bring it back, he could have taken it too."

Hsi-jen and Sheh-yueh reminded them, "That year when the jade was lost, Lin Chih-hsiao consulted a fortune-teller; and after Madam Pao married into our house we told her that the character he came up with was the *shang*[1] meaning reward. Do you remember, madam?"

"Yes," said Pao-chai thinking back. "You all said it meant we should look for the jade in a pawnshop. Only now is it clear that it meant that the jade had been taken by a monk, as the upper part of that character is the *shang* for 'monk'."

"I just can't get over that monk!" remarked Lady Wang. "When Pao-yu fell ill that time, another monk came and said we had a treasure in our house — meaning this jade — which could cure him. Since he knew that, there must be more to this jade than meets the eye. Besides, your husband was born with it in his mouth. Have you ever heard of such a thing before? But who knows after all what this jade can do or what will become of him? It was this jade that made him fall ill, this jade that cured him, this jade that he was born with...." She broke off here in a fresh fit of weeping.

Pao-yu, who had been following their conversation, was better able now to understand what had happened when his spirit took flight. He said nothing, however, just fixing it in his mind.

Then Hsi-chun joined in, "When the jade was lost, we asked Miao-yu to try the planchette and it wrote 'By the ancient pine at the foot of Blue Ridge Peak ... entering my gate with a smile you will meet again.' I think 'entering the gate' is most significant. Buddhism is the gate to sainthood; I'm only afraid Second Cousin can't enter that gate."

Pao-yu laughed sarcastically at this but Pao-chai knitted her brows, lost in thought.

"There you go harping on Buddhism again!" scolded Madam Yu. "Haven't you dropped your idea of becoming a nun?"

Hsi-chun smiled. "The truth is, sister-in-law, I've been abstaining from meat for some time now."

"Good gracious, child!" exclaimed Lady Wang. "You mustn't

---

[1] *Shang* (尚) meaning "monk" bears a resemblance to the upper half of *shang* (賞) meaning "reward".

have these notions."

Hsi-chun said nothing, but Pao-yu could not help sighing as he recollected the verse "By the dimly lit old shrine she sleeps alone." Then suddenly recalling the inscription for the painting of a mat and flowers, he glanced at Hsi-jen and tears started to his eyes. His abrupt transitions from smiles to tears puzzled the others, who could only assume that he was unhinged again, not knowing that his agitation arose from the verses he had memorized from the registers into which he had pried. Though unwilling to speak of them, he was convinced of the truth of these predictions.

Chapter 38
Alarmed by His Cryptic Talk, Wife and Concubine Reprove Their Witless Husband

The others saw that after Pao-yu's revival his mind had cleared, and by taking medicine every day he steadily recovered his health. This being the case, Chia Cheng turned his mind to other matters. As there was no knowing when Chia Sheh would be pardoned, and he did not like to leave the old lady's coffin in the temple for too long, he decided to escort it back to the south for burial and called in Chia Lien to consult him.

"Your decision is quite correct, sir," said Chia Lien. "Not being in office now you are free to see to this important business, whereas once you take off your mourning you will probably have other demands on your time. In my father's absence I couldn't presume to suggest this; but although your decision is excellent, this is going to cost several thousand taels and it's useless to expect the police to recover our stolen property."

"I have made up my mind," said Chia Cheng, "but since the Elder Master is away I wanted to consult you on how to handle this. You can't leave home or there would be no one in charge here. In my opinion all those coffins should be conveyed to the ancestral graveyard, and as I can't cope single-handed I'm thinking of taking Chia Jung along, the more so as his wife's is one of the coffins. Then there is your Cousin Lin's. The old lady left instructions that it should go south with hers. I suppose we shall have to borrow a few thousand taels to cover these expenses."

"Nowadays we can't count on others helping us out," replied Chia Lien. "As you are not in office, sir, and my father is away, we're in no position to raise a loan at present. All we can do is mortgage some properties."

"How can we, when this mansion of ours was built by the government?"

"I don't mean this mansion we live in, but there are houses outside which can be mortgaged and redeemed again after you resume office, sir. If in future my father returns and is given a post, that will make it easier. My one regret is that you should have to exert yourself in this way at your advanced age, sir."

"I'm simply doing my duty by the old lady. But you must be more prudent in running the household!"

"You can rest assured about that, sir. I shall certainly do my best, incompetent as I am. Besides, you will need to take quite a few servants south, and as that will leave fewer here I can cut down on expenses and get by. If you should find yourself short of funds on the way, sir, since you will be passing Lai Shang-jung's place you can enlist his help."

"It's my own mother's funeral. Why should I ask other families to help?"

"Yes, sir," muttered Chia Lien, then withdrew to raise the money.

Chia Cheng told Lady Wang his plans and asked her to take charge of domestic affairs, then chose an auspicious day to start this long journey. By now Pao-yu had completely recovered his health, while Chia Huan and Chia Lan were studying hard. Chia Cheng entrusted all three to the care of Chia Lien.

"This is a year for the triennial examination," he told him. "Huan can't sit for it while in mourning for his mother. Lan is only a grandson, so after the mourning is over he's still entitled to take the examination and you must send Pao-yu there too with his nephew. If he is a successful candidate, it will help to atone for our faults."

Chia Lien and the boys assented. After giving further instructions to other members of the family, Chia Cheng bade farewell to the ancestral shrine, had sutras chanted for a few days at the temple outside the city, then boarded a boat with Lin Chih-hsiao and others. He did not take leave of his friends and relatives, not wanting to put them out; thus only family members saw him off.

Lady Wang reminded Pao-yu from time to time of his father's instructions, and checked up on his studies. Pao-chai and Hsi-jen too, it goes without saying, encouraged him to work hard. Though he was in better spirits after his illness, he took more fantastic notions into his head: not only was he averse to rank and an official career, he had lost much of his former interest in girls. But this was not too apparent to other people as he did not voice these views.

One day, after returning from seeing off Tai-yu's coffin, Tzu-chuan stayed disconsolately in her room to weep. "How unfeeling Pao-yu is!" she thought. "When he saw Miss Lin's coffin taken south he showed no sadness, shed not a tear, and instead of consoling me when I sobbed he actually laughed at me. So all this heartless fellow's honeyed talk before was to fool us! It's a good thing I didn't take him seriously the other night, or I'd have been taken in by him again. One thing I can't make out, though, is his coolness towards Hsi-jen nowadays as well. Madam Pao has never liked too much show of feeling, but don't Sheh-yueh and the rest resent his behaviour? What fools most of us girls must be to have cared so much for him all that time — what can come of it in the end?"

Just then Wu-erh came in to see her. Finding Tzu-chuan in tears she asked, "Are you crying for Miss Lin again? I see now that it's no good basing your opinion of somebody on hearsay. Because we'd always heard how good Master Pao was to girls, my mother tried time and again to get me into his service; and since coming here I've nursed him devotedly each time he was ill, yet now that he's better he hasn't a single kind word for me — he doesn't even so much as look at me!"

Tickled by this, Tzu-chuan laughed. "Bah, you little slut!" she spat out. "How do you want Pao-yu to treat you? A young girl should have some shame! When he shows so little interest in all those who belong to his household by rights, what time has he to waste on *you*?" Laughing again, she drew one finger over her cheek to shame her. "Tell me, what's the relationship between you and Pao-yu?" she demanded.

Aware that she had given herself away, Wu-erh blushed furiously. She was about to explain that *she* wanted no special consideration from Pao-yu but he had recently shown too little to his maids, when someone outside the courtyard gate shouted, "That monk is back again. He wants ten thousand taels of silver! The mistress is worried and wanted Master Lien to talk to him, but Master Lien isn't at home! That monk is ranting crazily outside. The mistress asks Madam Pao to go and discuss what to do."

When Lady Wang sent to ask for Pao-chai, and Pao-yu knew that the monk was outside, he hurried all alone to the front crying out, "Where is my master?"

He called repeatedly but could not find him and, reaching the gate, saw Li Kuei barring the way, refusing the monk admission.

"The mistress has sent me," said Pao-yu, "to invite this holy man in."

Then Li Kuei let go of the monk who swaggered in and, seeing that he looked like the monk in his trance, Pao-yu had an inkling of the truth. Bowing he said, "Excuse my tardiness in welcoming you, master."

"I don't want you to entertain me," the monk replied. "Just hand over the silver and I'll be off."

This did not sound to Pao-yu the way a saint would talk; moreover, the monk had a scabby head and was wearing filthy rags. He reflected, "The ancients said, 'One who has attained the Way makes no show of it; one who makes a show of it has not attained the Way.' I mustn't let slip this chance, but agree to give him the reward so as to sound him out."

He replied, "Please have patience, master, and sit down to wait while my mother gets it ready. May I ask if you are from the Illusory Land of Great Void?"

"What 'illusory land'? Whence I came, thither shall I depart. I'm here to return you your jade. Can you tell me where it comes from?" When Pao-yu could not answer the monk chuckled, "You don't even know your own origin yet question me!"

Pao-yu had the intelligence after all he had experienced to have seen through the vanity of this earth, being simply ignorant of his own antecedents. The monk's question awoke him to the truth.

"You don't need any silver," he cried. "I'll return you the jade."

"And so you should!" laughed the monk.

Without a word Pao-yu raced in to his own compound, which Pao-chai and Hsi-jen had left to see Lady Wang. He snatched the jade up from his bed and dashed out, running full tilt into Hsi-jen who started with fright.

"The mistress said it was very good of you to entertain the monk, and she means to give him some silver," she informed him. "What brings you back?"

"Go straight and tell her there's no need to raise any money. I'll return him the jade instead."

"Not on any account!" She caught him by the arm. "This jade is your life. If he takes it away your illness will come back!"

"Not any more. Now I'm in my right mind again, what do I need the jade for?" He wrenched himself free and made off.

Hsi-jen ran frantically after him calling, "Come back! I've something to tell you."

He cried over his shoulder, "There's nothing we need talk about."

She chased after him regardless, expostulating, "Last time you lost the jade it nearly cost me my life! You've just got it back, and if he takes it away that will be the death of us both! You can only give it back over my dead body!" With that, overtaking Pao-yu, she caught hold of him.

"Whether you die or not I must give it back," was his desperate retort.

He pushed her with all his might, but she seized his belt with both hands and would not let go, weeping and screaming as she sank to the ground. The maids inside hearing this darted out and found them both distraught.

"Tell the mistress, quick!" Hsi-jen sobbed. "Master Pao

wants to give his jade back to the monk."

When the maids ran to report this, Pao-yu grew even angrier and tore at Hsi-jen's hands to free himself; but mindless of the pain she would not let go. And when Tzu-chuan inside heard what Pao-yu meant to do, even more frantic than the rest she completely forgot her resolve to remain aloof and ran out to help restrain him. Though he was a man and struggling hard, he could not free himself from their desperate clutches.

"So you're hanging on to this jade for dear life!" he sighed. "What would you do if I went away myself?" At that they burst into uncontrollable sobbing.

They were still locked together when Lady Wang and Pao-chai hurried over. "Pao-yu!" wailed his mother. "You've gone crazy again!"

At sight of her Pao-yu knew he could not escape. With a sheepish smile he said, "Why all this fuss? Why upset the mistress for no reason at all? I thought it unreasonable of the monk to insist on ten thousand taels, not one tael less; so in a pique I came back meaning to return him the jade, saying that it was a fake and we didn't want it. If he saw that we didn't value it, he'd be willing to accept whatever we offered."

"I thought you really meant to give it back," scolded Lady Wang. "All right then, but why didn't you tell them clearly? Why make them raise such a rumpus?"

Pao-chai put in, "If that's the case, well and good. If you really gave the jade back, that monk is so odd that he could cause fresh trouble for our family and that would never do. As for the reward, you can raise it by selling my jewels."

"Yes," agreed Lady Wang. "Let's do that."

Pao-yu made no objection as Pao-chai stepped forward to take the jade from his hand. "There's no need for you to go out," she said. "Her Ladyship and I will give him the money."

"I don't mind not giving him the jade," he replied, "but I must see him once more."

Hsi-jen and Tzu-chuan were still keeping hold of him. Pao-chai, having sized up the situation, told them, "Let go of him. He can go if he wants to."

Then Hsi-jen released Pao-yu, who said with a smile, "You people think more of the jade than you do of me! Now that you're not stopping me, suppose I go off with the monk and leave you the jade?"

In renewed alarm Hsi-jen wanted to seize him again, but in the presence of the mistresses she could not take liberties, and Pao-yu had already slipped away. She at once sent a maid to Pei-ming at the inner gate with the message, "Tell the servants outside to keep an eye on Master Pao; he's not in his right mind." The girl went off on this errand.

Lady Wang and Pao-chai went in now and sat down to ask Hsi-jen just what had happened, and she related in detail all Pao-yu had said. This so worried them that they sent word to the servants outside to wait on Pao-yu and hear what the monk had to say.

The maid on her return informed Lady Wang, "Master Pao is really rather crazed. The pages outside say he was at a loss because you wouldn't let him have the jade. Now he's gone out and begged the monk to take him with him."

Lady Wang exclaimed in horror, then asked what the monk had replied.

"He said he wants the jade, not it's owner," the girl said.

"Doesn't he want the money then?" asked Pao-chai.

"I didn't hear anything about that, madam. Later the monk and Master Pao were laughing and chatting together about many things, but the pages couldn't understand a word."

"Stupid creatures!" cried Lady Wang. "Even if they don't understand, they can memorize it." On her orders the maid hurriedly fetched one of the pages and, standing outside the window, he paid his respects.

"Though you didn't understand the talk between the monk and Master Pao, can't you repeat it to me?" asked Lady Wang.

"All we caught were phrases like 'the Great Waste Mountain', 'Blue Ridge Peak', 'the Land of Great Void' and 'severing mortal entanglements,'" he told her.

Lady Wang could not make head or tail of this either, but Pao-chai's eyes widened in alarm and she could not get a word out. They were about to send to fetch Pao-yu back, when in he came grinning and saying to himself, "Fine, fine!"

Pao-chai remained speechless while his mother asked, "What is this crazy talk?"

"I'm in earnest," protested Pao-yu, "yet you call me crazy! That monk and I knew each other before and he simply wished to see me. He never really wanted a reward but was just doing a good deed. After he'd explained that, he vanished. Isn't that fine?"

His mother, not believing him, sent the page to question the gateman.

"The monk has really gone," he came back to report. "He left word that Your Ladyships needn't worry. He wants no silver, simply wants Master Pao to pay him occasional visits. 'Just submit to fate and things will take their natural course,'" he said.

"So he was a good monk after all! Did you ask where he lives?"

"The gateman said he told Master Pao, so he knows."

But Pao-yu when questioned answered with a smile, "That place is far or near, depending on how you look at it. . . ."

"Wake up!" cut in Pao-chai. "Stop dreaming! The master and the mistress dote on you, and the master told you to study hard to advance yourself."

"What I have in mind will advance us all, won't it? Don't you know the saying, 'When one son renounces the world, seven of his ancestors will go to heaven'?"

Lady Wang lamented, "What's to become of us? First Hsi-chun insists on renouncing the world, and now here's another. How can I live on like this?" She broke down and wept.

Pao-chai tried hard to console her and Pao-yu said, "I was joking, madam. Don't take it seriously."

His mother stopped weeping to retort, "Is this a joking matter?"

One day, Pao-yu amused himself by reading the chapter "Autumn Water" in *Chuang Tzu*. Pao-chai, coming out from the inner room and finding him utterly absorbed in a book,went over to have a look and was dismayed to discover what it was. "He takes that talk about 'leaving the world of men' seriously," she reflected. "No good will come of it in the long run." But thinking it useless to try to dissuade him, she sat down beside him lost in reverie.

Pao-yu noticing this asked, "What's on your mind now?"

"Since we are man and wife, you're the one I have to rely on all my life; this isn't a question of my personal feelings. Of course wealth and honour are 'transient as drifting clouds'; but the sages of old set store by moral character and a firm foundation. . . ."

Without waiting for her to finish, Pao-yu laid his book aside and said with a faint smile, "So you talk about 'moral character and a firm foundation' and the 'sages of old'. Don't you know that one ancient sage taught that we 'should not lose the heart of a child'? What's special about a child? Simply this: it has no knowledge, no judgement, no greed and no taboos. From our birth we sink into the quagmire of greed, anger, infatuation and love; and how can we escape from earthly entanglements? I've only just realized that mortal men are like water weeds drifting together and then apart again. Though the ancients spoke of this, no one seems to have awakened to the fact. If you want to talk about character and foundation, tell me who has achieved the supreme primeval state?"

"Since you speak of the heart of a child," she countered, "the sages of old took it to mean loyalty and filial piety, not leaving the world and giving up all human relationships. The constant concern of Yao and Shun, Yu and Tang, the Duke of Chou and Confucius was to save the people and benefit the world; so what they meant by the heart of a child was simply love for humanity. What would the world come to if everyone took your advice and disregarded all natural relationships?"

Pao-yu nodded and chuckled, "But Yao and Shun didn't

force Tsao Fu and Hsu Yu[1] to take up office, nor did King Wu and the Duke of Chou force Po Yi and Shu Chi[2] to serve them."

Before he could finish, Pao-chai interposed, "What you're saying now is even more wrong. If all the men of old had been like Tsao Fu, Hsu Yu, Po Yi and Shu Chi, why should Yao and Shun, the Duke of Chou and Confucius be considered as sages today? It's even more ridiculous to compare yourself with Po Yi and Shu Chi. They lived when the Shang Dynasty was in decline, and because they couldn't cope with the situation found some pretext to run away. But we live under a sage Emperor, our family is deeply indebted to the state, and our ancestors have lived in luxury; while in your case, particularly, since your childhood you've been treasured by the old lady while she was alive and by your parents. Just think over what you said. Was it right or wrong?"

Pao-yu made no answer, just looked up and smiled.

Pao-chai went on to plead, "Since you've run out of arguments, my advice to you is to take a grip on yourself and study hard; because if you can pass the triennial examination, even if you stop at that, you'll be paying back your debt of gratitude for your sovereign's favour and your ancestors' virtue."

Pao-yu nodded and sighed, then said, "Actually it isn't difficult to pass. And what you said about stopping there and repaying my debt is not far wide of the mark."

Before she could answer, Hsi-jen joined in, "Of course, *we* don't understand those old sages whom Madam Pao was talking about. I just feel that those of us who've been hard at it since we were small serving Master Pao, and told off ever so often — though of course that was only right — all hope he will show more consideration for us. Besides, it's for *your* sake that Madam Pao has been such a dutiful daughter-in-law;

---

[1] Legend had it that the sage kings Yao and Shun wanted to make over the country to these men, but they declined.

[2] Po Yi and Shu Chi refused to cooperate with King Wu and the Duke of Chou, becoming hermits instead.

so even if you haven't much family feeling you shouldn't let her down. All those legends about gods and spirits are lies — who ever saw an immortal come down to earth? Yet when that monk from goodness knows where talked some nonsense to you, you believed it! How can someone with book-learning like you, Master Pao, take his advice more seriously than your parents'?"

Pao-yu bowed his head and said nothing.

Before she could continue, they heard footsteps in the courtyard and someone outside the window asked, "Is Uncle Pao in?"

Recognizing Chia Lan's voice, Pao-yu stood up and called cheerfully, "Come in!"

Pao-chai also rose to her feet as Chia Lan entered, beaming, to pay his respects to them both, after which he and Hsi-jen exchanged greetings. Then he presented the letter to Pao-yu.

After reading it Pao-yu said, "So Tan-chun's coming back?"

"According to grandfather, she must be," he answered.

Pao-yu nodded and seemed lost in thought.

"Did you read the end of the letter, uncle, where grandfather urges us to study hard? Have you written any compositions these days?"

Pao-yu smiled and said, "Yes, I must write a few to keep my hand in, so that I can wangle a pass."

"In that case, uncle, won't you set some subjects for us both, so that I can muddle through this examination too? Otherwise I may have to hand in a blank paper, making a fool of myself, which would reflect badly on you, uncle, as well."

"No, you should do all right."

Pao-chai invited Chia Lan to take a seat, and as Pao-yu was still sitting in his own place the boy sat down respectfully beside him. They cheerfully discussed writing essays; and Pao-chai, observing this, withdrew to the inner room. "Judging by Pao-yu's present behaviour," she thought, "he appears to have seen reason. Yet just now he stressed that this was where he would stop — what did he mean by that?"

Though Pao-chai still had her doubts, Hsi-jen was delighted

to hear how animatedly Pao-yu was talking about essay-writing and the examination. "Merciful Buddha!" she thought. "He seems to have come to his senses at last after that lecture we gave him!"

As Pao-yu and Chia Lan were talking, Ying-erh brought them tea and Chia Lan stood up to take it. He then consulted Pao-yu about the examination rules and suggested that they might invite Chen Pao-yu over. Pao-yu appeared very willing.

Presently Chia Lan went home, leaving the letter with Pao-yu, who went in cheerfully and handed it to Sheh-yueh for safe keeping. Coming out again he put away the volume of *Chuang Tzu,* then gathered together some of his favourite books on Taoism and Zen Buddhism and told Sheh-yueh, Chiu-wen and Ying-erh to take them all away. Wondering what he was up to, Pao-chai sounded him out playfully, "It's quite right and proper to stop reading those, but why have them taken away?"

"It's just dawned on me that these books count for nothing. I'm going to have them burnt to make a clean sweep!" Hearing this she was beside herself with joy. But then he chanted softly to himself:

> Buddha's nature is not to be found in sacred canons,
> The fairy barque sails beyond the realm of alchemy.

She could not hear too clearly, but caught the words "Buddha's nature" and "fairy barque" which caused her fresh misgivings. As she waited to see what he would do next, Pao-yu ordered Sheh-yueh and Chiu-wen to prepare a quiet room for him, and got out all his collections of the sayings of past sages as well as other famous works and poems written during examinations, which he had put in this room. Then, to Pao-chai's relief, he set to work in good earnest.

Hsi-jen was amazed by these developments. She quietly told Pao-chai, "The talking-to you gave him did the trick after all, madam. The way you kept refuting him made him see reason. Too bad, though, that it's rather late in the day — so close to the examination!"

Pao-chai nodded and answered with a smile, "Success or failure in examinations is fated, regardless of how soon or late one starts to study. We can only hope that from now on he'll stick to the right path and never be influenced again by those evil spirits!" Since they were alone in the room she went on softly, "Of course it's good that he's seen the light at last; but I'm afraid he may revert to his bad old ways and start fooling about with girls."

"Exactly, madam. After Master Pao put his trust in that monk he cooled off towards the girls here; now that he's lost faith in him, his old trouble may very well flare up again. I don't think he ever cared much for you or me, madam. Now Tzu-chuan's gone, leaving just four senior maids and the only vamp among them is Wu-erh. They say her mother has asked Their Ladyships to let her go home to get married; however, for the time being she's still here. Sheh-yueh and Chiu-wen are all right, but in the old days Master Pao used to fool about with them too; so it looks as if Ying-erh is the only one in whom he's shown no interest, and she's a steady girl. I suggest that pouring his tea and fetching his water can be left to her, with some younger girls to help her. What do you think of that, madam?"

"This is what I've been worrying about. Your idea's a good one." So from then on Ying-erh was assigned to wait on Pao-yu with some younger maids.

Pao-yu, however, never left his compound, just sending someone every day to pay his respects for him to Lady Wang. And she, it goes without saying, was pleased to know how hard he was studying.

A few days later it was time for the examination. Everyone else simply hoped that the two young masters would write good compositions and pass with honours; but Pao-chai had noticed that Pao-yu, though studying hard, seemed strangely detached and indifferent. As this was the first examination for which he and Chia Lan had entered, she feared they might meet with some mishap in the throng of people and horses; moreover ever since the monk's departure Pao-yu had stayed indoors, and though she had rejoiced to see him studying she was sceptical about his sudden conversion and afraid of some new misfortune. And so, the day before the examination, she sent Hsi-jen with some maids to help Su-yun pack the young gentlemen's things; and when she had made sure that everything needed was ready, she went with Li Wan to ask Lady Wang to send more than the usual number of experienced stewards with them, ostensibly to prevent their being jostled in the crowd.

The next day Pao-yu and Chia Lan, in clothes neither new nor shabby, presented themselves cheerfully to Lady Wang.

"This is your first examination," she warned them. "The first time in all these years that you've ever left me. Even when I wasn't keeping an eye on you, you were surrounded by maids and serving-women, never sleeping for a single night alone. Today, entering for the examination, you're going to be entirely on your own, so you'll have to take care of yourselves! Come out as soon as you've finished your compositions to find our family servants, then come straight back to set the minds of your mothers and wife at rest." She was moved to grief as she spoke.

Chia Lan had assented to each sentence, whereas Pao-yu had said nothing. But when his mother finished he came over to kneel before her, shedding tears. After kowtowing three times he said, "I can never repay the mother who gave birth to me. But I shall do as well as I can in the examination, to obtain a good *chu-jen* degree and make you happy, madam. Then I shall have done my duty as a son and atoned for all my faults."

This upset Lady Wang even more. "It's good, of course, for you to feel that way," she said. "If only the old lady could have lived to see you now!" Weeping she tried to raise him to his feet, but Pao-yu refused to get up.

"Even if the old lady can't see me, she'll know and be pleased," he answered. "So it's all the same whether she sees me or not. We're separated in form only, not in spirit."

This exchange made Li Wan afraid that Pao-yu was losing

his mind again, besides striking her as inauspicious. She made haste to say, "Madam, why grieve over such a happy occasion? Especially as Brother Pao-yu has recently been so sensible and dutiful, studying hard as well. When he and his nephew have taken the examination and written some good compositions, they'll come straight back to show what they wrote to our seniors, after which we can wait for news of their success." She told maids to help Pao-yu up.

He turned to bow to her saying, "Don't worry, sister-in-law. We're both of us going to pass. Later on, your Lan is going to do so well that you'll wear the costume of a high-ranking lady."

She chuckled, "I only hope it works out as you say, so that it won't have been in vain. . . ." She broke off there, afraid to upset Lady Wang.

"Provided you have a good son to continue our ancestors' line," rejoined Pao-yu, "even though my brother hasn't lived to see it, it means he has done his duty."

Li Wan simply nodded, reluctant to say any more as it was growing late.

Pao-chai was most dismayed. For not only had Pao-yu's words struck her as ill-omened, so had everything said by Lady Wang and Li Wan. Still, trying not to take it seriously she just held back her tears and kept silent. And now Pao-yu walked over to make her a deep bow. All present, though mystified by his strange behaviour, did not like to laugh. They were even more amazed when Pao-chai wept.

Pao-yu told her, "I'm going now, cousin. Take good care of the mistress and wait for my good news!"

"It's time you were off. There's no need to maunder like this," she answered.

"So you're hurrying me? I know it's time to be off." He turned to look round and noticed two people missing. "Send word for me to Hsi-chun and Tzu-chuan," he added. "Well, all I want to say is I shall be seeing them again."

As he sounded half rational, half crazy, the others attributed this to the fact that he had never left home before and was affected by what his mother had said. They thought it best to speed him on his way. "People are waiting outside," they reminded him. "If you delay any longer you'll be late."

Pao-yu threw back his head and laughed. "I'm going now! No more ado! This is the end!"

The others answered cheerfully, "Go quickly."

Only Lady Wang and Pao-chai behaved as if this were a separation for life. Their tears coursed down and they nearly burst out sobbing as Pao-yu, laughing like a maniac, went out. Truly:

> Taking the only approach to fame and wealth,
> He breaks through the first door of his cage.

Chapter 39
Pao-yu Passes the Examination with Honours and Severs Earthly Ties

Soon came the day for the examination to end, and Lady Wang was eager for the return of Pao-yu and Chia Lan. By the afternoon when there was no sign of them, she, Li Wan and Pao-chai sent servants out to make inquiries, but they did not come back, having no news. Others were sent, and when these did not return either the three women felt quite distraught.

That evening, to their delight Chia Lan came back.

"Where is your Uncle Pao?" he was asked.

Without stopping to pay his respects he sobbed, "Uncle Pao has disappeared!"

Lady Wang, dumbfounded, collapsed. Luckily Tsai-yun and others were at hand to carry her to her bed and revive her; but at once she started wailing. Pao-chai remained speechless, dazed.

Hsi-jen, dissolved in tears, reproached Chia Lan, "Stupid creature! You were with him, how could you lose him?"

"In the hostel we ate and slept in the same place," he told them. "And in the examination grounds our cells weren't too far apart, so we kept in close touch. This morning, Uncle Pao finished his papers first and waited for me to hand them in together. Then we came out together; but in the crowd at the Dragon Gate he disappeared. The servants who'd come to meet us asked me where he was and Li Kuei said he'd seen him, just a few yards away, but he'd vanished in the crowd. I sent Li Kuei and others to search in different directions while I took some men with me to search all the cells. But he wasn't there. That's why I'm so late back."

Lady Wang was crying too much to speak, Pao-chai had a

fair idea of the truth of the matter, while Hsi-jen was sobbing as if she would never stop. So Chia Chiang without waiting for orders went out with others in different directions to search. In the Jung Mansion, plunged in gloom and half deserted, the banquet to welcome the candidates back went untouched. Forgetting his own exhaustion, Chia Lan wanted to make another search for Pao-yu, but Lady Wang restrained him.

"Child, your uncle has disappeared," she said. "We can't have *you* getting lost too. Go and rest now, there's a good boy!"

Still Chia Lan insisted on going, till Madam Yu and the rest managed to dissuade him.

Hsi-chun, the only one to grasp the truth, could not divulge it. She asked Pao-chai, "Did Cousin Pao-yu take his jade with him?"

"Of course, he always wore it," was the answer, to which Hsi-chun made no reply.

Hsi-jen, recalling his attempt to snatch the jade from Pao-yu, suspected the monk of spiriting him away. Her tears fell like pearls as, sobbing and broken-hearted, she remembered Pao-yu's past kindness. "Sometimes when I provoked him he lost his temper," she thought. "But he always had the grace to make it up later, to say nothing of his warm-hearted consideration. When I provoked him too much, he swore he'd become a monk. For all we know he may have kept his word!"

By now it was already the fourth watch and there was still no news. Afraid Lady Wang would wear herself out with grief, Li Wan urged her to go and rest, and the others attended her, only Lady Hsing going back to her own quarters while Chia Huan skulked out of sight. Lady Wang sent Chia Lan to bed but herself passed a sleepless night.

At dawn, the servants came back to report that they had searched high and low without finding a trace of Pao-yu. Then Aunt Hsueh, Hsueh Ko, Hsiang-yun, Pao-chin and Aunt Li called in turn to pay their respects and ask for news. This went on for several days, with Lady Wang too grief-stricken to eat.

中鄉魁
寶玉都塵緣
沐皇恩賈家延世澤

One day, after the fifth watch, servants from the outer apartments came to the inner gate to announce good tidings. A few young maids rushed in, without waiting for the senior maids' permission, and burst out, "Such good news, madam!"

Jumping to the wrong conclusion, Lady Wang stood up elatedly to ask, "Where did they find him? Bring him in at once!"

"He's come seventh of the successful candidates."

"But where is he?" When there was no answer she sat down again.

"Who came seventh?" asked Tan-chun.

"Master Pao," they told her.

Then another shout went up outside, "Master Lan has passed too!" The maids hurried out and came back with the announcement that Chia Lan's name was the hundred-and-thirtieth on the list. Li Wan was naturally overjoyed, but while Pao-yu was missing she dared not show it. Lady Wang too was pleased that Chia Lan had passed but thought, "If only Pao-yu were to come back how happy we all should be!"

Pao-chai, the only one still overcome with grief, had to hold back her tears.

All who offered congratulations said, "Since Pao-yu was fated to pass, he's bound to turn up. Besides, now as a successful candidate, he's too well-known to remain lost."

Lady Wang half convinced by this gave a wan smile, whereupon they urged her to take some nourishment.

Pei-ming outside the third gate was clamouring, "Now that Master Pao has passed, we're certain to find him!" Asked what he meant he explained, "The proverb says: 'A successful candidate's fame spreads throughout the world.' Wherever he goes now, people will know about him and will have to send him back."

Those in the inner apartments commented, "That young fellow has no manners, yet he talks sense."

Hsi-chun, however, countered, "How could a grown man like him get lost? I suspect he's seen through the ways of the world and taken monastic vows, in which case it will be difficult to find him."

This set Lady Wang and the others weeping again.

Li Wan agreed, "Yes, since ancient times many men have given up rank and wealth to achieve Buddhahood and become immortals."

"If he's so unfilial as to abandon his parents, how can he become a Buddha?" sobbed Lady Wang.

"People shouldn't have anything unique about them," Tan-chun remarked. "We all thought it a good thing, Brother Pao-yu being born with that jade; but now it seems all this trouble stems from it. Don't be angry, madam, at what I'm going to say, but if he doesn't turn up in the next few days then there must be some reason, and you'd better consider him as never having been born. If there really is some mystery about him and he becomes a Buddha, this must be owing to your virtue in some previous existence."

Pao-chai said nothing, but Hsi-jen could not bear her mental anguish — her head reeled and she collapsed. Lady Wang compassionately told some maids to help her back to her room.

The officer in charge of recommendations presented the papers of the successful candidates to the Emperor, who perused each in turn and found them all perspicuous. Observing that the seventh candidate Chia Pao-yu was a native of Chinling, as was the hundred-and-thirtieth Chia Lan, he asked, "Is either of these Chias from Chinling from the same family as the late Imperial Consort?"

His ministers sent for them to question them, then repeated Chia Lan's account of Pao-yu's disappearance as well as of their antecedents. Thereupon our sagacious, compassionate Emperor recalled the Chia family's services to the state and ordered his ministers to draw up a detailed memorial on the subject. His Majesty in his great goodness then ordered the bureau in charge to re-investigate Chia Sheh's case and submit their findings to him. He also read in the report "On the Successful Conclusion of the Compaign Against Brigands at the Coast" that "the whole empire is at peace and the people are content." In his delight he ordered his ministers to reward those officials responsible and to proclaim a general amnesty.

After Chia Lan had left the court and thanked his examiner, he heard of the general amnesty and reported it to Lady Wang. The whole family rejoiced and only hoped that Pao-yu would now return home. Aunt Hsueh, even more overjoyed, made ready to ransom Hsueh Pan.

Then one day it was announced that old Mr. Chen and Tan-chun's husband had called to offer congratulations. Lady Wang sent Chia Lan out to entertain them. Presently he returned to her beaming.

"Wonderful news, madam!" he told her. "Mr. Chen has heard at court that our Elder Master has been pardoned; and Uncle Chen has not only been pardoned but is to inherit the Ning Mansion's noble title. Grandfather will keep the title of Duke of Jungkuo, and after the period of mourning is to be made vice-minister of the Ministry of Works. All the property confiscated will be returned. The Emperor was impressed by Uncle Pao's essays, and discovered that he is the Imperial Consort's younger brother, whose good character the Prince of Peiching has vouched for. His Majesty summoned him to court and when it was reported that according to his nephew Chia Lan he had·disappeared after the examination and a search was being made for him everywhere, the Emperor decreed that all the garrisons of the capital must do their utmost to find him. This decree should set your mind at rest, madam. Now that the Emperor has shown us such favour, Uncle Pao is bound to be found!"

Lady Wang and the rest of the family exchanged jubilant congratulations.

Chia Cheng escorting the old lady's coffin, and Chia Jung those of Ko-ching, Hsi-feng and Yuan-yang, had now reached Chinling where they had them interred. Then Chia Jung took Tai-yu's coffin to be buried in her ancestral graveyard, leaving Chia Cheng to supervise the building of the tombs. One day he received a letter from home, and the news that Pao-yu and

Chia Lan had passed the examination delighted him; but Pao-yu's disappearance so perturbed him that he felt constrained to hurry back at once. On the way he heard of the general amnesty and received another letter from home confirming his pardon and official reinstatement. Much heartened, he pressed on rapidly day and night.

The day they reached the Kunlu post station, it suddenly turned cold and began to snow, and their boat moored in a secluded spot. Chia Cheng sent servants ashore to deliver cards to friends in that locality, and to explain that he had no time to call and they should not trouble to call on him either, as the boat would be leaving again immediately. Only one page remained to wait on him as he wrote a letter to send home by a messenger travelling ahead by road. Before broaching the subject of Pao-yu he paused. Looking up through the snow, he glimpsed at the prow of the boat a figure with a shaven head and bare feet, draped in a red felt cape. This man prostrated himself before Chia Cheng, who hurried out of the cabin, meaning to raise him up and see who he was, but the man had already kowtowed four times, then stood up and made him a Buddhist salutation. Chia Cheng was about to bow in return when he recognized his son.

"Is it Pao-yu?" he asked in amazement.

The other made no answer, looking torn between grief and joy.

"If you are Pao-yu, what are you doing here, and in this costume?" Chia Cheng asked again.

Before Pao-yu could reply, a monk and a Taoist priest appeared, each taking one of his arms. "Your worldly obligations have been fulfilled," they declared. "Why delay your departure?" Then all three of them glided ashore.

Though it was slippery underfoot, Chia Cheng hurried after them but could not overtake them. However, he heard one of them chant:

> My home is Blue Ridge Peak,
> I roam the primeval void.
> Who will go with me to keep me company,

Returning to the Great Waste of infinity!

Chia Cheng pursued them round a slope, only to find they had vanished. Limp and out of breath, his heart misgave him. Turning, he found that the page had followed him.

"Did you see those three men just now?" Chia Cheng asked.

"Yes, sir. As you were running after them I came too. But then I lost sight of those three."

Chia Cheng was tempted to go on, but in the white wilderness there was no one in sight. Marvelling, he had to turn back.

When the servants returned and found their master gone, the boatman told them that he had gone ashore in pursuit of two monks and a Taoist priest. They followed his footprints in the snow and, seeing him approaching in the distance, went to meet him and escorted him back to the boat. After he had sat down and caught his breath he told them of his encounter with Pao-yu. They suggested searching the vicinity.

"You don't understand," he sighed. "I saw them with my own eyes, they were not apparitions. And I heard them chanting a most occult poem. When Pao-yu was born with jade in his mouth, I knew it was uncanny and boded no good; but because the old lady doted on him we brought him up all these years. As for the monk and the priest, I have seen them three times. The first time was when they came to explain the miraculous nature of the jade; the second time, when Pao-yu was so ill and the monk took the jade in his hand and intoned some incantation to cure him; the third time, when he brought back the jade and I saw him sitting in the front hall, then all of a sudden he vanished. Although that increased my misgivings, I thought Pao-yu fortunate to have the protection of these Buddhist and Taoist saints. Little did I know that Pao-yu was a spirit who had come to earth to undergo certain trials, and who managed to fool the old lady for nineteen years! Only now is it clear to me." He shed tears.

"If Master Pao was really a Buddhist saint, he shouldn't have become a *chu-jen*," they objected. "Why take the official examination then leave?"

"You don't understand that all the stars in the heavens, the saints in the mountains and the spirits in caves have each their own different nature. Pao-yu never showed any inclination to study, yet he'd only to glance at a book to master it. By temperament, too, he was different from other people." He sighed again.

They consoled him with talk of Chia Lan's success and the improvement in the family's fortunes. Then Chia Cheng went on with his letter, describing this incident and urging the family not to grieve. He sealed the letter and sent it off with a servant, then continued on his way.

Chapter 40
Chia Yu-tsun Concludes the Dream of Red Mansions

Chia Yu-tsun had been found guilty of embezzlement and condemned to punishment. He was pardoned under the general amnesty, but ordered back to his native place and reduced to the status of a common citizen. Having sent his family home first, he was making his way there with a baggage-cart and a page when, by the Ford of Awakening in the Stream of Rapid Reversal, he saw a Taoist priest emerge from a thatched shed to greet him. Recognizing his old friend Chen Shih-yin, he promptly returned the greeting.

"How have you been, worthy Mr. Chia?" asked Shih-yin.

"So you are Master Chen, Immortal One!" replied Yu-tsun. "How is it that last time we met you refused to recognize me? Later I was very worried to hear that your temple had been burned down. Now that I am lucky enough to meet you again, I am sure your virtue must be even greater. As for me, owing to my own inveterate folly, I've now been reduced to this."

"Last time you were a high official, so how could a poor priest claim acquaintance with you? As an old friend I ventured to offer you some advice, but you ignored it. However, wealth and poverty, success and failure are predestined. How amazing that we should meet again today! My humble temple is not far from here. Would you care to come for a chat?" Yu-tsun agreed willingly.

They walked off hand in hand, followed by the page with the cart till they reached a thatched temple. Shih-yin invited Yu-tsun in to sit down, and a boy served tea.

Asked how he had come to renounce the world, Shih-yin said with a smile, "It's easily done, with the speed of thought. Coming from the great world, sir, don't you know of a certain Pao-yu who used to live in the lap of luxury?"

"Of course I do! Recently it has been rumoured that he has entered Buddhist orders too. I met him several times, but never dreamed he would take such a decision."

"That's where you were wrong! I knew his strange story in advance, and had already met him at the time when the two of us talked before the gate of my old house in Jenching Lane."

"How could that be?" exclaimed Yu-tsun in surprise. "With the capital so far from your honourable district!"

"I met him in spirit a long time ago."

"Then you know, no doubt, where he is now?"

"Pao-yu means 'divine jade'. Before the raid on the Jung and Ning Mansions, on the day when Pao-chai and Tai-yu separated, that jade had already left the world of men to escape from calamity and effect a reunion. Then, former ties of affection severed, form and essence once more became one. It further showed its miraculous origin by passing the examination with distinction and begetting a noble son, proving that this jade is a treasure tempered by the divine powers of nature, not to be compared with ordinary objects. It was taken to the mortal world by the Buddhist of Infinite Space and the Taoist of Boundless Time. Now that its mortal course is run, they have carried it back to its original place: this is what has happened to Pao-yu."

Yu-tsun, though he understood barely half of this, nodded and marvelled, "So that's the way it was! I was too ignorant to know. But why, with such a spiritual origin, was Pao-yu so enamoured of girls before he became so enlightened? Would you explain that?"

"This may be hard for you to grasp fully, sir. The Illusory Land of Great Void is the Blessed Land of Truth. By reading the registers twice, he saw the beginning and the ending too all set down there in detail. How could that fail to enlighten him?

Since the fairy herb has reverted to her true form, shouldn't the jade of 'spiritual understanding' do the same?"

Yu-tsun was mystified, but knowing that this was some divine secret he did not press for a fuller explanation. "You have told me about Pao-yu," he said. "But there are many ladies in our humble clan; how is it that apart from the Imperial Consort all the others came to such undistinguished ends?"

"You must allow me to speak bluntly, sir. All noble ladies come from the realm of love and retribution. From time immemorial, carnal desire has been their cardinal sin, and they must not even immerse themselves in love. Thus Tsui Ying-ying and Su Hsiao-hsiao[1] were immortals with earthly desires, while Sung Yu and Ssuma Hsiang-ju[2] were writers of genius whose works were wicked. Anyone ensnared by love can come to no good end!"

Yu-tsun absently stroked his beard and sighed. "I have one more question, Reverend Immortal," he ventured. "Will the Jung and Ning Mansions be restored to their former prosperity?"

"It is an immutable law that the good are favoured by fortune while the dissolute meet with calamity. In these two mansions now, the good are laying up virtue, the bad repenting their crimes; so naturally their houses will prosper again with the orchid and fragrant osmanthus blooming together."

Yu-tsun lowered his head in thought, then suddenly laughed, "I get it! One of the sons of their house called Lan[3] has passed the examination; so that prediction of yours has come true. But just now, Reverend Immortal, you spoke of 'the orchid and fragrant osmanthus blooming together,' and you mentioned that Pao-yu has begotten a noble son. Is this as yet unborn son going to advance rapidly in his official career?"

"This belongs to the future," said Shih-yin with a smile. "It's

---

[1] The first was a talented and beautiful girl in a well-known Chinese romance and the second a courtesan in Hangchow at the end of the sixth century.

[2] Brilliant and romantic poets of ancient times.

[3] Lan means "orchid."